French
Trysts

ALSO BY KIRSTEN LOBE

Paris Hangover

KIRSTEN LOBE

French Trysts

Secrets of a Courtesan

ST. MARTIN'S GRIFFIN ❦ NEW YORK

Lobe
Kirsten

This is a work of fiction. All of the characters, organizations, and events portrayed in this novel are either products of the author's imagination or are used fictitiously.

www.stmartins.com

Library of Congress Cataloging-in-Publication Data

Lobe, Kirsten.
   French trysts : secrets of a courtesan / Kirsten Lobe.—1st ed.
      p.   cm.
   ISBN-13: 978-0-312-36320-8
   ISBN-10: 0-312-36320-6
   1. Courtesans—Fiction. 2. Americans—France—Fiction.
3. Paris (France)—Fiction. I. Title.

PS3612.O235 F73 2007
813'.6—dc22   2007016869

First Edition: July 2007

10 9 8 7 6 5 4 3 2 1

To women all over the world of every age who live

their lives passionately and courageously.

You are my inspiration.

We come running, we hurry

To know, oh Paris,

To know the intoxication

Of your days and your nights.

All the enraptured foreigners

Rush toward you, oh Paris!

—Offenbach's *La Vie Parisienne* operetta
  at Théâtre du Palais Royal, October 1866

CHAPITRE UN

Boldness rewards those who know how to seize their opportunities.
—MARCEL PROUST

Believe me. I didn't set out to be a courtesan. *Mon dieu!* Who does? It's not as though it was a lifelong dream. In fact, back in high school in Chicago's Elmbrook, for all my puritanical behavior I could've been voted "*Least* likely to be a courtesan." Let's just say, had there been a "Least likely to get *laid*" category, I would've been the titleholder hands down! I was such a goody-goody that I was, I kid you not, nicknamed Vanilla by my classmates for all my uptight propriety—check the yearbook!

Let's shoot ten years ahead, shall we? Last night, I found myself actually mentally debating, "Hmmm, what earrings are apropos for an orgy? Diamond posts or hoops? Definitely not hoops, they're bound to catch on something mid–orgasmic fuck frenzy. . . ." Well, I think it's apparent, that Vanilla title is long gone now, isn't it? By the way, I went with the 2-carat posts . . . a far more clever choice in the long run, as the sexual gymnastics got so passionate I think I started riding a man in one zip code and finished him off in another.

Possibly necessary sidebar: Hey, don't be afraid to admit you're a little hazy on what the word "courtesan" really means. At one time I only had a vague idea from my college French literature studies. I, too, just had the broad-stroke general idea, that is *until* all this fell in my lap. So, let me give you the crash course. And keep in mind—as you take this in—what follows is an *actual* quote given to me by a more experienced Parisian courtesan as I began my own adventure into this milieu:

> The Grand Courtesans were, throughout modern history, *the* women who were the most sought after, revered, and pursued by the wealthiest, most refined men of Europe. Their suitors were exclusively men of high rank and prestige, from the emperor himself to the bourgeois tycoon. All great and notable men fell under the incomprehensible spell of courtesans' sexual magic and charms: diplomats, aristocrats, barons, counts, marquises, lords, *vicomtes*, ambassadors, impérialists, princes, kings, et cetera. In fact, the men who had the *most* power and could have *any* woman they wished found themselves *willingly* powerless at the feet of these magnetic women.
>
> The most famous courtesans were referred to as *les Grandes Horizontales*—clearly a name not to escape subtlety or notoriety. The careers of these well-known courtesans became an important part of the social history of the French Second Empire, as they earned immortality and influence not only by their own remarkable talents and achievements, but also as the muses and companions of the most notable men of their time. *Les Grandes Horizontales* were not only themselves accomplished writers, playwrights, and social stars, but they also inspired, during their time, no less than the opera *Le Figaro* by Verdi; innumerable novels by Zola, Balzac, Flaubert, Colette, Proust, Dumas, and Dumas *fils;* poetry by Baudelaire and Théophile Gauthier; music by Franz Liszt; paintings by the likes of Delacroix, Renoir, Toulouse-Lautrec, Manet, and Courbet; posters by Mucha; sculptures by Clessinger; fashions by Worth and Poiret; operettas, plays, etc. . . . as they were also the worshipped muses, the idealized women for the most creative minds of the French literary and artistic world.

Ooh la-la! Right? Tell me that's not the fuel for fantasies! Now, back to how I came to embrace this lifestyle and its delicious enchantments.

I will readily admit, I have always possessed somewhat of a vicious curiosity—obviously that can get one into heaps of trouble. And you could safely say I am a ridiculously impatient girl. I hate to be bored and thirst for new experiences. *I love* to throw myself into situations that challenge, stimulate, and scare me. Note: not *scare* scare, like I'm foolishly swimming with sharks, a bloody carcass strapped to my back for fun, or running into oncoming traffic with a blindfold on for amusement. I think you get what I mean.

On reflection, I could wager that if you took my obsession with being a good, wholesome young girl and threw it together with my really active imagination, maybe someone could've anticipated this . . . *someone with a lot of psychology degrees on the wall.* So I managed to simultaneously rebel against myself and leap into a life that is very much like playing a role in a movie. Not so bad, really, as I'm the director, the star, and am in control of every scene (okay, not *every* scene; we'll get to that). But, seriously, I *do* get to live a lifestyle that is extravagant even beyond my childhood fantasies. You can be sure, I have given this "My God, I'm a courtesan!" idea a lot of thought, because it's clearly not something you circle under "career interests" when you search for a profession. I have psychologically, emotionally, and philosophically tried to unravel why I do this, and why I don't feel the slightest bit guilty or ashamed.

I think you'll be surprised to know I even consider myself a feminist. Or perhaps, better said, a truly modern young woman. I know it's not a life for everyone, but it is a fantasy for more than a few women. As Anaïs Nin, one of my favorite writers, once said, "I'm a writer, I would've preferred to have been a courtesan." She had a pretty good take on life, I believe, and I am equally convinced of her other famous line: "Life shrinks or expands in proportion to one's courage." Put those two ideas together, add the attentions of a wealthy older man, *et voilà*—you have my life!

It is actually pretty damn empowering to realize that since I've embarked on this existence, I think I have bettered myself in virtually every way: I have become conversational in four languages; learned how to reach multiple orgasms on cue (my cue, *merci!*); have read the lion's share of the Italian and French classics; become versed in opera (you name it—I can tell you composer, year, and original venue); have learned how to throw a formal dinner party for twenty at the drop of a *chapeau;* learned how to sail expertly, ride horses *fairly well*, ride men *brilliantly well;* can name the vineyard and year from a quaff of wine . . . and not to mention make a man come divinely. All the while acquiring confidence, knowledge, *and assets*. The truth is, for the time being, I enjoy it. I'll explain. A bevy of sexual tales awaits, I assure you, but frankly, if I am going to confess *all* to you, I'd better bring you up to speed.

What feels like a lifetime ago now, I was your average all-American college student at Northwestern University. Studying for a master's in French literature, quietly blending into the vast sea of other middle-class young women—all of whom had a passion for all things French as much as for devouring Ben and Jerry's while watching *Sex and the City*. Yes, there was a smattering of earnest, arty boyfriends that amounted to nothing except the welcome and long-awaited loss of my virginity. Are you sitting down? I was a holdout until age twenty-three. Yeah, weirdish. Vanilla, alright. Anyway, after I finished my degree, it seemed a charming notion to round off my French cultural obsession by taking a summer job in Paris, as an au pair to a rather wealthy family living in the 16th arrondissement. *Pourquoi pas?*

With my suitcase jammed with a distinctly Midwestern wardrobe emblazoned with Gap labels, I arrived at my new job and my new life. I had a pretty brilliant setup: my own spacious bedroom and bath in the Chevaliers' glorious apartment on Avenue des États-Unis, nannying from 7:00 A.M. until 4:00 P.M. for a precociously adorable two-year-old, and pocketing a cool four hundred euros a week for my troubles.

Troubles? Well, yes, let's just say, the wife, Béatrice, hadn't managed to shed that baby weight after two years, and while being an attractive if diminutive woman, that kind of über-womanly figure is considered a crime in France—an intentional act of marriage sabotage.

So, she, well . . . hated me on sight, being that I'm about a meter taller and about half her body weight. Toss in the fact that her husband clearly had designs on getting me into bed, and you could say she "tolerated me" while he "lusted for me" would be putting it best. As he wasn't exactly drop-dead sexy but did have drop-dead breath, I made it an art form to avoid his advances. Like when, get this, he "accidentally" entered my bedroom one chilly morning, clad in nothing more than his huge slippers and a smarmy expression.

I cut him to the quick: "Monsieur Chevalier, hmm, I guess that cliché, large feet—large penis, isn't applicable in France." *Parfait*.

I learned quickly in that single life-changing summer, everything from how to calm a screaming toddler to how to discreetly repel and endure the unwanted seductions of a married man. Still, I took it all lightly, as my main focus was just falling madly, crazily in love with Paris! So when that nanny gig ran its course, I took another and another, just too entranced with the City of Lights to even go home for Christmas. Frankly, I would be curious if anyone could resist the constant seduction of Paris, given the realization that if you just decide to stay here you could—spend your spring days sitting by the magnificent Fountain de Medici in the Jardins du Luxembourg listening to the soothing murmur of the water flowing as the sun shimmers through the tree canopy, sparkling diamonds of light off the water as the fragrance of the opulent blossoms in the gardens embraces you. All the while you sit in a peaceful reverie, enjoying the tranquillity, leisurely making your way through a fresh *brie et jambon baguette,* an ice-cold Perrier in one hand, a collection of Baudelaire's poetry in the other, while the charming voices of playing children mingles like music with the ancient church bells of St. Sulpice, resonating in your soul as they toll the twelve strokes of noon. And that's just lunch in one park, in one season! Imagine how many beautiful and varied visions just one park, say the Tuileries, can offer as it passes from day to night, from spring to winter. Then imagine how many thousands of breathtaking sights there are, how many new and delicious foods there are to experience, fragrances there are to smell, stories in history that each building and setting evokes. . . . The pleasures are endless, as Paris offers just a dizzying array of ways to fascinate, captivate, titillate, astound, and amaze you. For those with a taste for the new and unknown delights of this world, Paris is an addiction that has no antidote, a thirst that cannot be quenched, a lover that never disappoints.

You get it, right? Paris became my lover, my best friend, and my savior. This city grabbed hold of me passionately, and seduced me with its charms and secret pleasures, and I wanted nothing more than to remain drunk within its clutches.

To succumb to and embrace *la vie française* is a charming transition to experience, as the French live their lives with such a passion, it's simply enthralling to share in it. A passion for living well, eating well, dressing beautifully, for music, for history, for literature, for art, for cooking, for making love, even for driving! The smallest act, whether it be laboriously debating the selection of just the most perfect cut of *viande* at the *boucherie* or the extreme care they pay to keep their skin radiant—it's passion to *l'extrême*!

Par exemple: you know the sweet way we American children pull the petals off a daisy as we sit, starry-eyed, experiencing our first crush. And little breathy voices chant, "He loves me, he loves me not, he loves me, etc. . . . *he loves me!*" In France this little rhyme is far more rich and expressive and totally captures the different way they look at *amour*. "*Il m'aime . . . un peu* (he loves me a little), *beaucoup* (a lot), *passionnément* (passionately), *à la folie* (crazily), *ou pas du tout* (or not at all)." *Vive la différence!*

And really, who isn't utterly hypnotized by the mouth-watering aroma of freshly baked croissants filtering from a *boulangerie*'s open doors into the breeze. The mind-blowing architecture and staggeringly beautiful monuments soothe your soul's deepest desires for history and aesthetic delights. Ah, yes. . . . The blooming gardens of the Tuileries, the glittering fountains of Jardins du Luxembourg, the elegant boutiques, the magnetic pull of spending an afternoon on a sunny café terrace. And the *men*! I honestly don't think I was all that wild about men—felt the lure of their masculinity, a desire to discover what excites them—until I began living in Paris. Okay, I'm a late bloomer, but there's more to it than that. There is a sensual intrigue about the way men and women relate here that doesn't exist in the United States. It's difficult to explain, other than that there is just a universal appreciation for the differences between the sexes. And that creates a mystique, a power that each sex celebrates and wields in relationship to the other. It's *partout* (everywhere), as they say here—present in all interactions between men and women. Whether it's simply a new mother buying fresh *saumon* at the *poissonnerie* or a young man serving an older woman her *vin blanc* at a *brasserie*, there is always an element of seduction. Really. From the florist lovingly stroking the stems of the tulips you have chosen to the tailor tenderly caressing a lapel, this culture exudes sensuality. Between men and women it is almost a tango, with the *illusion* of ambiguous flirtation but the understanding that it's born of an unspoken dizzying, raw, wanton sexual desire.

Oh, don't get me started; I get all hot and bothered just thinking about it. They don't call this the City of Lovers for nothing.

CHAPITRE DEUX

When one door closes, another opens elsewhere.

—ANDRÉ GIDE

*L*et's fast-forward. After years of being on the receiving ends of wives' bitter dislike, and dodging husbands with a rapidly acquired precision, I had accumulated enough funds to embark on a new dream: to study for my Ph.D. at the Sorbonne. The focus being no longer French literature, because let's face it, that really is hardly impressive when actually living among the French, where virtually every citizen is as intimately knowledgeable about Balzac as about how to cook a divine *pot au feu*.

I chose art history, and for my thesis, the sumptuously erotic paintings of Boucher. Do you know the work of this eighteenth-century painter? Lusciously voluptuous female nudes languidly reveling in their full femininity, as they indulge in amorous affairs on opulent beds in disarray. So French, *n'est-ce pas?* Romantic scenes just dripping in warm golds, plump pinks, and creamy tones . . . delicious tempting images of women—often courtesans—living lives of pleasures of the flesh. I am also aware that they have had a strong influence on why I may have fantasized about and ultimately adopted my current profession. "Profession" may not be the right word. It's really more of a lifestyle, a mentality . . . oh, so difficult to label. But never mind titles, it's time I tell you precisely how this all came about.

My small savings gave me the means to ensconce myself in an adorable little garret on rue Monsieur le Prince—just round the corner from Théâtre de Odéon in the 6th arrondissement. By little, I mean *très petit*; twenty square meters of living space on the *dernier étage* called a *chambre de bonne* (maid's room) in French. In fact, it was my very first apartment, as previously I had always lived with my charges' families. I loved my quaint flat, and absolutely adored living in the midst of the vibrant Latin quarter. I could walk everywhere in a heartbeat. St. Germain, Île de la Cité, the Marais. And if I woke up late, I'd grab *un pain au chocolat* at the *boulangerie* on the corner and still make it to class at the Sorbonne in ten minutes.

I lovingly decorated my *chambre de bonne* in the crisp white, cheery yellow, and warm orange hues of Provence. These colors are so ubiquitous in French interiors, you can find the most charming of furnishings at ridiculously inexpensive prices. I was quite content with my motley little collection of rickety furniture: an old oak desk, two odd cane chairs, and a three-legged table—all discards found on the streets in my *quartier*. Interestingly, somehow what would be labeled outright as junk anywhere else in the world has endearing charm when nestled in a French garret. Toss in a few pieces of cute pottery and an old chandelier, and it's picture perfect. Think interior decorator Jacques Grange, if he were destitute.

With my tiny budget, a weekly bouquet of fresh white tulips was the single self-treat I could swing. Actually, masturbating was a bigger and more necessary self-treat, but thankfully, that's always free! The blossoming flowers gave me the welcome and necessary illusion of luxury during these meager financial times. Honestly, a venture out to a *resto* was a rare event, but not even much of a temptation, as I busied myself learning to cook *la vraie cuisine française:* soups, crepes, quiches, all made with fresh vegetables bought at the bustling open-air rue du Seine *marché*. Looking back, with a crepe costing about twenty centimes and free masturbating, I could *almost* wax poetic about the pleasures of poverty. *Almost.*

Yep, my little abode was charmingly idyllic—sunny, with a parquet floor of oak so hilariously sloping that you could sail from one side of the room to the other without even moving. The building was built in the seventeenth century, so I guess all the fine craftsmen were busy in Versailles. That warm golden light, light you can only find in France, filtered through a single classic French window. Its large paint-chipped shutters opened onto a view of the bell tower of St. Sulpice. *Magnifique!* Ah, there was no greater pleasure than the delicious freedom to have my most breathtakingly beautiful boyfriend, Laurent, lean me over the window ledge and take me from behind as the bells struck midnight and a strong warm wind chased dark clouds across the moon.

Laurent? you ask. God, even the name still makes me flush and stops my heart. Oh, I was madly in love with Laurent—he was perfect for me: a budding composer, geniusly *amusant*, gentle, as fabulously curious about everything as I was—art, music, opera, architecture, history. . . . And unlike so many other men his age (twenty-five *ans*, *comme moi*) he *was*—strike that, he *seemed*— stable and mature.

Young Frenchmen, no matter how sophisticated they look, are often surprisingly insecure, immature, selfish, still a bit lost trying to define themselves and find their way. Perhaps this stems from the fact that a great many of them continue to live at home while they are in *université* and haven't been sufficiently pushed from the nest to be fully formed. For all their sexy slim hips and cutting jaw lines, they are often more interested in hanging out with their *équipe* (buddies) than developing themselves emotionally, intellectually, or sexually. In short, conversation with these men is often confined to subjects like soccer, new motorcycle helmets, and the new three-layer burger at McDo. And it often includes phrases like "G-spot? Is that a new band?" Ughh!

Where were we? Right. Laurent. I thought he was an exception. Did I mention that he was exquisite? Lean long limbs acquired from years of fencing (how sexy is that?), 196 centimeters tall (trust me, that's tall, six feet four, I think). With espresso brown smiling eyes and thick shiny hair the color of bitter chocolate, full soft lips that kissed with excruciatingly knee-weakening skill, the most beautiful French accent ever (they really do vary, and some are downright jarring). His accent always reminded me of cool water running over smooth stones. I guess it's rather obvious, I was out and out, head over heels in love. And so was he. He would even yell, *"Je t'aime, mon amour. Totalement and passionnément!"* from the street up to me as he would head off to the *conservatoire*. I would fall back onto one of those crappy cane chairs and just bask in the sun, wallowing in perfect happiness at my good fortune.

Like just about every living, breathing soul in Paris (pets included) we were madly in love—joined at the hip constantly, and, well, literally. Mmm . . . he was sooo good in bed, it was like having sex with a thoroughbred racehorse. (I'm not speaking from actual giddy-up experience; it's just a metaphor! I have done a few outrageous sexual acts, but that was Catherine the Great's gig, not mine!)

Laurent and I were completely content to spend every available moment in each other's presence. Thinking back, even the simplest activities were sublime when we were together. We would talk about art and music until the sun came up over a cheap *bouteille de vin rouge*, a baguette, and a round of Camembert.

And with the volatile hot water in my building—generally lasting all of fifteen sacred minutes in the mornings—we'd shower together every morning. Oh, you know that young blind love, waking in your lover's arms, he makes you breakfast in bed, and then pulls you into a warm shower to lovingly wash your hair and sweetly soap your back. Now, I'm aware that this lasts all of about six months! But, those mornings are the treasures of life, whether you know it at the time or not. I was lucky to have day after day, month after month of it. God, just exquisite pleasure, starting each day with that love drug that continually has you unconsciously smiling while humming away. Your pure innate joy deflects any problem or annoyance. You can even see it reflected back as people look at you and can't help but be charmed as you radiate a life force that's palpable and magnetic. Ah, love . . . it catapults everything you do together—from a walk in the rain to running to the *boulangerie*—into a magical, idyllic experience.

And as much as Frenchmen can be cavalier, Laurent was, thankfully, the opposite. Raised with three older sisters by a single mom, he had great sensitivity and a feminine side that was just a drop-dead sexy contrast to his über-masculine physique. Yeah, I tend to go for that in men: contrasts. Either a slightly effeminate exterior with a strong personality or the blow pop type: hard candy shell on the outside—delicious and soft on the inside. (Oh, c'mon, I am hardly the first person to compare a man to a lollypop. You're just lucky I didn't extrapolate that into the sexual domain!) Anyway, you remember being poor and in love. There's nothing quite like it. Because Laurent and I couldn't afford to go anywhere, we'd improvise and end up creating nights, *par exemple,* like our indoor picnic.

Three times a year the gardeners at the Jardins du Luxembourg cut down all the blooming flowers to lay in a fresh crop of new bulbs and buds, leaving heaps and piles of perfectly gorgeous pale violet and egg-yolk yellow irises, velvety soft peonies, and cherry red pansies for anyone who wishes. We'd gather up armfuls, as many flowers as we each could carry home, fill every spare vessel we had with these fragrant blossoms, and arrange them in deep borders, surrounding the classic red-checkered picnic blanket we'd laid on the floor. With baskets of fresh fruit, a cheap chilled Muscadet, and a baked chicken from the rue du Buci outdoor market, we'd feast like we were kings and sure no one in all of Paris was having a more divine meal.

As if his being gentle and loving (and hot as hell!) wasn't enough, man, this boy could make me laugh like no other. He would do great little spontaneous skits, assuming characters and giving voices to people we'd see at a distance or animals trotting by. Like when we'd see a cute little dog being walked by its nutty old kook-a-munga of an owner. Laurent would throw his voice, as though he were the dog, "Oh, for fuck's sake . . . there I sat in the pet store, a very high chance of going home with an energetic, lively kid, and who walks in and puts the cash down for me?! This wack job, and now I'm held hostage in her shit apartment, as big as a shoebox, and captive to her nauseating kisses that smell like a monkey's butt. If she ever lets me off this damn leash for even a millisecond, I'm so making a run for it!" I loved it when he would launch into that spontaneous wit. Taking a basic idea or common moment in life, and carrying it into a hilarious abstract scene. He was a master. It rocked my world. I don't know how important *humor* is in your book, but for me it's right up there, as imperative as, well, having a penis. And if someone's got *both*? I'm all over that creature like a cheap suit. Funny = sexy. I defy you to argue that.

I know I'm carrying on, but—and it may surprise you—though a courtesan, I'm still a hugely sentimental romantic, so please indulge me and let me tell you one last Laurent story, as this was the innocent time in my life, when money, power, and decadence played no role—*yet*.

It was St. Valentine's Day. As this semi-Hallmark-created holiday was just catching on in France, Laurent wasn't entirely sure what it was about. At some point, I blithered off a brief wrap-up of bullet points—a cupid shoots an arrow through the lovers' hearts, blah-blah; chocolate, red roses, blah-blah, and poetry are exchanged; professions of love, and all things red. (Skipping the fact that generally, in the USA, Valentine's Day is often a huge bummer, the pressure of society resulting in women sadistically, cruelly comparing themselves to other women in their offices, dorms, or neighborhoods, who flash their diamonds and flaunt their bigger bouquets and marriage proposals. Oh, please, you *know* I'm right.)

Anyhow, I only mentioned it to Laurent because he asked; I wasn't expecting anything. Frankly, he showered me with such attention and sweetness every day, it seemed greedy to hope for more.

Well, that day was a Wednesday, and he'd slept at his own flat the previous night, so we had planned to make dinner together that night at my house. We were going to make a second attempt at a

Champagne risotto (the first time we gave it a whirl we agreed it would've made an excellent mortar for brickwork construction); now we were shooting for something slightly more in the edible family. The splurge of a bottle of Champagne would be put to a frugal dual use, for both *la cuisine* and *les boissons* (beverages). Frankly, when you're a student there tends to be a lot of "dual use" activity: sheets doubling as drapes, a desk doubling as a dining table, pencils as hair sticks, pillow case as laundry bag, et cetera.

Anyway, that day, I scooted off to the Sorbonne, to class in some silly get-up of a peasant dress with slim pants underneath—*remember that microsecond trend?* I rode it out all winter, like a dope, thinking I was *so Bobo* (*bo*hemian *bo*urgeois). At any rate, I'm sitting in a lecture by Monsieur Melenic on the paintings of Watteau, when all sixty eyes in the room are drawn like magnets to some commotion in the back of the lecture hall.

Always trying to resist the alarm of the populace, I played it cool, eventually, casually glancing at the activity drawing everyone's interest. Oh my God! No fucking way! A very tall man dressed in red tights, wearing a tight red T-shirt, white boxers dotted with red hearts, and sporting red Converse high-tops, is leaping down the stairs, a quiver of arrows tossed over his shoulder, a bow at the ready, a dozen red helium-filled balloons bouncing about, and big red plastic heart-shaped glasses as his sole disguise. And he's singing! Loudly! "Oh my darlin', oh my darlin', oh my darlin' Alexandra!" (to the tune of "Clementine," simply because it's the only American song he knows!) and wildly seeking out my face in the crowd.

Ei yi yi! I half want to slither under the desk, disappearing, and half want to wave my hand overhead, "I'm over here, baby!" Needless to say, the *professeur* is *très* unamused and the students are roaring with laughter; all of them are wondering who this overgrown putto will descend on. Laurent sees me, continues the leaping, and lands at my feet, where he assumes one knee, and hands me the huge, distractingly active bouquet of balloons while pulling something out of his sleeve. The crowd of students howls as he recites a little poem he's written to me *en anglais*, and sweeps in for a kiss on my cheek before leaping back to the aisle. He bows to all, and bids a *merci* and *adieu* to Professeur Melenic, hightails it two stairs at a time, and whisks out of the lecture hall. I have turned beet red verging on purple, but I am so unbelievably charmed and amazed with this thoughtful and courageous to the edge of ridiculous act. That free-spirited sweetheart with endless creativity and great legs (even in red tights) is my man!

Fellow students ask, "Who sent you that Valentine's message? That guy was hilarious! And what a getup! You'll have to tell your boyfriend what a riot it was." Wow. I hadn't thought for a second that people just wouldn't instantly know, *that was* my boyfriend. Funnier still. They think it was some hired lunatic.

The rest of the lecture was a total loss, as the twelve huge balloons hovering above served as constant reminders of the *amour* of my dreams. I sat there with a stupid drunk-in-love grin, not caring at all if Watteau was an eighteenth-century painter or a grub-digging aborigine.

Get the gist? It was Bliss, with a capital B, I tell you. Thus, after six more dreamlike months together, when he asked me to move in with him I literally leaped up and down with joy. (So much so, the impact made the neighbors' crystal light fixture *fall from the ceiling*! Oops, *c'est la vie*, I didn't care—I was ecstatic.)

One week later, on a rainy *dimanche matin*, snuggled in bed together *chez moi* like two *petit pois*, Laurent upped the ante with his extreme spontaneity: He asked me to marry him! As you can imagine, I yelped out an instant, "*Oui . . .* yes *. . . bien sûr . . .* fuck, yes!" A general euphoria swallowed us up, and I wallowed in ecstasy for three beautiful days. Until Laurent, seventy-two hours *après l'offre en mariage*, left me. Yeah. Can you believe that shit?! Refusing to say anything but "I am sorry, I guess I feel too young for this kind of commitment. I need to be free."

As mid-love fest we'd gathered up all our frequent-flyer miles and booked two cheap tickets to Greece for the upcoming fall, I was sure he'd ring and we'd somehow still end up on a beach in

Santorini laughing about his brief and silly departure. So you can bet, I spent about the next four weeks eagerly awaiting what I was sure was Laurent's "I've been such fool, I love you . . . Please take me back!" telephone call. I actually looked forward to his groveling aplenty, possibly gifts of flowers and/or poetry, some romantic gesture, so we could fall back in step as the perfect soul mate couple who also happened to shag with abandon.

Like most women who've been walked out on, I spent every waking minute conjuring up the various responses I would employ when this event would unfold, all of which had as their central theme my initial hostile refusal, which segued into reluctant acceptance, with the effect of course that he comes back but I make him sweat . . . and then we'd go sweat together in the sunny Greek isles and dance beneath the moonlight. But my once-upon-a-time-future husband never rang, wrote, or arrived with said plea or apology. How appallingly crappy of him!

Okay, okay. I can see now that his brutal departure was your standard, run-of-the-mill "panic anxiety freak-out" that many a young man suffers from at least once. Still, I was devastated. Throw in a lot of tragic pain, feelings of abandonment and anger, and you get the mind-set. Try: I wished we'd made a suicide pact together, and then I'd say, "You first," let him off himself, and joyously carry on living knowing there'd be one less *connard* (asshole) in Paris.

I guess it's fairly obvious that when Laurent left me abruptly, I was so hurt and stunned that I just felt a total loss of control. Fold into that the reality that sometimes being an ex-pat can make you feel as anxiously out of your element as you are thrilled with trying on this new life for size. And if that "new life" gets ripped out from under you, you feel suddenly powerless—being an ex-pat alone can also seriously shake your core personality. Especially if there is a trigger that sets that into motion—you can find yourself with no roots, living away from everything that had previously always acted as your own internal ballast, that guided you to a safe emotional place.

Yes, perhaps there's something to the idea that I was ripe and ready to switch gears from men my own age, the life that I knew, and promises that disappear as fast as free Champagne. Still, I had no idea I was bound for a reign as a *grande courtisane de Paris*.

My metamorphosis happened in the blink of an eye.

About a month after the dumped *sans raison* incident, my best friend, Isabel, offered me an invitation that seemed fun and distracting. Isabel was one cool chick; she had more innate style and *joie de vivre* than any girl I'd ever met before. Like me she had long brown hair and was stick thin, but unlike me she somehow made the whole flat-chest/boy body look elegant and sexy. French girls have cornered the market on that! She was a young fashion designer, twenty-four years old—one year younger than me—and was working her tail off as a *stagiaire* (intern) at the couture house of Balmain. I'd met her two years before at the big group picnic (*pique-nique en français;* isn't it funny how every word is just prettier in French?) on the lawn of the Tour Eiffel, called Champ de Mars.

For people my age it's a standard summer *fête* to meet up with *tes amies* after work on the huge green lawn, everyone unpacking a round of Brie, a rope of *saucissons secs* or a homemade *céleri rémoulade*, sharing everything as bottles of chilled white wine empty rapidly. As the sun sets and the crowd gets so thick there's hardly a place to sit, the wine works its magic and it becomes one huge effervescent party under the starry skies. Such an enchanting way to spend a summer night—the dewy grass, the deep lavender sky, the festive moods, laughter, and new friends. For young Parisians on budgets, there is no better way to spend an evening than finishing a warm night drinking warm rosé, chatting up someone new as the Tour Eiffel starts its ten-minute sparkling show of glittering lights. Even if you were born and raised *dans Paris centre*, nights like this cloak you in the happy certainity that life really doesn't get much better than this.

Anyway, now that you *finally* get the setting. I was arriving with a couple of other au pairs I'd met working in my *quartier* (neighborhod). I vaguely remember them as, more or less, people with whom I had little in common other than similar employment, and, well . . . breasts. Not tons to talk about really, but as an ex-pat you take your friends where you can get 'em!

Isabel was part of a large group, sitting about five feet away, and as I laid eyes on this skinny androgynous girl, I knew instantly that I'd like her. She was wearing capri jeans, simple cotton espadrilles, and a tank top with this big floppy sixties flowery hat that was just the definition of "I just like the hat; I know it looks dumb, but it's fun and I'm not trying to be the most alluring, seductive girl!" She looked cool and relaxed in her own skin. Not something you see often in young French women. They are generally, in a word: self-aware and *guarded*. Okay, that's two words. But I had to throw in the *guarded*. Isabel asked if she could use my *tire-bouchon* (corkscrew—which I never did get back, come to think of it) to open a stubborn bottle of Muscadet, and we hit it off from word one. Okay, truth be told, she was also one of the only French women who's ever asked me for my number, and by crazy cool luck, about the only girl I'd met in France that I would've wanted to give it to. We totally connected when I made another of my major screw-ups—I'd realized there were tons of leftovers and I wanted to wrap them up with some of the Saran Wrap I thought I saw in someone's picnic basket. With my ever-shaky use of French, I asked her if she had any *préservatifs* that I could possibly use to cover the Brie. She fell on her back laughing so hard she wept! When she could finally speak without roaring, she explained that I had just asked for a condom to put the Brie in. Yeah. Great. Gotta love those faux pas *en français*! Always *très* grounding and humbling!

After a few weeks of marathon chat-fest rendezvous at cafés, seeing films together and helping her drill holes for drapery rods— not an easy task with three-meter ceilings, plaster walls, and no ladder, I can tell you! We were like Chinese acrobats teetering on chairs, constantly falling down laughing—I maneuvered her into the *très vide* (quite empty) "best friend" role I'd never thought I could fill in Paris. I adored her innate charm, her eager ambition, and her energy. And thankfully, she, like a gift from God, welcomed me into her crowd of young hipsters and smart creative types. Phew. Let's just say, after way too many years of playing *fausse mère à la* au pair, I was damn glad to not be chanting *"Alouette! Gentille alouette!"* and dabbing spittle off baby-smooth chins anymore. Now I was finding myself chanting, "You know him, Isabel? I want to meet him!" and dabbing drool off my own chin.

In two years we bonded like sisters, doing everything together, from trawling the *soldes* (sales) in boutiques twice a year to finishing each other's sentences. Sitting together on the Pont des Arts, devouring freshly baked madeleines from the *boulangerie* while leaning against each other as though the other's back was a bench. Sharing dreams and making each other laugh when things went from "super!" to *"pas* super."

So, knowing I'd been through hell and back when Laurent left, Isabel once again had my back, and with an eye to cheering me up and shaking me from my sullen catatonia, she generously snagged me a free ticket to the Balmain summer *défilé* (fashion show) and the cocktail party afterward at sunset in the beyond opulent Hôtel de Crillon.

I immediately wagered this was something Laurent surely wouldn't be at (to be honest, I think I stayed hunkered down at home for four solid weeks out of the sheer terror of running into him with another woman on his arm—hey, I never said I was mature) and an opportunity to wear the incredible dress Isabel had stolen from work for me as a "cheer up—here's a dress you could never afford" gesture. Please don't judge her for her thievery, and keep in mind she was working without a salary for six months!

So, slipping into the fabulous pale gun-metal gray silk dress cut on the bias designed by Nicolas Ghesquiere, was a sublime escape from my traditional Agnès B. boy-cut jeans and jean jacket, yet another look they refer to in Paris as *Bobo*. (Essentially anything chic with an edge, and generally involving one item that's cheap and borderline wrong.) I even ripped a photo out of *L'Officiel* magazine of a model with a chic-to-die hairdo—all pin waves with a diamond hairpin—and copied it to the T. Okay, not to the T: the hairpin was a cheap Monoprix barrette with glued-on rhinestones. Poverty and time on your hands can be very inspiring!

Standing before the crack-aged mirror in my apartment, I felt a distinct Cinderella moment. "You know, Alexandra, you clean up pretty damn well," I said to myself as I realized how beautiful clothes can transform your entire being, from your mood to the way you carry yourself. I smiled, and it occurred to me that, amazingly enough, life was going to continue and I was going to be *fine*.

The dark thunderclouds of sadness that had followed me for the previous month lifted magnificently and late afternoon golden sunlight flooded the room. I grabbed the black makeup bag that was about to make its debut as a "clutch" and happily set out for the hike down five stories of stairs to the street. A giggle escaped my lips as I heard my heels clattering on the wood stairs, a rhythmic melody as joyous as my mood. *Charmante!* There was no doubt about it; I was decadently going to treat myself to the pricey taxi ride to the Crillon. Nine euros to arrive fresh, feeling a new, chicer self in that fabulous dress—so worth every centime!

You know what? I think that if I can lay the blame anywhere for my new profession, I could safely pin it on the dress. No, seriously. This dress was a feast for the eyes, and *it*, if I do humbly say so, looked rather amazing on me. Completely transforming me from *une étudiante* to, if you squint a little, quite possibly, runway model. Trust me, I was *so* up for feeling like someone new. Keep in mind, I was at a place where the most tactile erotic experience in a month had been the shampooist at the *coiffeur* massaging my scalp. (Hey, you have to acknowledge it, the shampooing massage does occasionally have a crazy sexual effect.)

Here's the equation: take one freshly dumped girl plus sexual libido revived by slithery sexy dress caressing neglected femininity, multiply by a rare chance opportunity, and the result is an exponentially profound desire for new existence! Or something like that!

The fashion show was absolutely amazing. The head designer, Nicolas Ghesquiere, is a genius. And I took note—a terribly sexy man to boot. Hormones definitely up and running again. Thank the lord!

I perched on the edge of my designated seat riveted, straining over the sea of coiffured heads, to see every detail. The surreal alien creatures they call *"mannequins"* striding with their sensual confidence as the über-groovy music reverberated in my chest. The silk chiffons and gossamer light tulles floated and undulated in the air. The exquisite beading and glistening jewels shot prisms of light off every surface. The music, the dresses, the opulence . . . I was in awe on every level. I couldn't imagine what kind of woman would be so fortunate to wear clothes that remarkable *every day*. Well, hell, I guess that would be all the other women here? Lucky bitches. I glanced around the room. Wow. Yes, indeedy, it was a terribly heady experience to find myself among such a crowd of the *bon ton* of France as I had, of course, only previously glimpsed these people in magazines, films, and the odd sighting at Café de la Marie. Gérard Depardieu, Carla Bruni, Catherine Deneuve, Sophie Marceau . . . and *me*, way off to the back to be sure, but not getting chucked out on my ear, amazingly. *At least, not yet.*

The famous and almost famous rushed backstage after the show. I more or less followed the crowd, partly out of cluelessness of where to go and partly in hope of finding Isabel. All the while trying to span my entire hand over my faux clutch, as I suddenly felt my makeup bag had been hideously miscast as a purse and was convincing no one. Mental note: Chuck backpack, get real purse, you tomboy! I shuffled out of the way of photographers, attempted to appear properly jaded, and spotted Isabel hanging clothes back on the racks.

I rushed over and embraced her, full of genuine pride and admiration. "Isabel, that was sheer brilliance! God, I'm so impressed. What an amazing show!"

"It was cool, right? I only saw bits on the video prompter, but it went off without a hitch. . . . Except somebody seems to have swiped a necklace and I have to find it pronto or it'll be my head. So, give me a minute here and I will catch up with you at the cocktail gig. Do you know where it is?" she asked, as she jammed silk stockings into a plastic bag.

"Ah . . . that would be a no. Never been here before, *évidemment*," I say, smiling, but feeling very much the *poisson* out of water.

"Follow the fashion lemmings, my dear. . . . And the dress looks divine. Remember, if anyone asks, you bought it in London," she whispers, stacking hats into hat boxes.

"Righty-o! Scoot over to the reception when you can, angel. I will be the one standing alone, looking like a dork!" I quip, as I fall in with the masses headed to the Champagne reception. Still the *poisson*, now swimming upstream through wave upon wave of the full splendor of fashion-speak; utterings of the "*La collection est génial!*" type and "Fab-U-lus!" bounced off cheeks and walls. The ballroom was a blur of air kisses, glimmering jewelry, and the "beautiful people" in all their finery. And one not so fine: some weird old hag standing on a chair, raising her glass to the sky, and clad in a hat the size and appearance of a helicopter—who let her in?

I took command of myself, brought my dropped jaw back up to my face, and parked myself at the least bustling of the zinc bars. I was making quick work of my *deuxième flûte de Champagne*, eyeing the crowd and thinking, "Everyone's in black. To the uninformed eye this would very much resemble the chicest funeral wake on record." Another sip of Moët and then, "Isabel, get your ass over here *tout de suite*, this is starting to get painful." Then I saw *him*. *Oui, the* him, who would become lover *numéro un*. My first, and frankly, my favorite.

Three meters off to the right and the center of attention—the essence of exquisite elegance.

A bit of a risk here, to be so revealing, but I'm going for it. I'll give you a big hint: He is the president of one of the world's largest luxury goods conglomerates that owns the lion's share of top couture and ready-to-wear houses in Paris. (Wow, oops, that was less of a hint and more of biography, only falling short of including a photo!) Anyway, you get it: Two words from his mouth wield the power to make the Bourse (Paris stock market) plummet. Right. His last name alone is globally respected, revered, and known to all. Think: France's version of Donald Trump but deduct Donald's bad comb-over, scary eyebrows, cheesy pretentiousness. Oh, hell, don't think Trump at all, actually! Think: a dignified, trim man in his late fifties, graying at the temples, with an aristocratic heritage evident in his Gallic nose, his grand way of carrying himself, and his refined gestures. Okay, truth be told, his name is Jean-Albert.

But of course, he's dressed impeccably, in a charcoal pinstripe suit and the most beautiful crisp white shirt I have ever seen. Strangely, I feel myself instantly drawn to touch it. Oh, and on the downside, Jean-Albert's my height, 174 cm (5 feet 7 inches) and has not much in the way of lips. But clearly on the plus side: zillionaire. (*That does always seem to fall on the plus side, now doesn't it?*)

I watch him a bit, forget about Isabel, and get lost in thought. "Well, he's just dripping with power. Incredible, as that makes not-so-sexy men instantly sexy." Hence the historical sexual appeal of men like Henry Kissinger, François Mitterrand, and Napoleon. Monsieur le Zillionaire glances my way briefly, as he continues to carry on a conversation with Catherine Deneuve, which I can't hear but that I hope was, "Cat . . . chill on the plastic surgery; you're starting to resemble that woman from the film *Brazil*." (Doubtful, though.)

He's surrounded by flanks of fashionistas, bodyguards, and his very attractive, thin wife with shimmering copper hair. I look at her, all frozen smiles and silently "standing by her man," and think, "Hmm, I wonder if she enjoys being the woman on his arm?" Glamorous? Yes. But there's something in her eyes that's sad. My attentions wander back to him. Astonishingly, I find he meets my glance and shoots me a look akin to "well, *bonjour*, stranger," and adds an exclamation point to it by raising an eyebrow slowly—and damn seductively, I might add.

I feel that warm rush in my loins. Loins? You know what I'm talking about; that unmistakable ache that passes through you when you unexpectedly feel yourself drawn to a man. It'd been so long that I'd assumed I'd used up my quota!

Whatever indefinable magical aura this man possessed, I, like everyone in the room, fell instantly under its spell. Exciting and unnerving as all get out, I tell you, as I found myself "replying" in kind with my best effort in the enticing gaze repertoire—which, frankly, hadn't gotten out much.

By some extraordinary alignment of the planets preordained by the gods of fate—or, more likely, sheer dumb luck—he pries himself away from the throng of press, adorers, and, *mon dieu*, the wife, a mere moment after my demure but flirtatious smile. I know, amazing! Not really sure what I'm doing here with the seductive come hither look, so I nervously spin back to the bar and look in the reflection of the mirror in front of me to track what still seems to me astonishing: his imminent arrival. The room seems to fall silent save for the dull roar of my heart pounding in my chest as I realize, I am *so* out of my league here.

A moment later I feel the warmth of his body approaching on my left as an intoxicating waft of his fragrance arrives in tow. Or is that intoxicating smell the aroma of power? Who knows. Together they are hypnotizing.

He places himself next to me, so close our arms are touching ever so lightly. He orders, or rather immediately is offered, a glass of Champagne. He places his empty flute on the zinc bar and looks at me, not directly, but in the reflection of *both* of us in the mirror. Why this move is so incredibly sexy, I can't explain. Why have I never noticed the strangely intimate effect of this technique before? I make a mental note to employ this more at every possible occasion.

Then in a voice I have only heard before on the business news (but *en français* of course): "You are the only person here whom I have not had the pleasure of meeting before . . . and by far the most beautiful."

Okay, you and I both know that's such a lie—*and so works*. Man, he's good. Sure. Flattery usually works for me—and this is a completely staggering compliment as I wobble in my heels next to the most beautiful models in the world. And entirely untrue, of course, as Gisele Bündchen strides by like a Brazilian tigress of perfection. Why do women like that even inhabit the planet? Ugh. But his mission is accomplished; I am truly flattered and instantly putty in his hands *and wishing my ex, that bastard Laurent, was in earshot!*

I reply, or try to, with bemused admiration and sincere gratitude, but my nervous mouth becomes as dry as the Sahara and beyond my ability to control, "*Merci*, you are very kind . . . and clearly
have been drinking." (I could shoot myself! Did I just say that?!)

He laughs gently, smiles, and continues to speak to me while
we look at our reflections in the mirror.

"Do I have to beg . . . to know your name?" He inquires with a
seductive lilt, as he takes a long, slow sip of Champagne.

"Yes, on your knees, young man. I want to see pleading," I
throw back, like I'm talking to the boy who works at the café around
the corner.

Somehow, like an epiphany, I have a flash of insight and understanding. I instantly, innately realize that everyone on earth praises,
worships, and caters to this man, and I can captivate him *only* by
treating him like the insecure twelve-year-old *garçon* he must still
be somewhere inside. Genius of me, really. (And as a footnote: This
is the key to dealing with powerful men. Though it does tend to
parlay into my now very established theory that the most powerful
men in the world want to act like vulnerable babies, and to whine
and whimper during sex. Details on that to come. *And it's not pretty.*)

"On my knees? You know I can't do that. It'll be immediately
photographed and splashed across newspapers by the morning,"
Monsieur le Zillionaire counters, clearly amused.

"Morning? I was hoping it'd make the evening paper, as I do so
love a good laugh before bed," I answer, zipping full-speed ahead
on the sassy autobahn.

Our flirt-a-thon is interrupted briefly by the sudden arrival of a
couple obviously hoping to be allowed a moment of his attention.
With a brush of the hand, he dismisses them, and they flee at once.
Cool move.

A chuckle slinks out of his mouth as he silently taps his crystal
flute to mine and holds my gaze in the mirror. Simultaneously
noticing our image reflected to infinity between the large mirrors
on opposing walls, we smile in mutual recognition of this fun-
house illusion. Surreal? *Oui.*

"You really are an obstinate young woman. Do you know who I am?" he asks proudly, with an accent as thick as foie gras. I offer him a coy semismile back, having clearly embraced the new cocky Alexandra that must have been lingering just under the surface for twenty-five years.

"No, should I? More importantly, do you know who *I* am?" I reply, feigning both ignorance and indignance. It's the dress talking. *And* the Champagne.

"Well, well, well. As I said, I do not. But my curiosity continues to grow," Monsieur le Zillionaire replies, with a sly smile.

I glance down at his pants, assured my follow-up comment is on target—and *it is*. His swollen sex strains the zipper of his trousers. His eyes follow mine as we acknowledge his ever-increasing interest.

"Growing curiosity? Yes, I can see that. Charming of you to rise to the occasion," I add, raising an eyebrow.

A loud, voluptuous laugh escapes his lips. It's clear he's not the slightest bit embarrassed; on the contrary, he's terribly proud. *Remember: He's French.*

"I'll have you know that, thanks to you, I cannot turn around now and face the press," he says, gesturing back to the beckoning photographers and movie cameras.

"Right. Whatever are you going to do, monsieur?" (Yeah, that would be me, going full stop: *jeune femme avec beaucoup d'attitude*.)

"Whatever you wish, Mademoiselle." (Staggeringly sexy retort, huh? I told you this man is good. Suddenly the lack of lips doesn't seem like such a detriment.)

"Hmm." I pause, not so much for drama as to try to come up with some clever, seductive idea of a reply. I wish like hell I could hit pause and really take some time to debate down to the most clever and witty possibility. Not an option, carry on, girl. Well, here goes nothin'. And I launch into the only thing I can think of: "Meet me tomorrow at three."

"But I have a meeting with the Minister of Finance," he protests.

I brazenly continue as though he's rudely interrupted the teacher, "Cancel it . . . as I was saying, meet me tomorrow at the *glacier* (ice cream stand) in the Tuileries at three. Order me a *vanille* (oh, the irony!) ice cream and have it ready when I arrive."

And with that I give him one last full-on penetrating look. His response? Well, he is all but purring with satisfaction. I grab that hideous wannabe clutch and prance off. Okay, more like try to put one foot in front of the other and not knock over the approaching waiter balancing a tray of Champagne flutes as I simultaneously fight to maintain this total façade of assuredness, *and* before he has a chance to yell something like, "Oh, get over yourself, girl! You're not all that!"

I hurriedly make my exit, and by more of that dumb luck run smack into Isabel at the bar across the room. She's quite obviously trying to hit on the hot actor Vincent Cassel. (Who, by the way, is married to the gorgeous Monica Bellucci, but as I've said, *and you must get the hang of this*, in France there are no barriers to seduction. It thrives on the forbidden. Trust me on that, I so know whereof I speak.) She instantly throws in the towel and retreats after seeing my wild-eyed expression.

"Isabel . . . wow, Vincent Cassel? Did you tell him he's your sexual fantasy? He's mine, too . . . Hell, he's every woman's fantasy." Clearly, I'm attempting to address her little *tête à tête*, though all I really want to do is recap my brush with a zillionaire, squealing like giddy little girls. Isabel had already glimpsed my *par hasard* (by chance) meeting of Mr. Rich Guy—no lips and *sans doute* that took precedence in the flirting with famous men de Paris competion.

"Alexandra . . . Stop . . . Just tell me what in the hell you were doing talking to him?!!!" she demands excitedly, handing me another Champagne off a passing tray. Best friend across the board there.

"I know . . . Do you believe it?! I am sure he was only hitting on me because I'm the *only* woman here he hasn't slept with!" And I unload the story with the enthusiasm of a ten-year-old, line by line, gesture by gesture. Like a perfect partner in crime, she falls into peals of laughter and howls with delight as I recount the whole scenario.

Unwilling to drop this subject, as it's the most fun thing that's happened to me in the last four weeks (not counting the previous

record holder: the high-drama thrill of a mouse running across my
face as I slept the night before. Oh, the glamorous life I'd been living!), I keep turning over the details.

"But let's be serious, Isabel. There's no way he'll show up at an
ice cream stand! It was a riot to see his expression, though. I could
die laughing!"

"Alexandra, where in God's name did you come up with that
absurd suggestion? If you had a chance *at all*, you blew it there,"
she says, trying to gently bring reality back to my world.

"I know. Just always thought that'd be a funny proposal. Oh
well, I enjoyed the whole thing anyway. Really, I can't thank you
enough for this invite! How thrilling . . . But, c'mon girl. You gotta
say, for an old guy, he *is* rather sexy," I say, scanning the room to lay
my eyes on him again. It appears he's just leaving as cameras flash
wildly by the exit and bodyguards trail out the door.

The next morning I woke in a post-*reconnaissance* reality check:
"No way he'll ever turn up in the Tuileries today, but *mon dieu*,
what fun it was to play the demanding bitch card." I swear I could
get the hang of this! Honestly, that felt more *me* than when I'm
talking to men my own age and trying to shave my personality
down to their meager desires.

With the gunmetal gray slip dress hanging in my armoire like
Batman's costume in Bruce Wayne's closet, I switch back into my
daily uniform of jeans and your classic white shirt. Real life to resume whether I prefer it or not. Time to step out of the dream and
back into my daily routine; gotta hustle over for some more of that
mind-numbing thesis research in the dark bowels of the Bibliothèque Nationale.

With a homemade *baguette du poulet* and an Orangina Light
tucked into my bag for a quick lunch in the sun, I head out onto rue
Monsieur le Prince, debating where to park my *derrière* for today's
little budget lunch. With all the beautiful options, sometimes it's
damn hard to choose a locale. It occurs to me, "Hey, it's two
o'clock, and I do *have to* pass through the Tuileries. That's the plan:
déjeuner sur l'herbe, and then it will be around three. It wouldn't hurt

to check. Then again . . ." I look down to critique my look—or lack thereof. Oh, foolish of me to even consider this. Sneakers and my fourteen-euro Ober jeans, which are like the equivalent of Wrangler, for God's sake! Like that's chic. Damn, I do have to start shedding the student-with-a-master's-in-poverty look and embrace dressing like *une femme élégante* soon.

Still, I stop in the gardens, devour my lunch in ten minutes, and just linger . . . and linger. As though my legs have a life of their own, I am magnetically drawn toward the *glacier*. Pathetic, really. Subconsciously fooling myself that the warm autumn sun is just so darn enchanting that I am compelled to sit and have cigarette after cigarette on the stone ledge overlooking the *glacier*.

My thoughts wander as I let a tiny black ant crawl up my hand and tour through my arm hair. Somehow it feels good, and I laugh at realizing it's yet another of my strange triggers for sensual pleasure. Ants crawling on me, international license plates, the smell of toast, licking fresh figs, the caress of my own hair blowing across my face, the smell of a new book—it's a wacky list, I admit.

Thoughtlessly, I let my cigarette burn to the filter, and that's my cue to give up on this latest round of random thoughts. I pack my backpack, place my new ant friend gently out of harm's way, and head off toward rue de Rivoli. Halfway there my cell phone vibrates and I negotiate it out of my front jeans pocket.

INBOX: 1 TEXTO
Tell me U R not there waiting! Meet U 4 apéro later at Café Noir. We gotta find U a new homme? Bisous, Isabel

I smirk. She knows me *so* well. Taking a heavy, deep breath of acceptance of my predictability, I turn toward the rue de Rivoli, when I hear, "What? Are you *that* impatient? I'm only four minutes late!" And I whip around in a virtual cartoon-quick spin in my disbelief.

It's him. Monsieur le Zillionaire. Ten meters back. Standing there in all his refined elegance. With two scoops of *vanille* on a cone and a big smile, complete with no lips.

I will never forget this moment. I knew instantly that my whole life was about to change in a compelling, significant way. And that even if I wished it, there was no way I was *not* going to throw myself into it madly and with total abandon. The sunlight literally beat down with such intensity that it radiated into an all-white flash, and I just stood a second, living those last fleeting moments of my old life. And with a single step toward him and a flick of my hand through my hair, I set off on my journey.

CHAPITRE TROIS

Sex pleasure in woman is a kind of magic spell; it demands complete abandon; if words or movements oppose the magic of caresses, the spell is broken.

—SIMONE DE BEAUVOIR

We should clear something up right now. Since I'm inviting you to come along for the ride, I think it's only fair you have the big picture, so we understand each other. First, I would like you to know that I didn't quite *get* the role I was assuming when I embarked on my adventure. You see, this small-town hickster from Elmbrook spent a fairly kooky first few weeks under the impression I was being pursued by Jean-Albert to become, well, a serious girlfriend. What with all his exuberance and attention, he appeared to be so astonishingly smitten that I thought he might even have been considering leaving his wife for me. Are you laughing out loud? Fair enough. May I attribute this heinous miscalculation to my youth, my sense of awe, to the overwhelming headiness of it all? That might be fair in the USA, but in France—at least in this high-powered world of old money and immense power—nothing's as simple as that.

In matters of all extramarital liaisons involving sex, or heartfelt emotions, or both, there are historical traditions—"cultural guidelines" if you will—just as strict as the rules that apply to how to decant and serve a fine Château Lafont.

Sans doute, these distinct perimeters must be acknowledged and adhered to with as much innate comprehension as possible. All well and good if you've grown up saturated with it: seeing your *père* slink off with his mistress as your *maman* turns a blind eye, or having observed the universal acceptance of these affairs and courtships as often as you've slathered your *croissant chaud* with *confiture*. But as we all know, that wasn't my past by a long shot. I was well versed in knowledge of the proper way to shuck corn and keep snow out of your winter boots variety.

Sure, I was well aware from my au pair forays that married men cheat for fun and distraction, but boy oh, boy, I was not hip to how or when one actually assumes the mistress or courtesan role. Nor, clearly, what makes that role so uniquely different from a brief dalliance. So, like a bit of a dork, I spent the first two weeks of this overwhelming ride into Jean-Albert's center of gravity—extravagant dinners, white-tablecloth lunches, endless flower arrangements arriving at all hours, small but pricey gifts bestowed at every meeting—thinking, my God, this guy is going absolutely bananas for me! He has all but canceled every one of his previously scheduled evening rendezvous to see *me*—to meet *me* for a walk in the rain, to take *me* to the opera and place *me* at his side in the family box! And then there's that sweet afternoon he rang and begged eagerly to know my exact location so he could whisk by and "feel the exquisite curve of your warm waist beneath my fingers . . . if only for a few moments"?! Oh, yes, a lot of self-absorbed cluelessness going on there on my end! I was sure he was fixin' to leave his wife and marry me. Charmingly naïve? Nah, just ridiculously ignorant to the intricate mating dance of the Paris haut monde. No, dear girl, you're not the be-all-end-all who has captured him like no other. These men—well, they pretty much *always* lavish over-the-top gifts and expressions of love and adoration and passion beyond reason. It's *not* that I was so worthy and so spectacular; it's just the modus operandi, the protocol of the game between cat and mouse. Note that in this scenario of courtesan and lover, the cat is the woman and the man is willingly the mouse who enjoys getting batted around and living in danger. Leave it to the

French to always twist a seduction into something far more risky and shocking. Thus, it was only when Jean-Albert unconsciously let slip the following that I truly understood my situation: "It's my wife's birthday this weekend; what do you think I should offer her? After twenty-five years, I am running out of ideas, and this year she really deserves something exceptional." Ooh la-la. Reality check time, Alexandra. And not a moment too soon! Jean-Albert was not going anywhere. The old ball and chain may be 24k gold and emblazoned with diamonds, but it's on tight and good and locked. Thank God I tuned in at this point, or surely soon enough I would've been launching into my usual routine—calling him my boyfriend and mentally starting to plot our wedding. Need I add, of course, arranging our wedding to be so well covered by the press that Laurent the *pièce de merde* would have to endure it plastered across all kiosks and magazine covers throughout Paris and beyond? Petty of me? *Oui*. Malicious? *Non*. Malicious would be actually sending him an invite and/or catalogued photos of all my gifts. Ahh. Enough about *merde-tête* Laurent. Now on to the next detail you should be informed of.

At this revelation and wake-up call—having been effectively clued into the notion I was being pursued as a companion and *not* a future wife—I acquired some serious *rules*. Truthfully, they're pretty much the same ones I cooked up once I decided to play and stepped into the life of a modern French courtesan.

Rule number one: I don't take cash. Well, I do, sometimes, but it's not like, "Thanks for the blow job, here's five hundred euros." More like, I'm invited to Gstaad or some such locale, and obviously don't have an au courant arctic ski wardrobe, and my lover (they are not "clients"; it's not like they send me a W-2 form at tax time!) offers me "spending money" for the day to shop, and outfit myself as he spends the day in some big hostile takeover meeting.

As a matter of fact, I often don't need to do anything but— would you believe—sign my name. Perhaps you're in on this, but I have to say, I sooo didn't know this was an option. At a certain level of wealth and a boutique's or an establishment's familiarity with your spending habits, you can simply run an account. Clarification: I don't have an account in my name, but after the initial shopping forays to the likes of Chanel, Fendi, and Cartier, the staff is formally *made aware* that my purchases will be covered by Monsieur Mogul.

And gang, this whole "walk out of the shop scot-free" idea also is applicable at Michelin-star restaurants like the Ritz, Taillevent, Guy Savoy . . . anywhere the extremely wealthy dine. Cool, huh? Who knew? I also have the coveted Centurion American Express credit card (commonly known as the "black card") from each of my lovers, as it's de rigueur to cut out that indiscreet cash transaction. *This card is light years* plus *chic than the Platinum AmEx, only offered by invitation to the most exclusive individuals, and requires the cardholder spend a* minimum *of a quarter of a million dollars a year.* As I've never tried to max them out, God only knows what the limits are!

Needless to say, going full stop with *les cartes de crédit* of these elegant men of the haute monde *de Paris* would be *très declassé* and a ruinous mistake.

It's something that is implied: We treat each other with the utmost respect. It's a tacit agreement; what he says and does in the bedroom is private, whether it be about his business or his sexual fantasies *(whoopsie daisy, until now, at least! But I am being fairly vague as to their actual identities. Sort of–ish).*

Perhaps you are wondering what the distinction is between your standard mistress and a courtesan. *Beaucoup!* This is where we differ:

1. I don't have any obligation nor will I take on any man I don't find enticing or *très couchable* (fuckable). If he's not in some way sexy or attractive to me, I say, zip up your *pantalons* and take a walk, Monsieur!

   In fact, historically, courtesans have always had an infinite number of aspirants to choose from; one might make her choice based on love, which is known as an *amant de coeur* (a relationship without any monetary transaction), or based on a man's financial generosity, or simply for her own amusement. The choice is *always* hers to make. I am very much of the same mind as one of the *grandes courtisanes* of the nineteenth century, Marie Duplesses. Here's how she put it: "I am always frank, I intend to remain at all times absolutely free in my movements and mistress of my own fancies: I give the orders, I do not receive them. I do not feel compelled to receive a lover whenever he expresses the wish to see me."(Yipes, intense woman, huh?)

     I'm in total agreement with her philosophy—I have free will to take another lover or . . . *three*, if I so wish. I am in no way bound to monogamy *(quelle horreur!)* nor obligated to be around for tedious things like a man boring me to death with stories of his wife.

2. Unlike your standard mistress, I harbor no real illusions of a future, a marriage, or children with any of my lovers. I ask for no assurances, expressions of love, or emotional commitments. That said, they do always seem to fall in love and promise the world. It's quite *charmant*, really.

3. They have no keys and no access to my *maison*. Even the man who bought it for me is forbidden to visit without invitation.

4. I am not a *"femme galante"* (the seventeenth-century term for "kept woman"), or a mistress in the traditional sense of the word. *Au contraire.* While, yes, they "keep" me living well, I am entirely free. Free to leave them all, free to refuse sex, free to act like an entitled bitch and get away with it, or free to act simply as a tender friend. Mistresses cater to their man. I don't have to. While my sensual skills are certainly employed, it is very much their job to please me as well. They have to bend over backward to please *me* sexually (not literally backward, of course; I've tried it and I don't get much pleasure at that angle).

5. I don't have to meet him in secret locales, fear the press discovering us, or wear dark glasses and slink out the

back entrance. Read: He never keeps me a secret, I'm
very much known as his mistress, and frankly, the
French press acts very much as the American press did
back in the JFK administration: They all know but
consider it disrespectful and/or pointless to plaster a
man's private life on magazine covers. There is respect
and acceptance within the public and press, and
between my patron and myself. Everyone
acknowledges his or her role and follows suit with
dignity.

So then, no, in case you were wondering, he doesn't
ask me to do anything humiliating or involving black
leather masks with zip mouths, fisting, or peeing. *Strike
that.* To clarify, one man did ask to *watch* me pee, but
that's not so disturbing, is it? You know, I'm seriously
asking, as I have to admit many of the edges of decency
have blurred and I have kind of lost track of society's
guidelines of late.

With some men it almost seems as if we're husband and wife, as
we share some very sweet nonsex times, like picnics, going to art
shows, and long walks *après* afternoon tea. Except that in France, the
wives of these men are generally aware that their husband has taken
a lover (long-term or temporary, paid or otherwise kept), and they
must endure this silently and with grace. Yes, I know, it's really unfair
and a raw deal that after helping these men become magnificently
wealthy, supporting them emotionally for decades, *and* raising their
children, they get relegated to being an emotionally neglected wife
kept around for social events and a proper family image.

Case in point: At François Mitterrand's state funeral, there stood
his wife and, right next to her, his mistress, Anne Pangeot *and* the
child she'd had with him. *Et voilà!* Fidelity exists, I'm sure, *mais pas
du tout en France*! And you can be sure this is a tradition as old as
Notre Dame and as universally accepted as the *espresso après le dîner*.
In fact, the higher up the aristocracy or moneyed ladder, the more

understood, expected, and, amazingly, *encouraged* this behavior is. I bet you're damn glad you live in the States, now, aren't you?

I digress. I do that a lot, and I hope you'll get used to it. It's a French thing I've adopted. Convoluted conversation intermixed with *not* answering questions directly. It has its charms and is fantastically useful. It's almost like an elegant dance: undulating in *grandes arabesques*, intentionally complicated, seductively coy, and intriguing. See? The French can look at *anything* sensually, even evasiveness!

But back to what I *do* accept as my tokens of appreciation. Are you ready? Well, you already are hip to the free apartment. I know it's rather obscene, and to be honest, I'm good in bed but the perks are really off the scale. Sorry to be so bold, but as you can imagine, being neither humble *nor* a mediocre lover are qualities that make a very successful courtesan!

Of course, I will be happy to receive any goodies a lover chooses to drop in my "trick-or-treat bag." That's really the fun part. With the exception of a Hermès horse bridle—with the idea that the gifts reflect the elegance of the man offering them—they do tend to be of the sparkling variety. (And we are not talking body glitter or sequins, *mes amies*!)

The very first big *cadeau* came from my first lover, Monsieur le Zillionaire Jean-Albert, as an anniversary present for our first five weeks together. Yes, a mere five weeks. I know, not really something one celebrates normally.

It's a divine story, really, so I will share it. I also promise to tell you the not so divine stories as there are a few situations when being a courtesan is decidedly . . . "unpleasant," to put it with an elegant spin.

L'histoire . . .

onsieur le Zillionaire—who, truthfully, I wasn't even sure I was worthy of—and I were finishing a late lunch of *canard sauvage rôti aux figues caramelisées* at the Ritz Hôtel one afternoon

(Hilarious! I say that so casually, as if it *wasn't* me a month before ordering in Pizza Hut because I was too sad to leave my flat.) when he, in his divinely chic gray Dior suit with immaculate white cuffs asked challengingly, *"Tu veux nager dans la piscine à l'hôtel maintenant? C'est une idée charmante, non?"* (Translates as: "Would you care for a swim in the hotel pool right now? It's a charming idea, isn't it?")

Having somehow, upon meeting Jean-Albert, instantly switched to never refuse an opportunity to impress this amazing man with my spontaneity, I smiled and replied (and I'll start translating to English again for you, or you're really going to get *fatigué* thumbing the French-English dictionary!): "How delicious! Although, I can't say I've anticipated this, and certainly haven't brought my *maillot*." Can you sense my determined self-editing of slang and sloppy diction? At this point I was still in sort of a frenzy, and thought it was imperative that I speak with a more refined vocabulary. Until the nocturnal activities, that is—then it's no-holds-barred, my dears!

Jean-Albert counters, *"Chérie,* pick out whatever you need from the hotel's boutique and meet me poolside in half an hour. I'll have chilled Champagne awaiting you." And with that he signs his name to the *addition* and places a tender kiss on my forehead. A bit too much like *mon père* . . . eeek, the first cringe among many to come.

He smiles mischievously and goes over to whisper to the hotel concierge that the brunette in the beluga-black dress, yes, that's *moi*, a full thirty years younger than he is, should have carte blanche in the boutiques. Frightfully fun moment.

I have to admit, being new to this man, this lifestyle, and having been living on a very restricted student budget, I did feel a fleeting temptation to go absolutely mad shopping, cramming everything my heart desired into dozens of huge Ritz shopping bags and dashing for the exit. But then I realized I actually *enjoy* this man's company. From the moment he asked ever so elegantly to be my *protecteur* (how's that for being *très* French and vague?) upon our meeting for the famous ice cream date, he's been lovely . . . and has yet to even ask to sleep with me. *Sérieusement.* He's brilliant, charming, infinitely tender, witty, sexy in a world-weary way, and so kind to me. Who knew a thirty-year age difference could be so negligible? In fact, this whole experience is all quite fascinating *and more to the point,* I probably wouldn't have gotten as far as the revolving door before security would have stopped my shopping spree.

Smiling to myself, I browse the shops, choosing a simple chocolate brown one-piece by Eres (I've learned *tout de suite* that this man is chic beyond words and wishes me dressed quite classically and modestly). I only add a pack of cigarettes for him to the bill. Always include some gesture for him. These men want to be taken care of too, I surmised. I'm a quick study, *n'est-ce pas?*

Of course, like most young students with a recreational budget as tight as a virgin, I had never even been to the Ritz, and certainly not to the famous opulent indoor pool. So this invitation was all quite in keeping with my passion for the new unknown. And to be treated like a princess was very much a new, intoxicating treat. That *merde* head Laurent had never so much as offered me a pair of socks.

In the changing room of the spa, after slipping into my bathing suit, I put my hair up into a loose chignon (Jean-Albert's favorite) and took a quick glimpse in the mirror. "Well, it's fair to say," I thought, "I can give up my lifelong hope of ever sprouting a bust. At twenty-five, if it hasn't happened yet, it's not gonna. I suppose it's okay; Jean-Albert miraculously adores them small. *Adorable* of him to tell me my *oeufs au plat* (fried eggs) are his favorite meal."

I wrap myself in the plush terry robe, slowly make my way to the door marked "*Piscine,*" and attempt to enter with a false sense of familiarity. Surely fooling no one! Especially when my eyes lit up and damn near fell out of their sockets at my first glance of this sumptuous Grecian-style room: Doric columns of marble at every turn, magnificent frescoes on the ceiling; elaborate mosaics on every exposed wall, and illuminated chandeliers casting a shimmering light that transformed every surface into gold. *Mmmm.* Add the soothing fragrance of heliotrope filling the air, I assure you, as much as the smell of money—I swear money has a smell.

"*Mon ange . . . Je suis ici,*" I heard from the far end of the pool, and I looked over to see my new zillionaire. *New?* Wait, what am I saying? Make that my *only* zillionaire lover (that is at *that* time), gesturing for me to join him on a chaise longue to his left.

I lie back into luxury, still in my robe, and am happy at that moment that yesterday I had taken him up on his offer of a full day of facials and a pedicure and manicure at Institut de Guerlain. The old me of a scant five weeks ago would've been sporting a far less *jolie* set of *doigts des pieds*. Think: toenails *à la* hyena claws.

We light cigarettes—he lights mine, *bien sûr*—as an attendant appears instantly and gracefully pours the Cristal into two chilled crystal flutes. As I take a sip I think to myself, "Hmm . . . I'm definitely acquiring a taste for Cristal and this new lifestyle. Haven't even slept with this man and get to live like this. . . . Kissed him a bit. And yes, sadly it was like kissing a trout, one who's gasping for his last breath of air, no less. And frankly, trout have bigger lips, I think. But really, that was a mere ten unpleasant minutes among all these hours of pure bliss. I'm sure a host of surprising sexual demands awaits me (that's an understatement, I can tell you now!) but in this moment, it's all good."

I steal a glance at Jean-Albert and behold that regal profile. He's so elegant, it's simply captivating to be around him. I know I am out of my mind, but it almost feels like being in the presence of a king. More surprising: I am surprised at how quickly he immersed me in his life, this little corporate titan of mine.

He asks to see me almost every day. Sometimes for nothing more then a cup of tea at Hôtel Meurice. Seriously, we have tea dates constantly—this man may love a steaming cup of Lapsang Souchong as much as sex! My first tea-aholic sex-ophile. Though, come to think of it, I bet in Britain that's rather common!

But I have divined that Jean-Albert needs me, *or someone like me,* to counter the enormous pressure and responsibility of running a vast empire. And I can say now, as I look back to the early days of this new profession, there had been a great deal *less time* spent supine engaged in sexual acts (deviant *or otherwise*) than chatting over the aforementioned tea.

Moreover, I think the thrust (if you'll forgive the pun) of being a courtesan to powerful, wealthy men is really giving them an outlet to let down their steely guard. Offering a world where they can be playful, free to say anything, to be childish, and most important, to let someone else take control. They are forever in charge and "*Oui*, Monsieur"–d to death, and part of them wants—*needs*—to be bossed around. Stranger still, he and I are really comfortable together; there's something familiar between us, an alchemy of spirits. Who'd have guessed? Could my soul mate be a guy who has *shoes* older than I am!

Champagne in hand, we begin to speak about my thesis, on Boucher, which I tell him I've been working on diligently for about a year. He offers, "Between eighteenth-century masters of that style, obviously Boucher and Géricault reign supreme, but, I have to say, I honestly prefer Géricault. In fact, I recently bought his painting *Scène Erotique* at Sotheby's."

"You bought that?! I adore that painting," I semiyelp, and thankfully edit "*get out*" and/or "no *way!*" and a simultaneous shoulder slam out of my response. But, "holy shit"—seriously—that painting had been estimated at four to six million euros, and when the hammer fell, it had gone for 8.3 million to a "private bid by phone." I guess that would be the man next to me. *Cool*.

He continues: "Yes, well, when another Géricault series went to the Frick Collection in New York, I thought, why not at least acquire the piece that initially inspired the series?" He talks like it's the most natural decision on earth.

"Yes, why ever not, darling?" I add.

Jean-Albert acknowledges my jest and smiles in rebuttal. "To tell the truth, I just bought the Fragonard as a salve, since that day I had also lost out on Maurizio Cattelan's *The Ballad of Trotsky*, and I wanted *something*." He laughs hard at his own petulant-sounding honesty. "More serious and important, *ma chérie*, are you almost finished with your thesis? Is there anything I can offer you to alleviate any of the workload? A secretary? A research assistant?" He asks with exquisite politeness.

"Terribly generous of you, *mon petit chou*"—that means little cabbage in French, and believe it or not, is a term of endearment. Go figure. Maybe it's kind of like "pumpkin"—"but I wouldn't dream of it. This thesis is my undertaking and I need to do every step of it *seule* (alone)."

"*Soûle?* Alexandra, you make me laugh, sweet girl! With your accent, it sounded like you said, '*soûle*,' meaning drunk!"

"Yes, well, with afternoons like this," I say, raising my empty flute to the attentive attendant's lightning-fast refill, "I shall certainly be *soûle*!"

I suddenly realize that since meeting Jean-Albert, I haven't touched my thesis. Not even thought about it once. *Merde!* In fact, I've completely stopped my research at the Bibliothèque Nationale and have assumed this new itinerary of glamorous dinners, exciting rendezvous, and all the necessary time-consuming preparations one needs to be ready to set off on an evening of being the courtesan mistress.

Oh, God, don't kid yourself; this job is no cakewalk! It's such intense pressure to be utterly perfect in every way. But in some twisted way I love that, and need challenge to thrive. Interestingly enough, clever banter and the ability to speak intelligently on a host of subjects is truly more vital to a courtesan than talent in the bedroom. While prostitutes may be obliged to perform immediately and wordlessly, a courtesan must offer sparkling witticisms and hold her own at grand dinners, where she is a reflection on the man she accompanies.

This is not a job for the occasional magazine reader or demure wallflower. *Obviously!* To be a good companion, one must be brilliantly well read about every subject under the sun, from string theory to Palladian architecture. I quickly learned that to be the young consort of this genius businessman and highly cultured individual is a crash course unto itself. I had to research Jean-Albert's business empire immediately, and instantly become well versed in the diverse subjects passionate to him: *par exemple,* the literature of Anatole France and collecting Andre Arbus furniture. (*Oui,* I digressed again. You're getting accustomed to it though now, *non?*)

So with the better part of the Champagne imbibed in a mixed emotional state of guilt (the ignored thesis) and exuberance (the new extravagant and cerebral lifestyle), I took a moment to bask in the silence.

Glancing across the room, inhaling deeply the dizzying pleasure of it all, my gaze is suddenly caught and held by a sparkling reflection at the center of the pool. Is it a piece of glass? A sequin? A crystal fallen from the chandelier into the depths? "There's something in the pool. Do you see? Right there, Jean-Albert?" I ask, pointing. "Really? No, I don't see it, darling," he replies convincingly.

"Oh, yes, I'm sure there is." And I, in my role as the ever curious girl, leave my robe in my wake as I dive in and descend to the depths. As expected, the water temperature is like a sublime elixir after the Champagne and glazes over me as I glide underwater. And what's that I hear? Extraordinarily, the majestic music of Haydn's Symphony No. 9 is piped underwater as well. *Très chic.*

I make my way down the length of the pool in one breath. Spot the shimmery object and grab it in my clutches. Still submerged, I can hardly contain a yelp of excitement at this incredible moment of finding . . . a ring. The *jeune fille* in me recalls the French equivalent of "finders keepers" as I sail to the surface to get a better look at my find.

Standing hip deep in the pool, unable to contain my delight, I bellow, "*Regarde!!!!* It's a huge diamond ring! . . . I think it's real!" Of course, in one fell swoop I unwittingly reveal my inexperience with anything remotely luxurious, not to mention being childishly possessive.

"*Oui, ma chérie, c'est un cadeau pour toi sur notre anniversaire . . . cinq carats pour cinq semaines ensemble.*" (Apologies, obviously, I couldn't resist retelling it in the true French phrase, which translates as, "Yes, darling. It's an aniversary present for you. Five carats for five weeks together.")

Amazingly—and thank God—I didn't wet my pants. I could've theoretically, I guess, seeing as I was in a pool. But instead, I swayed on shaky legs in shock, repeating, "*Pas vrai*" (translates as "no way," *sort of*) about a hundred times before I fell into a hypnotic daze.

Monsieur le Zillionaire comes over to the side of the pool and kneels down to me. "You like it? . . . *Bon*. Shall we celebrate . . . a bit more privately now? I keep a suite here . . . Come, Alexandra, let's spend the afternoon in each other's arms . . . Do you know? . . . *Je t'aime* . . . I love you to distraction. *Vraiment* . . . and believe me, I'm as shocked as you are," he confessed with an expression of blissful unconsciousness that, may I say, any actor, poet, or painter would despair of portraying with gesture, language, or brush, such was its sincerity.

His voice, full of such certainty, was simply mesmerizing. It was as though silk velvet were being passed slowly over my warm, naked body. The entire afternoon, with all its surreal, dizzying pleasures, had the kaleidoscopic quality of a dream. I was both deliciously *lost* . . . and yet entirely *found*.

That second, with his words, "*Je t'aime*," hanging in the air, and the sparkling rock on my still wet finger, was—I can see clearly now—the precise moment I realized, no denying it or calling it by any other name: I had become a courtesan.

One elegant, sophisticated married zillionaire, one proclamation of love and acceptance, one bottle of Cristal, one 5-carat emerald-cut diamond ring . . . and one suite at the Ritz. Search your soul . . . would you have resisted?

LES CADEAUX DU MOIS
(Gifts acquired this month)

I made a killing, really.

The diamond ring, appraised for insurance purposes only (okay, I was dying to know its price tag): 89,000 euros

Lanvin black crepe dress: 750 euros

Day at Institut de Guerlain: 620 euros

Sheets stolen from the Ritz—I'm kidding!

A fresh bouquet of lilies each week from the florist Christian Tortu: approximately 600 euros, minimum

A pumpkin Hermès cashmere wrap, bought simply because "you look cold, chérie": 850 euros

A SHORT LIST OF REQUIRED READING

Niccolo Machiavelli, The Prince

Jean-Paul Sartre, Intimacy

Maurice de Talleyrand-Périgord, Memoirs of the Prince de Talleyrand

Karl Marx, Communist Manifesto

Günter Grass, The Flounder

Anthony Levi, Cardinal Richelieu and the Making of France

Vladimir Nabokov, Butterflies

James Joyce, Ulysses

Johann Wolfgang von Goethe, Faust

Italo Calvino, Marcoraldo

Albert Camus, The Stranger

André Malraux, La Tentation de l'Occident *and* Et pourtant j'étais libre

Jean Genet, Notre Dame des Fleurs

Stendhal, Le Rouge et le Noir

François-René de Chateaubriand, Mémoires d'outre-tombe

Leo Tolstoy, Anna Karenina

Aleksandr Pushkin, Eugene Onegin

CHAPITRE QUATRE

You will do foolish things, but do them with enthusiasm.

—COLETTE

Are you a smidge curious about how that afternoon unfolded after the diamond on the bottom of the Ritz pool? Thought so. Now we get to the part that felt very much less the me I'd known for twenty-five years and more like a nervous young woman in over her head . . . *albeit adorned with a dazzling new piece of jewelry.*

As I told you, I'm going to be wildly, brazenly honest about *this* whole affair—and all the others. So, frankly, as I made my way with Jean-Albert at my side to his amazing suite overlooking the Place Vendôme, all I really wanted to do was stare at this ring for hours, call all my friends, and laugh at my good fortune. But he had other plans. *Très différent* plans.

Jean-Albert gallantly pushes open the door to "our" suite and steps aside for me to enter first, my eyes falling upon a *chambre privée* the likes of which I had only previously seen in a coffee table book about Versailles.

He goes about drawing the organza drapes closed as I seat myself on the enormous bed and scan the room. A tall candelabra on the Louis XVI *guéridon* (table) was lit and already at half wick. More of that Cristal sat sweating in an ice bucket on a silver tray nestled on the canopied, gilded bed, lavishly swagged in silk brocade, tied back with huge ornate tassels of gold. The most exquisite bed linens were already turned down, *mais oui*. (Can I steal those? I'm sure I'd sleep like a *bébé* on them!) A black garment bag emblazoned with the Lanvin logo was draped gracefully across a gilded *fauteuil* (chair). Hmm. That would be my "walking out of the hotel elegantly *après le* sex act" dress, I'm guessing. *Bien sûr.* It all became quickly obvious that the plans for this little stolen moment were not so spontaneous, but in fact had been very much set in motion earlier in the day.

Oh man, and that sex act has suddenly become unavoidable. Just as all this is filtering into my consciousness, I realize I am not so sure I am ready for what's coming. I had never *ever* had sex with someone I wasn't absolutely dying to see naked, and this guy, for as much as I like him and find him sexy, I am not so sure about the sex idea. I semishuddered already on our second date, when at the opera I leaned over to whisper, *"Merci pour les grands bouquets des fleurs"* and caught sight of long, gray squiggly hairs leaping out of his ears. His ears, I might add, resemble dried apples. (I'm off apples now forever, I fear. Sometimes one's imagination can be a hindrance!) Segue back to *le suite* and the disrobing scene.

Tenderly peeling off my damp robe, Jean-Albert says in low tones, "You have such a beautiful body . . . For so many nights I have tried to conjure you *nue* and what it would be like to lick you absolutely everywhere." (That's nude, of course, and yes, I agree, it would've been cooler if he'd said, "I have imagined you in a parka, watching TV with me as I just hand you a hundred euros every ten minutes." Alright, maybe not "cooler" per se, but *easier*!)

My thoughts raced: "What's my problem? What? Am I out of my gourd? This man is incredible! Take him, you silly, lucky girl! Yeah, well . . . Perhaps, it's just that he's older . . . a lot older. And God knows what sex is like with a man who, as he once told me, actually grew up in a village where there was a town crier, pounding on a drum, calling *"Citoyens! Attention! . . . Aujourd'hui!"* for daily news updates. (I kid you not!)

Okay, if I'm going to survive this, perhaps I should switch back to role playing, as I gotta keep reality at bay. So I offer in response, "You have been a *mauvais jeune homme* (bad boy) . . . and made me wait so long. You deserve a scolding." (*Cliché* to die, but in the right mind-set at least.)

"Oh, yes. I *am* a bad boy. Punish me!" he pants, sliding right into that cliché like a bespoke suit.

My thoughts were swimming . . . *Olympic relay style:* "I don't know if I can pull this off. A dominatrix I am not. Geesh, what have I gotten myself into?"

I take a moment to fight—and, amazingly, win—against the desire to run screaming out of the room. Hell, even leaping out the window was an option. But I summon all my strength to demand, "Pour me some Champagne, light me a cigarette, and then go . . . kneel by that mirror!" Gesturing to the mirror embedded in the enormous walnut door to the *salle de bain.*

Jean-Albert, le mauvais jeune homme, follows my orders promptly, handing the lit cigarette and flute to me, and then strips himself of his robe and shorts as he gets down on his knees. All the while, peering at me apprehensively, like I'm going to drag him off to the guillotine or something.

Meanwhile, I am thinking, "This is *amazing* . . . I bet very few people on the planet have ever seen that expression on his face!"

Taking a long sip of Champagne, I stride over to him still in *maillot.* As I let my robe fall to the floor, I kick a pedicured foot onto his chest, pushing his ass back onto his feet. "Rules! You will do exactly as I say!" I demand with aplomb, throwing the empty flute and cigarette into the fireplace. Drama? I got it in spades, kids.

"Absolument, chérie!"

"And don't interrupt me! Or I will tie you up on the bed and leave you there . . . Do you hear me? Not another word from your mouth, young man!" I am just channeling the vixen chicks in Helmut Newton photographs, and so wishing I had a whip and some fucking evil stilettos to play this out to the hilt.

Jean-Albert nods silently. And in that colossal, awe-inspiring moment twenty-five years of polite modesty and sexual inhibition were swept away in a flood tide. The greedy awakening of the pleasures of the flesh mingled with the power I wielded—took hold of me entirely.

I grab the belt of his robe, whip it out in a flourish, and standing behind him, wrap it in tight knots, joining his wrists behind him as I simultaneously push him parallel to the mirror. He whimpers in pain.

"Shut up! If I want you to talk, I will tell you!"

I could almost fall down laughing. I've got to be the only person who would dare say such a thing to this mogul control freak. *Peut-être*, I should tell him to buy me this hotel while I'm at it. Power is *délicieuse*, for damn sure!

Employing the mirror again—we do seem to make good use of mirrors, this man and I—I stand in front of him and thrust my crotch in his face. "Push my bathing suit to the side . . . with just your tongue," I command, feeling a surprising wave of heat and getting wet as I hear the words pour out of me.

His head dives into me at once. A probing tongue eagerly forces itself against my flesh. My suit is quickly moved aside as I notice veins in his forehead strain and swell as he works with a focus bordering on delirium. Well done, Monsieur, you made quick work of that little project.

I step back slightly, so as to have him lose his equilibrium, and to force him to balance his whole weight on my *chaton* (I think you get what this is a "polite" word for *en français*) as he teeters on his knees, submitting willfully.

"Don't stop until you make me come!" I say, as I grab a fistful of his hair and yank back his head. He nods passively, but I can see his eyes are awash in ecstasy and his sex is as hard as stone in his appreciation.

Caught up in a daze of sensual pleasure, I close my eyes as I feel the arrival and warm flick of his tongue on me. Alternately delving inside me and sucking at me with a tug I can only describe as . . . perfection, I find I am totally caught off-guard to be succumbing. . . .

Succumbing, indeed; he's doing the "suc"-king, and I'm doing the "cum"-ing. Oh yes, there's something to be said for experience. This man is amazing at the job I've set before him. I open my eyelids slightly, as much to get my bearings as to sneak a peek at a scene I can't believe I am in at all, let alone falling into with such raw passion.

He notices me watching the two of us, with my drunken desire. My lids at half mast, one hand on the back of his head as I guide the rhythm of his stroke, and begin to moan, "Deeper . . . I want to feel your tongue deeper." He's watching me. And I'm watching *me . . . and his tongue* working with an almost religious fervor. I'm about to slip into a blinding orgasm when I realize he's probably dying to fuck me . . . God, I am dying to fuck *him* . . . should I untie him and let him loose . . . in every meaning of the word?

"*Arrête* . . . come take me on the bed," the newly unleashed nymphomaniac in me hurls at him.

I quickly and gently untie the knots binding his wrists, slightly grimacing to see they've made red, raw impressions in his skin.

I wait behind, hands on my hips, watching him climb onto the bed not unlike a little boy. My inhibitions and unwillingness have completely evaporated and are replaced with this new surprising combination of sexual bravado, confidence, and delight.

I stride over as Jean-Albert pushes the silver tray off the bed, ice bucket pouring all over the floor. Funny, with normal men in normal life I would be leaping around, frantic to get a towel, terrified at the cost of that minidisaster *and surely killing the moment*. Not with Monsieur le Zillionaire here. It's all just play through and live with abandon. That's sexy. *Quite*.

I crawl up on the bed like a tigress in heat, after whipping off my bathing suit and tossing it at his head. He catches it midair, bringing the still warm crotch to his elegant Gallic nose and inhaling deeply. Surprisingly erotic, *if predictable*. Another point for the geezer with gray hair! Me-ow.

Taking him in my hand as I straddle his slim hips, I lean over and announce, "I'm going to fuck you so hard you aren't going to see straight." With that, I guide his throbbing cock inside me and start pounding him so violently our hip bones are crashing together.

"Oh, please, stop . . . you're hurting me. Gentle. I've never done this before," he cries weakly, lying through those meager lips. *Clearly better at business than at lying when naked.*

"You love it, *ferme la bouche!*" I add, as I lean over and bite at his neck.

"Oouchh . . . oh, it hurts!" he whimpers. (Listen, my friends, fear not. That is such a lie! I have the hips of a kitten. No way is he in pain. So, I continue my "torture fest," twisting and pinching his hard nipples as he writhes in pleasure beneath me.)

And you know what? I realize, I'm so loving this. I'm on top, where I love to be, and calling all the shots. And what's more, I can see in his eyes that he knows he's playing for me as well. My fantasy. His fantasy. Has become my reality. And . . . I am addicted.

"I'm going to come!" he says, more as a question than a warning.

"No! You will wait for me. I will tell you when you can come." And I bend back and run my finger between his legs, resting it just under his *bijoux de famille* and gently pressing in increasing rhythm with my thrusts. I can feel him swell and throb inside me, and I feel the wave of orgasm crest.

"Come . . . *now!*" I demand, looking fiercely into his eyes.

"AAAAaaaaah, *mon dieu . . . Bordel! Putain! Ooh la-la!!!!*" He screams in increasing waves of ecstasy.

Upon hearing him . . . and feeling the warm pulsing explosion inside me, I thrust once more. "Oh my God . . . oh . . . fuck!" I'm coming with such mind-blowing intensity, the room has all gone blue. I have no awareness of time, my own name, or even if I'm the man or the woman. I very well could be melting into a liquid pool and I simply don't care or want for anything.

We are both silent for several moments afterward. Stunned at the strange way it's wildly intimate, freeing, and utterly . . . an extension of this unique thing we are together. This delicious incomprehensible rapport we have: two naughty kids who have found a playmate—*on every level.*

I laugh, he laughs. "Wow, baby . . . what the hell were you even yelling?" I ask, back to being Alexandra. And knowing that the show's over, and he's quite fine with that.

"Did I say something? I don't even remember speaking! But you . . . you, Alexandra, yelled out 'Fuck!' I used to loathe that coarse word until I discovered it stood for Fornication Under Consent of the King. Now I positively find it titillating!" he says, as he roars with laughter, taking me in his arms. He showers me with tender kisses all over my face, my chin, my nose, my eyelids.

"*Je t'adore* . . . you are a gift from God!" he whispers. He nuzzles into the nape of my neck as the musky, dizzying fragrance of sex hangs in the air. A delicious moment. I find I'm smiling so hard my cheeks hurt.

After lying in each other's arms for the better part of an hour, he gets up to shower as I linger in bed, searching my mind for a pang of guilt or a hint of regret. *Non, je ne regrette rien!* Picking up the ice bucket, I catch sight of my sparkling ring . . . *Bizarre!* The ring is like the *cerise sur le gâteau* (the cherry on the cake). A great perk but not even necessary, as that sex was like a gift to me. His attention is a gift to me. This whole experience is beyond a dream. That this man is so truly fascinating, so inspiring, so incredibly attentive. Calling me, complimenting me, sending me thoughtful books and gifts as though he has nothing else to do with his days. To have so much adoration and attention from someone so respected, so successful, and so busy . . . Overwhelming!

He has made me feel, in five short weeks, as though someone finally understood that this other person inside me exists and has just been hoping she would be given the venue and encouragement to be set free. Someone knew that there was a creature inside me that wanted to experience all this—the nights at the opera, the pressure to be as well read and articulate as I have also hoped to be. To allow me to play the bad girl, to release my pent-up sexual intensity, to welcome me into his life, to be known as the woman he has chosen. And to inherently know I will not stay in this world with him, but he will make it beyond amazing as long as I wish it to last.

Generous man. Great lover in all respects. That was "titillating," alright!

Now, let's see what that Lanvin dress looks like!

THE FIRST LOVE LETTER FROM JEAN-ALBERT
(Hand delivered by his driver, Charles, at eleven the following morning.)

Dearest Alexandra,

Infinitely happy remembering our accordance in flesh . . . the honey smooth skin of your belly . . . our laughter set to an inexpressible felicity . . . am exquisitely exhausted by your expert caresses and deliciously drunk with your sublime kisses . . . I implore you to be cruel enough to worsen my addiction by seeing me *ce soir* at 8:00. I will be under your window, praying you have granted me this wish . . . Until then, let me give you an amorous, respectful kiss on your celestially beautiful neck.

Your J.A.

LES CADEAUX DU MOIS

1 Christian Dior clutch purse: 875 euros

4 weekly flower arrangements from florist Stéphane Chapelle: 600 euros

1 Philippe Model chapeau: 375 euros

1 pair Roger Vivier talons (heels): 525 euros

1 Lanvin beige crepe dress: 740 euros

1 Vertu Black Ascent cell phone: 4,250 euros

CHAPITRE CINQ

> I would myself become an imaginary character, endowed with beauty, desirability, and a sort of shimmering transparent loveliness.
>
> —SIMONE DE BEAUVOIR

To be honest, it's kind of fortunate for me to be living a gajillion miles from family and childhood friends. Over the phone, through the mail, and in cyber communication, there are no telltale signs that my life has accelerated into this heady extravaganza. Can't quite imagine what the parents would say if they glimpsed their demure little Alexandra, clad in nothing but earrings and scandalously high heels, walking on the naked back of France's corporate titan while he bellows like a hyena whose foot's caught in a trap—*in an octave on par with* Maria Callas. C'mon, I had to add the last bit, it's true! Last week. *Chez moi.* The neighbors must think I'm skinning live cats as a hobby!

Frankly, my mother might say, "Dear, wouldn't a lower shoe be better for your back?" And my father might pipe in with, "Man, that's gotta hurt!" Don't get me wrong. My parents are lovely, modern, and cool people. I adore them. In fact, I was the black sheep of the family for my rigid, uptight propriety. So really, they might very well be relieved to see that I had finally let down those steel walls and annoying, saintlike ways. Still, as my life in this arena winds its way between the surreal and the shocking, I am keeping references to all the extravagance and decadence to a scant minimum. I hold reality at a healthy distance, continuing my courtesan lifestyle as though it were a secret identity. So in phone calls and letters I gloss over all the drama with broad strokes and hope they don't discover this until/and if, I choose to tell them. I'm keeping my fingers crossed on that. Legs? Obviously not!

Which brings us to, *Ooh la-la!* My big debut on the arm of Jean-Albert at a very sha-sha private dinner for his megaempire. A *smoking* affair (that's "black tie" *en français*, but yes, there was actual smoking as well, to be accurate) where all the head honchos of every component of his conglomerate come to pay tribute. Meaning: the pleasure-loving plutocracy with money to burn congregate with their kind—"smart society"—and toast to their extreme wealth and to the ever-increasing desire by the masses to pay exorbitant prices for whatever these wizards deem objects of desire, the so-called "luxury goods." Not that that's what it said on the kelly-green crocodile cigar box that was hand-delivered as the invitation! I know. Can you believe it? What the hell kind of money was wasted there? Jean-Albert called that Friday evening at six to confirm.

"*Chérie,* you will be ready by seven, *oui?* I am sending a car to retrieve you," he yells over the sound of the helicopter he's in. (Cheap tip here. No charge. It sounds very much like he's sitting next to a loud air conditioner, so if one wanted to feign similar circumstances, one could try that "I'm rich enough to die in my own helicopter" angle, say, for getting dinner reservations at overbooked *restos.*) "*Mon chou,* can't you come pick me up yourself? I don't want to just meet you there," I say, overwhelmed in anticipation, staring at the heaps of garment bags he had sent from all his design firms—each vying with the others for me to wear their label.

"You are so right! *Bien sûr.* How foolish of me. I hadn't had a second to think of it. I will be below your window then at seven fifteen. Look for the silver Maserati. I feel like getting into trouble tonight!"

"I assure you, darling, with me at your side, you will! And thanks for the dresses. But I'm at a loss which to wear!" I reply, noticing that my stomach is starting to get squishy. Damn, all this gourmand cuisine is starting to mess with my figure. But I do love that whatever I say, he does. That's cool as all hell.

"Wear the Dior, I promised him you would. *À tout à l'heure, mon ange!*" And he clicks off.

So much for fretting about the dress. I have to admit, I am a tinge nervous. Two months of being the woman in Jean-Albert's life—the "other woman," I should say—and I still haven't quite acquired all the confidence I pretend to enjoy. Frankly, I am such a nervous nellie, my *régles* (period) has just stopped altogether from the stress. Fear not a little Zillionaire is on the way—Jean-Albert's a member of the vasectomy club. Phew, that would be *très* complicated.

I help myself to a nip of the Dom Pérignon he sent over last week after he spent the evening with me. Oh, how he was appalled to see: (1) My apartment's size and lack of opulence; (2) that my selection of beverages consisted of tea, Coca-Cola light, and *jus d'orange;* (3) that I hadn't a "proper bed," whatever that means. A futon is a bed, Monsieur. *Weirdly, rich guys prefer beds to be quite high up from the ground; it all caters to their towering regal power position; unless of course they're on their hands and knees licking your boots, that is!*

Now, time to put myself together. My little courtesan dressing routine is becoming a ritual:

Une douche avec huile d'amande. *Panic not, a douche in French is a bath. Bathe with almond oil; your skin will positively glisten and radiate light!*

Hair pinned up in low chignon; optional hair stick, tortoiseshell hair comb, or other accessory.

Maquillage: *light neutral tones; matte light cinnamon lipstick.*

A spritz of Guerlain Vega parfum; again, it's one of his companies. Thank God he doesn't own something like a tire company, right? Anyway, I have enough to last me now until the next millennium. And it will make killer Christmas gifts for friends back home!

Gown or dress for evening. Pantsuits only for day; the only women who wear skirt suits during the day here are girls for hire (pas moi, *the low-class mistresses who linger at hotel bars) or secretaries.*

And I should wear the new 2-carat diamond studs he gave me last Monday for our two-month anniversary. I know. This man does love to celebrate a holiday. Fine by me. Christmas with this dude is going to be bananas!

And can't forget the ubiquitous talons en soie *(silk satin heels) or jeweled slingbacks. Thankfully, they are always sent along with the bags-o-pricey-dresses.* Et voilà, *courtesan to go*, à vôtre service*!*

Jean-Albert arrives promptly at 7:15 P.M. Rare in France, but he knows I go into instafoul mood if he keeps me waiting. As I once told him, "I wait fifteen minutes for a date, and after the first five, I am casting off sexual favors by the minute. (After twenty minutes a man is lucky if he gets a peck on the cheek.) I will wait thirty minutes only for the pope; all others get the door."

I sure am taking to this sassy *femme* thing like a horse to water, eh? But, as I said, being all passive and demure is dull as hell to these men. And as for "waiting for the pope"? I swear that seducing the pious isn't my thing—though one lover did ask me to dress up in a nun habit and garters once. I passed. That's a sure, one-way express ticket to hell, don't you think?

Climbing into the car I see, as ever, that Jean-Albert looks seriously dashing in his tuxedo. Hard not to, when they are handmade by the finest tailors in the country. With a light shimmer of sheen in his *sel et poivre* hair, I find myself thinking he is positively gorgeous. Take note: Maseratis have that effect, *even if the man is lipless, with dried-apple ears.*

We zip through Paris in a blur, and the sexy hum of the engine (really—it makes a Porsche sound like a blow-dryer) further ignites our moods. We are one very happy couple: the zillionaire and the courtesan. (Not exactly a good title for a children's book though, is it?)

Circling the chic Place des États-Unis, we arrive at the elegant

Baccarat *hôtel particulier* by 7:30—just as John Galliano jumped off his Ducati motorcycle, adjusted his skirt, and threw his cigarette to the curb. Somehow he made it look chic, don't ask! He and Jean-Albert exchange *Bonsoir*s as I stand at Jean-Albert's side and take in the enormous scene.

Dozens of chauffeurs seated like lifeless, inflatable dolls in polished to the nth Bentleys, Mercedes, and the odd Rolls-Royce. Swarms of photographers snap wildly as the designer Alexander McQueen arrives with Kate Moss on his arm, both clad in gray flannel suits, some sort of rebellious fashion statement, I'm guessing. Side note: It does get to be tiresome—read: horrifying—to always be "hanging" with supermodels in the periphery. Just when you're thinking, "Hey, I don't look bad," one will appear at the table and annihilate your belief in justice in the world. Digression number twenty-one, *I know*.

Jean-Albert introduces me to Monsieur Galliano, as *mon amie*—his friend. Freak not, as interestingly this means "lover" in French, while *ma copine* means "my friend," as in, we're not fucking. Trust me, this language has delicate nuances, and you can get both inappropriately furious or in crazy situations if you don't catch them! Still, hearing him use this title for the first time stuns me, as it clarifies just how significant this is for us both. (In case you're curious, his wife's in Geneva at a spa. Rumor has it she's having plastic surgery after catching wind of my existence. I shudder to think she'd be so reactive, though—I am *so not* his first foray into *les liaisons dangereuses*.) This is *my* first real introduction to his entire world, the beau monde, and it's semiscandalous. For me, this is big shit. Sorry, make that *grande merde*.

The other arriving guests, the security staff, and even the maître d'hôtel, all murmur, "Bonsoir Monsieurdame" in decidedly quiet, respectful tones to us as we make our way through the vast entrance. I laugh to myself, remembering when I was working as an au pair, I once asked the *voiturier* (parking attendant) if I could possibly use the *toilettes* here, and he, gesturing at my sneakers, dismissed me instantly. The silly girl in me is half-tempted to start singing aloud, "Times they are a changin', my friends." Thankfully for all involved, I stifle said impulse! But zounds, this is the most magnificent and beautiful restaurant I've ever seen. And in Paris, after the last two months of Guy Savoy, Senderens, Taillevent, that's saying somethin'!

Pausing while our coats are whisked away, Jean-Albert gives me the lowdown on the building: Once the private mansion for the renowned Vicomtesse Marie-Laure de Noailles, the Baccarat firm has now purchased this nineteenth-century masterpiece of architecture and created a sumptuous restaurant and museum to exhibit its sparkling creations. Design god Philippe Starck has kept the bare bones of the Louis XIV style while transforming the interior into a mélange of Baroque and modernity, with his witty and famously irreverent sensibility for playing with scale.

Upon entering the vast entrance we are met with a grandiose crystal chandelier immersed in an aquarium. Another, twice the size, hangs from the ceiling, rotating slowly and majestically as it lights the wide stone stairs leading to the first floor. Groovy, sophisticated, and chic, a tough combination to pull off, Jean-Albert and I concur. We wind our way up the wide red-carpeted *escalier*, passing a huge, oversized two-meter Louis XVI chair revisioned by Starck in white leather with silver crystal legs at the foot at the *premier étage*. The chair is five times normal size and has all the makings of fantasies.

"Let's order a dozen and have an *Alice in Wonderland* tea party sometime!" I joke to Jean-Albert.

"Ha-ha! I do so much like the way your mind works, Alexandra. Always to the extreme. You know, I should hire you!" he says, laughing.

"You couldn't afford me!" I throw back, kidding, as clearly *he can* and, in essence, kind of *has*.

We both burst out in giggles and continue on past a fabulous piece: an arm made of crystal reaches out from a huge twelve-foot crystal mirror holding a glass lamp. "That's something you don't see every day," Jean-Albert comments. We pause, stopping briefly for a photographer on the stunning illuminated stairs, and I try to

imagine if my "dumb struck in awe" expression is going to translate on film. Hope not.

"*Merci, merci*, Monsieur!" the photographer chants, as he almost
bows with gratitude. *Okay, this is getting ridiculous*.

But Jean-Albert is being as gallant as I could ever have hoped,
his hand alternately gently around my waist or arm in arm. We
make our way to the large square dining room where the one hundred dinner guests are expected. The gorgeous room is humming
with voices and a refined level of excitement buzzes through the
crowd. I am simply beaming with happiness. As much to be there
as to be with him in this beautiful room. The ornately carved walls
of *boiserie* are festooned with enormous cameos of aristocracy in regal profiles, all powdered wigs, huge noses, and Louis's this and
that. As my eye climbed the staggering five meters to the ceiling it
delightedly fell on the four ornate crystal chandeliers, each as large
as a Renault *voiture*, and casting shimmering golden light on the
endless sea of crystal tableware. Wow. Toss in all the women in dazzling diamonds and it's seriously blinding!

The guests are all beginning to take their designated seats after
seeking a precious moment or word from Monsieur le Zillionaire. I
tell you, it's quite an amazing scene to behold; the assembled elegant crowd all paying homage to Jean-Albert, the room so sumptuous and vast; damn, if it doesn't feel very much as though a king is
receiving his courtiers. (I know, I make that parallel a lot. It's a
common thought of mine these days!)

Left alone for a few moments, I try to appear at ease, walking
about, casually taking in the room, and like clockwork my nervous
clumsiness shatters anything resembling dignified poise. I walk
slap bang into the sommelier—spilling Champagne on his jacket,
tripping over a waiter, and finally coming to rest next to an older
gentleman in a wheelchair who's watched my speedy descent into
complete gracelessness. He amusingly offers, "Perhaps you'd be
safer in one of these?" He laughs, tapping his wheelchair. I smile,
wink at him, and make a quick getaway back to Jean-Albert, who's
scanning the room. He spots me and summons me with a smile.

Finally, we are all seated. Jean-Albert has placed me on his right, with a very sophisticated couple "of a certain age" *juste en face* (just in front of us). Looking at this chic woman I feel instantly revealed as the Midwestern hick that I am just beneath the Dior gown and diamonds. (Now, that woman *looks* like how I'd like to *feel* . . . refined and dripping with wisdom and elegance!) My attention travels to my right, where I am delighted to find as my dinner partner the marvelous shoe designer Bruno Frisoni.

"*Enchanté!* Alexandra, lovely name. Did you notice the ceiling, yet? Rather amusing, *n'est-ce pas?*" Bruno points out a hand-painted banner emblazoned on the ceiling; large letters facetiously inform diners: THERE'S NOTHING TO EAT TONIGHT (CE SOIR, Y'A RIEN À MANGER).

"Oh, that's so great. I adore this place!" I reply, positively giddy.

The ravishing claret-haired femme fatale seated in front of me meets my gaze and gives me a knowing smile. Not condescending but somehow along the lines of, "Your naiveté, dear Mademoiselle, is endearing." *You get the gist.* My eyes dart away, as it feels as though she can see right through me. I sit quietly, allowing the hum of conversation and music to engulf me.

Jean-Albert assumes his role, stands, and with that, the string quartet instantly ceases playing their enchanting motet. It's brutally abrupt, and I find I'm somewhat annoyed, as I had just been swept up in the music, trying to place how the piece felt so familiar and moving. Suddenly, I remember, and my contented expression fades. A host of memories flood back. Recalling how on a beautiful summer evening my ex, Laurent, introduced me to that piece and all the joys of French classical music from the seventeenth century. He played dozens of works by Marin Marais and Lully on his violin as the entire neighborhood fell into reverie. Oh, it was sublime. I'll never forget that sense of complete peace, and how I was just *full:* madly, wildly in love. Dammit, why did he leave me? I muster to regain my composure, as the present reappears and the past fades slowly back into the shadows.

Reaching for his glass, Jean-Albert passes his hand tenderly over my bare shoulder. Ah, yes, Jean-Albert. He really is marvelous. Every gesture, every word that falls from his mouth is either fascinating, elegant, or intriguing. He truly is a masterpiece, even with those small feminine hands and terrible kisses. I smile at him, suddenly feeling a wave of pride. Not for me, but for him, strangely as though I were his mother or something. Weird.

He clears his throat and draws the full attention of the room with a tap to his crystal Champagne flute. Off the cuff he makes an eloquent speech—*somehow!*—about double-digit profit increases, and he wraps it up with a sincere toast of appreciation to each of the company presidents and directors. After the bevy of "here-heres" and polite applause, the festivities begin in earnest.

Champagne flows like water. The crisp white Porthault tablecloths are laden with dazzling crystal candelabras and decorated with luminescent glassware, in what appears to be every bloody example of their collection. Damn, are there ten different pieces of stemware?! Wish that bastard Laurent could see me now. (Alexandra! Stop thinking about that poop for brains! If you must, lose yourself in the food. *D'accord. Avec plaisir.*)

The delicate *amuse-bouches* of a chilled *soupe d'asperge avec des huîtres* arrive and are sipped, followed by a butter-smooth foie gras with a delicate mango chutney on warmed blinis. My God, it's a genius innovation; the combination melts in your mouth as if a dream.

Between stolen moments with Jean-Albert and Bruno's witty banter, my eyes dance about the room in ecstasy. Everyone very much resembles extras from an opulent Merchant-Ivory film set in turn-of-the-century France. It's a mesmerizing image indeed: There is something terribly intoxicating about a room full of bare shoulders, waistcoats, and fine manners.

As per tradition, with each service one should alternate one's attention with dinner partners. By the arrival of the *brochettes de Saint-Jacques et mousse de fenouil,* I have found myself sufficiently inebriated to engage in a conversation with the previously mentioned staggeringly beautiful woman seated across from me.

Her face has qualities of nobility and courage, credulity, and cunning. Impeccable woman, intimidating beyond words . . . *sans alcool. But with alcohol, I'm launching into a chat almost unbeknownst to my mouth, which is already in action.*

"*Wow.* I have to tell you, your necklace is breathtaking. I'm Alexandra, by the way." Okay, that didn't come out nearly as lovely as it appeared in my mind. Definitely drinking too much Champagne in an attempt to quell nerves.

"*Merci* . . . and yes, of course, I remember your name. We were introduced when you sat down," she says, with grace personified. Right. I can hardly grasp names in those moments, too busy trying to *appear* calm.

"I am Marie-Hélène de Saint Florent," she generously offers as a refresher course, "and the man accompanying me this evening is Monsieur de Bellemont."

And she gestures to the older gentleman with a sweep of her glittering wrist. Her gold cuff, encrusted with emeralds the size of walnuts, casts vibrant green hues off the silver and crystal as she gestures. Monsieur de Bellemont appears about sixty, harmless and charmless, and with such a craggy, wrinkled face I was seriously tempted to grab a piece of paper and do a rubbing.

Okay, we've determined a few things: I'm the only one here without the "de" aristo thing. I'm giving off more of a "duh" title, if any, I fear. And we know she's one gorgeous, self-assured woman; the man accompanies *her*, and that "*this*" evening" means they're not married. And she has jewels up the ying-yang. Hmm, interesting.

"*Enchantée . . . encore.*" Alright. It's official, I'm as bad at speaking to elegant women as I am expert at chatting up chic men. Who knew?

I continue in hopes of possibly stumbling into intelligent conversation. "I have never seen so many emeralds," I blather. Great, Alexandra, way to establish you're a hick from the Midwest. What's next? For the love of God, don't ask if they're real or you'll get tossed out on your *derrière.*

"Oh, emeralds are my passion. I wear nothing but. Make note, Alexandra, it is definitely wise to choose a favorite stone above all others, to make it all that much more simple for the man—*or men*—in your life to offer you gifts." She states this with such authority, I feel like I should start taking notes.

"Ah yes, one stone above all others. Noted," I parrot, and help myself . . . no, more like try to *lose myself*, in a second glass of the Château Margaux '86.

Gotta admit, partaking of extraordinary cuisine and wines is all new to me, and I find I keep drinking and eating too much, aware that this may all be a once-in-a-lifetime chance. I mean, seriously, how does one leave so much as a crumb behind of anything created by master chef Joel Robuchon? (I must be careful with all this consumption, as my tummy's starting to pooch, and with my stick legs, in no time I could end up looking like a pony.)

The uniformed *serveurs* (waiters, all of whom are gorgeous, *not just by chance, certainly*) glide through the room silently making finished plates disappear into thin air and seamlessly reappearing to place silver-domed plates at every setting. A delicious hush falls upon the room as the waiters fall into position, standing formally one behind each of the hundred guests. And with a precision of great elegance, each simultaneously and in unison extends one hand, unobtrusively lifting the domes to unveil the *homard rôti aux betteraves* (roasted ruby red lobster with julienned beets).

Such an unfathomably chic moment to witness, I know I shall never forget it. And it confirms, without question, that living well is just one sensual pleasure after another.

Each huge lobster is ceremoniously surrounded by pale silver *truffes noires* risotto and three crystal bowls, each sitting in its own ice, of beluga, sevruga, and osetra caviar. (Reader: Please insert another of my king and court references here.)

As the waiter unveils my lobster—and while I am ridiculously attempting to discreetly check my lipstick in the reflection of the silver dome—I notice my blazing red lobster has just one claw. The Château Margaux inspires me to pipe up.

"*Quel dommage*, my lobster only has one claw."

"Oh. Terribly sorry, Mademoiselle. They often fight with each other in the tank," the *serveur* replies apologetically.

"Well, take this one away and bring me the victor!" I reply, mentally celebrating the return of some wit.

Amazingly, this silly comment sets off a surprising wave of laughter at the table. A welcome relief, as I always imagined the beau monde to be lacking in *any* sense of humor. Jean-Albert gives me a sweet, sly smile, and there's a twinkle in his eye, as if to say, "That's my girl!" Hate to say it, but it seems obvious: I'm much funnier slightly drunk. *(I can definitely see a stint at Alcoholics Anonymous in my future if I have to keep up these stressful dinners.)*

"Adored your quip, Alexandra . . . Do I detect an American accent? Have you recently arrived to France?" The gorgeous red-haired diva asks, leaning toward me and lowering her voice.

"American, yes? But actually, I have lived in Paris for three years. I initially came as an au pair, but I am doing my Ph.D. on Boucher at the moment." Christ, Alexandra, why stop there? Why don't you just tell her how you were cleaning your rusty kitchen stove today!

"Very good for you! I find it fascinating that Jean-Albert has attached himself to you. Clearly, you are a clever and charming young woman . . . As well as possessing other talents," she whispers, as her gaze intensifies in a curiously appreciative fashion. Well now. I'm getting it. She's referring to the bedroom. Very delicate of her.

"Tell me, Alexandra, like many Americans I read about, do you believe in all those New Age ideas *or* astrology?" (Go ahead and note the casual snobbery.)

"Absolutely not. But then again, Pisces never do," I say, clearly verging into standing up, grabbing the mike, and launching into a comedy routine. Somebody stop me . . . *or at least take away the alcohol.*

"Ha-ha, well done. I should think we might have a great many subjects to discuss together," Marie-Hélène says, regally pulling her shoulders back with such exquisite grace as to resemble a peacock spanning the full glory of its splendiferous tail.

She adds, "You study art, *oui*? You do realize, this is an art as well?" *This?* I think to myself, as in *dinner*? Oh, of course. I get it. Bloody wine is killing brain cells a plenty *ce soir*.

"Yes, I fully agree, conversation is an art," I respond, thinking, "Phew, right answer, right answer!"

The red-haired beauty, dripping in emeralds, looks directly at me and whispers, "No, my dear. Not conversation per se . . . but the role you have agreed to play . . . as a courtesan to a man like Jean-Albert." She ends with a tilt of her head as if to add, "Call a spade a spade, young lady."

How does one respond to something like that? I search possible mental files and "zip" comes up. Only that my friend Isabel said last week, *after hearing I was still seeing Jean-Albert,* "You're a mistress now?! That is *so* not you!"

I had told her, "Mistress? Not exactly. I call the shots, and it's more stimulating—excellent choice of words—than being with men our own age." She acknowledged both points, but I could tell she was either flabbergasted or jealous or both. But this woman tonight? What's her angle?

"Alexandra. Allow me to offer you an invitation for tea next week. We simply must get to know one another better." And Marie-Hélène slips a large beige engraved calling card with emerald *(bien sûr)* green edging from her small lizard purse, and places it in my outstretched hand.

MARIE-HÉLÈNE DE SAINT FLORENT
40, AVENUE FOCH
PARIS, FRANCE 75016
TELEPHONE: 01462482810

"I shall ring you on Monday. Tea would be delightful. I look forward to our next acquaintance with impatience," I say, miraculously and thankfully struck with momentary semieloquence. I take the crisp card and put it into my long, slim purse, next to my tiny wad of cash, which I realize does make a lot of outings with me—but rarely gets used these days. For the first time in my life I have extra money. Meaning: I could actually afford taking taxis now, which with my new diamonds would make sense. The cash to insure them? Not quite yet. How bizarre is that?

After our final exchange, Marie-Hélène and I nod respectfully to one another and resume conversations with the men at our sides and enjoy the last sparkling moments of the evening. Double-cheek air kisses, hearty handshakes, and candles burned to the wick. *La fête est finie.*

Before the clock strikes midnight, the guests have all streamed away into their awaiting cars and must be home untying those *cravats* and placing the jewelry back into velvet cases. Jean-Albert has given the keys to the *voiturier* and we make our way up to his suite at the Ritz.

A very drunk kiss in the elevator (that would be me; he never loses his dignity. Clarification: That is, unless he's naked!) and I slide my hand in his shirt and pinch hard at his right nipple. "Arhhh! Alexandra, you vicious girl!" he yelps. Predictable and perfect response. Like clockwork, he instantly goes into a sexual frenzy every time. Trust me, I know better than to do this if I'm *not* in the mood, as he's unstoppable, but right now, I want him. *Badly.* The extreme tenderness he showered on me tonight, his delicious appetite for life, and the seductive effect of his extreme power—throw in copious amounts of Cristal and fine wine, and I am one ravenous lioness.

We race to the door, rip off our clothes, and make love for hours. Okay, not hours. But long compared to nanosecond relations with young men. (News flash: Now I love older men; they can control when they come and wait until they are given permission. As they say in life, "Timing is everything." *Certainement!*)

Given the green light to accelerate into ecstasies, he moans out his traditional and somehow endearing *"Bordel! . . . Putain!"* and collapses beneath me. Yes, beneath me.

Gotta say, he's good. Insatiable desire is just plain sexy.

It was a metaphysical experience—oh strike that, I don't know about the "meta" part, but the "physical" part—oh, yes! And a damn fine one at that.

The next morning I awoke with such a hangover I felt like I had been embalmed. Stayed in all weekend. Not working on my thesis, but reading *Memoirs of the Prince* by Talleyrand, which Jean-Albert had given me. Not being prepared with a full critique by the next time I see him would be, well, unacceptable. To both of us. I make a mental note: New self-imposed pressure and discipline must be employed in regard to drinking Champagne in public venues. Ouch! My noggin's killin' me.

NOTABLE OBSERVATION UNIQUE
TO LIFE AS A COURTESAN

You find yourself quite often at openings, dinners, and receptions where you are one third the age of most of the assembled guests. Your eye seeks out a face of equal youth and you think, "Oh, thank God, someone my own age to chill with!" Then, without fail, you realize that this young face belongs to a waiter or a chauffeur. Not to mention, you will be seated around a dinner table, feeling strangely out of place, and it will hit you, "That's because I'm the only one there who's *not* famous, *not* a billionaire, and *not* the recipient of the Légion d'honneur. Right, I'm the courtesan. I'm almost famous, almost rich, and hell, I *should* get the damn Légion d'honneur for my services to the great men of France!"

CHAPITRE SIX

It is not enough to conquer; one must also know how to seduce.
                                                        —VOLTAIRE

The following Monday, having recuperated suitably and given substantial thought to Marie-Hélène, I felt it was time to get our tea underway. Rang her and initially got a gentleman possessing a *très raffiné* voice: *"La résidence de Madame de Saint Florent."* Sheesh. That's a whole lot chicer than me grabbing my cell phone out of my jean jacket and barking, "Speak to me!"

Marie-Hélène and I made superpolite chitchat, the tea invitation reissued and designated for Wednesday at four. She explained that she is occupied Tuesdays, "holding her *salon*." Hmm. I'm assuming she doesn't mean embracing her living room but something akin to receiving guests for a stimulating social exchange. (See? I'm catching on!)

Tuesday, I saw Jean-Albert for a quick dinner at the *resto* Black Calvados in the chi-chi 8th arrondissement. Would you believe they have some *plat* on the menu that's "foie gras, vodka cubes, and popcorn balls"? Oh, you know I ordered it. Surprisingly good mélange on the tongue! You don't say that phrase every day, now do you?

Afterward we made a mad dash back to my flat for a round of

playing a hilarious sexual skit, where he was a shoe salesman with a mad foot fetish—a lot of toe sucking and him pawing me as I pretended to be uninterested. Couldn't tell you why, but it worked for me. And of course, it worked for him. This man loves a good talking down. Go figure.

I spent the better part of Wednesday *matin* debating outfits for that afternoon's tea and trying to imagine what this extraordinary woman and I would possibly have to talk about. Somehow, my asking, "Have you the foggiest idea how to defrost a twenty-year-old freezer?" didn't seem likely. Still, I was flattered by the idea that she wanted to meet me again, *sans* Jean-Albert, as I'm starting to notice I'm making a great many "friends" who have simply deduced I am an *entrée* to him. I suppose insta–faux friends go with the territory—that is, when the man you're with *owns* almost all the territory on rue Faubourg St. Honoré and avenue Montaigne.

Wednesday afternoon: Casually and elegantly clad, *I hoped*, in a fitted black cashmere turtleneck, high-waisted black sailor pants with the ubiquitous six gold buttons at the waist, and the new short camel trench from Vuitton, I made my way into a taxi just as the sky opened up, first with a crash of thunder, then a flash of light illuminated the dark sky, and as a finale, clouds loaded with inexhaustible rain unleashed a torrential downpour. Paris in the winter is just one gray day after another, with slight variances of dark clouds and rain showers. Amazingly, it's still gorgeous, in a romantic, melancholic way.

"C'est là! Arrêtez ici, s'il vous plaît," I command the cab driver, as I spot number 40 on the über-chic avenue Foche.

This famous avenue is one of the tree-lined wide streets that radiate off the Arc de Triomphe like spokes and are positively bathed in the patina of old wealth. The avenue sports building after building of stunning landmarks, impenetrable elegant white limestone buildings of neoclassical ornate facades, tracery ironwork gates, and sumptuous custom silk draperies peeking around vast windows. I arrived at number 40, which was clearly one of those buildings that looms over you as you look up thinking, "Who is so bloody fortunate as to live here?" (And one can be damn sure is loaded with masterpieces and art of museum quality.) In truth, the Baccarat building has nothin' on Marie-Hélène's hacienda.

I got positively drenched as I sprang from the taxi and sprinted into the huge vaulted entrance. So much for polished-casual elegant; try dripping wet rat. Under the awning I grabbed my compact out of my purse to see just how much of a raccoon I resembled. Dead-ringer. Super. I tried to quickly wipe away the remnants of a once carefully applied makeup job, as I've come to understand fixing one's makeup in public is *très, très déclassé* in France. *God, what isn't?*

I pressed the round brass buzzer, announced myself, and the enormous carved-oak doors opened as if by hidden hands. The owner of the *très raffiné* voice appeared; a distinguished, gray-haired gentleman of about seventy, dressed in a dark single-breasted suit of the uniformed staff variety. With watery blue eyes beneath tired lids, he introduced himself while bowing slightly, "Mademoiselle Alexandra, I presume." (Well, I did just say that into the speaker phone, mister.) "I am Hugo. (Curiously, all menservants seem to be named Hugo.) Madame is waiting for you in the drawing room. Please follow me . . .

"Pity about the rain," he adds, and thank God, because I was starting to think he might be an automaton for all his trancelike gazing and controlled movements.

Hugo opens and offers me a black umbrella with a cane handle. Good, because I didn't relish the idea of huddling under his, *with him*. It's just that Hugo is one of those men who seem as though they smell—of mothballs, at best. I'm not being mean, but some members of the older generation in France haven't ever embraced the whole hygiene thing. If you've ever been to France you know I speak the truth. Still, I'd gladly swap these wet, smelly wool pants for your fussy uniform, buddy.

Hugo proceeds to lead me through a courtyard situated around a perfectly raked long, rectangular garden of small pebbles—man, this gravel lawn is the size of a tennis court, for God's sake. And at these real estate prices, luxurious beyond belief.

Trundling behind on the cobblestones, it's all but impossible to avoid the puddles. *Merde alors!* Within minutes all hope is lost of a second wearing of my new lamb suede boots from Michael Perry. Pity, these beauties deserved better than only *une promenade*.

Entering tall glass-paned doors, Hugo takes my wet umbrella, places it in a silver cone receptacle, and escorts me into the foyer. The de rigueur chandelier of immense scale and innumerable tiers hovers overhead, and I am greeted by a trio of life-size female nude sculptures on pedestals.

"Hello, ladies" pops into my head, and I cringe that my "amuse yourself with silly jokes" reflex almost escaped my lips. I know Jean-Albert would laugh at that too, though. This Hugo would just think I was bonkers. Right, Alexandra, get a grip: Assume some semblance of sophistication.

"The drawing room is this way, Mademoiselle," Monsieur de Mothballs announces, directing me up a set of curving stone stairs and through a long corridor lined with Renaissance tapestries. It occurs to me, "Fuck, should I have brought something? Like flowers? A book? Christ, I need *A Young Courtesan's Guide to Old School Etiquette*." Where does one find that? Actually, it wouldn't surprise me to find out such a book exists in France.

Hugo deposits me in a large well-lit room flanked by marble fireplaces on either end. Towering arrangements of lilies dot the room, as do silk settees, ottomans, and armchairs of various pastel tones. An interior frozen in time—*in a good way*.

An obscene array of crystal vases, glass sculptures, and crystal bowls are arranged carefully on every surface. Uh-oh. I am just too nervous, definitely gonna be my usual bull in a china shop and demolish something before this afternoon's over. The only question is, just which priceless object will take the fall? My money's on the antique Lalique vase on the *guéridon*.

Caught up on calculating the odds, I suddenly hear, "Ahhh, Alexandra, how lovely to see you again." Marie-Hélène enters the room in her full splendor. Her voice is calm, slow, and suggestive, as if she had just left her bed, which is impossible given her impeccable state of adornment. She approaches me with such a seamless glide as to appear to be moving on an unseen conveyor belt. (Can't be RollerBlades. Unless they're Chanel or something.) In two words: killer entrance.

"*Bonjour*, Marie-Hélène. Thank you again for your invitation. Your home is simply enchanting," I say, as I run a hand through the wet hair stuck on my cheek.

Marie-Hélène looks like utter perfection. That flaming auburn hair has been set free of its previous upsweep and is cascading in shiny waves over her delicate shoulders. She's taller than I had thought; easily five foot ten, and in those heels, a grand gazelle, again teeming with emeralds. Ah, yes, *she* chose the perfect ensemble for tea: a soft, yellow silk blouse paired with a wide fox wrap tossed over one shoulder. Tailored cream wool crepe pants with wide sweeping hems that fall just that perfect 2 cm over her bisque leather boots, which have a dozen self-covered buttons trailing up the ankle. Very wealthy lady of leisure meets modern suffragette—*by way of Dior*. What was I thinking with wool sailor pants? God, this is neither a resort nor a yacht party! Clearly it's not enough to get free fabulous clothes; one needs a bit of style to wear them.

"Dear girl, you are soaked to the bone. We must get you out of those wet clothes . . . and tea? No, that won't do. . . . Hugo!" She raises her voice above her usual kittenish tone.

"*Oui*, Madame?" Hugo arrives with such speed it's as though he was simply hovering behind the door, awaiting his next command. Maybe he was, actually.

"Please set up the tea service in my boudoir and bring in a tray of liqueur and spirits, if you would be so kind, and then I shall not need you again until the dinner hour."

"*Très bien*, Madame." And off Hugo scoots.

"Alexandra," she says, taking my hand in hers, "let's see about finding you something dry. You're about *ma taille*. . . . Thirty-six, *oui*?" And we make our way through another set of double doors, through another set of rooms. The second contains wall-to-wall, floor-to-ceiling leather-bound books, large Parisian club chairs, and a black pony skin rug hugging the parquet. *Bien sûr*, the library, right. Have to get me one; the teetering piles of books willy-nilly in my apartment have all the charm of a garage-sale stand.

I follow her into what appears to be the north corner of the building, through an ivory inlaid walnut door, and into a shimmering white cloud of creamy marble and gold leaf. Is this the bathroom? Christ, it's twice the size of my whole flat!

"This is my sanctuary, my *salle de bain*, and there . . . my boudoir," she explains, pointing through an open door into a coral-pink nest of shantung silk and shell-pink velvet. Her fastidious taste is apparent everywhere.

The room is suffused with shimmering light, all warm peaches and apricots, Fragonard-perfumed candles alight on every table. It's sheer femininity and pure sensuality; one immediately wants to curl up on this sumptuous velvet chaise longue and while away the day, *neither alone nor dressed*. Hugo arrives with a large trolley, one stubborn wheel with a mind of its own making his efforts a struggle. He silently sets up the tea service, all twelve sparkling silver pieces: the sugar bowl overflowing with the pretty pale brown cubes of *sucre cru;* a three-tiered plateau of tea cakes; *bonbons pour grignoter; macarons, nougats,* and *fruits confits* of every hue. Two round porcelain plates of small cucumber and *saumon* sandwiches; Sèvres tea cups with handpainted Napoleonic bees; and below, a silver tray of twenty or so liqueurs, mixers, and wines.

Nice eats, as we'd say back in Elmbrook, Illinois. I know, I know, completely inelegant of me.

"Shall I pour?" he inquires, steaming teapot in hand.

"I think not; that will be all, Hugo."

"Very well, Madame." And he does another one of those semi-bows and backs out of the room.

I stand shivering, pretty much stunned and unsure what to say or do next. Thankfully Marie-Hélène jumps in. "Oh, let's get you something fun to drink . . . a grog, perhaps?" Incredibly, she's quickly slipped off her boots and is on hands and knees hunting on the lower tray of alcohol. "Lagavulin? A Fernet Branca?" she asks, as sweet as can be.

"What's a Fernet Branca? It sounds like the name of my sixth-grade Spanish teacher!" I say, getting down next to her on the marble floor.

"*Artichaut* alcohol . . . maybe not the ticket today. Better for yachting when cold waves spray over the stern." (But of course, I should've guessed. Note: Wear these pants while drinking a Fernet Branca on a yacht one day.) "I'm bored with tea. I'm going to have a martini; would you care for one?" she asks, still lingering on the floor next to me.

"May not be a wise choice. Last time I had a martini, I woke up on a picnic table in the Bois de Boulogne!" I say, *clearly* feeling more at ease.

"Alexandra, that's a riot! You're outrageously funny . . . a very important, indeed, an *essential* quality for women such as ourselves. You know the Greeks thought that laughter made the soul immortal? I am in full agreement. Martini it is, then," she continues, surprising me in every way there, as I sit pondering, "Women such as ourselves?" Huh? "I hope you have a picnic table, or perhaps a stretcher, as strong alcohol knocks me off my feet," I say, by way of a *deuxième* warning.

She laughs uproariously as she begins to gather all the necessary bottles and ingredients. "Don't worry. I will catch you!" she almost murmurs, pouring in the vermouth with great aplomb.

"Do me a favor, push that button behind you, sweetheart . . . and by all means unburden yourself of those damp boots," Marie-Hélène commands, pointing to my left with one hand as she drops in crushed ice with the other.

I do as I'm told on both, and as I reach down to unzip my boots, I hear *"Shhhhnkk."* The two walls of mirrors pull back automatically, in a three-step process where each panel unveils a larger, and then a larger, deeply set closet of dizzying volume and a staggering range of colors of what is clearly haute couture. And on the opposite side, tray upon tray of silk scarves and *foulards;* stacked shelves of easily two hundred pairs of heels, mules, and lace-up high-heeled sandals. Handbags line the upper tiers, by color and skin. Never have I seen so much crocodile, alligator, and lizard. Mouth agape, I kick out both legs from under me and just sit on the floor in awe, and gawk, "That's amazing."

"Yes, isn't it? I adore my dressing room. Every woman should have a special place in which to celebrate her femininity. Dare I say? I do have an obsession with *accoutrements*."

Jamming my wet *chaussettes* into my boots, "And possibly a reptile fetish?" I joke, standing up again.

"Dearest Alexandra, my fetishes are far more perverse than that! Here you are." She smiles mischievously as she hands me my glass. "To new friends . . . and long, wet afternoons!" she adds.

"Sounds like something Jean-Albert would say!" I chime in, as I take a deep sip. Mmm, a *vanille* martini. How decadent, delicious, and girly! And *so* Marie-Hélène, I'm starting to gather.

"Yes, he is quite the sexy man, isn't he? You have hooked yourself the biggest fish in France, Alexa. May I call you Alexa? It so suits you. Do tell, was meeting him by design? I'm ever so curious," she asks in her butter-soft tone, as she places herself in front of her closet. Strike that, *closets*.

"Alexa? Yes, I was called that when I was a little girl. And 'by design'? Oh God, no. Quite *par hasard*. I met him at the cocktail following the Balmain *défilé* . . . We had this hilariously seductive chat, and I found myself entirely charmed." I realize I'm zipping through my martini lightning quick, possibly inspired by the storm still brewing outside.

Polishing off her drink, she sets about the task at hand. Reaching deep into her closet, she grabs pieces with innate accuracy. "Here, what about this? And these cashmere leggings are simply sublime. I have them in every color. After a fresh bikini wax I find I am positively in ecstasies to slide into these." And she holds out a dove gray, deep V-neck cashmere sweater and matching slim leggings. They are both heavenly, feather light and unimaginably soft.

"Lovely, you sure you don't mind?" I ask, trying to compute

the comment about *après* a bikini wax and looking for somewhere to change. The modest old Vanilla in me still rears her ugly head when changing clothes around other women.

"Not at all," she replies, and hands me a fresh martini. "This time, let's toast to rich men and great sex. One cannot live without them both!"

I laugh. "Yes, but if you had to give up one, which would it be?" and I drink what is quickly starting to go down like water. And quickly making me a free-speaking chatterbox . . . *on unstable legs.*

"*Quelle question! Enfin*, I see you have deduced my *métier*. It's true, this *appartement*, its contents, even Hugo, are *absolument* the acquired trappings of my position. No different from your own role, Alexa, though you are new to it. We are the rare fortunate, modern-day courtesans to a select few—*of our choice*—of the beau monde of France."

"Really? I suppose you are right. It does feel unlike any exis-tence I have ever known . . . or even dreamed of!" I say, rather re-lieved to have permission to say it out loud. I have been trying to put a mental title to what I have been doing for weeks.

She refills my glass as she continues, "Alexandra, I suppose I should admit, I initially extended you an invitation as I always seek to acquaint myself with any woman who presumes herself in any way qualified to seek a position on par with my own. It is generally a painful afternoon during which I unearth a host of disappointing qualities possessed by said woman, and end up completely con-founded as to what a man saw in her. I might add that without excep-tion these women are quickly revealed as the blatant social-climbing gold diggers they are, and I discard them rapidly. But you? Dare I say, I have a wickedly sharp skill for reading people . . . and you, you may be a surprise, especially since you're American. I like you. Which surprises the hell out of me!" she tosses in, exhibiting a flash of casualness—clearly just slightly affected by the alcohol. While I'm over here, *massively* affected by the alcohol. It's been proven time and again: Take one dose of Nervous Alexandra, and add available alcohol = one smashed small-town girl capable of anything.

"Life as a courtesan? Hmm. For all the surprising power I suddenly feel over Jean-Albert . . . or with any man now, I suppose, it certainly is an enormous amount of pressure and work, don't you find?" I blather, looking for some reassurance that I am not alone in finding this role tremendously demanding. Having thrown out that question, I also toss all my former modesty aside like my wet socks as I embark on a martini-induced struggle to extricate myself from my damp sweater.

Marie-Hélène replies slowly while I battle with the sleeves that seem to have become as complicated as a Chinese straitjacket. Through the wool I hear: "Absolutely . . . *sans doute* . . . It takes years of reading, acquiring knowledge, refining one's mind, and honing one's talents in everything from nineteenth-century Russian literature to seducing a man with a single glance. But remember that since your power comes from your own wealth of self-confidence and from the effect you have on men, unquestionably, this will provoke envy or disgust from jealous women who either pretend to take a moral high ground or secretly wish to be in your shoes. And they are always exquisite shoes at that, *n'est-ce pas? Mais franchement*, you must accept it or ignore it . . . My, my, Alexa, you have such beautiful small breasts," she whispers as she steps closer, offering to take my wet things.

"Oh heavens no—they're bee stings. Utterly pointless to even wear a bra." I say, suddenly aware I'm topless and not all that embarrassed, amazingly enough. So un-me.

"No, my sweet, more than a handful is too much," she purrs, and reaches in to tenderly caress my right breast. "Mmm, and your skin is as soft as a *pêche*."

I neither push her away nor speak, swept up in a strange, unknown wave taking over my whole body—humming, for lack of a better word. Curiously, I'm reminded instantly of what it felt like the *first* time a man touched me there . . . dizzying, drunk with pleasure. I'm drunk again—in both senses, I realize.

Ooooph. She glides her hands down to my waist to help steady me as I try to take off my damp pants and underwear. Again, damp . . . *in both senses*. Marie-Hélène takes my limp hands, places them on her shoulders, and pulls off my clothes in one gesture. Standing in front of her, suddenly wearing nothing but a hazy, contented expression, I put a hand over my *chaton*, in an act of returning shyness.

"Alexa, my dear, you have a gorgeous figure . . . don't be shy. If I had your body, I would prance about naked!"

"You are far too kind. I have always had the body of beanpole, and truthfully, was teased relentlessly as a teenager. Boys used to say, 'You're a pirate's dream—a sunken chest!' I still think of myself as that young kid who was constantly mistaken for a boy. I swear, the first time I bought a bottle of perfume, the saleswoman said to me, 'You *do* realize that that's for *girls*!' It was torture!"

"Oh *mon dieu* . . . How charming of a story . . . Jean-Albert must be beside himself in delirium to have found such an innocent creature," she says, as she helps me into the leggings, sliding them up over my hips as her hands follow my every curve.

"Innocent? Not so much of late. I find I'm discovering an unknown side to myself . . . a side far more . . . *creative*, shall we say?"

"Ah, the blossoming of a rosebud . . . delicious. There is so much I should like to open your eyes to, my sweet Alexa," she says, wrapping one arm around my waist, leading me into the coral-pink boudoir. We pass the trays of small, pretty sandwiches begging for attention. "I'm famished. May I sneak a little something to eat?" I ask.

"Oh dear, I'm a terrible host. You nestle up on this divine chaise and I shall bring them to you . . . Another martini? Oh, no, let's try some nectar of the gods. Champagne! A far better accompaniment to *saumon fumé*."

And she makes her way back to the silver cart, plucking various amusements with delight and placing them on a large silver plate. Returning, she hands me a flute of Veuve Clicquot after taking a sip from the glass, and places the plate at the foot of the chaise—curiously, out of arm's reach.

"Something to tempt you with . . . Let's see if you find anything you like." And with that Marie-Hélène begins to slowly peel off her sweater, revealing a pale pink embroidered demicup bra and those enormous emeralds against her bare skin. In her midforties, she has the body of a woman a decade younger. For all her compliments, I find I am rather envious of her whippet-thin, toned, long limbs. She's like a ballerina. I realize I have never seen a woman naked at that age—damn nice to know you can still look seriously sexy.

Glimpsing her breasts slipping out of her bra as she steps out of her trousers, I am aware that I am studying her appreciatively, with an interest bordering on fascination. She feels my gaze and clearly enjoys it. I see her nipples swell and redden as she unhooks her bra and lets it fall to the floor. *Just what is going on here? Weren't we just talking about great sex with men?*

Standing in nothing more than her matching pale pink string, running her hands through her silken hair, Marie-Hélène brazenly asks, "So, as I said, have you found anything to tempt you . . . anything that you like?"

"Ah . . . God, yes . . . wait . . . meaning?" I stumble over my words, unsure if she's just simply speaking of the food or . . . this whole scene. She laughs again, that surprisingly deep and haughty laugh that makes me pull back and check to see if it's still her. Seriously, I'm too drunk to figure this out. Is she seducing me or simply changing clothes? Sober, I am sure I could get a handle on what's unfolding here.

"Alexa, you luscious creature . . . I mean the food, of course. What on earth did you think I meant?" More of that laugh again, as she comes toward me, kneeling on the end of the chaise. Looking at me intensely, she scoops her slim index finger into the creamy *chantilly* atop a cream puff and raises it to my—unbeknownst to me—opening mouth.

Her eyes meet mine with unremitting candor. We hold each other's gaze tauntingly. I feel only the wet glide of her warm finger sliding slowly into my mouth.

She slowly removes her finger, licks it, and smiles mischievously.

Case closed . . . on that question.

THE SECOND LOVE LETTER FROM JEAN-ALBERT
(Hand delivered by motorcycle messenger.)

Dearest Alexandra

Mon amour, I'm bathed in an impenetrable happiness, all the more exquisitely so, as the bliss of moments spent with you is always beyond dreams and expectations. Am still delightfully dizzy, thinking about the sensual graceful swaying of your beautiful hips . . . There is not a single gesture in you that does not genuinely embody sensibility, beauty, generosity, sensuality . . . femininity! . . . A light kiss on the fresh sacred corolla of your soft mouth . . .

Your J.A.

AS A COURTESAN, DON'T EVEN THINK OF LEAVING THE HOUSE WITHOUT . . .

1. Impeccable grooming. Opt for a subtle French manicure—never a fire engine red or striking color, even if it's Chanel's latest must wear of the season. Hands and gestures are to be admired for their fluidity and elegance. Thus, merely lightly glossed in discreet nude or buff. As for the pedicure, I don't care if that fashion doyenne Diana Vreeland pushed red for all seasons and all time, the palest shell pink or bisque is the rule. No polish with an opalescent shimmer—it's trash, trash I tell you! And don't even think of sporting a bit of a longer, if well-shaped, toenail. Again—it's the epitome of *déclassé.* Those have been known to slice delicate five-hundred-thread count sheets into shreds during passionate lovemaking . . . at least courtesan-style lovemaking!

2. At least one fresh witty quip and anecdote at the ready. This should be historically based or *au courant*—derived from current events—but

must be unique, not common knowledge, and something one can weave into conversation without appearing forced.

Par exemple, this doesn't work.

While taking a sumptuous bite of the world-renowned duck à l'orange at the famous restaurant La Tour d'Argent, overlooking the gloriously illuminated buttresses of Notre Dame, don't try to make some joke about the odds that the two-hundred-euro poultry you're chewing is tainted with the deadly avian flu.

Timely? Yes. Funny? *Non.* A downer? Totally.

And yet this does—*surprisingly*—work.

I wasn't sure how this would go over, but I went for it, doing an entire reenactment of the following story, and Jean-Albert cackled so hard I thought he'd wet his pants:

One Saturday, as I perused the shops of St. Germain, some German tourist with his son stopped me to ask, in all his non-English and non-French skills, where the Musée d'Orsay was. Knowing that it was Bastille Day, and there was no sense giving him directions when the museum was just going to be closed, *and seeing as we had not a common language between us,* I found myself launching into a physical performance. Not an easy task, I assure you, as I needed to convey myself as representing a museum that was closed, then progressing into a massively complicated mime of an accurate reenactment of the taking of the Bastille, complete with cannons blaring and the battered flag waving over head . . . and, you know what? The German guy *got it.* He nodded. *"Ach, sehr gut, danke."* Maybe that one's funnier in person, but I thought, here goes, I'm going to be me, but I could very well be setting my own future aflame with this. Conclusion: If it's amusing, try it. Lighthearted wit is always an elixir for overworked men.

3. The de rigueur accessories. Fresh breath mints. The new squirty ones with liquid centers are sublime and easy to discreetly sneak into one's mouth. The old school favorites, Fisherman's Friends mints, with their medicinal aftertaste and cumbersome size, have all the charm of sucking on a urinal cake. Sorry, a ghastly notion!

Also falling into this list, your traditional and ubiquitous extra pair of La Perla, Sabbia Rosa, or Fifi Chachnil panties (available at the lingerie shop Emilia Cosi on rue St. Sulpice). Nothing in vibrant colors, *mais bien sûr*, and surely nothing *à la* Fredericks of Hollywood with a whistle a danglin', in polyester with satin rosettes, or bearing any rhinestones, sequins, or beading.

A tiny flacon of perfume, preferably sprayed to cloak you in a balanced distribution of fragrance. Ideally a couture scent created exclusively for oneself, as with men of a certain age and caliber you can bloody well bet they have a serious memory backlog of other women who have passed through their arms wearing Guerlain, Hermès, Yves Saint Laurent, and Chanel. Better to mix your own oils than march around reeking of the same Chanel's Coco that is on scent strips in all the magazines.

4. Cell phone with speed dials locked in with numbers of chauffeur services, private taxi on call, elegant florist to send quick thank-you bouquets, ready-to-wear boutiques in every major city, *absolument,* with manager name reference, such as Pierre at Dior on avenue Montaigne (for last-minute or unforeseen need of the perfect strappy *talon* or matching handbag). Also have at the ready the numbers of the Michelin-starred restaurants that one frequents habitually.

5. Cash. Imperative. Tip well and hard. Note: fine line here, *not* vulgarly or blatantly. Generally, *after* a service is rendered rather than *before.* An implied incentive sends a very dangerous message that one thinks excellent service is (a) not an entitlement but something that need be demanded; (b) insults the establishment, as though such gestures were indeed necessary, when in fact, such restaurants are unequalled in their service regardless; (c) portrays the instant image that you are *très nouveau riche* and need to flash your wealth.

In general, you want to ensure faithful, polite discretion combined with excellent, respectful service. Therefore, one must "extend kindnesses" (how's that for a more chic euphemism? Far better than the cheesy "butter up" or my least favorite, "oil the palm") to the maître d's with whom you're acquainted, your driver, your concierge, the PR people, personal shoppers, or liaisons at couture houses and boutiques. Hell, even the coat-check girl who, you never know, can save you in pinch. Oh yes indeedy, once a clever if homely coat-check woman at the *resto* Senderens tipped me off to the presence of Jean-Albert's wife dining with her lady friends just as Jean-Albert and I were arriving for a *dîner tous les deux*. How ugly . . . or, should I say, "unnecessarily unpleasant" would that have been? I do have to admit that even the idea that I have to come up with precisionlike replies to possible confontations with a lover's wife does pretty much suck, to put it succinctly. The old me, *the vanilla Alexandra,* used to try to pre-think insightful comments to impress *professeurs* and boyfriends' parents. I guess that that mentality has gone the way of my stocking the bath with generic shampoos and lotions—banished, and never to be seen again, much like . . . fuck, Laurent is the name that comes to mind, *ggggrrr.* I still am furious at that boy!

CHAPITRE SEPT

Everything you want is out there waiting for you to ask.
Everything you want also wants you. But you have to
take action to get it. —JULES RENARD

Regarding that afternoon with Marie-Hélène, did I leave the Isle of Man and adventurously visit the Isle of Lesbos, you ask? Not really. Vague of me, isn't it? A daring erotic seduction if ever there was one, right? Gay Paree, indeed. In retrospect, ironically (or maybe not so ironically), my mental image of the two of us languidly lazing the afternoon away, lying together on that luxurious chaise, is not unlike one of the frothy images of frolicking courtesans in a Boucher painting. I find myself wondering, "Just exactly how much have my studies influenced my recent actions?" *Beaucoup*, it seems. We should all be glad I wasn't studying cannibalism!

But seriously, I'd better watch what I'm doing here, as I clearly am intrigued, and clearly am *such* a *succumber* to the power of suggestion. Marie-Hélène certainly was the temptress feline, igniting a spark and fanning the fire, but aside from allowing a few small kisses—*alright, more than a few*—I *mostly* played it off, reassuming some of the vanilla flavor that I still have in my back pocket. *There's very little left, to be sure.*

Frankly, Marie-Hélène is one seriously sexy woman, and while

I would never have guessed she partook in dalliances with both sexes, I found the whole experience very eye-opening. *Literally!* I am not saying I wouldn't go there, but at present my head is spinning more than enough for me to indulge in every sexual fantasy I ever had. Did I just say that? God, Freud would have a field day with that. This is just *entre nous* and between us girls, anyway, right?

She *finally* put some clothes on—a magnificent Chinese embroidered robe—and we spent the remaining moments before sunset talking our heads off as we lay together on that cloudlike velvet chaise. Fascinating woman. It seems she's convinced herself that she wants to be a guide to me—in her *milieu*—of *la vie d'une courtisane.* Apparently, to be something of an adviser, offering instruction, advice, and the like, as she wishes someone would've once done for her.

It's kind of like—if you extract the seduction aspect, *mais oui*—having an older sister who is protective and worldly—*and* can tell you the sexual tricks to make a man lose his ever-loving mind. And some to lose yours. Tip *numéro un*: She suggested that when a man is about to come, inhale deeply, as it tightens the walls of your *chaton* and makes him come with insane pleasure. Trust me—it's the clincher (pun intended) in great sex. Jean-Albert went into ecstasies.

What else? There's so much. The woman is a gold mine for stories and witticisms. I find myself thinking about her—curious about her—more than I think of Jean-Albert. I can see completely why men shower her with adoration and opulent gifts. She's positively captivating: exuberant, beautiful, brilliant, elegant, sensual, and wicked fun. I love that she feels no rivalry, that she's extremely generous in spirit. *And she's clearly tactile to the extreme, as well.*

Among other things, Marie-Hélène warned me not to get too attached to Jean-Albert. To consciously keep reminding myself, as she says, "It's all light-hearted frivolity, my dear. Guard your heart. Take your wisdom. Better your mind, and fill your bank account."

Good heavens! I do have to catch myself, as sometimes the tenderness, and the constant flow of attention and compliments from him, make me want to believe *it* could be possible. Then I remind myself, he's married, has been for years, and will always remain so. In those moments I settle in to thinking that all this is just a wonderful jaunt, a foray into a different existence where all my senses are alive and operating at full throttle. There's definitely been an internal shift in how I think of myself, my abilities, and my power. Frankly, when Laurent exited so brutally, I felt I had failed. Failed to enchant him . . . failed to . . . oh, you know what? He failed *me*! See, a new perspective indeed. The old me would've rattled off a list of all *I* thought that *I* was lacking, Now? Screw it. He blew it. Done. *Motherfu$%#@#r!*

Why the new burst of anger at Laurent, you ask? Okay, truth be told, this past Friday was the day he and I were to leave for that Greek getaway. The one we'd planned so intensely with Lonely Planet guidebooks and through a ton of research on the Web, putting together the whole itinerary of island hopping and the various ferries that would propel us from one paradise to another. I knew that the trip, and traveling in general, was hugely important to him, so I just couldn't fathom he'd cancel, and, well . . . to be honest, I didn't cancel my ticket either. Despite all the thrilling drama and the new life with Jean-Albert, I sadly (or maybe romantically? You choose) thought maybe, just *maybe*, he'd call, and we'd spontaneously leap into action without any deliberation. In my fantasy, I'd figure out what to do about Jean-Albert *après* the sunny, dreamy vacation with my young love.

So after a quick, sly call to the airline impersonating Laurent's "assistant" and confirming his flight—all of which to see if he already had—I found out that he was booked to go. Thus, come Friday morning, with not a word to anyone—not even to Isabel—I packed a small bag with a ton of bikinis and a few sarongs and ventured to Charles de Gaulle Airport with the intent of just plopping down in the seat next to him and forcing a reunion. Hell, I had a six-hour flight to convince him, and with my newfound confidence and our sincerely beautiful history—and toss in a fair number of tiny bottles of alcohol—I was sure he'd resume his place as my grand *amour*. With a mission and a faith constructed on memories, and clad in a killer Lanvin dress that had been tailored to my every curve—however small these curves were—I leaped from my taxi and beelined to the check-in counter. Just as I was excitedly fishing through my new Fendi bag for my passport I glimpsed Laurent coming through the huge revolving door . . . with a woman at his side. Laughing and clearly carrying her bag. For the love of God, I hadn't for a second imagined this shit scenario! A final peek at her showed my nightmare realized—a tall gazelle of a brunette with a quiet, intelligent appearance, simply dressed, and clearly older than he. Ugh! They were so picture perfect, and so comfortable together, it was all I could do to slink off discreetly out of eyesight and not just fall down dead right there. I fled to one of those hideous public toilets to sob like there was no tomorrow, and threw myself into a cab to make the horrifically painful trip back to my flat with bag-o-bikinis and zero hope left for our reconciliation. Now maybe you get why my anger has refueled, and why my determination to really throw myself into my new world is without question. If Laurent can move on and be happy, then I sure as hell will give up the idea of him and move on further—*higher!* And be happier! Now if I could just stop dreaming about him, it would make it a helluva lot easier!

Also, in my new ever-changing world, it seemed that Marie-Hélène was quickly replacing Isabel as my confidant. When Isabel rang a week later, strangely, we had this weird awkwardness, acting not at all like our old selves:

"Alexandra, have you fallen off the planet? You never call anymore! Where has Jean-Albert been keeping you?" she says, and it sounds like an accusation.

"Sorry, I know, I have been rather silent. I have been just wildly busy. But, 'keeping me'? It's not as though I am being held hostage as a sex slave, you know?" I smile to myself, thinking, if anyone's the slave, it's Jean-Albert, for fuck's sake.

"Right. It's just you never come to meet the gang for an *apéro* anymore. We miss you. You know, there are some wacky stories about you flying around. I don't know how to respond to them. Is it true you're sporting some big diamond now?" she says, as though wearing expensive jewelry is akin to having taken up with a cult.

"Ahh, kinda . . . it was a gift for . . ." I begin to respond, thinking, "Why do I have to defend myself?"

Isabel interrupts: "Listen, I just don't want you to get hurt. Remember, these men have a woman in every corner, in every city. Just don't start thinking you're *special* . . . like he'll marry you or something . . ." she says, with more than a hint of condescension.

"Geez, don't worry about me. My life's never been more exciting, fulfilling. Truly, I have learned more in virtually *every* arena of life in the last four months than in the last four years!" I reply with indignation, and add, to soften it, "And Isabel, remember one of my favorite lines: 'Before you criticize someone, you should walk a mile in their shoes. That way, when you criticize them you're a mile *away*, and you have *their* shoes.' And I'm wearing a killer pair of Roger Vivier today that you'd love!" I say, laughing.

"Okay, okay . . . Very funny . . . Let's drop it, Alexandra . . . So, tell me, how's the thesis going? You still hope to finish by summer?" (Hrmph! She barely laughed; that joke used to kill her.)

"Great . . . Yeah . . . summer, absolutely." (Total lie.) "How's the job at Balmain? Still digging it?" I ask, changing subjects pronto.

"Love it. I just got promoted. Official design assistant. Crap salary, but it's something. Maybe I can stop thieving the place!" she adds, laughing.

"Good for you! And the love life, Isabel. Anything new on that front?"

"Funny you should ask. Met a sweet man, Mathieu. He works in perfumes. We met on a blind date. So far, so good. No diamonds for me; just great sex, and damn, is he hilarious! But you wouldn't like him, he's young and poor!"

"Sounds nice." (Me, a smidge pissed at being judged by a best friend who used to think I shat gold.)

"Hey, on Saturday, we are all planning on getting stoned and piling into Olivier's old Citroën—thinking a road trip to Euro Disney or someplace silly. Wanna come? Or are you on-call to Jean-Albert round-the-clock?" she tosses in, with thinly veiled hostility. *Very thin veil, there.*

"In fact, we have a dinner at Vaux le Vicomte on Saturday, so can't, sorry to say."

"Well, well, well, looks who's all *parvenu!*" she retorts.

(Being a bit of a harsh girl, aren't ya, Isabel? And did I ever think that kind of thing was fun? Guess my version of fun has definitely changed. Like when Jean-Albert and I were at the restaurant Prunier two nights earlier and he joked, "Let's eat our body weight in caviar!" It was so absurdly funny, we seriously tried to finish the heaping bowls, and roared in laughter about taking it home to feed it to the dog. C'mon, that's funny. It *was. Hey, it's rich guy humor. On a different level, I guess.*) "But have a great time, and give my love to the gang. I'll try to pop by the café next week."

"Fine, enjoy . . . and Alexandra?" Curtly.

"Yeah?"

"Don't lose your way," Isabel says coldly, to wrap up.

"You either. Take care."

I press "end call." Don't know what I meant by "you either," but *please,* she's just jealous. Dating those young pups who can't even take her out to a cheap bistro.

I tried to shake off the residue of that chat: "Well, she should just chill. It's not like this was all my *big plan.* Sorry that my life catapulted ahead of yours and I no longer see the charm in mindless pastimes." Oh, I'm getting dumb defensive. As Marie-Hélène would say, "Some people will just simply be evil with jealousy. Let them go. Life's too short to care what someone else thinks."

True enough, and time to climb into action and get ready for an evening *chez moi* with Jean-Albert. He was to spend the day in London, acquiring yet another *parfum* company, so I promised him dinner *or* a massage when he got in. A generous act on my behalf, as I have never offered him anything before except my company. A massage? Hmmm. It's fair to say I am better at the cuisine part, as every man I've ever given a backrub to *begs* me to stop. On the other hand, my bad massages always lead to fantastic sex, so maybe I'm doin' something right. Jean-Albert's a sport. Up (literally) for anything. I could probably whack his back with an eggbeater and he'd find it erotic.

What a nut he is. *Par exemple*, last Sunday he made a quick exit from brunch with "the wife" and asked to meet me in front of the monkey cage at the zoo in Jardin des Plantes. I'm standing there waiting, leaning against the fence eating licorice, when I hear behind me, "Oo, oo! Aa, aa!" And wouldn't you know, he's leaping up and down wearing a gorilla mask—and probably a two-thousand-euro Lanvin suit—doing monkey impressions, and he finishes by throwing himself into the bushes. I died laughing! What lunatic would be so elegant *and* so bananas? The guard, thankfully, didn't recognize him when he came over to tell him, "Monsieur, do not destroy the foliage, or I will ask you to leave!" I just stood there laughing and totally stunned, and he acted like it was the most natural thing in the world for him to do. Such a kid, this man. *Aren't they all, though?*

But for all Jean-Albert's charm and amusing antics, he can still be a bit of an annoying elitist. And I don't know why he even comes over to my flat. (It's got to be a novelty or something to him, as every other environment he's in is just over-the-top chic.) Because the other two times he has been here, he snorted about the size of my flat, and that there was nowhere to sit, while picking up this or that, saying, "And what, exactly *is* this?" Last time it was an old, chipped house number made of tin I'd once pried from the dilapidated door of the composer Erik Satie's house in Trouville. Laurent had taken me there last summer for a little weekend on the Normandy coast . . . God! We had a ball, devouring *galettes de jambon*, drinking *cidre*, and meandering through the old streets. Laurent scolded me at the time for taking it, but I was compelled. Needed a lifelong reminder of that beautiful day. Fucker. I still think of him every day . . . like, twenty times a day. Unreal. In the words of someone I recently read, and don't ask who as my mind is just aching from all the required reading of late:

> It is impossible to fall out of love. Love is such a powerful emotion that once it envelops you it does not depart. True love is eternal. If you think that you were once in love, but fell out of it, then it wasn't love you were in. There are no "exit" signs in love, there is only an "on" ramp.

Yeah, well, I'd like an "off" ramp, please. No time for sentimentality, as number one, he doesn't deserve it, and number two, I have to make cassoulet for dinner, and that takes hours.

I hustled about my tiny kitchen, mixing white beans with huge white chunks of goose fat. Yeah, yuck. But, hey, that's what the recipe says to do . . Sometimes with French cuisine you're better off not knowing how it's made! Think: *fromage de tête*. Do not translate. Or your appetite may not return for weeks.

Later, around 6:00 P.M., in a moment of divine inspiration, as I am wrapping the Camembert in pastry dough and thinking it looked rather dull—OK, really like an albino horse apple—I was hit with a neat idea. After four very ridiculous failed attempts, I managed to cut out a pretty convincing likeness of Jean-Albert's profile and laid it on top of the flat surface of the dough. A quick brushstroke of egg yolk, *et voilà*, something new (*anything* charming) I can offer my generous beyond comprehension lover. Fat chance he's ever been served something with his image carved into it. Cool.

At eight, as I was putting the finishing touches on my lipstick, he called to say he was going to be arriving late. Crap. Apparently the drive from Le Bourget private airfield is about an hour, add rush-hour traffic, and double that. I endured the wait with remarkable and rare patience. In truth, I have *no* patience. I am fairly sure that when God was handing out that skill, I must've been in the ladies' room or something. So I rang up Marie-Hélène, who talked me down from fury, and even made me laugh with yet another of her takes on being a courtesan.

"Alexa! You realize we are the modern incarnation of a living Venus, the goddess of love, sexuality personified! Rejoice in your good fortune! You know, the men of polite society find the protocols of privilege suffocating; it is boredom, snobbery, envy, and ambition, not to mention lust, that drives these men into raptures, making them willingly fall at our feet. Make him kiss your toes!"

"He already has!" I roar.

"Good. Never forget; desire is excited by the presence of a spirited soul—unpredictable, independent, and mysterious. And indeed, those with extreme wealth have unique needs."

"Unique needs? You can say that again! In the words of F. Scott Fitzgerald, 'The rich are very different from you and me.' Wait, you *are* rich! But of course, I get your meaning."

"*Bien sûr*, I am financially secure, due to the extreme generosity of these complicated creatures! They need, almost crave, amorous intrigue, a world of *galanterie*. To balance the enormous pressure and power they live with *every* moment of their lives. Give them a sounding board, a second childhood, intellectual conversation, and mind-blowing sexual adventures and you own them body and soul!"

"And now I can add 'give them cassoulet' to that list," I toss in.

"My dear, as I told you, I think cooking is a mistake. *Trop, trop domestique*. Too catering when you should be *hiring caterers!* The key is to be alternately dominant and then submissive. In turn ferocious, and then pliable. Keep this all in mind, my dear Alexa. Now off you go, have a lovely night, and do promise I can take you to my coiffurist Saturday afternoon. We have to be perfection for the dinner at Vaux le Vicomte . . . Jean-Albert will have to let me drag you away from time to time; I want to present you to a lot of gentlemen."

"Oh dear, I don't think I can handle more men like Jean-Albert! *Merci* for the sage advice. *À samedi après-midi, Marie-Hélène!*" (I gotta get that woman a nickname! Marie-Hélène is just such an effort to get out all the time. Something about her does seem to resist nicknaming. MH? No. Think on that.)

"*À bientôt*, sweet rosebud." And she clicks off. So now she's also calling me rosebud. Never in my life have I had so many names. Jean-Albert with his *petit chou, bébé d'amour,* and *princesse.* And no, I *do not* want to know how many other women he's *petit chou'd* and *princessed.*

Jean-Albert arrives a scant five minutes later, and as suggested by MH (that *kinda* works), I'm all Mademoiselle Carefree, and charming. She was right; he dropped his harried expression at the door and swept me into his arms.

"*Mon amour,* forty-eight hours without you is an eternity," he whispers into my hair, still wearing his coat. "Dreadfully sorry for the delay, but I did bring you something I picked up at Graff in London," he says, as he rifles through his inner coat pockets.

"The queen's jewels, I hope!" I joke, as I realize, once again, he has something like a stalagtite stuck in his nose. God, his nose is just a magnet for yucky things. Certainly the size has something to do with it; his nose enters the room several seconds before he does!

Jean-Albert hands me a red velvet box and throws his coat on the bed.

"I was kidding! You shouldn't have! . . . Should I open it now?" I ask, hoping for a yes.

"*Absolument.* I just thought it was very *you* . . . and that you might enjoy wearing it to the *dîner* at Vaux le Vicomte."

Beside myself with excitement, I slowly creak open the hinged box to see . . . a dazzling, long necklace of sparkling small diamonds, a lasso of glittering cascades.

"*Jean-Albert! Ooh la-la!*" As I tear it from its box, the strands unravel, revealing that it's one very long chain of diamonds, all of the same size. (Now, having become kind of an expert on stones, I can say they're about a carat each, and probably, given Graff's, *damn close to D flawless.* And just as an aside, trust me, as a courtesan one better brush up on diamonds. Anyone can grasp the basics of the four Cs: color, cut, clarity, and carat weight. It's the *vrai—* real—diamond adorers that appreciate the brilliance, fire, and scintillation that the cut and polish create in relation to reflecting light. And only bona fide connoisseurs will be able to extol the three effects of the scintillation—the sparkle, contrast, and pattern. In short, just be sure you're not being slipped Austrian crystal or zirconias!)

"This is unreal! You're my king!" I say, as I instantly go to the mirror and drape the magnificent necklace around my neck. . . . King? Did I really let that slip?

He stands behind me, helping me arrange the strands in varying styles. "See? You can wear it as one long necklace, or twice around, or tight like a choker of five strands. Very you, I thought. Alexandra: never the same."

Looking again at the two of us in the mirror, I realize I'm almost crying. So touched and so grateful. This man has given me a completely new belief in myself. And oh yes, this night is off to a rousing start! (Now if he'd just blow his nose.)

"Baby, I adore it . . . and I adore you. You're so good to me!" I say, hugging him tightly.

"*Je t'aime, Alexandra*," he says tenderly, still in my embrace and sounding somehow all of about twelve years old.

I fight with all of my being not to say "I love you" back, and not to let a tear fall from my watery eyes. Dig deep, girl. Be strong. I succeed on both counts and extract myself from his clutches. *Phew, close one.*

Jean-Albert lights a cigarette as I clear off my desk and throw a white, linen tablecloth over it, hiding the ink stains. Charmingly, he makes himself at home, getting a bottle of Veuve out of the fridge and bringing two flutes from the cupboard. I light an old bronze candelabra I borrowed ages ago from Isabel and am suddenly hit with a pang of sadness at our disintegrating closeness. What a drag that I can't call her excitedly with some of these stories to share. We could—*we should*—be falling on our backs and giggling, trying to add up the value of all these insane gifts and how we could live for years on them in Bali or somewhere. Miss her.

"Ah, dinner? It smells wonderful. I thought I'd opt for the

massage, but now I think otherwise," he says, opening the oven for a peek, and bringing me back to the moment.

"No idea if it's going to work, *chéri*. First attempt at cassoulet. But it's not like I have massage oil, so if the meal is a bust, you're getting an olive oil rub down!" I tell him, putting the silverware and plates on the makeshift dining table.

"Well, I doubt it will be as good as my *grand-mère*'s, but then again, she doesn't look as good in the kitchen," he says, grabbing my ass as he nuzzles into my neck with that nose. Yes, stalagtite still present. Cripes, it's hard to find *anyone* sexy with "a bat in the cave."

"I thought your *grand-mère* was no longer alive," I say, remembering a sweet story he'd once told me of how he used to help her brush her hair each morning before *petit déjeuner* . . . I think I *half* fell in love with him that night.

"Correct, she has passed."

"What a compliment! I look better than a dead woman in the kitchen!" We both laugh as I discreetly tuck the Camembert into the oven.

Jean-Albert puts on a CD he left at my apartment the first night he came by, Césaria Évora—she's a gorgeous, big black woman who belts out hypnotic, sensual Portuguese music. Undoubtedly, for the rest of my life I will be carried back to that night whenever I hear it. It's become the soundtrack of this dream, as has the music of Serge Gainsbourg, which Jean-Albert plays ad nauseam in his car. He's like a teenager, this pushin' sixties lover-o-mine.

We settle into the cassoulet and it's, well, rather disappointing. Didn't soak the beans overnight first, and to be clear, that's not good for digestion. Think Gas-X maximum strength. Actually, don't just *think* some, *bring* some!

Add in Jean-Albert doing his traditional talking with his mouth full (which is strangely common in France), yet not commenting on or complimenting my grand efforts, and I'm starting to think Marie-Hélène was oh so right about my making dinner being *trop domestique*. Still, I'm rather sure the profile pastry shell will knock him dead. It's a sure hit, *sans doute*.

"Want to open another bottle of Champagne, darling?" I ask, trying to steer his attention elsewhere while I retrieve the baked cheese *pièce de résistance*.

"Are you trying to get me drunk, Alexandra? I have a very important meeting about Samaritane *demain matin*." He pops the cork out the open window, a tradition we started at the Ritz, and I think, he feels it is very "bad boy" of him.

"Seems that *connard* minister, Frédéric de Fallois, has it in for me and is talking about it being a fire hazard and wanting to shut it down. So absurd, the building's been there for a century!"

"Really? That would be ridiculous. Didn't I just read that you put nine million euros into a huge renovation there? Isn't it in his best interest to keep it open? It's two thousand French jobs, working at an impressive profit margin, not to mention that the building's a landmark!" I remark, with newfound informed authority. Annual corporate statements have become required reading—that goes with the courtesan job.

I arrange the perfectly browned *fromage* in pastry on a bed of roquette leaves and finish with a garnish of halved cherry tomatoes. I place my masterpiece at his setting and resume my seat. He just carries on.

"Yes, all true, but he and I are always fighting like cats and dogs. He took a wrong turn after studying with me at the Polytechnique and likes to tell himself he could've been as successful as I am had he not chosen politics. Never!" (Hello, are you ever going to notice the goddamn cheese of your head!?) "I think he's a fool, pompous and arrogant. Now he's even publishing his poetry. *Mon dieu*. Baudelaire he is not. I am sure he despises me because I once slept with his wife—that's the wound that motivates him to destroy me." And Jean-Albert finally shuts up.

I note that very indiscreet confession, but stash it in my mental files, as I'm far too engrossed with his reaction to my little creation *en fromage*—I just sit back rather childishly, awaiting praise and amazement. Jean-Albert finally looks at the pastry, pauses, smiling, "Well, that's cute of you. People are forever putting my image on things—posters, T-shirts, I even have a watch with my profile. Don't you dare start marketing these without giving me a cut," he says, as he jams a hunk of bread through it. Disappointing as hell. What the fuck does it take to amaze this man? Don't answer that! Surely it's something sexual. It does get a bit annoying that he has seen it all, done it all. Do I have to get this man an island for a Christmas gift? *Better ask Marie-Hélène how to handle that next month.*

My mood is a bit off. The "cute" comment has swept the wind from my sails. I know I shouldn't have expected him to do backflips, but just "cute"? I suddenly have no desire for him tonight, despite the crazy, lovely gift. When we finish eating I throw the dishes in the sink, and he's upon me like a bee on a spring flower—*complete with a hard stinger.*

"I have a bit of bad news, *mon amour,*" he says, taking my hand and leading me to my bed. "The dinner at Vaux le Vicomte *demain soir . . .* "

"Yes . . . where you want me to wear the necklace?" (Me trying to *remind* myself: Be happy, you lucky girl. You have a staggering new necklace. That's a big deal, even if it's the financial equivalent of buying a pack of gum for him.)

"It seems . . . I shall have to bring my wife. She has come with me every year and it . . . it just wouldn't be correct not to escort her. She doesn't deserve any scandal or the gossip that would occur if we didn't arrive together." Caressing my cheek gently and with what *appear*s a truly sincere sweetness. "You do understand? I would vastly prefer to be with you, but this is one of those events where wives are de rigueur."

"Fine. I will wear the necklace to the movies then. It'll look killer at *Shrek 3,*" I reply curtly.

"Alexandra, come now. I still want you to come. I need you to be there. I, I . . ." He stumbles on his words. "I just feel better when you're in the same room. Will you please? Come with anyone you wish, but promise me you'll attend. *Alors,* I could even have you escorted by that male model in the Dior ads you said was haute."

"I said, he was *hot*, not *haute* . . ." (Jesus, way to show your age, Jean-Albert.) "No, that's quite alright. I will come, but you will owe me." Why did I say that? Now I look like I mean more gifts, and I so don't. *At least, I don't think I do.*

"You are the best ever. Now, let's get to bed; I'm dying to hold you in my arms," he said, dragging his feet and dropping with sleep.

I trotted off to the bathroom to wash my face and put on one of those La Perla nightgowns he had given me. Face still dripping wet, I catch my reflection in the mirror and take a mental time-out. You know—one of those pure moments in life where you stop all the rushing about and pause, exhale, really seeing yourself in this place, at this moment, and in this chapter in your life.

Palms on my chin, leaning on my elbows, I just looked intensely, *deeply* at my face. So familiar, and yet the more I look, the more abstract the image becomes, as if I'm seeing myself with new eyes. My thoughts a-jumble. "Who are you becoming? What is this all about? And what is the inexplicable reason that you are just compelled to continue this story?" So strange. I can't resist this man. Or Marie-Hélène . . . Or these experiences. All these "transparent" days and nights—with the conscious feeling that I am asleep but on the point of waking up. It's dizzying. Addictive. Sometimes I feel I have all the power in this relationship, and then there are moments like this, cooking at home, I feel like I'm giving him too much of me; then he has the power. Will I ever be calm with this? And, geez, will I ever get my period again? The doctor ran all those tests and said it must've stopped from sheer stress. I have to chill, like Marie-Hélène said: "Keep it all lighthearted frivolity." Right.

The spell is broken. Reality returns. Back to Geezer Zillionaire on bed. Now, with the lights out, I won't have to see that nose chock-full of snot. I think to myself, almost laughing out loud, "Thank God for my sense of humor; saves me every time!"

I crawl into bed next to him, and despite snoring already, the slightest hint of the existence of a woman at close proximity instantaneously rousts his manhood into action. I thought older men became, shall we say, less firm in the bedroom with age. Not this one. It's like steel every time. Mixed blessing *ce soir*, as I'm so not game, especially for any antics, role playing, etc.

"Alexandra, thank you very much for dinner; it was really lovely of you. No one ever cooks for me. I'm quite touched," he whispers, reaching around me and caressing my breasts.

"You're welcome. I love to cook," I say, all matter-of-factly, facing the wall.

"And as for that dinner *demain soir*, I am so sorry. Let me make it up to you."

"Don't worry about it." I interrupt, wishing we could just sleep.

"No. Listen. You know I find your flat *charmant*. Truly. I think one of the reasons I so much like to stay over is that it has always reminded me of my own little studio as a student, and I have so enjoyed the experience of what felt like I was stepping back into that carefree time of my life. But I would like to offer you a situation more becoming of a woman such as yourself. Allow me to find you a proper"—oh, here he goes again with the "proper" this or that—"apartment."

Huh? Okay, I'm awake now! Does he mean, like, buy me one, or set me up with a good realtor? Of course he means *buy*. I should know that by now.

"As you please. If it makes you happy and you will prefer the idea, I would be thrilled. We'll see if you remember all this in the morning, *chéri*," I say, nudging him in the ribs with my elbow, and suddenly I'm (oh, *quelle surprise*) a lot more of a happy camper.

I let him enjoy a few spare crumbs of affection. Read: taking me from behind. Have to admit that position has become a new favorite of mine. It's harder to come like that, but really, it seriously sends shock waves through your body that reverberate like a long, hard strum of harp strings. Damn, even my metaphors are getting pretentious, but a new apartment? That's big time, as we'd say in the States.

Lying there in blissful silence, La Perla gown still crammed up around my waist, strands of new diamonds sparkling in the light of the fading candles, my zillionaire lover's hand on my breast, I almost burst into hysterical giggles thinking, "You know what *this* is, Alexandra? This is all definitely the dead opposite of your old vanilla-girl behavior. Good. I've finally put that whole uptight young girl to bed. Or Jean-Albert has!"

I fell asleep laughing.

NOTABLE OBSERVATION UNIQUE TO LIFE AS A COURTESAN

One quickly discovers that what older, rich men find sexy is very different than what rocks a young Frenchman's world. *Par exemple* (and there are many!): Older men have spent their youths creating sexual fantasies of women from images like Courbet's paintings, Rodin's watercolor nudes, their aunt's Chanel open-toe heels—not inundated with images of women *à la* Pamela Anderson, chicks shakin' it in videos clad in tummy-exposing spandex . . . nor are they even remotely acquainted with a Brazilian bikini wax. Thus they are hugely turned on by the delicacy of a woman's wrist, a bare foot, a well-fitting crepe dress. And they are, across the board, fiends for a woman not to wax or trim her pubic hair. It's "full bush" or bust for men of a certain age!

CHAPITRE HUIT

Paris is a courtesan.

—BALZAC

In the morning Jean-Albert did his usual internal-alarm-clock thing—waking up at 5:00 A.M. and dressing quietly. Not that he has to dash home and slink into the matrimonial bed. Apparently he and Madame are already at the "separate bedrooms in different wings" stage.

I opened one eye just long enough to see that it was still dark out, and knowing full well that after a night's sleep, my hair always looks *très* Loretta Lynn. I chose to spare Jean-Albert that frightening vision, and I fell back into the arms of Morpheus. (Not another man, silly rabbit; it's a metaphor, mythology? Right.)

Kneeling on the bed with his coat on, Jean-Albert leans over, and speaking softly with a soothing tenderness, says, "*Bonne journée, mon amour* . . . and don't think I forgot that *today,* we find you a new apartment." The gentle vibrations of his whisper travel through my body, and I feel that intoxicating wave of morning desire.

"Oh, baby, you mustn't trouble yourself with that; but you can give me something I *do* want," I beg, pulling him down on top of me, and delving into his open coat in search of that sexual-trigger switch: *his right nipple.* Secret—this is all done on "automatic" with my eyes closed again; dare I say, the morning coupled with sobriety demand it.

"God, how I wish I could stay," he moans, as he halfheartedly slips out of my arms. "And as for the apartment . . . your happiness is my happiness. *À bientôt, chérie.*" He blows me a kiss, bows slightly, and silently closes the door behind him. God. Everything he does is so elegant, it's just staggering.

I sit up like a lightning bolt. Damn. It's only 5:00 A.M.! I am dying to call Marie-Hélène; she'll positively faint and fall over. Can't call Isabel; she'd ream me out and shatter the fun. I lie back against the pillow and wallow in my amazement. I actually hear myself say out loud, "An apartment? Yipers, how cool!"

Okay, I pretty much spent the entire day wallowing in amazement. And made that call to MH at a respectable 11:00 A.M.

"Marie-Hélène, you were so right on the dinner idea being *trop domestique.* I felt the first pangs of insecurity and self-doubt . . . Realized that's not really why he pursues my company. I think on some level, he likes that I *can* cook for him, but it's simply superfluous— it's just not the draw it is with normal men."

"Precisely. I made that mistake early on a few times, myself. It's a bonus, but not the prize they seek."

"Wanna hear about the prize?" I say, almost bursting with my news.

"Do tell!" she commands enthusiastically.

"Well, for starters, a rope of nice diamonds . . . *from Graff!*"

"My, my. Perhaps you should be the one sharing *your* tips in the bedroom. And?"

"Then he launched into telling me that he should really escort his wife, not me, to the dinner at Vaux le Vicomte," I say, twirling the new necklace through my fingers.

"Hmm, yes, 'the wife,' that happens. It's a good wake-up call to keep emotional distance. I hope you handled it with grace."

"Not sure about that. I always opt for humor when put off-balance. Have to remember that. Grace. Yes. Grace personified. Never the wrong approach. But listen, then the guilt or something made him burst out with an offer to buy me an apartment. I mean, he said, 'find' me one, so I think that means 'buy,' correct?" I ask with the same interest that I once used to question the professor at the Sorbonne about brushstrokes. (Hey, where did that thesis go, Alexandra? Oh, who cares. I'm on the cusp of acquiring real estate. Far more fun than huddling all day in dark rooms in the Bibliothèque Nationale doing research!)

"Darling! Bravo. You have shot to the top of the game. While Jean-Albert is renowned for his legendary generousness, I don't believe he has ever purchased an apartment for any woman . . . The protégé is quickly assuming the title as *la grande courtisane de Paris* . . . I would be elated to pass the crown to you."

"Ha-ha! I don't know about any of that, but it's all incredibly exciting . . . That is, until I start to imagine tonight at the big dinner; he wants me to come despite the fact that he'll be with his wife. That sounds like a nightmare," I say, staring blankly out the window.

"*Au contraire! Écoute*, this will be brilliant. I will introduce you to a host of marvelous, important men of whom you will surely have your pick. You will look smashing, he will be aching to be with you, and you will taunt him into insanity by being fawned over by all the men of his ilk." Marie-Hélène states this as though she can see it as a premonition.

"You're so optimistic! It will probably be more like me seeing him with the respected wife and feeling like a stupid young *boy* from Elmbrook impersonating a woman, dressed in a gown . . . who has sex for jewelry," I reply, joking—make that, *half joking*.

"*Ridicule*! You shall come with Monsieur de Bellemont and me, and I trust I shall make all the necessary arrangements. Oh, I do find this positively enthralling. Do come with me to my coiffurist, Alexandre, at four today. I will send Hugo round to get you at three-thirty. Bring all your gowns, jewelry, and *accessoires* and we will prepare for the evening *ensemble*. We will create you into a complete masterpiece and the evening will be *un beau rêve* (a beautiful dream)."

"I have to say your enthusiasm is contagious. But will you hold my hand if I start to feel I'm in over my head?"

"Darling, I will hold more than your hand. As you well know, I'll take any and every part of you, my rosebud!" she says, all wickedly sexy.

At 3:30 I stash my makeup, *parfum*, three pairs of Fogal stockings in different shades, four possible pairs of heels, the three diamond pieces of jewelry from Jean-Albert, three evening bags (real ones now; the makeup bag no longer makes public appearances, thank God) in my old Samsonite baggage. (Note: Get chic luggage ASAP; this is a crime against aesthetics!)

I drape four evening gowns in their garment bags, throw two fur wraps over my shoulder, and drag it all down the five flights of stairs. Could've let Hugo help me, but no way I'm letting him see the squalor I live in. Weird. I used to cherish this flat, but now it reminds me of Laurent. (And that was another life ago. No, four months ago actually. Strange. It feels like a lifetime ago.)

Hugo speeds me over to the Alexandre salon in the 16th arrondissement. He waits in the car with my evening's wardrobe as I hustle in to meet Marie-Hélène. One of the staff leads me into a charming private room with walls the color of aubergine and a Murano chandelier in silver blown glass (how chic; I must remember that). There I find Marie-Hélène well ensconced and already well under way in getting her shimmering red locks secured in a French twist (*mais oui*) with a few soft tendrils gently caressing her neck and cheeks.

Leaning in to give MH a double-cheek air kiss, I accidentally trip on a blow-dryer cord and take such a digger (Elmbrook word there for stumbling fall) as to damn near careen through the gilded mirror and take down the chandelier, as I go horizontally airborne. *Almost.* But as I've spent the better part of my life being disastrously clumsy, I have acquired miraculous midair talents for reducing the damage by half, so I more or less merely skin my palms on the counter and lose my self-respect for a few fleeting seconds. The two salon assistants gasp while Marie-Hélène raises a graceful hand to her open mouth, "My sweet Alexa. Are you alright, dear girl? You had better get that out of your system, because tonight, I can assure you, one simple trip down the red carpet would annihilate your reputation in the blink of an eye," she says with a smile, though she is clearly serious.

"I think we are safe. But you're serious? Not a very forgiving crowd *ce soir*, I'm guessing. Would it be on par with the time Naomi Campbell fell in her platforms at the Vivienne Westwood fashion show? God, wasn't that replayed ad nauseam?" I ask, thinking, "Wow, the lighting in here is incredibly forgiving. MH looks about ten years younger, and, well, I look . . . about the same, which puts me at fifteen, which is just ridiculous."

"Naomi who? Now off you go! No time to lose. You do grasp the extreme importance of this evening, *oui*? We have a lot of people to astonish, and every element of your *toilette* must be impeccably attended to!" Marie-Hélène watches herself in the mirror as she speaks and clearly enjoys the dichotomy of giving me marching orders when she looks so drop-dead feminine and enchanting.

By the way, I am thinking she *so* knows who Naomi Campbell is, and it's just silly that she wouldn't dream of admitting it. And P.S., I will never get used to the French reference of dressing and doing one's hair and makeup as *toilette*. No matter how long I live that will bring a white porcelain toilet to mind, just the way whenever anyone ask's me, "Would you like to *prend une douche*?" I will forever conjure up the semiwacky American "douche" visual well before the French "take a shower" pops up. MH surely is loading this night up with a lot of pressure, right? I'm not sure she gets that it hasn't been my lifelong dream to charm the Parisian bon ton. Frankly, until a couple of months ago, the idea that I'd even be going to a fête like this seemed as likely as . . . Patrick Swayze making a big comeback. *Not!*

Next, as per Marie-Hélène's command, I'm entrusted to a team of three people—all of whom get their flurrying hands on me pronto. As soon as my *derrière* hits the chocolate-brown leather salon chair, I'm offered Champagne—I immediately pass. I know me, I will get drunk too soon if I start now. Oh, you know what? Screw it! Okay, sure, one *flûte*, and yes, I am aware I am sliding into the lush category about two decades earlier than most. I *do* employ some discipline and refrain from the petit fours. Arriving *ce soir* with a tummy pooched out would result in a ton of "baby in the oven" gossip. And can someone tell me why as I get older, if I so much as eat a turnip, my belly pops out like Buddha himself?

So there I am in a slight recline as a young Russian blonde (faux color, but well done for a change) on a small stool unburdens me of my crocodile JP Tod's (gift from Jean-Albert, who I think may have some driving shoe fetish. Seriously, he brought these to me during our first-week *ensemble*, insisting I wear them whenever heels aren't apropos. I think I'm finally getting accustomed to wearing shoes that cost as much as my tuition, but during the first few wearings I was doing some pretty careful stepping, attempting to keep them pristine. Now the goal would be to wear them in the rain without cringing).

Anyway, the Russian starts applying a *miel-paraffin* foot masque that feels like warm caramel being drizzled over my toes—which you have to admit is a rather nice concept. Followed by a *concombre et noisette* scrub; then she places each of my feet in a heated velvet slipper. All the while my hair is being softly misted with a sheen of *huile d'amande* for shine before it's set in huge steel rollers that resemble martini shakers. Meanwhile, my eyes dart from the woman buffing my feet to the man brushing out my hair as an older woman who has the tiniest hands I've ever seen rubs a delicious-smelling orange-scented cream onto my now uniformly shaped fingernails, so free of the usual red, nibbled hangnails and cuticles I swear I barely recognize them. Madame of the tiny hands proceeds to apply the French white-tipped manicure with a surgical precision. Hey sister, if you ever tire of doing manicures, you could always get a job cutting diamonds—or even possibly doing circumcisions. Right. The latter's probably a helluva lot more nerve-racking and helluva lot less glam. Smaller tips too, I'm guessing. Pun not intended!

Après two very pampered hours of power brushing, extreme polishing, and championship spritzing from head to toe—feeling very much like I had just been in a repeat of that scene in Oz where the Tin Man, the Lion, and Dorothy all get gussied up before they go off to see the Wizard—I was released from the clutches of my *prémaquillage* team to be handed over to the makeup artist, Clotilde, who was previously assigned by MH to exercise a careful hand while she applied a "mere scrim of a warm bisque base with dusting of tonalities of *cannelle* (cinnamon)." All matte, *bien sûr*, "*sauf les lèvres un peu plus brilliantes*." That was achieved as Clotilde unpleasantly cloaked me in her cabbage breath (the only downside to the entire experience).

Enfin, moi et mon visage sommes finis and submitted to the ruthlessly discerning eye of Marie-Hélène, awaiting me in the lounge to give me the thrice-over inspection. I was seemingly stamped with an ACCEPTABLE label as MH entered my *salon privé* and beheld the handiwork of *l'équipe du salon* (team).

"Exquisite . . . you are sheer perfection. Alexandra, you shall be the belle of the ball!"

All lovely of her, but this phrase struck me as very Disney animation Princess–ey, and somehow that killed the charm. Sometimes my name sounds a smidge too kids' storybook, you have to say.

Seven hundred euros later—which used to be my monthly rent, frighteningly enough—I had one *très élégante* hairstyle, ten pale-nude fingernails (with just the slightest hint of the French manicure—that's really the idea; so they look just pristine rather than blatantly white at the tips), and one seriously amazing makeup application. I should note that Alexandre himself decided on a sleek side part for me, with a low chignon interwoven with my long rope of diamonds. Which probably added an extra two hundred euros to the bill! The makeup artist, Clotilde, contoured, dusted, and all but airbrushed my face into something familiar to me, but truthfully I was just a canvas for her genius. It then occurred to me—you know when you see movie actresses at the Oscars and they look amazing, and then you see paparazzi shots of them *au naturel* and they look like hell? Well, it's due to the talents of these skilled individuals who create that illusion. Hmm. Good to know. Expensive, but good.

Marie-Hélène and I dash back to her apartment to choose the perfect dress for the evening. Hugo drove, of course, it's not like we ran to the *métro* . . . Actually, I used to love the *métro*. Loved people watching and eavesdropping. Suddenly I am not such a fan of going underground. Unless it's a wine cave. Oh dear, how snobbish of me! MH is rubbing off on me. And not all in good ways.

Chez elle, each of us with a Champagne flute in hand, and wearing nothin' but stockings and a string, we lay out my evening's options in her boudoir. As an aside, I would be pleased if you noticed I have made great strides in becoming entirely more comfortable scantily clad, and I attribute this newfound confidence to Marie-Hélène's compliments and assuredness. As I shed each of these ex-vanilla qualities I'm just so happily surprised. I thought I had given myself over to the idea that I'd be a lifelong rigid woman who flinched even at communal dressing rooms. Okay, truth be told, it's being nakedish in the *light* that made me squirm. If the lights are out I can be a wildcat on all fours, writhing in free-spirited bliss, but you see, while I was given a metabolism that keeps me trim, I have also been given an unfair propensity for cellulite, so beaches and hot pants have always been nonoptions. Until now. I am getting over it . . . slowly (I still keep my back mostly to the wall). I digress. Back to the boudoir scene already underway . . .

With the potent scent of lilies wafting around us, and me with my tummy of butterflies, decisions had to be made and *tout de suite*. We were expecting the arrival of Monsieur de Bellemont in an hour, and then were to make the forty-minute drive out of Paris to the château.

"I love this caramel silk chiffon one," I say, holding up a one-shouldered sheath with pearl and gold Lesage beading on the shoulder and running down to the hem.

"*Non, je pense c'est trop!* I propose you wear the gown with the *least* trim or embellishment. Remember, women who have nothing to say wear dresses that shout. Women such as ourselves must adorn ourselves with quiet elegance. In short: simple lines for complicated women."

"*D'accord*, and *j'adore* the concept. Okay, embracing that notion, Marie-Hélène, that leaves me with the cream halter neck with the open back that cascades dangerously low, by Alber Elbaz . . . I think the back's so low, I won't be able to wear stockings . . . Can I pull that off?" I ask, sipping the last drops of my Champagne.

"Oh, more than that . . . it's fabulous. The silhouette will just cling over every naked curve, and you will exude a youthful raw sensuality. A total contrast to what will be a plethora of very fussy, overly nipped and tucked women falling into their traditional trap of bows and ruffles."

"Or I could just look foolish! *Mais d'accord*, I'm going to trust you on this . . . as in every matter, come to think of it!" I say, already stepping into the dress and shimmying out of my stockings. We partake of another quick *flûte de Champagne* as she adjusts the back of my dress.

"Alexandra, this is divinity. Your dress just dips to the most erotic curve of your back, where the sweetest hint of your derriere commences," she coos, trailing my vertebrae with a gentle caress to its descent. "You look sublime . . . Just the one ring, the small earrings (small? 2-carat is huge to me!) and skin, skin, skin. I am like a proud mother. *Tout est parfait!*" she says, making a little double clap with her slender hands.

Standing before the mirror, I am delighted. It's one drop-dead dress, and thanks to the handiwork of a great many people, I am rather fetching, if I do say so myself. How insane it is that it takes this many advisers and creators, and obscene amounts of money to get to look this good!

"This is, hands down, the most fun I've ever had playing dress-up! But now we have to actually go, right? This will be awe inspiring . . . The whole haute monde of France? I'm scarified," I say, hand to forehead, suffering a bout of extreme trepidation.

"Heavens. Think of it all as a movie and place yourself as the star. Dare I say, that's the mentality I had to assume when I began, and before you know it, you'll become the woman you aspire to be." Marie-Hélène soothes me, handing me my cream satin purse.

I take a deep breath and feel a surge of something, but what? Love? Adoration? Desire for her? A warm, indefinable pleasure sweeps over me, and I am ready in every sense. To her—and to my—surprise, I kiss her cheek and hold her in a close embrace before we descend the stairs.

"My dear rosebud. Now, let's go set Paris on fire!' she says triumphantly, like the crescendo of an aria.

At precisely 7:00 P.M., Monsieur de Bellemont arrives in his carriage to retrieve us. Alright it's not a carriage, but a Mercedes. A hyperlong one at that. As a Midwestern girl, I have zero knowledge of cars, but this one looked like it had been stretched out about an extra two meters—so big one could have given birth back there with a whole birthing team. Theoretically speaking, of course.

On the lengthy drive to Vaux le Vicomte, like a good soul Monsieur de Bellemont stays relatively silent, save for his incessant nose blowing. To be brutally frank, he is a man unburdened by charisma.

Thankfully, as it allows Marie-Hélène and me to sift through a few last-minute pointers and vital details. We hash out who she wants me to meet, what I need to know: their positions, their status in the gilded ladder of aristocracy, their worth, their marital status. Not to mention—and equally as important—whom to avoid.

Apparently, nouveau riche money is to be avoided, as are men under the age of thirty-five. Marie-Hélène claims both are unstable. And a man must be from a good family—which is not as easy to decipher as it might seem. I mean, *I'm* from a good family, for sure: We all remember each other's birthdays, keep in touch, and adore one another. But no, in France, a good family means: of a *nom de famille* respected for centuries, a historically relevant family, and it generally includes the "de" factor or titles à la *chevalier* (knight), *comte* (count), *duchesse, baron,* or *marquise.* You get the idea. Tough criteria, huh? Being such a lover of French history, I am, admittedly, entertained by it all. Better said, put a title or a number (*par exemple,* Louis-Philippe III) by somebody's name, and I'm there!

As we drew closer to the château, the sun was setting in a brilliant twilight of pale gold and indigo blue. It couldn't have been a more beautiful evening to have a lavish party in a French château. I craned my head, searching for a glimpse through the trees of this French architectural monument.

To be properly prepared for the soirée, you can be damn sure I did a lot of research, fully aware that for everyone else invited, this was just another in a string of glittering dinners. Which is all very well if you happen to be a birthright member of the Parisian demimonde, but I just checked, and I am not. Not even close. You neither? Great, then let me bring you up to speed. (A mini private history tutorial to follow; invoice me later.)

Vaux le Vicomte is one of, if not the most beautiful, châteaux in all of France. Built in 1661 by the *Surintendant* of Finances to Louis XIV, Nicolas Fouquet, the magnificent opulence of the château, its expansive gardens and fountains, had never before been seen on French soil. It is an exceptional building, both because of the genius talent of its designers—the master architect Le Vau, the painter Le Brun, and the gardener Le Nôtre—and the scandal that broke after Fouquet threw an enormous fête to celebrate its completion in honor of the king.

At the opening night soirée, the staggering brilliance of the evening sent all six thousand invited courtiers into raptures. An elaborate supper was served on 432 solid gold plates and 6,000 silver ones, while 1,200 fountains framed the entertainment. Instantly, all the splendor and magnificence sent the king into a jealous fury that his *Surintendant* should possess a château far more regal and majestic than his own. (Rumors circulated that Nicolas Fouquet had pilfered the state's cash reserves to finance the masterpiece of all the most creative minds of France.)

Fascinatingly, King Louis XIV waited until *after* the festivities— the elaborate feast by Vatel, the performance of a play by Molière, followed by a ballet, and finally, fireworks—and then had Fouquet arrested and thrown in jail. (Harsh, huh? But it gets worse.) The king proceeded to confiscate the château, *all* the furniture, tapestries, marble statues, and paintings, and imprisoned Fouquet for life—until his death twenty years later. It was said, "When the lavish banquet commenced at 6:00 P.M., Fouquet was king of France; by 2:00 in the morning, he was nothing at all!"

Rule to be learned here: Do *not* try to outshine a king who anoints himself the Sun King! The king, in turn, sequestered the very same architects, painters, and designers who had made Vaux le Vicomte and had them design and construct the château of Versailles in his honor.

As the Mercedes fell into a stream of arriving limousines, we made the final approach to the château, stunningly majestic in the evening twilight. My heart leapt. Never had I ever seen anything so beautiful, so lavish!

Spectacularly bathed in a pearly mist, trails of thousands of candles lining the gardens and staircase, it shimmered in the night air. My hands were almost shaking as I squeezed Marie-Hélène's.

Monsieur de Bellemont graciously escorted the two of us, one on either side, up the long, red-carpeted stone staircase. About thirty elaborately uniformed French soldiers stood, one gallantly arm-raised, sword in hand, as a regal welcome to all. Their faces firmly maintained a stony expression of seriousness: at once both intimidating and dazzling. I smile at one of them, a young beauty with a chiseled face, as he lets his eye wander and take the slightest notice of us. Ha! They're not *all* immune to women's charms. But of course not, they have French blood in their veins!

"Oh, screw the wealthy bourgeois, gimme him!" I whisper to Marie-Hélène.

"*Ça suffit*, time to assume your grace, Alexa," I feel moderately scolded. *Pardonnez-moi*, but this is just so unreal, I'd frankly kill to whip out a camera and take about four hundred shots of this evening. But I can't be a tourist. I must play this out with blasé self-assurance—role playing indeed. . . .

Dazzled, we move through the vast entrance flanked by colossal Doric columns and Corinthian pilasters, and through the elaborate doors adorned with medallions of Roman emperors. We pass into a long *couloir* of sumptuous delights: marble sculptures line every niche; gold leaf tracery borders the ornate cornice; a profusion of graceful caryatids and rich allegorical frescoes draw us into the stunning central rotunda. It's all of such a staggering scale, and beautiful beyond comprehension. ("Mercy," as my mother would say.)

Crossing from one side of the château to the other, we come into an enormous oval room, two splendorous stories in height. The massive dome looms overhead, painted in a *trompe l'oeil* and giving one the magnificent illusion of looking up into the azure sky. Zounds! Marble busts of ancient Romans flank the walls as gigantic candelabras flicker a golden light across the room and out through the gallery's open doors. Beyond, the view unfolds across a seemingly never-ending succession of opulent gardens and elaborate fountains, stretching as far as the eye can see.

The room is alive with festivities, as about a hundred guests have arrived and glide about mingling, Champagne in hand, filtering who's who, eyeing and assessing one another. The rustle of dresses and the sounds of voices dance about the room to a sonata by Mozart.

Women are fewer in number and solidly belong to the "of a certain age" category. All of them drip their finest jewels, setting off myriad scintillations throughout the room. It's like a high-society laser-light show. And don't forget the ubiquitous haute couture, paired, as ever, with immovable tornado-proof hairstyles. The array of gowns is enchanting: every color of the rainbow in satin, silk, and organza; yards of embroidered lace; legions of ruffles and bows; a plethora of bugle-beaded *décolletés;* ostrich-plumed straps; and gold bouillon–trimmed bodices. Just how many poor souls worked their fingers to the bone for this *grande soirée*?!

Several gentlemen sport their glittering medals of the Légion d'honneur, others are draped in the red satin sashes with swords at the hip that designate membership in the exclusive Académie Française. Impressive crowd, as there are only forty members at any given time and about two dozen of them must be here in one corner alone.

Monsieur de Bellemont plucks two flutes of Champagne off one of the many silver trays passing through the room and hands one to Marie-Hélène and me. And thank God: Never before has a drink been so necessary!

"This is simply extraordinary! I'm overwhelmed!" I whisper to Marie-Hélène.

"Yes, it is lovely, isn't it? I see some people I should like to introduce you to," she says, her eyes scaning the room. "Indulge me this, if for no other reason than because men like to compete, to feel they are the fortunate object of desirability. We need to push Jean-Albert off his high horse of self-certainty. Tonight we must create the illusion or reality, preferably that you are pursued by many. Are you ready?" she asks with sincerity. That would be, um, a no. . . .

"Not quite. May I step outside and see the gardens for a moment, *ça va?*" I need a moment alone to gather my wits.

"*Mais oui*, you must take a promenade through the *jardins* at some point this evening, but *dépêche-toi!*" she says, meaning "hurry back," surveying the guests with a studied air.

I glance back as I depart, seeing her resume conversation with Monsieur de Bellemont, gesturing with such languorous, sensual movements it's all I can manage to not plop down right there on the floor and study her.

Inspired, I employ my best effort at grace personified as I make my way toward the open arched doors leading onto the vast terrace and gardens. Passing through the crowd, I feel the distinct sensation of conversations falling into whispers and heads turning my way. Am I being paranoid, or is everyone checking out the young American mistress? Or is it the dress? My ears prick up and pick up: "That's Jean-Albert's new . . ." *"Oui, elle est américaine . . ."* How bizarre. Word travels fast in this so-called polite society. *Hmm.* Am I to feel embarrassed or somehow honored? Still haven't discerned what it all means, but I have a hunch I will know better by the night's end.

Ignoring the gossip, I venture outside, dawdle on the opulent terrace, and peer into the lush gardens beyond. It's a gorgeous, luminescent sight: the night sky asparkle with flickering stars and the garden alit by a flotilla of small candles. My thoughts race as quickly as the clouds chase the moon. What a vision.

"Count your lucky stars, Alexandra. Well, not literally: there are millions tonight. Yes, this beats the hell out of going to Euro Disney in a beat-up Citroën! This is *insanely* beautiful. A few months ago I would've bet this evening was as likely as a one-legged man tap dancing. No girl from Elmbrook ever got to see this world from the inside. Well, I'm not really *in* this world . . . wait, yes I am. Kinda. My lover is the wealthiest man in France. How weird does that feel to say? I never even cared about money before, and now . . . all this? Too wild! And Marie-Hélène is a godsend. Without her, I surely would've balked at even continuing with Jean-Albert . . . it's all just so . . ."

My mental pep talk is suddenly interrupted by a soft, female hand on my bare shoulder. I imagine Marie-Hélène has come to retrieve me. I turn around to say, "It's fine now . . . I am . . ."

And before me I see the silhouette of a beautiful red-headed woman, her features semiobscured since the warm glow from the château only serves as a backlight: coiffed to perfection; wearing an elegant strapless black dress; glimmering in a choker of large diamonds; and poised with all the feminine fragility of a delicate bird.

"You are fucking my husband, *non*? You may share his bed . . . *on occasion*, but I hope you are well aware he will never leave me," said the face that looked like it cared for nothing but Champagne and jewels.

Jean-Albert's wife. A nightmare.

A COURTESAN'S LIST
OF DON'TS

1. Don't get "come" in your eye. For some bizarr-o reason the sensation is akin to pouring hot lava mixed with gravel directly into your cornea. And dear God, if you happen to wear contact lenses you may as well rip your eyeball clean out of the socket; it's very likely less painful.

2. Don't try to light a cigarette while wearing an elegant hat with a veil. Yep, I have to admit I do still occasionally blow my cover with this whole graceful-as-a-swan façade, like when I accidentally set the veil

of my Philippe Model hat on fire lighting a Dunhill Superlight at
the Prix de Diane horse races. Had to rip it off and stomp on it.
Sure, men just love that. It's a huge turn-on!

3. Don't allow any lover to brand you in any physically identifiable way.
    I know this sounds very cattle prod—oriented, but what I'm getting
    at it is: no love bites left behind; no inner thigh bruises; and no rug
    burns on knees or tailbones. Sometimes, in the heat of the moment,
    it is surprisingly difficult to get away unscarred from the frantic
    fucking.

4. Don't ever say "I love you," "I need you," or "call me." Instead,
    always act like you're half on the verge of leaving him. Men need
    to fight an ongoing battle to win you.

5. Don't yell out the wrong name during sex. Partake in a bevy of
    universal terms of endearment that can never fail to sound
    convincing and appropriate. *Par exemple:* baby, darling, sweetheart,
    mon ange. All work in a pinch—*or with a pinch.*

6. Don't get dressed in the dark, in a rush, or thoughtlessly. Like the
    time when I was running late to meet Jean-Albert, and jumped in
    a taxi, and in my mad rush, put my seamed Fogal stockings on
    backward. Marching around with the blatant seam running down the
    front felt the dead opposite of sexy. Though I may have unwittingly
    started a trend: Believe it or not, Jean-Paul Gaultier saw my legs and
    exclaimed, "Genius!" I think he was just being kind.

7. Never ask for a gift—and never refuse one. Like a complete ass, in
    the first weeks of seeing Jean-Albert, he offered me a gloriously
    beautiful Mont Blanc Meisterstruck Fountain pen, and I said,
    "Thanks no, I'm really attached to this Bic rollerball . . . had it for
    months. It's like my lucky pen." Duh . . .

CHAPITRE NEUF

Each player must accept the cards life deals him or her:
but once they are in hand, he or she alone must decide
how to play the cards in order to win the game.

—VOLTAIRE

*W*here were we? Oh, right. Jean-Albert's wife scaring the bejesus out of me. This is kind of where it started to feel less of an amusing game of sexual adventure and amusing perks, and more like, "Hello Alexandra, people's hearts and lives are in play here. Be very careful, young lady." Noted.

I took a deep breath as much to stall for time as to not faint and fall down. I recovered something of my composure and finally responded: "Yes, you are correct. I am Alexandra. And I am very sorry to meet you under these circumstances. I assure you I have no intention of pursuing your husband to the extent of which you speak. If you so choose—at your behest—I will take my leave from him. I am a woman of my word." And I passed my hand over my heart. (The hand flashing the diamond ring from her husband; mixed message and subtext delivered.)

Sort of graceful, right? Hey, could *you* have come up with something better given the sneak attack? Mentally, it was all hands on deck for a retort, and after three glasses of Champagne, I could only summon about half the mental troops into action. But you know what? I sincerely meant it. I'd have left him had she demanded it. *I think . . . possibly.*

She finally replied, in carefully chosen words, "No, my dear girl, I am simply letting you know I am *aware* of your existence; you are not the first and will not be the last. Just know your position and respect the code of honor." And with that she was gone.

"My dear girl"? Effectively condescending on her part. She's no amateur to this scenario, clearly. And "code of honor"? Sorry, I didn't get the manual. Did they hand it out in university? Because I have been a little too busy with your husband's head between my legs to make it to class lately. (Yeah, I agree, that's what *not* to have said! Would have made for an interesting catfight, though. And possibly to the cover of *Le Monde*.)

Well, we are off to an interesting evening. Let's hope it goes up from here. *Sheesh.* I take my shaky legs back inside and make a bee-line for Marie-Hélène, who's chatting up her geezer du jour and a younger, handsome couple.

Slipping my arm through hers, I shoot her my shocked expression. She tilts her ear toward me, while still elegantly continuing to follow the conversation.

I whisper, "Jean-Albert's wife just confronted me. Terrors! Still, she literally said, 'Continue but with decency.' *Très bizarre, non?*"

"Dare I say, you have passed yet another of the tests in the life of a courtesan. The wives often say as much. They generally are relieved to have someone take on the sexual appetites of their husbands. Let it go. There is much yet to be done tonight." She says this as though the experience were as common as a hangnail. Unflappable, this woman!

The fête is now in full swing, and the entire château is bustling with life. All the guests have arrived, imbibed sufficient *coupes* of social lubricant, and are reveling in the glorious setting. Standing with this group all a-chatter, I feel a gentleman's hand pass swiftly over my lower back, a warm finger brushing against my exposed flesh. My head ricochets around in anger. Who the hell thinks they can touch me?

"You look good enough to eat! Meet me on the terrace." Jean-Albert's voice hangs in the air as he maintains his dignified stride, heading toward a group of men near the open doors.

Ahh. I feel at once calmed, and instantly thrilled. Aware that all my desires awaken in his presence. Maybe leaving him *is* beyond my ability. Oh God, am I addicted to this man? Captive to this lifestyle? *In love?* I darn near shake my head in front of everyone, trying to shake it off. I'm in deep. *Mon dieu.*

And another visit to the terrace? Ugh, that was just loads of fun the first time! And where is that wife of his? Gotta keep her in my sights.

She's ensconced in conversation with five other women of similar age, beauty, and rank, clearly speaking about their jewelry as they rant and rave. (By the way, when women like this rant and rave, the extent of their gestures are hands held daintily over mouths in midwhisper. This is one very self-aware, contained crowd.)

The music floats up on the air and dances out into the moonlight as I make my second trip to the terrace. I am delighted to find the Champagne is starting to work its magic, and my inhibitions are disappearing as fast as the bottles are being emptied. In short: Gossip all you want, gang!

Jean-Albert spots my exit and follows closely behind. I don't turn or acknowledge him until we meet under the cover of darkness on a far corner of the long terrace.

"*Bonsoir, chérie.* Please take this and put it somewhere safe." He hands me a document, folded twice. (Guess it's not drink tickets. Another annual report? Spare me one night of reading!)

When I look at him, kisses seemed to spring from his eyes. I am sent instantly into a broad, happy smile. Some men's eyes are so magical they have that effect, don't they? It's fucking great to have their gaze on you. It instantly transforms your mood. And if you've been angry, you become something like docile, accommodating. In other words, you think: "Fuck me, boy . . . and make it sooner rather than later."

"What is this, *mon ange*? By the way, there's been an auspicious development: I just met your wife. She's fairly angry and possessive. So I am guessing it's not divorce papers," I say, joking slightly, and suddenly longing to have his hand in mine and feel that safe beautiful feeling that the world is fine. Just fine.

"*Non, mon amour.* It's the deed to your new *appartement. A cinq pièces* on rue Faubourg St. Honoré, just around the corner from my *hôtel particulier.* The meeting today with that *connard* Frédéric de Fallois went surprisingly well—I think he's actually here tonight, in fact—I just made a large contribution to his next campaign, and now Samaritane is safe. So I wanted to share the good fortune. Dear girl (what? is the whole family going to call me that?!), the *appartement* is nothing ostentatious or vulgar; just a beautiful little place for you to unleash your fantasies."

"Or *your* fantasies! Baby, that is just so incredibly generous of you. Are you sure you want to do this?" I ask, placing the papers against his chest, for no other reason than to feel the warmth of his body on my hands.

"Absolutely. I love you, of this I am certain, I have no doubts at all," he replies with intensity.

"Oh, Jean-Albert. Remember the line by Voltaire: 'Doubt is not a pleasant condition, but *certainty* is absurd.'" Sure, it's a little pretentious, but I love that all the voracious reading allows me delicious retorts like this . . . It's time well spent, as I well know Jean-Albert eats that shit up with a silver spoon.

"Darling, if Voltaire were here this evening . . . looking at you . . . so *ravissante,* I'm certain he'd retract that line"—okay, that is a good comeback; now I'm eating *his* shit up—"and I want you closer to me . . . and I can promise you nothing more than my eternal devotion," he continues, as I simply swoon.

I'm rather misty-eyed. Stop, Alexandra. Public venue. Wife within hundred meters. Photographers aplenty. Emotional outburst aborted. For the time being.

It's a very sweet, romantic moment—until Jean-Albert immediately mangles it with the following line (yeah, those same men often have a knack for this too): "Do something for me to get me through this night. Take off your panties and give them to me. I need a part of you with me." He asks like it's as normal as asking for a *stylo*.

"Oh, you are incorrigible. You have got to be kidding," I say, realizing that of course he is not. But, called to duty, I instantly reassume the role of playful Alexandra that he's after.

"One apartment for one tiny pair of underwear . . . Okay. I'd say that's a very fair deal. Obviously, I can't give them to you here . . . now."

"*Certainement* you can." He looks like he's about to beg.

"No, but I promise, at some point this evening I shall put them in your possession. You do realize you're stark raving mad, right?" I say, making a gesture as though I were about to pinch his nipple. *In the stark raving mad department, I am quickly following in right behind.*

"*Ooh la-la.* I do love the anticipation," and with a quick double kiss to my cheeks and a hastily whispered, "*Je t'aime,*" he's up the stairs and rejoining the crowd.

And . . . I'll be damned, back at the side of his wife. *Merde alors!* New apartment and great dress aside, this is a huge mind fuck. Is he terribly twisted or what?

Somewhere within the château a bell is rung, and all the guests begin to make their way from the Oval Salon toward the Salon of Muses. My well-studied mental floor plan of the château has long since evaporated, but my eyes scan for Marie-Hélène while I join the exodus to the next astonishing venue. By luck, MH soon hastens up behind me. "Where have you been? I had a marquis who was primed for your return!"

"Oh, the usual dinner party moments. After the wife confrontation I received a deed to an *appartement*, then promised to hand over my underwear to a billionaire. *C'est normal,*" I joke.

"Yes, well then, let's get this evening underway . . . I have arranged for a rather surprising twist to tonight's festivities. For a mere two hundred euros your place card has been, shall we say, resituated to your advantage."

Unquestionably, this woman is unflappable . . . and industrious . . . and fun. I suddenly have the distinct feeling one has when one is strapped into a roller coaster and headed for a 360-degree turn: There's no exit and nothing you can do but grin and bear it. (But for the love of God, Alexandra, don't be the fool and put your arms over your head and squeal . . . At least not here; that can be saved for some crazy sexual soirée!)

Monsieur de Bellemont cavalierly goes to check the seating plan elegantly displayed in a gold-leaf eighteenth-century frame. Christ, everything in this place is gilded from top to bottom. Just curious, is the *papier de toilette* gold leaf?

Thankfully—*parce que* I'm getting a little too overwhelmed to play explorer—Monsieur de Bellemont leads Marie-Hélène and me around the dining room's huge U-shaped table as they escort me to my designated seat. Draping my fox wrap over the back of the Louis XIV red velvet chair, I wait to sit until more people have taken their seats. It seems chicer, but I could be dead wrong on that. Marie-Hélène hovers a moment and says, "I am intentionally placing you in front of a gentleman whom I think you should take as a lover. Make it happen, my Alexa, and trust me, I know what I am doing. And fix your lipstick." (Bossy, *n'est-ce pas?*)

In a move that quickly evolved from newly acquired to a habit, I mechanically slide my hand into my purse, my finger glazing over the pale mauve Guerlain lipstick. As I trail the color over my lips, I ask, "*D'accord*, but do tell! Who is the man? Don't suppose you brought me the sexy young guard from the front steps?"

She simply smiles and glides off, taking her seat on the other side of the room. Oh this is hell, I'm alone, and well, look over there. Now entering the room is my lover . . . and his wife. Isn't this just intimate fun? Survey says: "No."

Okay, time to feign looking very much at ease and at peace, the dead opposite of what I feel right now. Tough, as the man I *might* love is over there, with the hand that always cups my left breast as we sleep together now around his wife's waist. Just when did I sign up for this surreal life? I pull my eyes away and let them wander up to the magnificent painting overhead.

"*Bonsoir*, mademoiselle . . . I believe you and I are to be dinner partners. I am Frédéric de Fallois. *Enchanté*." The owner of one of *the* sexiest voices I have ever heard announces himself, and my gaze immediately falls from the Le Brun painting on the ceiling to settle on him. Okay, Marie-Hélène *is* one clever, dangerous woman. Frédéric de Fallois is drop-dead gorgeous—that is, if you like 'em graying at the temple, tall, fit, and refined to perfection. And you know what? I'm finding I do!

"*Bonsoir*, Monsieur de Fallois. It is a pleasure to make your acquaintance. I am Alexandra."

He interrupts with, "Ah yes, I know . . . Alexandra . . . I was told you were to come this evening, and may I be so bold as to tell you I had arranged to be placed near your person," he says, exuding sensuality so thick I swear I could reach out and grab it.

"My person"? These people never tire of aristo-speak. Wait. He arranged to sit by me? I thought Marie-Hélène was behind this. I look over his shoulder, a strong, square one at that for a man of fifty-five-ish, and catch MH's eye. She looks at me, mystified and somewhat miffed, shakes her head, and it's clear Frédéric wasn't her intended target for me. Yes, indeedy, the plot's suddenly as thick as a Ladurée *chocolat chaud*. *Very*.

What the hell is going on here? Clueless and giddy, I continue, "*Vraiment?* I would be ever so delighted to be enlightened as to the reason for your ensuring we dine in close propinquity." *Propinquity?!* What the hell am I saying? Dope alert! What a failed attempt at that aristo-speak. Clearly that skill is hard-wired in the DNA. *Or not!*

"We share a common business interest, as it were . . We are both involved financially with Jean-Albert . . . If you don't mind my putting it frankly." His finger traces his beautiful lower lip. "Yes, I prefer people to be frank with me, thank you, but I believe you are mistaken regarding any financial association I might have with monsieur," I reply, trying to appear haughty, while in reality my heart is beating so fast, I can hardly think straight.

"My deepest apologies. Perhaps I am mistaken. Nevertheless, it is a great pleasure to see you again," he offers, placing his napkin in his lap.

R eader: Can we just have a sidebar over here for a minute? This man, is, how shall I put it? "The shit," we'd say in Illinois. Next to Jacques Chirac (who's really on the way out) this silver-haired, ice-blue-eyed wonder is one of the most powerful men—France's Minister of something. Sorry, gotta be vague here, but I can tell you it's not Minister of Agriculture!

Not only does he have all French businesses in a stranglehold of fear and obedience, but he alone has the ability to open the cash reserves of this country. He wields the power to permit or deny all banking and business transactions—from mergers and acquisitions to dissolving industries. Remember, he had Jean-Albert wetting his pants about Samaritane, and now he has me wetting my pants, for oh, so very different a reason.

Let's be frank here. Jean-Albert is charming, generous, and elegant, and he has a great mind, full of playfulness and tenderness—even if it is tainted with a smidge of sexual deviance. But Frédéric? Ah, he could be a garbageman and women would still fall at his feet. A quintessential sexy French man from his full lips to his strong hands. Add to that powerful and clearly intense, and you just want to rip his clothes off, knock everything off the table, and have him take you right there, hard, fast, and loud . . . Got it? *I thought you would*.

"To see me again? I assure you, had we met before, I would remember it. You're not exactly forgettable, *Monsieur*." I am flirting unabashedly. Not very cool of me, as I did just receive a rather large gift. Not to look a gift horse in the *bouche* here, but my reality is all obscured. I implore you to take it on the chin when your lover's twenty feet away with his wife . . . and laughing at something she has just said. No way I'm going to sit here like a wallflower.

"Oh, do call me Frédéric . . . and I am certain you are the same young woman who I used to see pass by my office window at the Bureau Matignon . . . pushing a stroller with a cherubic *jeune fille* in tow," he says, leaning in and running his hand through his thick shiny hair. This move is so sexy I could melt into my shoes.

"My God! Sorry . . . *Mon dieu!* You are right . . . I did pass that building every day on the way to the École Maternelle when I was an au pair . . You can't remember me from that, could you?" I have lost all grace and am just flustered beyond reason . . . or elegance, clearly.

"Indeed, I do. My assistant, Renaud, and I used to have an ongoing daily bet if you would be wearing those interesting jeans with the holes or the short black capris, I believe you call them." Frédéric laughs, his eyes flickering with a flash of desire and amusement. The waiter arrives and sets about pouring the wine, a Château Clinet '78. I'm so dying for a drink, it's all I can do to stop myself from telling the waiter, "I love you."

Frédéric resumes, "Then recently, I saw a photograph of you with Jean-Albert at some fête and I knew it was you—even minus the ripped up jeans and *avec* the new look."

Okay, I'm speechless, and frankly, in awe. A month ago, when the photo of Jean-Albert and me at that Baccarat dinner somehow appeared in *Figaro* magazine, I only thought of how I hoped Laurent would see it, and if it would tear him to pieces. Wait a sec. I am almost positive . . . yep, this man is also . . . "You are married? Are you not, Frédéric?" I ask, thinking, "Oh God, another one."

"True . . . twenty-six years, in fact." He pauses briefly to quaff the wine. "Allow me to be clear. My wife and I have an understanding, not to mention that she loathes these types of affairs."

(Yes, yes, "the understanding." For the love of God, is this built into every French marriage?)

"Affairs? . . . I'm quite sure I understand your meaning . . . in both senses," I answer, suddenly noticing the famous Le Brun masterpiece painting on the ceiling. (At this point, dinner is served, though, for the life of me, I can't recall a single morsel of what we ate.)

I do remember asking, at one point: "Do you, dear Frédéric, enjoy the irony that the painting overhead is entitled *The Triumph of Fidelity*? Isn't it absolutely riotous?"

"*Touché!* Made all the more entertaining to you, perhaps, that I want to see you again. *Privately*," he says, sliding a prewritten card with his cell phone number and *details* under my plate. I leave the card and plow on. "Ah. One better than that. Did you notice the phrase painted on the banner there?" I ask, pointing to the wall where two beautifully painted majestic eagles appear to brandish a banner spread between their beaks.

"*Quo no ascendat?*" He laughs raucously. (God, I love men who laugh freely and loudly. I swallow his laughter like bread and wine.)

Frédéric continues, "*Oui, c'est vrai:* Latin for 'What heights will he not reach?' Bravo! Alexandra, for as much as I do not like him, I believe Jean-Albert has unearthed a jewel in discovering you."

"And is it your intent to play jewel thief?" (Alexandra *avec* attitude is back. Once again, verbal taunting seems to be working with a powerful man.)

"*Bien sûr.* I am a man who knows what he wants, and takes it," he announces, eye fucking me so hard I can feel my chest flush. Cue: full swoon. So many Frenchmen are wishy-washy; this boldness is very rare, *mes amies*.

"Jean-Albert is just such a man as well. And, by the way, he is coming this way," I say, thinking, "Oh, this is getting really fucked-up. What's next? Frédéric's wife of twenty-six years sneaking up at the dessert service?"

Frédéric and I both watch as Jean-Albert slowly makes his way across the room, playing out a few social greetings. I decide, right there and then, that maybe it's time to go full-stop. I mean, never in my life will I be in this kind of a situation again. These men are playing me like a pawn in a chess game. "And," I think, "*I can trump them both*."

I rise off my seat slightly, and with a quick sweep hook my thumb in the waistband of my panties and slowly, as discreetly as I possibly can, shimmy them off and onto my shoe, just as Jean-Albert appears. "Speak of the devil . . . and he appears!" Frédéric says, setting the tone. With a faux gesture of friendship, Jean-Albert puts his arm on Frédéric's shoulder and says with as much cool-headed authority as he can muster, "Yes, and I noticed you two are getting acquainted? Frédéric, you seem to have your eye on all my most valuable acquisitions." They exchanged a glance of respect mingled with a glint of acknowledged rivalry.

"In fact, Alexandra and I are old friends, Jean-Albert. And do not forget, I have the final word on just *who* retains *which* acquisitions in France." ("Old friends"? Geez, what a bunch of hooey!)

"I will have you know . . ." Jean-Albert begins, as his voice strains with a tinge of anger.

I cut them both dead. "*Mes mauvais garçons*, while I would be terribly entertained to see you two take this battle to a field in the countryside and duel until the death, I suggest we all simmer down and enjoy the dinner . . . It is a positively splendid evening!" I say, sweeping my hands widely, as if any of this were my doing.

Oh, by the way, I have no idea how I ever got into a situation with two men of this level. I mean, I know "how" but, it's *so* not about me possessing a beguiling beauty or rare magnetic charm. Yes, women in my position as a courtesan have to possess certain talents and be educated in a vast array of subjects, but this is about power. *Their* power. These men can have anything they want—and they need to one-up one another, to bicker over something. And to-night it's me. Only because I came out of nowhere and somehow crossed their paths and fell into place as a possible conquest. And without question—and take note, ladies—once you have found an *entrée* into this world, or any elite echelon, whether it be of wealthy aristocratic men or rock stars, once you are in—*you're in*.

It's suddenly as though you have a stamp of approval on your forehead. They accept, acknowledge, and pursue you with the as-surance that you're a member of their private club. Quite odd, re-ally. Oh, but do keep in mind that this is only applicable to men. We women are far more cerebral about who is worthy of our attentions, *non*? Anyway, I doubt they'd be amused by the idea that I had such gas last night from the cassoulet that I spent the better part of the night making the bathroom into a gas chamber. That's just between you and me, of course.

Dessert is served, and I do remember *that*—as a woman with a sweet tooth, I can never forget dessert: a *fondant au chocolat avec un coulis de framboise* and sprinkled with—get this—*des feuilles d'or* (edible gold leaf). I laughed so hard, I blew the delicate little flakes clean off the plate! Both Jean-Albert and Frédéric seemed at a loss for what to say next, so I jumped in—many thanks to the wine.

"Jean-Albert, darling, may I borrow your *pochette* (pocket square) for a moment?"

He leans over the table and gallantly hands it to me. I take it ever so gently from his open hand (a small attempt at grace personified), drop my hand beneath the table, and make as though to wipe something from my shoe. Then I slyly exchange the *pochette* for my tiny lace *coulottes*.

"*Merci, mon ange.*" And with that, I reach out to arrange my panties in his breast pocket, leaving just the top of lace peeking out. The frilly beige lace set against his couture tuxedo is so blatantly my underwear, it's ridiculous! Both men look at the new *pochette des panties*—then look back at me and burst into laughter. With Jean-Albert beaming, taking some absurd joy in being the lucky recipient of my dirty laundry. *Silly boys.*

"This is a wild filly you have here, Jean-Albert. Do you think you can bridle her?" Frédéric positively cackles.

"Messieurs, I prefer to be untethered. And frankly, neither of you have a big enough lasso, shall we say, to snare me." I admit I am enjoying the exquisite pleasure of role playing. But c'mon, first I was a jewel, then a pawn, and now, I'm off the chessboard and a racehorse? If anyone calls me a "wild card," I'm outta here. Gentlemen, can we please ditch the misogynist clichés?

"*Pardonnez-moi*, I must dash back to my seat, the play is about to begin. *À bientôt, chérie?*" Jean-Albert says, by way of a request.

"*Peut-être.* Give your wife my best," I add. Okay, I'm officially not enjoying the constant magnet-like need for him to return to the wife. And one should never let men think they possess you. At least never men like these men. Holy smokes, I'm starting to sound like Marie-Hélène!

Everyone rises and makes toward the theater, where we are to see a presentation of the very same play that was inaugurated at Vaux le Vicomte that scandalous opening night in 1661: *Les Facheux* by Molière.

Frédéric quickens to my side, taking my fur wrap and draping it gently over my bare shoulders. "Alexandra, I am very sorry for the ludicrous horse comment. Please excuse my indelicacy. It is simply that it is not every day one meets a vibrant young woman such as yourself. And somehow, perhaps it's destiny—by way of Jean-Albert—that we are to meet, *enfin*."

Moving toward the theater, I consciously slow our pace so as to not have to follow behind Jean-Albert *et son épouse*.

"Destiny? Perhaps it's just that you don't happen to meet many young American women. We are, as a rule, something to contend with. More outspoken, self-possessed, and less constrained in words or actions than French women." (Man, have I always wanted to say that to a Frenchman!)

"In actions, you say? I should like very much to become better informed on the subject. It would be my personal effort at improving Franco-American relations," Frédéric coyly replies in low tones, putting his arm through mine.

He looks away for a moment to nod to a gentleman, and I steal a glance at him. Damn, Monsieur, you're so motherfucking attractive, I just want to reach out, take your face in my hands, and kiss you until neither of us can see straight. Rosebud blossoming? I don't know. But Marie-Hélène has it right; discovering new aspects of one's desire and sexuality *is* intoxicating. I'm finding these older men's faces are just so enthralling; like maps of a life rich in ambition, accomplishment, and tactical thought. Lately I am just ignited with desire by knowing eyes punctuated with deep crows'-

feet. (Don't get me wrong. To a point. It's not like I'm becoming a geezerophile, to coin a word.)

Taking our seats in the upper box of the theater, we most inelegantly, accidentally turn in the same direction, and bump into one another. A flutter of electricity shoots through me. And you know where to, I'm guessing. You have to admit, as a woman, that wave of sudden passion is dangerous. And delicious. (And if it ever fades from my life, I will just stay home eating chocolate all day.)

"Oops!" I say, without thinking. Frédéric bursts into a smile, reaches out, takes my hands in his, and sits sideways on his seat looking up at me with a beseeching expression. I am still standing, realizing that, once again, I find myself presented with a married man, utterly undeterred by the consequences of flaunting an affair publicly. What's with these guys?! I'm starting to believe that powerful men seek, and maybe even require, the danger of being caught misbehaving flagrantly. Perhaps it is to offset the security they have achieved in every other aspect of their lives. It's just a theory, really. It could also be that they're just horny bastards.

He begins to speak as the curtain goes up and the lights dim. "Did you say 'oops'? You are positively adorable. So fresh. So desirable, impetuous. I am simply besotted with you. What must I do to see you again?" My heart beats violently to see this man doing a very convincing line reading of French charm. Clearly, with age, these Frenchmen really hone the art of seduction. Frédéric has every gesture, every possible appealing quality at his disposal.

Hmm. How to answer that question effectively? Especially since I am quite sure I would give my right arm to spend one night in this man's bed—and I am also quite sure he doesn't want me to indulge him so easily (i.e., willingly fall flat on my back *tout de suite*). Looks like we are going to need to dip back into the bag of tricks I found when I met Jean-Albert.

"Frédéric, you know I am with Jean-Albert. If you wish to see me, I demand blind obedience. You must wait for *me* to tell *you* when and where," I say, not even looking at him, pretending to be far more interested in the orchestra beginning below. (Full stop: BOW, Bitch on Wheels. That should do it.)

"I will be available to you as much as my schedule permits. So, you promise to call me? May we meet again in the coming days?" he almost begs, with as much eagerness as a little boy. (I find myself thinking, "God, if only he was this imploringly gentle in business, maybe the economy would pick up!")

"*Oui*. I think it should be my pleasure to educate you as to the hidden charms of American women," I tell him, turning back to him. Our eyes catch and we hold each other's gaze with such intensity, it's almost hypnotizing. I feel a deep throbbing overwhelm me. Oh-la. Frédéric is so gorgeous I try not to slide out of my chair and slip over the banister.

"Alexandra, many of your charms are not so hidden *ce soir*." And his hand glides over my shoulder and ever so slowly over my breast, settling in my warm—make that, suddenly very warm—lap. Kinda wish I had those panties on right about now.

"You will call me then? . . . *Magnifique!*" He sits back and beams; a wicked smile of triumph passes across his face.

Jean-Albert, in his box directly to our right, notices at once, and looks over, concerned. The wife spots his glance and shoots me a look of, essentially and expectedly, "die, bitch." Interestingly, that look is the same in any language.

Thus begins a rapid-fire exchange of fleeting glances between Jean-Albert, Frédéric, the wife, and me, each of us displaying varying states of pleasure and displeasure, arousal and fear. Having just acquired one apartment, and one new, far sexier lover, all at the minimal cost of one pair of underwear, I am feeling rather amused with myself.

Moi: I will take an order each of arousal and pleasure, *merci*.

Three hundred and forty-five years after that first scandalous fête at Vaux le Vicomte, the decadent games of the wealthy are still played with robust enthusiasm. Except this night, under an ink black sky ornamented by the shimmering sliver of a golden moon . . . a young American woman is the victor . . . La-di-da!

I think.

LES CADEAUX DU MOIS

Two-hundred-square-meter apartment in the 16th arrondissement: 1.6 million euros

Déménagement *(moving expenses): 4,000 euros*

1 Hermès riding crop: 300 euros

2 Yves Saint Laurent suits: 4,200 euros

1 J. Mendel fox scarf: 870 euros

1 Alber Ebaz evening gown: 3,400 euros

THINGS YOU AREN'T ALLOWED TO HAVE AS A COURTESAN

I. Your *règles; en anglais:* your period. This is something bizarre, right? You can't beg off from a sexual adventure with this or menstrual cramps as your reason. Don't even think about it as they don't want to hear mention of it—even the ones that don't mind playing through at that time of the month. Explaining, even casually, that it's that time of the month unnerves these men. It's an unwelcome reminder that you belong to the sect of humans who actually inhabit the earth with nonfantasylike attributes of reality. Not to mention that it brings up the awareness of fertility, family, children, responsibility—all the things they seek to escape with you. In short, you suddenly are a woman like all others, which pokes a hole ever so briefly in their well-scripted fantasy. But it's a bummer that goes with the job, and does not outweigh the perks of jewels, jets, free-flowing Dom Pérignon, and worship.

2. No personal problems of any kind. Sure, you can discuss the quandary of which gown to wear with him to the next ball or that you're unsure of investing in bonds or mutual funds. (Jean-Albert once asked that a calculator be brought to the dinner table at Le Voltaire as he went into ecstasies for hours, showing me the concept and nuances of investing in derivatives. Totally helpful? *Bien sûr*, but God, I was fighting to listen as the singer Bryan Ferry was sitting within earshot and eye fuck, and I was pretty damn tempted to throw myself in *his* lap . . . or to try to lure him to the loo for a secret snog.)

　　By "problems" I mean anything that exhibits self-doubt or internal struggle, or could be construed in any way as depressing or negative. *Par exemple*, if you're struggling with the question of your life's purpose, better keep that to yourself. Don't bring up worries about aging, missing your family back home, or the story about arguing with the clerk at *la poste* . . . If something seems possibly too domestic, trivial, or common—it is. Edit! It does become a tinge isolating to not have the ability to speak freely about your life and thoughts, and weirdly, does—over the time—seem to have the unexpected benefit of making one's life appear to be chock-full of nothing but fabulous venues for amusing stories and divine adventures. Okay, I will admit it, for a certain amount of time it's pleasant to live with your head in the sand and focus on all the pleasures of the senses.

3. Never make any mention or request for anything in the ever-so-ambiguous future. Not a "call me" or a "what do you say we go away this weekend?" should ever drop out of your mouth. No mention of a rendezvous or any future together. The deal is that he offers and you either refuse or accept. If he asks for *dîner à mercredi*, and you're busy, you simply say no, and spur him to keep asking and offering until he hits on a date or invitation that tempts you. Remember, these men need to work to have a precious moment of your time, otherwise it will seem too easy and that will bore them. If your sister's wedding is approaching and you think arriving on his

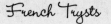

arm would make a splash, don't kid yourself. The last thing he wants to do is meet your family and watch your dad shake it to "Hava Nagila." *Way* too real.

To summarize, refrain from any behavior that may threaten the fantasy that you are a free-floating, immaculately conceived, exquisite angel with a radiant life force unaffected by issues of the world.

CHAPITRE DIX

The desire of the man is for the woman, but the desire
of the woman is for the desire of the man.

—MADAME DE STAËL

The next morning, you can bloody well bet Jean-Albert called lickety-split, desperate to reaffirm his claim on me and mark his territory. After securing the safety of Samaritane, I instantly became the next tricky acquisition to track and protect. That has to be the first time anyone ever equated my worth with that of a luxury department store. Maybe, the first time any woman has. Trust me, it's not all that amusing! You're not missing anything in not sharing in this experience.

He rang and asked me to meet him the following night at his suite at the Ritz. I was going to say, "our suite," but I guess I haven't been handed the deed to that palace . . . *yet.* I'm *kidding.* I'm not a greedy monster; I haven't even asked for any of these treats. Treats is really downplaying it, I know. I realize I feel calm about the rendezvous awaiting me for a change. I no longer feel compelled to prepare clever anecdotes or titillating references in advance. After all the hoopla of late, I am feeling rather confident that I can hold my own in any situation. I know for a fact I didn't feel that self-assured even a month ago, and that's pretty damn cool to realize. Who the hell was it that said, "Fake it until you live it"? But P.S.: that damn sure doesn't apply to orgasms. I'm a big believer that if he's not getting you there, no sense in letting him think he's Casanova. In short, "Work, keep at it, boy, until I'm screaming so loud the Champagne flutes shatter."

Whoops-ee! I digressed again. Sorry, so much to tell, back to the *soirée* in question. I was saying, among other things, that I no longer spend hours laboring over what to wear to meet Jean-Albert. I don't keep my clothes on that long anyway! (Alright, I'm semiexaggerating: we *have* had several rendezvous that were merely long walks through the Jardins du Luxembourg, or like the day we drove to Fountainebleau for a ride on a merry-go-round. Jean-Albert looked hilariously absurd, with his knees up by his shoulders astride a pink pony, I can tell you!)

And with my closet chock-a-block bursting with generous freebies from all Jean-Albert's design houses, pretty much everything is a fabulous option. (Except the Vuitton Empire line dresses; I look very six months pregnant/matronly in those. By the way, who the hell can wear that look, anyway? Right, Natalie Portman, and no one else on the planet.)

I threw on a pale blue bateau-neck sleeveless dress and a pair of lace-up Chanel wedge espadrilles. Hair up, as always, and the stack of three big cuff bracelets in beige Bakelite that I found for a song at an *antiquaire's* shop on rue de Beaune. I bounded down the stairs and waved to Jean-Albert's driver not to bother getting out to open my door. You have to say, it's really the height of vulgar to not even open your own damn car door! Charles (le driver) thoughtfully slipped in my favorite CD by Coldplay, asked if the car temperature was to my liking, handed me a small bottle of Evian, offered me a cigarette, and then off we went. Yeah, pow-bang-zing! That's a helluva lot of service in just the first three minutes. It's astonishingly true that the real luxuries in life are not the big things like owning couture or private jets but the little things, like the precision of efficiency and endless beyond-perfect service. People always anticipating your slightest desire and at the ready for your slightest whim. Extreme wealth is the public's way to buy being treated like royalty. There's so much bowing, catering, ass kissing and kowtowing, red carpets, palaces, enormous jewels, and fleets of limousines, the *only* thing missing is the bloody crown!

I've also come to notice that the fragrances and textures of living in luxury are so unique, from the ever-changing and ever-divine scents that inhabit these venues: every room in every home, restaurant, or mode of transportation is carefully controlled to smell fresh, rich, and grand. Then there are the lusciously fine sheets ironed with *lavande* water, the heady scent of fresh rubrum lilies blooming in every room, the deeply sumptuous Pratesi bath towels—surely they are what God has in his *salle de bain*: the richly embroidered fabrics that serve as drapery; the expertly woven silk failles that cover the pillows; the meticulous antique tapestries that cloak the walls; and on and on! For eyes, body, hands, and face, all that comes into their world is a textural orgasm. With one exception: Kleenex. So far there are no Bulgari tissues, so we are all even steven there!

But, for the love of God, let's get on with this night, *d'accord*?

Zipping over Pont Royal, I catch myself smiling at the skyline of the Grand Palais in the reflection of the tinted window. It's starting to become a silhouette against the setting red sun. Man, even the sky in Paris is sexy. Unquestionably, this city was created by God for living all of life's sensual pleasures. And I'm on my way to taste some more!

I have to admit, I feel a certain sense of sassy attitude entering the Ritz these days, *bonsoir*-ing the entire staff: "Yeah, that's right, I'm one very expensive fuck, people. You got a million euros? That won't cut it, kiddo. Call me when you hit a billion." I'm kidding. *Kinda.* I know I haven't done anything to earn anyone's respect or made any monumental contribution to the culture. But having Jean-Albert at my feet has me thinking all crazy on every level.

And I must confess, all this recent sexual awakening and freedom has me checking out men left and right. I find myself eyeing the crotch of the flower delivery boy, thinking, "I bet his head would explode if I dragged him in here and gave him my new Japanese squat trick." What's that? you ask. Hold on to your hat. It's a comin'—and so will the man in your life!

Jean-Albert greeted me at the door with a swarm of kisses. Love him for that. Never does he fail to make every greeting and departure an event. And the parts in between are rather eventful as well, I should add.

"Oh, *mon amour.* I love you in that dress. The cut, the silk crepe . . . You are Audrey Hepburn reborn!" I'd swear he was gay if I didn't know better, this man *looooves* to talk fashion.

The hypnotic fragrance of heliotrope candles by Diptyque fills the room: a *bougie* burns on every table. See? Told ya.

"A new fragrance for our love den, *chéri?* I love it . . . it's like emerging from a swim in the sea and having sex on the beach in the sun," I say, knowing that's character perfect.

"Interesting thought, and very Alexandra. The aroma of heliotropes always reminds me of falling asleep on my *grand-mère's* lap at her *maison de campagne* (country home), the smell of dew on the wet garden wafting in on the breeze from the sea, a tray of warm *madeleines* cooling in the kitchen," he says, as he takes off his suit jacket and hangs it on a chair.

"Very Proustian of you, *mon amour,*" I say, without thinking. My God, I just called him "my love." This is something I have always wanted to hold back. Crap.

"*Mon amour? Enfin* . . . you love me just a little bit then, my darling?" he exclaims, reaching for my hand. Deep breath over here. This is a lose-lose moment. I either relinquish the love I have held hostage or I say "no" and crush him. Racking my mental files for an out, I spy a prop, a possible escape route. I pluck a buttercream rose from the bouquet on the dresser and launch into a French version of the "he loves me, he loves me not" children's game. You know it *en française* now too. "*Il m'aime . . . un peu* (he loves me a little), *beaucoup* (he loves me a lot), *passionnément* (he loves me passionately), *à la folie* (he loves me crazily) *ou pas du tout*

(not at all). Phew. Very French of me to *not* respond directly and let
the question hang in the air as though I've answered it.

"Oh, I love you so," he responds, reassured, and gestures toward the bed. "There ... on the pillow ... two little things to
amuse you. *Allez.*"

I scoot over and spring onto the bed, landing on my knees to
discover the latest in treats. Out of the corner of my eye I see something familiar yet out of place. What's that? Hey, those are my ini-
tials. On the pillowcase and on the breast pocket of one of those
Dior bathrobes; he's had my monogram embroidered in pale gold
bullion with a regal crest atop. I burst out laughing at how fun and
chic it is, and at such an unnecessary but delicious idea! I'm starting to really dig them. What's next in the absurd extravagances? I
got it! He should name a yacht after me! Kidding. The wife would
go ballistic.

"Have I been knighted without knowing it, *chéri*?! Oh, this is
fabulous, what a riot," I say, whipping off my dress and trying on
the robe.

"*Oui, bien sûr.* You are the queen of my heart," he replies dramatically, placing both of his hands on his chest. "I'm glad you like
it; there's another like it being sent to your new apartment ... and
look in the pocket, *mon ange.*"

Oh goody, more jewelry? Wouldn't that rock! My hand scram-
bles through all the pockets until it hits on a small blue velvet box.
I look up at Jean-Albert, now sitting on the edge of the bed in front
of me, and give him a broad smile. Cracking open the little hinge, I
instantly notice— Hey, this isn't an elegant box, it's all cheaply
made and *velveteen*, not velvet. Yikes, spoiled courtesan alert!

Shimmering in the center of some seriously cheesy blue poly-
ester is a matte silver sphere, about the size of a large jawbreaker.
Got a clue? I didn't. Chic reference to "jawbreaker," right? I know,
"You can take the girl out of Elmbrook, but you can't take the ..."

"Okay, Jean-Albert. It's a silver ball. What am I to do with this,
exactly?" Feel free to read disappointment in my voice.

"Haahaaha! It's a platinum orb for my queen. They are quite

the rage in Japan," he says, rising and taking it out of the box. "See, you twist it slightly at this center seam . . . *et voilà*!" he explains excitedly, placing it in my hand.

My new little platinum orb is vibrating in my palm like the dickens! Wow, quite a little motor in there! It's interesting, but I'm still lost.

"*Tu vois*, my dear, you take this, turn it on, and put it in your *beau chaton*. Thus, anytime, anywhere you wish, with this pulsating orb inside you, you can quite discreetly find yourself having an orgasm. Marvelous, isn't it?" he exclaims, as though he invented it. Christ, maybe he did.

"Wow. I have to say, that's a *unique* gift, baby." I'm not sure if I think it's the coolest thing ever or really creepy.

"May I assist you in christening it?" he says, gettin' all sexy on me. Christen it? Hey, it's not exactly a yacht you can slam a bottle of Champagne against. (Clearly, I can't quite give up the fantasy of the boat named after me!)

Jean-Albert takes the silver sphere from my hand and rolls it slowly down my neck as he parts my robe and trails it down ever so gently to the edge of my *chaton*. The little orb throbs against my clit and instantly sends a shudder through me from head to toe.

"Oh, mmm, I'm starting to like your little *cadeau*, baby . . . go lower . . . slow now . . . *doucement* . . . Ahh! Yes, there . . . Faaa—ucck!" I scream. Okay, I have a verdict: coolest thing ever.

Jean-Albert rolls the quivering sphere over my lips, yes, those lips, and suspends it just below me.

"*Tu es prête, ma chérie?*" he asks sweetly. *Ready?*

"*Ah, oui . . . s'il te plaît!*" Trust me, speaking French in bed is always a good thing.

And with that he slides the ball inside me and pushes it deeply with his finger . . . which he then takes out and sucks. The rest I don't remember, as I was very busy trembling and quite possibly levitating. All I know is he stripped himself quickly and pulled me on top of him.

"May I join you?" he asks, while caressing my hips tenderly.

You know what, buddy, I'm feeling *très agréable* right now, you could tell me you're gonna behead me after this and I'd happily nod. I'm not capable of talking, so he takes my nod as his cue and slides his sex just slightly inside me. Pushing deeper, I can feel both the vibrating tremor and his hard sex sliding against the walls of my *chaton*. It's insane pleasure. Somehow in the dizzying midst of this explosive new sexual escapade, a flash of an image I'd seen in a Kama Sutra book comes to mind. If ever there were a moment to play geisha, this is it, I tell myself, as I endeavor to pull my feet up and place them flat on either side of his narrow hips.

Keeping him and my new favorite object on the planet inside me, I lean my shoulders toward him as I keep squatting on his hard cock. I begin to slowly ride his sex, lifting my hips by bending my knees. Raising my ass up to just the verge of him pulling out . . . and then sliding him back in as deeply as I can take it. My thighs start to ache and burn as I glide up and down on his shaft . . . I'm dying in pain but can see that in just a few more strokes he's going to absolutely lose it!

"Ohhh, mon dieu . . . Putain! Bordel! . . . Ooh la-la!" he erupts, shaking and convulsing with the mother of all orgasms. Just seeing the unbelievable, completely consuming pleasure he feels instantly pushes me over the edge. We both collapse, reeling and swimming through the swelling tides of pleasure that roll in again and again.

"Domo arigato," he says, speaking into my damp hair like seaweed caught on his cheek—*charmingly thanking me in Japanese.*

I die laughing, and with him still inside me, the shaking of my laughter spins us both into small echoing shudders of pleasure. The effect of which only makes us both roar with laughter and starts the ball rolling again, as it were.

Major footnote: I'm not kidding. This Japanese squat trick is the biggest gift I can give you, from one woman to another. Fair warning: once you pull this trick out, the man in your life will beg for it endlessly. Bonus: fuck the Stairmaster. Employing this move

makes for rock-hard thighs *and* killer orgasms. And I don't see anyone screaming in ecstasy at the gym, do you?

AND THE THIRD LOVE LETTER FROM JEAN-ALBERT
(Written on Ritz Hôtel stationery and left in my purse
when he did his 5:00 A.M. departure maneuver.)

My Princess,
Can I tell my impatient fingers that tomorrow evening, at tea time,
they will have a chance to check if the smooth warm texture of the
fragrant skin they are obsessed with is all just a dream? Did you
hear me this morning murmuring, "I love you" as I was leaving
our bed? Perhaps not, so I'll repeat: *I love you.*

Your J.A.

P.S. There is something I know about you that you do not
know . . . *how beautiful you are asleep.*

CHAPITRE ONZE

Where your life leads you, you must go.

—OSCAR WILDE

eedless to say, Marie-Hélène and I had a lot to rehash. With Hugo at the wheel and the midday sun streaming in the open windows, we were off to rue Faubourg St. Honoré, to check out my new apartment.

Passing through the dizzying traffic by the Arc de Triomphe, a cool breeze whipping through our hair, life seemed as perfect as a bowl of *cerises*. (That's cherries, if you hadn't guessed as much.)

I have to admit, for a woman who's seen it all, I had Marie-Hélène rather boggled.

"Sweet Alexa, fate has played you an amazing hand of late. While I still don't know how Frédéric de Fallois switched his seat with the marquis, in truth he will be a pleasant diversion, and there is no reason why you can't have all three men!" she says, blowing cigarette smoke out the window.

"Three!? Maybe we can hold off on my meeting the marquis awhile; I don't think I can handle three men right now. Just the one night at Vaux le Vicomte, I already felt very much like a ball in a pinball machine ricocheting back and forth. I may need a little time to acquire the skill of juggling men. How many men are you *seeing* at the moment?" ("Seeing" seemed like a good euphemism.)

"Three. It's the magic number. I am of the complete belief that it takes three men to fulfill all the needs of one woman. One must be heinously wealthy and madly in love with you. He is the one who offers you the moon and the stars, trips and jewels, and that you retain at all costs."

"Check! That'd be Jean-Albert." I count off, as I dig through my purse for the apartment keys he had sent over that morning.

She continues, "You need another that is staggeringly beautiful, the one you really want to have sex with. He's ultimately disposable but really satisfies you. With him you can experiment and hone your skills in the bedroom. Generally, he's the young one, takes it all too seriously and ends up proposing."

"Hmm. Sounded like Frédéric until you got to the young and proposing part. I so don't care. He's just unfathomably sexy, don't you think?" I ask, as I start checking the street addresses for *numéro deux*.

"Yes, I agree he is that. But something tells me he could be trouble . . . Just a hunch. Anyway, the third man should be the tender lover, the sensitive, caring soul. He is the one you sneak off to when you need to be taken care of. As a rule, they are the ones that offer rare books and *objets d'art* instead of bank accounts and jewels. This man is the one you have to protect yourself from falling in love with." She finishes just as Hugo pulls over.

"C'est numéro deux, Mesdames," he announces, as he opens each of our doors.

Standing on the sidewalk, Marie-Hélène and I look up at the classic French nineteenth-century building shimmering in the sun. Graceful wrought-iron balconies adorn a beautifully proportioned facade of ornamented columns and pilasters, with stonework of voluptuous foliage and flowers, all typical of Second Empire architecture.

"The building looks a little like a wedding cake, *non*? A bit fussy, wouldn't you say?" I ask, feeling a pang of, "Am I really going to take this apartment as a gift?"

"Alexa, the address is *top*, and I'm sure you'll assume it." (Very French phrase, meaning to acquire the mentality to make it feel *naturel*.) We use the largest of the seven keys, a five-inch shiny steel number, to enter the large glass-and-ironwork doors. Ooph! It almost takes the two of us to push the tall, heavy doors ajar.

"If I ever come home alone drunk, that will be hell," I murmur. Marie-Hélène chuckles lightly.

Stepping into a huge rectangular cobblestone courtyard, we're met by four large green square planters of flowering magnolias, one punctuating each corner. A quartet of matching green benches sit, one under each tree, and in the center is a large Carrera marble fountain of fish spouting sparkling jets of cool water. And put there by well-meaning hands: blossoming blooms fill flower boxes on windowsills on every floor. Chic to die.

"OK, this is charming as hell. Certainly beats my so-called courtyard, with its abandoned broken baby carriage, an old wheelchair, and half a bike. I am so going to love living here. Apparently, my apartment is on the *sixième étage,* so I imagine I will get to fall asleep each night to that sweet trickling fountain. Nice touch, huh?" I toss out, as we make for a curving stone staircase just to the right, behind another set of glass doors.

Marie-Hélène and I take a pass on the beautiful but *petit ascenseur* (elevator) after sizing it up. "Adorable, but I prefer to walk. It's got to be a hundred years old. With my luck I'd get trapped in there and they'd find me a year later, a carcass, albeit still sporting a wickedly sexy pair of heels!"

"Alexa, you're bananas!" MH says, as we glide up the wide stairs, eyeing the quality of the chandelier. *C'est très bien,* by the way.

"Marie-Hélène, I've got *you* saying 'bananas'! How funny is that? I'm corrupting you!" I laugh, trying various keys in the door of the apartment, which already bears a brass plate engraved with my name. Cute move, Jean-Albert. No aesthetic detail escapes this man!

"As you well know, I was already corrupted, my dear, and I'm simply trying on your casual slang. It seems to be a striking and charming contrast that these men find appealing."

"I'm not sold that it works for you." I smile over my shoulder as I push open the large double doors. "Though I am sold on this apartment!" I bellow, leaping into the room.

The two-hundred-square-meter apartment is not grandiose by Parisian beau monde standards. Just a bright sunny flat of *cinq pièces* (five rooms) with very pretty details: elegant parquet oak floor; a classic marble fireplace in both the *salle à manger* and the *salon*. Lovely three-meter-high ceilings that climb to an elegant cornice trimming all the rooms. A terracotta-tiled American-style kitchen, outfitted with all new Gaggenau appliances and a charming oval-shaped window that looks out into the courtyard below.

I scamper about excitedly and grab Marie-Hélène's hand.

"Come, let's find the bedroom, and where the hell is the master bathroom? I saw a small room with a tiny porcelain toilet by the *salon*, but there must be another!"

(And by the way, I hate those "toilet only" little bathrooms; absolutely no way to pretend you're just going to powder your nose or wash your hands, as there is rarely so much as a mirror. Not to mention, they are always just off the main room, so if you really have to use the facilities, you can damn well bet that all and sundry lounging in the living room get an earful of every drop. Enough said.)

Hand in hand, we saunter down a long, wide hall that stretches fifty feet or so.

"*Voilà*, the bathroom. Beautiful, but the tub looks a little like what would be placed next to a guillotine to catch the decapitated heads, or am I wrong?" I exclaim.

In the center of the cheery all-white marble bathroom rests a large patinaed copper bathtub, very eighteenth century, and while very "decorator showroom," it's very brutal in its severeness. Flanking the elegant marble sink are twin white armoires of painted oak for storing towels and linens . . . and, in my case, a perfect place for my growing collection of sex toys, oils, and accessories.

"In fact, the copper tub is called a *baignoire* and is a rare piece, Alexa. Isabel Adjani has one very similar. A very nice detail. Jean-Albert has an eye, no question," MH replies. We move on.

"Onward, to *la pièce de résistance*—*la chambre d'amour*! Or for acts of *amour*, at least," I announce, leading the way. Making our way to the northeast corner of the building, we turn the crystal doorknob and enter what will be, joy of joys, my new bedroom.

"Love!" I yelp, dashing about the room. "Look, double windows on both sides! And check out the terrace." A set of French (but, of course) glass doors opens onto a short—but ten-foot-wide—terrace overlooking the chic Place Vendôme and a view going all the way up to Montmartre in the distance.

"I will put the bed there—actually, better ditch the futon and get a real bed—and then I can lie in bed at night and see the lights of Sacré Coeur!" I squeal, as I mime lying in a bed. Marie-Hélène smiles and lingers on the terrace, looking over Place Vendôme. "Well, what do you think?" I ask.

"Better still, you are a stone's throw from Cartier! I'm delighted for you . . . And I can see you're pleased. The *appartement* has charm, but I frankly thought he'd have opted for something *un peu plus grande*," Madame Buzzkill offers.

"Really? Remember, Jean-Albert and I have only been together six months. I'd say this is *extremely* generous. You know the deed says it was 1.6 million euros. I know your apartment is probably twice that."

"Three times, to be sure. But remember, purchasing this apartment for you is nothing to him. I just read he bought an Asian Mirogui from Christie's auction house for twenty-one million dollars," my elitist *amie* shoots back.

"I know. He showed me the piece, from the Yuan period, a blue-and-white jar. It's lovely, but the price is staggering. To own any one thing that valuable? Madness. Oh, whatever. *I am* elated with the flat. Now I just have to furnish it. God what a task!" I say, looking around, suddenly plagued with the magnitude of the project.

"That's the fun part. I will take you to my *antiquaire*, Chloe

Chevalier. She has a splendid gallery right down the street at 92, rue du Faubourg St. Honoré and she will set you up in no time. In fact, she was the mistress to Baron de Rothschild for decades. She even had a daughter with him. And a very intelligent woman, in that she parlayed her courtesan existence, the wealth and connections, into a very respected and successful business. Oh, and I must give you a bit of advice: Change the locks and don't ever give *any* of your lovers the key."

"At the *moment* I only have one lover . . . And frankly, while my little velvet bag of scruples has recently popped a small hole, I am going to stand firm on not allowing any men other than Jean-Albert to visit me here. It's the least I can do, right?"

"Proceed with the best intentions, of course. But, I am sure any lover will prefer your *appartement* to his own. And remember, hotels are for amateurs."

"Yes, except of course, Jean-Albert's suite at the Ritz . . . which is right there!" I say eagerly, pointing over the terrace. We burst into laughter, and I teach Marie-Hélène how to high-five. It's not pretty. She looks like she's making a bid at Christie's. As I've said, you can't alter genetic codes.

We conclude the first viewing and agree to meet on the weekend to see the Bonnard exhibit at Musée d'Art Moderne. I have Hugo drop me back in St. Germain after we deposit Marie-Hélène at Guerlain to get their famous blue-gold facial. (Would you believe they actually slather your face with pure liquid gold and rare blue seaweed? What's next? Bathing in beluga? Geesh.)

Back in the 6th arrondissement, coming into my old building, I grab my mail from the *boîtes aux lettres*. No bills. Well, that's a nice little perk these days. Yep, I'd say my living expenses are about zip these days. I put down cash for the odd French *Vogue* or baguette, but pretty much everything else gets put on Jean-Albert's *plastique*. A vastly more expensive lifestyle, and I am actually saving money? Groovy. Oh, *pardonnez-moi*, make that *splendide*!

As I climb up the five flights, the rickety, dusty stairs suddenly seem horribly shabby. And upon entering my teensy apartment I'm stunned by the contrast a few hours can make. What I once thought was a dreamy little garret now has all the charm of a roadside public toilet. How did I ever live here? The walls are stained and cracked, the grubby floors are like a skating rink, and the bathroom—filthy, yuck, zero elegance! Sitting on my crappy old futon bed, which I now realize feels a lot like sitting in a canoe, my thoughts skitter: Marie-Hélène thinks the new apartment should be *more* grand? That's absurd. Sometimes, for all her advice and tender concern, she can veer into being too much of a hovercraft. A little too interested in having me recap every element of my *soirées,* from the lurid sexual details to making me guesstimate the value of gifts I've received. Maybe for as much as she wants to guide me, part of her still feels threatened. I mean, really, it's not as if the courtesan lifestyle breeds a sense of camaraderie among women. Thankfully I am still able to see how unbelievably fortunate I am. Nope. *Her* disappointment is not going to rain on my parade, I mean, *please.* I'm twenty-five years old. If I ever even finish my thesis on Boucher and get a curator job, I still couldn't swing an apartment like that!

(Yeah, and what about that thesis? It's getting sadly neglected, like a three-bean salad at an elegant picnic. I will get back to it when things calm down, but now . . . I have a hankering for a sexy Frenchman.) And more fun still, in contrast to my relationships with Frenchmen my own age, *I* have the power to demand that he charm the pants off *me.* That's never the case with the young pups I've known. I always felt like I had to turn cartwheels to get a crumb of their attention. "I don't miss that at all!" I actually say out loud, unhinging and opening the windows.

Leaning on my elbows out the window, I savor the final days of my view of St. Sulpice. It's been a great first apartment, but now it's time to move on. And up! God, so much to do. New furniture? What a project. Gotta do something with this stuff; no sense in keeping it, it would be laughable in my new place. Oh, and I should thank Jean-Albert, I suddenly remember.

He's number one on my speed dial. Not just because we speak

constantly, but because when he gave me this killer fab Vertu cell phone, he'd already locked it in. I had a little thrill when I first saw the phonebook list. He's constantly reassuring me with his attentions and placing himself as a priority in my life. It calms all those voices of insecurity every woman feels: When you know absolutely that a man is crazy about you, there's a beautiful peace that cloaks you against all the little troubles life throws at you. It's what makes you wake up happy and fall asleep smiling; it's like a protective shield. Damn, I was going to say, "and gives you an optimism for the future," but I guess that doesn't apply here. I did feel that way once—with Laurent. It was like a drug. I imagine that's how you feel on your wedding day. Just overflowing with joy. All those questions answered and the future before you. I will have it again. I never really wanted to be married before thirty-five anyway. Too much to discover, to learn about life and one's self. This just reeks of defensiveness, doesn't it? Pee-ew! I fling off that reverie and proceed to push *numéro un.*

"*Oui?*" Jean-Albert says abruptly, and by the way, he pronounces it *"whey"* while kind of inhaling, as all Parisians do.

"Hey baby, just saw the apartment and wanted to say again, it was so amazingly generous of you. And I think . . ."

He interrupts, "*Vraiment désolé, chérie,* I am on a conference call. Ring you *à plus tard.*" Click. Well, that was no fun. I often get that cold tone when I ring him during the day, and yet, when I don't call him, he goes ape-shit on me. "You forgot me, you have someone new!" Blah, blah. I can't win. Fine, Mr. All Business, let's see if your rival is more sporting. Where the hell did I put Frédéric's number? "Oh Christ. If I lost it, I'll die," I think, rummaging through my desk. Ah, *voilà!*

Number in hand, I notice that Frédéric's also written an e-mail address in his elegant scrawl—lebateauivre@wanadoo.fr. Funny, that's the title of a poem by Rimbaud. One of my favorites, actually. Boy, these Frenchmen are just chic to the core.

My hands start to tremble as I dial, and I feel that old feeling, like when I first moved to France. Something along the lines of, I'm going to make an ass of myself, but here goes. Screw it. Frédéric's the one who pursued me. Right. I hold the cards. He finally answers, after what seems like eternity.

"*Oui.*" Man, these dudes are curt.

"Wild filly, here. You busy?" I say, instantly thinking, "Fuck! This man's life is soooo busy with calls from Putin and meetings with Chirac, what the hell am I saying? He'll never remember that foolish reference. Hang up while you're ahead!"

"Alexandra? How divine to hear from you. I'm just about to head into a press conference. I'll be at my office later, e-mail me, as the cell phone is an unsecured line, *d'accord*?" that voice that makes me melt says to me. Me! The girl with the beanpole body from Elmbrook!

"*D'accord, comme tu veux. À tout!*" I say, adhering to Marie-Hélène's advice: Always say less on the phone, and leave them wanting more. *And* I *tu*-ed him, giving him the less formal version of "you." Riotous, I bet *no one tu*-s him. Well done, except the *à tout;* that was nowhere of me. Gotta lose that.

E-mailing? Is that sexy? I think not. Well, perhaps I should look at it as an opportunity to develop my skills to enchant through the written word. Oh, yes indeed! It's a very eighteenth-century courtesan concept: a few exquisitely chosen words to captivate a man's attention. Pity it has to be via the cyber world; I'd so prefer to dash out a few lines in beautifully calligraphied script, and have my manservant deliver the crisp letter sealed with the stamp of my signet ring in glossy red wax . . . Oh, what a time that must have been! I was *so* born in the wrong century!

I settle in at my desk and turn on my computer. I shift in my seat and tap the keys anxiously, hoping something clever will come to me. Nothing. Bloody hell, this is harder than I thought. Couldn't I just skim a volume by Verlaine and plagiarize a little something? No, the crap deal with sophisticated men is that they've seen, read, and done it all, so one *must* be original. Despite my initial idea that I should adapt my vocabulary with them and learn to communicate in refined aristo-speak, I've come to understand that my casual slang and sassy off-the-cuff free-speaking is what really engages them. So I'll stick with that. When in doubt, be yourself, *n'est-ce pas?*

I type in his address, and then write:

Hey cowboy, are you game for a ride on an untamed filly *ce soir?* No saddle necessary; bareback riders only. Bring large lasso. Riding crop: optional.

Oh, this is so dumb. Kinda funny, though. Have to remember, in his busy day of serious market capital and debt margins business, this will be the highlight. I'm sure of it. But location? Need to choose that. No, maybe leave that to him; gotta give him the illusion of some power. Done.

I hesitate before pushing the send button. Then laugh out loud with the realization, this is so much fun, I can hardly believe it. OK. SEND.

What to do now? I definitely owe Isabel a call, have blown off her last three text messages. I push "Isabel" on my cell phone.

"*Allô.* Alexandra? Hey girl, it's been a while!" she says, sounding in good spirits.

"Hi, doll. Is it OK I'm calling while you're at work? Yeah, and sorry for the absence. Life has been chaotic of late." (Yeah, better to downplay the hoopla.) "How's life, sweetie?" Gosh, it's nice to hear her voice.

"*Fantastique!* Remember I told you about this man I've been seeing, Mathieu?"

"Yeah. He sounded lovely." And another poor young pup, if I recall correctly.

"It's been a beautiful whirlwind. We are just madly in love, and moving in together! Isn't that great?"

The sound of sewing machines purring away behind her.

"Isabel, that's marvelous. I have to meet this man who's won your heart!" So she's in love. Real love. I feel a pang. Is it jealousy?

"Yes, I'm moving into his flat on Saturday. So let's try for a dinner next weekend . . . you can bring the old man! I have to thank him for the last raise. You know my salary checks come from his office?!" She laughs.

"Nah, he's no fun." Actually, Jean-Albert's heaps of fun; I just can't fathom that double date. Isabel might drink too much and beg him for her own company or something. "Actually, I'm moving too. A small apartment on rue Faubourg St. Honoré. And since I'm starting afresh, I thought maybe you'd want some of my furniture. You always said you loved the armoire. It's yours!"

"Really? That's terrific of you! Rue Faubourg St. Honoré, eh? How pricey is the new place? I mean, that's a splashy address." Of course she knows Jean-Albert's the source of the new digs, and is slyly making me acknowledge it.

"It's a bit more for sure, but I am sick of living with the memories of Laurent here." An answer which is both evasive and contains fragments of the truth. (Very French answer, actually. Damn, this culture is overtaking me.)

"Still miss him, Alexandra? I saw him last weekend. He's alone. Asked about you."

"Well, the anger has abated a little, but I'm glad to know he's alone again. If he meets someone, I don't want to know. I saw him with a woman a few months ago and it was devastating. Did you tell him about me and Jean-Albert?" I say, half hoping she had and half not.

"He saw the photo of you two in *Le Figaro*, like everyone did. He said he blew it with you, and he regrets it." (I hear a muffled "Izz?'" as a voice in the distance calls for Isabel.) "Listen, Nicolas and I are going into a design meeting—I have to go. Let's chat *demain* about dinner, and again thanks for the furniture offer . . . hey, and I miss you. *À bientôt*." And she clicks off.

Semi-dazed, I can't seem to put down the phone; my mind swims. I think, "So, Laurent knows he 'blew it' . . . and he 'regrets it'? Good, because I still want to pummel him with my bare hands. Never have I suffered so much for any man. I was so sure of our love, and he just ran away and ripped my world out from under me." Funny, isn't it? How just when you think, "My life is perfect, I'm in

love! I can *finally* let down all my protective shields and trust this
fabulous man," you get fucked. Not fucked *literally*, of course; that
was why you were so happy to begin with. The other "fucked." The
one that involves less screaming in pleasure and more screaming in
anger. Oh, enough about him! I have my plate full with men who
adore me . . . Or so they say.

I leaned against the windowpane and looked out into spring's
rays of sunshine for an answer. What to do next? For distraction, I
set about editing what to take to the new apartment and what to
leave for Isabel. Amazingly, after only an hour's time, I have only
piled the new clothes, recent gifts, and all my books—I would never
part with my books—in a corner for the movers. I leave behind all
the furniture, the sorry collection of cheap dishes from Ikea that
Laurent and I bought when we were to move in together . . . Hell
no. I so don't need any reminders of him anymore.

That done, let's see if Frédéric read my e-mail.

"You've got mail!" I hear in that cheesy voice. Cool. Something
from my mother. I'll read that later when I can figure out how to
tell them I'm moving. And junk e-mails from Eurostar and Promo-
vacance. Funny, I don't see myself getting in line for their cheap
flights to Tunisia anymore. And, *enfin!*

No way.

Frédéric.

Open file.

Chère Wild Filly,

Hélas, I am terribly distraught to have to report that I am obliged
to host a dinner at the embassy *ce soir*. You could extinguish this
agony of not being able to see you with a single word. If you would
extend the invitation by a single evening, you need only to respond *"oui."*

For, if you grant me a rendezvous *mercredi soir*, I will sweep
you away for a magical evening of endlessly paying tribute to
every delicious centimeter of your exquisite naked form. To strip
you tenderly of your clothes, lay you gently on the bed, and simply

devour you with my eyes . . . to watch you fall asleep, to match the
pace of your breaths with my own, until the first rays of sunlight
slip through the drawn curtains, waking you softly. . . . Mmm, I
think that it would be incredibly sexy to awaken alongside you, to
drink in the fragrances of your warm perfumed skin, to trail my
finger over the gentle curve of your breasts, awakening your desire
so passionately that you find yourself soothingly caressing yourself, your hands traveling all over your creamy flesh, in turn
stroking and delving deeply . . . to allow me to observe the beauty
of you profoundly lost in the act of self-pleasure. Consummate
with the raw pleasure of slipping inside you, penetrating your
body and spirit. I imagine there is nothing more intoxicating than
to watch ecstasy shudder through your body and emerge through
your eyes, pass over your features. Dreaming of this moment . . .
on the edge of my seat awaiting your allowing me this . . . to become a beautiful reality. Soft kisses all over.

Yours . . . in every sense,

Frédéric

Wow. Oh, wow. Give me a minute here to get my wits. Mother of
God, that's sexy beyond comprehension. Class, we have a new winner in the writing contest. Quite a provocative first correspondence,
for damn sure. Phew. *Ooh la-la.* If I were a man, I would need
about, oh, about a hundred cold showers to chill down to anything
remotely resembling a state of normality right now. My *chaton* is
purring like one contented little kitten.

Damn, I love Frenchmen. OK, that's definitely going in the
Saved Messages.

And for once in my life, I am utterly powerless to play any mind
games. This man has suddenly fulfilled what I had truly believed
was just an unattainable sexual fantasy.

Yes, indeed. He will get his wish. I hit "Reply" and type one
word: "Oui."

Come on, can you blame me?

Je pense que non.

NOTABLE OBSERVATION UNIQUE
TO LIFE AS A COURTESAN

You notice that more often than not, you're making love to Chopin's *Nocturne* with a Dyptique Figue burning bedside. Gone are the CDs by Massive Attack and Moby and incense bought on the street. And I can't tell you how many times I've heard Césaria Évora as a distant soundtrack during a blow job. It's almost become an uncontrollable Pavlovian reaction: I hear "Sodade" and find myself falling to my knees!

CHAPITRE DOUZE

Imperiously he leaps, he neighs, he bounds,
And now his woven girths he breaks asunder;
The bearing earth with his hard hoof he wounds,
Whose hollow womb resounds like heaven's thunder;
The iron bit he crusheth between his teeth,
Controlling what he was controlled with.

—*VENUS AND ADONIS*, WILLIAM SHAKESPEARE

Had that little dinner with Isabel. Didn't go quite as smoothly as I hoped. Not by a long shot. Thought treating her and the new man, Mathieu, to a gourmand dinner at the fabulously elegant Le Grand Véfour would have slid in right next to the free furniture acquisition in my "Alexandra's a fabulous friend file." But nope, reverse effect. *On both ends.*

I guess in retrospect I should've anticipated that because my life had changed so much there'd be a few gaps in our banter and references, but I haven't much time these days to anticipate this kind of potential glitch. I am a smidge too busy juggling studying the wines of the Loire, reading a biography of Madame de Staël (a highly fascinating woman—love this quote of hers: "The pleasures of the mind are made to calm the tempests of the soul." Genius!), and would you believe . . . going to art auctions with Jean-Albert to help him choose pieces for his collection—he's thinking of opening a museum. (Can't say I had had many boyfriends in my life before who were "thinking of opening a museum.") And let me just say, it feels more than a little absurd to have not even finished my art history thesis and be whispering, "*Absolument, bébé*, you must bid ten million euros on that Anish Kapoor painting. Sure, many would do so simply because it's a wise investment, but I totally agree with you, one should never buy anything one isn't mad for, and I find it a compelling piece loaded with passion and assuredness." Go ahead and laugh, because we all know I have zip-a-doo authority in contemporary art, and only meagerly more in French paintings, but how could I *not* play along? My life as a courtesan is just an endlessly amusing escape to live out my wildest fantasies and have the most extravagant experiences. Which is partly why I thought it would be so fun to share dining at this famous restaurant with Isabel and her man. I chose this restaurant partly because it is one of the finest in Paris and partly because it's virtually impossible to get a reservation unless you're Jacques Chirac or Johnny Hallyday. Who is Johnny Hallyday, you ask? A geezer old rocker, France's version of Elvis, strangely worshipped despite his heinous addiction to plastic surgery and a voice that sounds like someone's stepping on a ferret.

Anyway, I thought Le Grand Véfour was a divine, if slightly self-ish, choice, as it has always held some special power in my dreams and fantasies of Paris. I had read about it years ago in guide books and magazines, before I even moved here. Drooling over the photos of the exquisite nineteenth-century gilded jewel-box interior, with its every crystal chandelier and handpainted panel so perfectly preserved that I was sure it would feel exactly like stepping back into La Belle Époque era. *And it is!* And the menu: chef Guy Martin's Michelin star (and yes, it does take years to mentally grasp that a *tire company* somehow became the most revered reviewer of fine cuisine), French haute couture fare, if you will, at its most delicate, masterfully presented and delectable.

Since the day I arrived in Paris, schlepping about as an au pair on a strict budget, and with the criminally inelegant wardrobe to prove it, at least once a week I made the pilgrimage to walk through the Palais Royal, dreamily strolling through the regal arched arcades, under the leafy canopies of the long *allées* of trees, just to peek through the window of the famous Grand Véfour. Always pining and hoping that at least once in my life I could go there even if just for the prix fixe *déjeuner,* which seemed a bargain at 78 euros (*sans* alcohol, and like that's any fun). Heaven forbid the luxurious idea of actually feasting on the chef-tasting *menu plaisir* of 256 euros or . . . God, who could ever go à la carte with an *entrée* (remember, that's a starter here in France), coming in at 74 euros for a few tiny frogs' legs, and as a *plat,* the Prince Rainier III pigeon for 88 euros?! Such must be the meals of kings . . .

So you can imagine how incredibly elated I was when Jean-Albert casually asked one night, "Dinner at Véfour *ce soir?*" Let's see, that would be a *yes,* and I will need a new pair of underpants; I've just wet these. Hell, had someone—even Quasimodo himself—invited me to a dinner like that in my poverty student life I would've shown up with bells on. (Get the subtle "bell" joke?)

Back to the Isabel soirée at Véfour. I can offer you a possibly helpful bit of advice based on what I learned that night: One always thinks after attaining any marked success that one can just slip back into the familiar, and I'd wager that turns out to not be the case about 99 percent of the time. So when friends say, "Remember me when you're rich and famous," and you think, "How absurd, of course we will still be soul sisters," *think again.* The brutal truth is, it's more like "Yes I remember you, but what the hell do we have in common now?" Not insurmountable if one can keep in mind to curb the glamorous stories and button up your lips about your latest acquisition (in short, go back to your shared habitual haunts and keep things "real"), but like a dope I didn't understand this that night. And though I know I may sound all hifalutin saying all this—I mean it's not like I'm Bill Gates going back to his high school reunion or something—it seemed the gap between our daily lives spread before us, and neither Isabel nor I could quite navigate our way back to our former seamless connection and intimacy.

You decide just how wrong this dinner of old girlfriends went . . .

From the moment I was dropped at the restaurant by Jean-Albert's driver, just as Mathieu and Isabel were walking over from the *métro*, the night was off to a rocky start. One of Paris's famous out-of-nowhere downpours had recently started to fall, and Isabel and Mathieu had clearly been attempting to stay dry by dashing from one covered awning to another, with no great success, just as my car pulled up on the narrow street to the left of Le Grand Véfour.

Like precision clockwork, the driver steps out into the rain, clicks open a large cane-handle black umbrella above my open door of the black Mercedes as the shivering, drenched duo Mathieu and Isabel huddle together observing my every move. The chauffeur, with his gallant and experienced skill, ensures that not so much as a drop of rain pelts my suede eyelet trim jacket, and that I have only to make five escorted steps to the front door, whereby the maître d'hôtel spots me and gestures to an underling to graciously open the doors at once. Hard to be like, "Hey guys . . . how the hell are ya?" after an entrance like that. And yet, that's exactly what I did say! Their surprised expressions and stunted replies spoke volumes. Pretty much saying, "It seems Alexandra's newfound pretentiousness has instantly thrown off the balance and set the tone for the whole damn dinner to awkward." *Et voilà*.

Not great, right? After Mathieu and I were introduced, we were ensconced at my favorite table (to the far right corner, commanding a view of the gardens of the Palais Royal lit by the gas sconces) I make another stab at reestablishing our old rapport.

"Hey, Isabel . . . I got a chance to chat up Nicolas (Ghesquiere, head designer at Balmain, where she works) at a dinner party the other night. Man, he's brilliant, and I really dug the way he speaks so quietly and purposefully. It's so soothing and engaging, don't you think?" I say over the menu.

"You think? Actually, he doesn't speak to me much. Sort of places himself in an ivory tower and sees the staff as worker bees. But I did get a chance to see Sophie Marceau up close the other day, she came in for a fitting for the Cannes film festival, and we were all falling over ourselves at how lovely she is. She autographed the drawing I did of the dress we did for her. God, it would be totally cool if she wears it. At least, I hope she will, she's had another made for her by Lacroix. Cross your fingers she opts for the Balmain, so I will be able to clip pics from *Figaro* of her in it."

"Yeah, I met Sophie at an auction at Christie's—love her to pieces! She's a pal of Jean-Albert's, so she sat next to us, and amazingly we both ended up bidding on the same Giacometti lamp. Waiting for our piece to come up for bid, we started whispering to each other; she had all these wild stories of who the other bidders were and what they did. She told me about this one older woman, 'You know, that old fossil of a woman . . . over there in the fraying beret? She's the last descendant of Balzac. She can't give it up, going so far as to try to look and dress like the famous dead writer himself. She's so living in a different era, I bet she hasn't even a clue we're bidding in euros, not francs. And the old man who has just placed his hand on her knee, he may look all innocent, prim and respectable, but he owns almost all of those back room gay porn palaces in Pigalle! Rumor has it he likes to sleep in chains and collects anything that was owned by the Marquis de Sade.' Isn't that amazing? Damn, Sophie's just a riot, don't you think? I swear I spent the whole time busting a gut. Hey, if you want, I could call her and ever so subtly help push for her to wear *your gown*."

I know, I *know*. That recap of meeting Sophie didn't come off as casually as I'd hoped. Then the sommelier arrived, and assuming Mathieu was proficient at selecting a wine, asked him whether he had made his selection. The poor boy looked like someone had just demanded the secret code to deactivate a global nuclear war. "Terrified" would be a fair summary. So Mathieu nervously hands me the *carte de vin*, accidently sweeping it over the flickering flame of the candle and managing to set the wine list aflame. Both he and

Isabel blushed purple as the waiter doused the flaming papers in an ice bucket. I tried to make light of it: "Next time I need a light for my cigarette, I know who to ask!"

Such a deafening silence fell upon us, I swear I could hear myself blink. Tough crowd.

So I focused on the wine list, choosing a '95 Château Poujeaux Cru Bourgeois Moulis for the table, and we continued with the awkward fest.

Mathieu *did* try: "Isabel tells me that despite your Midwestern American upbringing, you're dating some French big shot, but she won't tell me who. So will you cough up his secret identity?" he asked, with a sweet, timid smile.

"Secret? Geez, he's the furthest thing from a secret. I swear, I am getting a little sick of seeing his face everywhere, he's so omnipresent even in his physical absence! You really don't know? Make a guess," I say, thinking this might be fun. *Might*.

"Okay, is he famous famous, wealthy, or powerful in business?" he asks, as the *amuse-bouche* arrives.

"Ah . . . all the above," I answer, thinking it's a little weird that they haven't even commented on the stunning interior.

"Does he work in big business, fashion, or the arts?" Mathieu asks, playing along.

"All the above . . . OK, maybe I should give you a clue. He signs *both* of your paychecks. Not literally, but in the bigger sense," I throw out, while approving the *vin* and trying to choose from the gorgeous array of breads being offered. Olive *petit pain*, sesame rolls, and chewy triangles sprinkled with *poivrons*. No chance they'd just leave the whole tray if I asked nice? Just once I'd like to eat myself silly on fabulous bread.

"*Pas vrai?* Jean-Albert? Are you serious? Isn't he almost *soixante ans* and married?" Mathieu's face suddenly switches from impressed to shocked.

"Well, yes, that would be a *oui* on all three," I say, thinking, "C'mon, it's pretty trippy but *in a cool way*, unless Mathieu is moral boy."

"Oh, I see." He wraps up his foray into conversation. *Is this French boy judging me?*

Isabel excuses herself and goes to the ladies' room. Mathieu immediately leans in and explains, "Hey, I am entirely *not* judging you. I have just heard Isabel go on and on about this new man in your life, and how it's just shot you to the pinnacle of the world in which she aspires to be recognized, and I think she's pretty jealous, so I don't want to make a big production in front of her, but I really did want to know who it was . . . And I seriously don't care if he's married or older; I'm just trying to make Isabel feel better. *Putain*, that's a serious catch, Alexandra. Bravo! You're with the man all French boys want to be one day and all French women would kill to be with!" he adds, raising an eyebrow approvingly.

"I assure you, Mathieu, it wasn't my master plan. In fact, never would've met him if Isabel hadn't invited me to one of Balmain's fashion shows. Let's shush, Isabel's coming back. Hey, think she'll get over it?" I whisper, glad to see Mathieu's a sweetie after all.

"Give her time. Isabel adores you. I'm sure she's just *verte* with envy at the moment."

But Isabel has barely sat down before there is more colliding of worlds.

"So, Alexandra, are you still game to make our annual retreat to Hossegor to see the surf championships in August? So far it's eight of us; I gotta book that campsite soon."

"Ah, umm, *merde*, I think I'm supposed to go with Jean-Albert that week to Venice for the Biennale . . . really sorry. I will definitely go next year; it's just that I think it would be good for my art-world connections to go. You understand, right?" *Camping in hot tents with unbathed friends for a week versus a suite at the Gritti Hôtel on the Grand Canal and fresh Bellinis at Harry's? You have to see my point here!*

"Sure. I get it," Isabel replies curtly, inelegantly hacking into her ninety-one-euro *turbot meunière avec shitakes, jus parfumé au raifort* as though it were a slice of pizza. *Never realized before her table manners were not very refined. Oh, for God's sakes, it's not like I'm* marrying her. All this courtesan stuff has given me such a ruthless eye for anything less than sheer perfection. And Jean-Albert, for all his billions, still blathers with a mouth full over dinner. It totally repulses me and makes me lose my appetite; don't think I haven't been so annoyed as to want to stab him with a butter knife! Regardless, I'd better give Isabel a break; she's a good egg.

"How about we go to the newly redone Guerlain spa Saturday and make it a girls' spa day?" I ask, feeling like I'm extending an olive branch.

"Are you nuts?! I *so* couldn't afford it." She cuts me dead. "Anyway, I have to work . . . like every Saturday lately."

"Sunday then . . . my treat, it will be great. After all that work, you completely need to de-stress and be pampered, *n'est-ce pas?*" I ask, nodding to the waiter for another bottle of wine.

"Sunday is the only day I have to go to the market, do laundry, clean my apartment . . . *pas possible*. But thanks," Isabel adds, without so much as a hint of a smile. Alright, so maybe she's not such a good egg–good sport these days. Mathieu snuck me a grimace of understanding, and Isabel caught him looking at me and glared at us both.

O-K! That went about as well as Hitler arriving at the gates of heaven.

Topping off the night, both Isabel and Mathieu clearly ended up feeling weirdly uncomfortable by the fact that I just signed my name for *l'addition* and, in truth, it probably emasculated Mathieu.

I get it. Loud and clear. I sure as hell need to hold my tongue in the future, about the people I'm meeting, the grandness of what I am doing, etc. Eeks. Clearly a reality gap has opened up between us, and there seems no easy bridge. It's just unfair and bee-zarre, because as I have said, I bloody well know it's not like I have done anything noteworthy to deserve all this nonsense—well, maybe the recent trick of making Jean-Albert come by just stroking him with feathers was rather notable!—I was just in the right place at the right time and chose to go for it. Almost any woman could have this lifestyle . . . *Sets your thoughts awanderin', doesn't it?*

I walked away from Le Grand Vefour sad that there was a growing distance between us. And also thinking of how sweet and pure
Mathieu's and Isabel's love is. Mathieu had been just charming—
doting and adoring to her, and gorgeous in that *young* way . . . You
know, the boyish smile, the energetic naïve ambition and untainted
idealism about life and love. After I came home to my new, fabulous apartment, I stretched out on my new bed, gazed out at Montmartre, and let my thoughts untangle.

"I'm alone. Yes, it's beautiful here . . . a dream come true in so
many ways. Intoxicatingly exciting, but . . . I don't know. The idea of
Isabel and Mathieu now getting ready for bed, joking and standing
next to each other in *their* bathroom, brushing their teeth, spitting in
turns—strangely domestic acts like that are such unadulterated happiness. *Unadulterated?* Hrmph! There's a word that's not too applicable to my life these days."

My thoughts wander all over the map. I make every attempt to
cast off the recent memory of the rather twisted sexual adventure
of playing nude blind man's bluff with Jean-Albert the last time he
was here. Amusingly, I do have a little snapshot memento slyly
taken with my cell phone while Jean-Albert was fumbling about
stark naked. He'd die if he knew it's the image that now appears
when he rings me. If he ever really fucks me over, I suppose I
could sell it to the press. I'm *kidding*. Not to mention, in France,
can you believe, a cavorting naked shot would probably only *help*
his image!

Am I jealous of the "real couple" Mathieu and Isabel are? Was I
showing off to them because I was jealous? I desperately seek reassurance of my own good fortunes. Lying in bed, hands behind my
head, I began to compile a mental list of all the thrilling and life-
changing events of my new life, making a conscious effort to savor
the new luxuries, to wallow in my new magnificent butter-soft Frette
duvet (at a ghastly four thousand euros for the whole shebang), the
soothing fragrance of a bouquet of pale peonies bedside, a closet
bursting with couture, an apartment teeming with newly acquired

antiques. Better than counting sheep! I eventually exhausted myself into a certain peace and drifted off to sleep.

*Y*eah, yeah, yeah, enough of the 'poor me' crap," you're saying. So what about that rendezvous with Frédéric last *mercredi soir?*'

Well. It wasn't quite the ball out of the park experience I had hoped for. For all his erotic romantic writing skills, and my ravenous desire for him, Frédéric turned out to have his lazy shortcomings. Literally, if you get my gist. Sticking with the self-imposed rule of keeping any dalliance with Frédéric away from *chez moi*, I agreed to meet him at the gloriously masculine Hôtel Raphael. I know, I know, Marie-Hélène distinctly said, "No hotels." And it turns out that she was right on the money!

We arranged to meet at 8:00 P.M. Actually, the power-control hound that he is, Frédéric said, "Arrive at eight sharp, all will be taken care of, my wild filly."

My fantasies ran wild; the thrill of seeing him *swelled* as I was getting ready for the appointed hour. A bit of a warning, girls: The pleasure one takes in getting dressed for a date should never outweigh the pleasure one takes in getting *undressed* for a date.

Two pre-rendezvous glasses of Champagne and the marvelous playing dress-up routine was hard to top for any but the *hardest* of men. I have a feeling you are starting to grasp Frédéric's weakness. Oh, I'm just being evil rude to snipe about his less than performance-ready state! But as all women know, it's a crushing blow to find oneself on a first date, facing a long task—"long" may be a poor choice of words—make that an *arduous* task of battling a flag at half mast.

Having verged on excited delirium in the taxi on the way there, I was ill prepared for anything but the most sensual of seductions. Ever so slightly tipsy, clad in a virginal Chloe strapless white eyelet dress and a pair of come-hither pale blue suede mules by Roger

Vivier, I was betting on a killer night. And yes, the juxtaposition of wearing a virginal dress and fuck-me-hard heels pleased me very much. Trust me, it's very French: allowing yourself to parlay your mood as you so choose; not adhering to anything but your own agenda, which you can let others decode. Useful approach, *non?*

Handing the nine euros to the taxi driver, I felt a tremor of "What am I doing? Kind of feel like I'm cheating on Jean-Albert. An absurd notion; he's married. *Let it go.* That seems to quickly be turning into my modus operandi. How scary is that?! All justifications and worries were swept away by the immediate arrival of a large man in a dark suit following close on my heels as I made my way into the hotel.

"Mademoiselle Fee-leey?" says the huge creature, sporting a discreet earphone and indiscreet black sunglasses, as he strides up alongside me.

"Pardon?" I reply, a bit taken aback. Instantly, I'm thinking, God, don't let Frédéric see this oaf with me or he may have second thoughts about my worthiness.

Then it hit me. "Fee-leey." Filly. *Wild Filly.* Oh, Christ. Part of me thought it was hysterically funny, just as much as a part of me thought, "Seriously, is this all a new low?"

"*Ah, um, oui. Je suis* Mademoiselle Filly," I choked out. Well, at least it's not Mademoiselle Bareback. Hey, this was one tough mo-ment. It was hard not to feel like a call-girl. Really, only the chic am-biance and knowing who I was there to meet kept it all one small step above feeling like I was going to answer to the name "Peaches N. Cream" or "Donna Matrix."

Luckily, the huge creature simply said, "Monsieur awaits you in suite 635 . . . *Bonne soirée*, Mademoiselle." And with that he was gone.

"*Merci*, Monsieur," I said to his receding back, and continued in my intended general direction. Not ever having been to the Hôtel Raphael before, what followed was a theoretically confident stride toward anything resembling a landing strip for me to crash, pause, and catch my breath. As luck would have it—and someone with a well-tuned sense of direction had obviously designed the hotel with this in mind—I landed in the bar.

Assuming that belting a huge nervous, "Ahhh!" out loud was not exactly apropos, I opted for another glass of Champagne instead. I inelegantly "slammed" it, as we'd say in the Midwest, and I charged it to *chambre* 635. Hey, all is fair in love and war, and while frankly, this night is neither, to be sure, tonight we "have a round-trip ticket to debauchery" and I'm *so* not putting this on Jean-Albert's *carte de crédit*.

Yep, Frédéric's going to have to pony up a credit card soon, if you don't mind my sticking with the horse metaphor!

I galloped. (Okay, kill the horseshit. Oh, but it's so fun, I may corral a few more jokes out of it, bare with me!) I made my way up to the *sixième étage,* and after a wrong turn found myself finally in front of the door to *chambre* 635. I counted myself fortunate that the huge lurking creature with the dark glasses wasn't now guarding the door, and took a second to fix my lipstick, inhale deeply, and knock gently three times.

"*Entrée!*" echoed through the door, in that voice of sex dipped in cognac.

The room was dark, save for the flickering light of a few dozen votive candles placed throughout. Nice touch. Definitely preconceived. I loved it that such a busy man had made a real effort.

My eyes took in the enormous canopied mahogany bed to the left, varnished to a gleaming dark caramel brown, a lot of unnecessary bureaus and armchairs, and a commanding figure standing in the center of the room.

Said figure in the center of the room was, of course, Frédéric—*buck naked!*—wearin' nothin' but his wedding ring. So French, I had to stifle an explosion of giggles!

(A side note: Keeping in mind that I had not had *that* much sexual experience before I lived in France, I still do have to point out that Frenchmen have no inhibitions or shyness in exhibiting their manhood in, shall we say, its boyhood. I bet Napoleon marched into battle flaccid and blowing in the wind. In fact, I'd absolutely wager my ring on it! But back to this millennium's French political naked *homme.*)

Frédéric's expression, poised as he was au naturel, was haughty, condescending, and with an undefinable air of a high dignitary. Well, well, well. It felt as though I'd arrived at a conference of political intrigue where he'd come to the table, thrown down a badly worded treaty, and said, in no uncertain terms, "Take it or leave it." (Not your average first date, in other words.)

"*Bonsoir*, Alexandra, you are a feast for the eyes," he said ceremoniously.

I edited out my first retort of, "Why, thanks—you're hung like a chipmunk!" and blurted out a slighty less offensive "*Bonsoir*, Frédéric . . . You sure cut to the chase, don't you?"

"*Oui*, and I took the liberty of bringing all that you requested," he says, turning around to get something from a huge Hermès box on the dresser.

Oh please, don't turn around, dude. You have a nice body . . . *really* great legs. But sometimes, I have to say, when seeing these older men naked I get flashbacks that remind me of my childhood friends' dads and stuff. It's all got to be in the right context with older men or one can lose one's desire in the blink of an eye. Turned out I was blinking a lot here.

I resist just dropping my purse—from the shock of him already stripped to just the ring—and place it on the bed to approach naked man stage right, more out of curiosity at this moment than desire. He continues chatting away.

"As per your command, one well-polished Hermès riding saddle," he intones, as though the press were all there taking notes. Wait a minute. *Is* the press here?! Head check! All clear. Phew.

Taking the heavy—albeit amazingly beautifully crafted saddle—in my arms, I realize that I am kind of a novice in horse-oriented sex, and am not really sure how to properly address said object. Though I am *quite* sure I am not throwing this on *my* back. Well, *pretty* sure. *Très* Helmut Newton or not, I'm the one doing the riding, and nobody's gonna yell "Giddy up" if I'm getting naked. Addendum: unless it's me, okay?

Frédéric resumes the presentation, "And one very small bridle . . . it's the smallest they had in stock, certainly one can be had *sur command* (by special order), but that would take some time."

Alright, I am so not even taking the bridle in my hands. Surely that would be some heinous "no turning back" moment in my life. One day I *do* hope to hold an *enfant*, and if that bridle thing so much as brushed my palms, I could never look at these hands as pure and decent enough . . . Not to mention that the bridle's *really* too big. And it's true, a *couture* bridle would have really rocked.

"And I did run with your idea, my creative *jeune fille*, and I brought you a lasso, a riding crop, and a small whip," Frédéric says, as he pulls each item out of its trademark pumpkin-orange velvet bag. Okay, when you are, say, a twenty-five-year-old woman and you find yourself on the receiving end of leather horse whips *twice* in one month from older wealthy men, there's no more kidding yourself: You are a courtesan, a mistress—one rather naughty girl. Definitely a head trip and not for the weak of constitution. In moments like this, one must be unflappable and at the ready to play along.

"Lovely . . . looks like you've cleaned out Hermès. Still, I'm rather disappointed you forgot chaps and spurs—and really, no oats? No feed bag? I'm kidding, darling. Well done! Frédéric, you really missed your calling, *chéri*. You would have made an *excellent* stable boy."

And predictably, the mere mention of a role for him to assume has him dragging all the Hermès accessories to the canopied bed. *Sooo* predictable. Strangely, the strong scent of saddle soap and money has a small effect on my desire. Not to mention, if I can manage to keep all this stain-free, I will have a pretty credit balance to play with at Hermès, when I return all this nonsense tomorrow.

I did my darnedest to steer clear of the leather goods. Honestly. I only *really* employed the lasso and the whip. Frighteningly, they *seemed* harmless next to the bridle-and-saddle combo. After Frédéric had stripped off my pristine white dress—"Yes, lay that out of harm's way, if you would, Monsieur"—I stepped back into my seducer mode, as he clearly wrote a persuasive but utterly inaccurate tale of all the romantic and sensual acts he'd lavish on me given the granted wish of seeing me. *Yeah, yeah.* Talk about the old bait and switch!

At the starting block I was a bit annoyed to see Frédéric seemed shockingly passive, just lying there like an inanimate totem pole, arms at his sides, waiting for me to do everything. It felt like I was playing tennis alone against a backboard for a while there. Then I remembered, "Ah yes, these men are all talk, but when it comes down to it, they want to be taken care of." One brazen sexually demanding bitch called to duty.

"So you want to fuck me, cowboy?' I bark, straddling him naked, one arm behind me holding his sex firmly in my hand.

"Oh God, yes, I do!' he explodes, pulling me down to take my right nipple in his mouth.

"Well, you've got one ticket to ride, baby," I whisper, as I run my tongue over his upper lip. Mmm, love that lip. So full and beautifully curved, I think I could come just sucking it.

Grabbing a fistful of his hair, I yank back his head and kiss that mouth I have pined to taste. Our warm, wet tongues tease and taunt each other, biting and sucking lower lips with wild intensity. With one hand behind me still caressing him, I push his head back, running my tongue along his strong neck to his collarbones. Soft nibbles with teeth pressing against his flesh as I climb to his shoulder. There I bite hard and viciously. He groans in pain mixed with pleasure. (Take note: Really. Men go wild at this!)

"C'est bon . . . J'adore ça!" he says, starting to writhe beneath me.

Convincing and yet, for all my efforts, I can feel he's totally flaccid. Not a pulsating, throbbing cock in the room. (And trust me, had there been a hard cock in the room, I would've headed there, as nothing makes me crazier than to watch a man with a steel hard-on, on the verge of losing all control.)

"I want to lick you, take you in my mouth," he bellows, trying to move his head down between my thighs.

"Wait! As I demanded from the start, you must act with blind obedience."

(Just saying it made me think, "Damn. Pity he didn't bring horse blinders . . . that might've been somethin' to rouse this boy.")

"I'm entirely yours . . . Do as you wish." (Like I didn't know that already, buddy.)

I swivel around, facing away from him, and thrust my *chaton* mere inches from his face as I slowly take his sex in my mouth. Running my wet lips in progressively increasing strokes over the shaft of his sex, simultaneously running my tongue in wickedly taunting flicks from the base over every pronounced vein . . . to the head . . . taking his balls gently in my mouth as I let one and then two fingers explore his ass . . . Sitting astride him naked, my entire face buried in his lap, gyrating my hips in rhythmic beats . . . caressing his cock with my breasts and licking every inch of this man. I even slap his cock against my face . . . Ooh la-la.

Nothin'. Zip. No hard-on whatsoever. Hey, that's my best work. What's the problem, mister?! After a good hour of focused oral attentions, I discover I am now one very randy beast, all my juices are flowing, and he's attempting to sit up, his hands still on my hips, semidazed.

"*My God, what have I done?! Vraiment désolé,* in all the excitement of preparing to see you, I foolishly forgot to take one of my magic blue pills. I'm so sorry . . . am so stressed, it's a necessity," Frédéric announces, bounding from the bed to scavenge a small pill box from his jacket pocket.

Wahh!! Blue pills? Is this possible? I'm not even thirty and I'm fucking—OK, not actually, technically, fucking him yet—a man who takes Viagra?! Despite all my exhausted efforts and frustration level, the likes of which I haven't seen since my math SATs, I somehow manage to keep my libido lingering in the not entirely sexually *dis*interested mode and stick out the wait.

Chalk it up to my youth, but my ability to deal with sexual disappointment hasn't been very impressive in the past. Maybe it's because I hadn't really felt I deserved great sex until now, and I always just dashed away after any less than pleasant experience, feeling it was my fault. That sure as hell isn't the case anymore. If there's one thing I am *very* confident about these days, it's blowing a man's mind in bed. So surely this is a test on some level, and I am committed to see it through. (Listen, kiddo, you can bloody well bet we are both gonna come—if it *kills* me!)

Frédéric popped not one but two blue pills in his eagerness to perform, and came back to the bed with a chilled bottle of Dom Pérignon and two glasses.

Hope he knows what he's doing there. I don't have any experience with anything stronger than aspirin, but doesn't alcohol kinda magnify drug reactions? I opted for trusting him on that, since clearly he's done this before.

So, strangely enough, we passed the downtime (as in downward dick, sounds a bit like a yoga move, doesn't it?) chatting like dear friends. Once he poured the Champagne and we both slipped under the covers and leaned back against the pillows, Frédéric dropped the whole sensual predator act instantly. It was a charming relief. He launched into sweet and profuse apologies, and adopted what for him must be construed as a demeanor of extreme humbleness. Frankly, he couldn't stop talking. It was a true pleasure to see him let down his walls of formality as he literally inched closer and closer to me and opened his heart. Very moving to see his face fall into a childlike wistfulness as he told a touching story of how he was trying to live the life that his father always wished he had pursued, of working at the pinnacle of French politics. He clearly felt an enormous responsibility to live out and honor this dream that his father had had to abandon to raise his family. I let him unravel and simply listened, offering an occasional quiet, soothing comment.

Apparently feeling more relaxed after drinking the lion's share of the Champagne, Frédéric then began to speak of how the incredible pressure of his position is sometimes just unbearable for him, and that he has no one to confide in. He went on and on, about how all his contemporaries are rivals and adversaries—all his university friends are bitterly jealous of his success and achievements, his family resents his frequent absence, etc. As he spoke I felt such compassion for his state of isolation, of how he was envied and had to bear such decisions. To put it succinctly, he's definitely justified in feeling that as a world-renowned politician, his life has got to be endless shit. I reached over and took Frédéric's limp arms and wrapped them around me and just lay with him, holding him close. Given this gift of rare intimacy, very much without judgment or pressure, he grabbed me tightly and squeezed me into him with such desperate force that I thought he might cry. For all his previous boisterous talk, there was just a little boy there in my arms, needing reassurance, someone to listen and to make no demands.

With Frédéric in my arms and his beautiful voice trailing into deep sincerity, I felt attracted to him in a much more cerebral way, on a more connected level. So when the stirrings of the "blue magic" took effect, I was anticipating something more like making love than just fucking. *Mistake.*

The Viagra-Champagne combo definitely kicked Frédéric into something resembling high gear. Meaning: What was once a dead ringer—"dead" being an operative term here—for an abandoned cocktail frank left overnight after a party now revived to a short, hard stack of nickels. (Too mean of me? Hey, I'm just givin' the facts!) Still, I was charmed that he had been speaking so freely and trusting me with his personal stories and secrets, so I was more than a little surprised when he assumed a new role as sex fiend from hell.

Discovering he was now up to snuff, Frédéric leaped up, grabbed the lasso and the horse whip, and pleaded with an almost religious fervor: "Tie me up, Alexandra . . . and thrash me. Even if I beg you to stop . . . don't!"

"Thrash me"? Oh dear. Clearly he was one of those men who can't be gentle or sincere during sex because they'd feel too vulnerable, or find it too real. Yep, Frédéric was doing the old switch-a-roo; shedding his previous gentle nature in lieu of "I'm Mister Alter-Ego Crazed Sex Machine." I find that tiresome. Not to mention schizophrenic.

A command performance had been demanded, so I played it out, though I was disheartened to see that sex for him *had* to be about power . . . losing it and yet, in fact, insisting on how it was to be.

Fine, you big loon. I snatched the lasso from his hands and trussed him up like a Christmas goose with an apple in his mouth, and then whipped the dickens out of his hard ass, while he licked me furiously and finally came like a wild man. Mission accomplished.

In truth, it was *kinda* fun. Learning new ways of making a man come had become an interesting project. And oh Christ, seriously seems to have replaced my Ph.D. thesis research. Wonder if I can get a Ph.D. in innovative sexual proficiency? *Très possible*—this is France, for crying out loud!

I agree, it was a far stretch from the promised *lettre d'amour,* but not exactly a total loss. I gained a great deal more knowledge into the inner mental workings of these men, learned a little patience, and oddly enough, felt I had really provided a valuable service to Frédéric . . . *in many respects.*

He was all dreamy, dazed and smiling when I left, and I almost laughed, thinking that his peaceful, agreeable state may very well benefit this damn country. Wouldn't that be something?!

I made way out of the Hôtel Raphael—the large orange Hermès box carted behind me by a bellboy, realizing I was fairly relieved that Frédéric, while being briefly emotionally open, wasn't as adoring or sincere as Jean-Albert.

In fact, Frédéric had asked me almost nothing about myself, and had used me more as a psychiatrist and sex therapist than anything else. Boy, oh, boy, is it ever true: "Everyone seems normal until you get to know them!"

Seriously, as much as I find the sexual aspect of my life these days liberating, and of course the idea that I'm fucking the two most powerful men in France is *quite* amusing, I really do adore Jean-Albert and only want to give *him* happiness. He's so good to me, and he cares about me, who I am, how I feel; the way he looks at me with interest, the questions that he asks me, the rare talent for listening carefully, the optimism he offers with his thoughtful responses. Not to mention—but of course I will—that he works so hard to charm and please me.

As I get out of the taxi, with a giant Hermès box under each arm, I pause under the starlit sky, enjoying the cool night air. Paris. Stuff from Hermès. An apartment in the center of this magical city. Wow! I pause a split second, trying to decipher if I feel very connected to my life or if it seems very surreal. All I know is, it's still all so new, unknown, and thrilling. Well, maybe not *all* thrilling— some of that nonsense with Frédéric was downright bonkers. I guess Marie-Hélène was right: Frédéric is simply lover *numéro deux*: the sexy one who's impossible to get attached to.

As I put the key in my lock at midnight, I was somewhat sorry I hadn't given Jean-Albert a key to come and wait for me.

Then again, reeking of sex and saddle soap, nipples sore from having been bitten all night, and walking like I'd ridden a horse bareback for a month . . . it's probably for the better.

Wild filly? *Indeed.* Bridled? *Absolutely not.*

An impressive stash of Hermès goods to exchange for something I truly desire?

Oh yes . . . *Yee-ha!*

(That's the last horse joke, I promise.)

NOTABLE OBSERVATION UNIQUE TO LIFE AS A COURTESAN

You find that you're no longer impressed by a man saying (which used to be impressive enough), "I'm a successful banker." Now you think, "Yeah, well do you own your *own* bank, or not?" Or your ears perk up when you catch a man saying, "I keep all my yachts in Port Grimaud in St. Tropez off season." Right. *All* your yachts . . . as in *numerous.* Good. And obviously, you do become a bit of an expert on private planes, "Do you have a Gulfstream 550 or a Challenger? Because I really prefer the headroom in a Gulfstream." Gross, isn't it? Come on, I'm just an observer.

HALLELUJAH! . . . YET ANOTHER
COURTESAN SEXUAL TIP

Gonna be technical here for a few moments. And I'm confident you'll stay with me, as what woman in her right mind would see the above and say to herself, "Oh, who cares about mind-blowing orgasms?"

Le G-spot is ground zero, really, so let's get at it, metaphorically and literally!

The facts: As we all know by now, this *plaisir central* is an area approximately the size of a large pearl, located about two thirds the length of your middle finger inside your *chaton*. (Essentially at twelve noon.)

- *Secret:* Pleasure derived from the G-spot is thought to be more intense and more long-lasting for women in their thirties and beyond. Interestingly, at that age, changes in tissue inside *le chaton* allow easier access to the G-spot. Let's hear it for getting older and better!
- *Another Secret:* Women who have delivered a child vaginally are more elastic internally, and the penis is thereby able to stroke the G-spot more easily, resulting in a far more powerful *petite mort* (yes, orgasm translates as "little death" *en français*).

Your lover can stimulate the G-spot with his finger or tongue (a *bisou minou en français*, which literally translates to the "kiss of a tiny kitten." *Mon dieu!*) through the combined pressure of pushing down on the pearl (clitoris) while arcing the tongue *or finger* upward in a beckoning motion. (Come hither indeed. *Faites attention:* The finger or tongue must be approximately one to three inches inside the vagina for this to work.)

The G-spot can also be stimulated more directly during sex with the woman on top. Female-superior position.

Tip: If a woman experiences one *petite mort*, she can usually have many more in one session, as long as stimulation continues. Practice makes this more probable. What good news!

Fact: A penis that curves upward has a natural ability to exert more pressure on the G-spot.

The best positions for G-spot stimulation are rear-entry—man entering from behind (*à quatre pattes en français*—aka, woman on all fours). But if a man's penis curves upward, face-to-face sex may prove just as fabulous.

Try other sexual positions with a man whose penis curves downward: the doggy-style position is ideal for the woman in "polishing your pearl" as the curve works against the front wall.

Tip: Once you're in doggy style, lean farther forward with your head down and arch your back, creating the perfect angle for hitting your G-spot. We really should rename this position the Opera Box in honor of the French courtesans' passion for discreet sex in their opera box balconies. Imagine how enthusiastic the man in your life would become about the opera if you suggested this decadent *soirée*?!

CHAPITRE TREIZE

Wine keeps neither secrets nor promises.
—MIGUEL DE CERVANTES, *DON QUIXOTE*

Vendredi à 13.40

Déjeuner with Marie-Hélène at the legendary Fouquet's on the Champs-Élysées. It's a June afternoon drenched in light. Two courtesans dining *tête à tête* in the choice far right corner, well situated for a perfect view of the departing and arriving men of smart society who religiously dine in this chic enclave that's so regally draped in burgundy and gold.

Consumed: two delicious entrées of *soupe de poissons avec Gruyère et croutons*, two glasses each of Château Haut-Brion '97, followed by *un steak au poivre cuit* (cooked) *à point (pour Madame)* and *un saumon grillé avec citron, cuit: rosé*. One absurdly expensive bottle of Evian on the table, de rigueur and ignored. One basket of sliced baguette, virtually ignored. (Eating too much bread is considered a bit rude to the chef, and a bit for *ploucs*—for peasants.)

Dessert is served: two perfect *crèmes brûlées à la lavande avec des tuiles croustillantes à la violette, un espresso et un café crème,* three cigarettes in ashtray. One burning in hand.

Mood? Marvelous, *merci.*

Conversation in progress:

"I told you, Alexa. I had a hunch Frédéric was a lot of . . . *work!*" Marie-Hélène laughs, as she cracks her silver spoon through the crisp, browned shell of the *crème brûlée.*

"Pfff! That's an understatement. I felt like a one-man band over there. Pah! Pah! Pah! Watch this, people! And how about *this*?! *And* I will attempt this move while also juggling two balls and tootin' his horn!" I giggle, miming the whole scenario.

We both fall into peals of laughter. However, with MH, never so loud as to cause people to stare. That would just not be "grace personified."

"Are you going to keep seeing Frédéric? You know, I really think you should. He has enormous . . ."

I interrupt, "Hey, you can't use the word 'enormous' in *any* respect with Frédéric, unless it's to describe his ego."

"*Oui, je sais,* I was going to say enormous connections, and he is a man of such high esteem, that with both him and Jean-Albert in your thrall, you will have established yourself at a virtually unmatchable level of distinction. You could set yourself off on a glorious path, not unlike the great Anglo-Saxon courtesan Jane Digby in the nineteenth century."

"I'm assuming this is some kind of test, Marie-Hélène? Yes, yes, I read her diaries as per your suggestion. And I have to agree, she had a marvelously decadent life. What was it again? She marries a British cabinet minister, then has an affair with an Austrian prince, then a German baron, a Greek count, then the king of Bavaria, and she ends up marrying an Arab nobleman?" I ask, feeling rather pleased that all the Champagne of the last few months hasn't killed *every* brain cell.

"A *Bedouin* nobleman, to be specific. But well done, Alexa. You would have to agree, given just one life to lead, a woman must make it as adventurous and rich as her wildest dreams."

"You can bet your tiny *derrière* I'm trying! This all reminds me of that line from Rimbaud, 'I myself became a fabulous opera.' I have always loved that idea. Bold self-creation to the heights of one's imagination!" I rattle on, raising my silver spoon triumphantly.

"*Fantastique!* And I also passionately adhere to his line, 'Morality is the softening of the brain,'" she counters.

"Spoken like a *vrai* hedonist, sweetie. But really, all kidding aside, I know. *Frédéric de la Horse Sex* is truly a feather in my cap. Actually, I did enjoy it more in retrospect than I did in the moment. His switching mental gears from 'confessional child' to 'beat me hard—I beg you!' was a little jarring. But, it *is* quite something to get inside the mind of someone like Frédéric. Fascinating. I actually cannot fathom how these men manage the extreme pressure of having to be accountable for so many people's lives and futures," I say, glancing around at all the powerful men in the room: their faces are deeply lined, with tired eyes and, very likely, hardened hearts.

"Dear, it's not for us to worry about. We are their escape, their sanctuary. *Ça suffit pour l'instant.* Where are you headed now, my Alexa?" Marie-Hélène asks as she reaches for her lime-green ostrich-skin wallet.

"I am off to shop at Bonmarché. Now that Chloe Chevalier has bought up every piece of Empire furniture left in France for my flat, I think it's time to get, *oh*, say, a cup, maybe a plate and silverware! This is very weird, you know. To just receive so many material gifts. Don't you ever have that little angel on one shoulder and the little devil on the other and hear them arguing it out?" I ask, watching MH sort through her credit cards, deciding which of her lovers will pay for our long and lovely lunch. Yep, I'd say, this would be as good a time as any to ask that question, *n'est-ce pas?*

"The angel fell off years ago, I think the time I was making love to a *duc* as the *duchesse* watched and did a watercolor of us coupling," she says matter-of-factly. BTW, she always says, "coupling," "amorous adventures," "indiscretions," "making love"—not fucking. Fair enough. As she likes. But you know me, I'm more of a no-holds-barred, call-it-like-you-see-it girl. In other words, American through and through.

Marie-Hélène leaves a thirty-euro tip for the waiter (that's on top of the service charge already included in *l'addition*) and we sweep out of the *resto*, making a grand exit, to the delight of all the ancient men present. Just curious: Do any of you men actually still fuck your wives? Sorry, make that still have "amorous adventures" with your beloved spouses? The odds are on par with that of Donatella Versace embracing the *au naturel* look. Zero!

Marie-Hélène and I exchange a quick double-cheek air kiss at the curb, and she adds her traditional extra peck on the mouth, just to let it be known she's always game. *Noted.* MH *may* get her little wish. I'm starting to get really curious about what she's like in the bedroom. *Ooh la-la.* Can only imagine what tricks she has up her sleeve. And between her legs . . . and with those lithe hips . . . and that mental repertoire of lusciously lurid skills. Oh, don't get me started. One, because in that arena, I am a total amateur, and two, I am not altogether sure I'd ever come back to men. (Did I just say that? Blame it on the *vin* at lunch. *In vino veritas!*)

I nod to one of the taxi drivers waiting on the Champs-Élysées, and he jumps out and opens the door. Hate that with chauffeurs but like it in taxi drivers. Couldn't tell ya why.

We scoot through traffic: down the avenue, over the glittering gold-leafed Pont Alexandre bridge, and through St. Germain. Arriving at Bonmarché, I tip the driver well—after all, he told me I look "the vision of spring itself" in my floaty sundress with a matching buttercream Birkin bag in the crook of my arm. Bet he'd have cardiac arrest if I told him I tied down and *chaton*-whipped the esteemed Minister Frédéric de Fallois to get this ludicrously expensive purse at Hermès. *Oui*, that's probably something *not* to share with the dear old man. Then again, as a world-wise man of Paris, he's probably seen it all—and possibly guessed as much!

Now inside the chicest of Parisian department stores, I immediately employ—as I have recently learned to do for efficiency and excellent service—a trio of salespeople to make a running inventory as I set about knocking out the long list of things I need.

"More of those Frette *reine* (queen) bed linens that are pure heaven." I try not to even look at the price, as it's just ghastly exorbitant. Oh cool, the precise wineglasses that we drank from at that Baccarat dinner; I'd better choose a service of twelve. Thinking of having a dinner party soon. God, what a cast of characters that will be! (Baccarat Empire *verre*: 231 euros each.) Oh, and what the hell, the matching *carafe du vin* (738 euros).

Jean-Albert loves to come for tea—hell, he just loves to come!—so I should absolutely invest in a proper tea set. This will do: adorable with hand-painted pale little birds. (Porcelaine aux Oiseaux collection tea set by Bernardaud: 133 euros a cup. Teapot, *sucrier*, and *lait* pitcher: 860 euros.)

Something to eat off and with . . . that is, when I'm not letting Jean-Albert lick *chocolat noir* off my naked tummy: Hermès's Balcons du Guadalquivir *assiette en porcelaine* (91 euros each) and Puiforcat Guethary silverware (each *fourchette* [fork] 51 euros, each *couteau* [knife] 64 euros) . . . etc.

I add a couple of tall Lalique vases for all of the flower arrangements, a few tablecloths, and a dozen silk napkins, each in muted gold, deep red, and bronze tones—which actually is the color theme of my interior now, inspired by the Gustav Klimt painting *Hygieia*, which I covet! And no, I am not looking to get it—the original—from Jean-Albert. That would be like ten times more expensive than my apartment, and as I've said, I'm not greedy. OK, in truth, we'd looked together at a print of it and *he offered*, but then we discovered the painting was destroyed in a fire in 1945. Tragic loss. For the painting and . . . me. (I'm kidding. Sort of.)

Frankly, as I make my way to the bottom of my dream apartment wish list and have run the staff ragged, I feel like somehow this all should've been more fun. OK, sometimes it *is* kinda weird to have people know you're a courtesan to a zillionaire. And while I'm not embarrassed, I do think it would feel more exciting if I could buy all this with money *I* made. Part of the charm is definitely lost in that the salespeople certainly know my story, my means of acquiring all of this.

One, everyone remotely connected to fashion has caught wind of this *jeune fille américaine*, Mademoiselle Nobody de Nowhere, who has somehow captured the attentions of Monsieur le Zillionaire. It's wacked; people I have never met now address me by name, which I find both unnerving and uncomfortable. And two, no one my age could ever swing dropping 21,050 euros on outfitting their kitchen. Unless it's Paris Hilton, and I'm damn sure her taste doesn't lean toward discreet elegance.

Anywho, I am surprised to find myself strangely not that over-the-top thrilled by this shopping spree. Maybe I will be when I get it all home and unpack. I'd *better* be. I'm far too young to get jaded and "all fancy," as they say back in Elmbrook. Okay, truth be told, I'm a bit lonely. And I haven't wanted to say this, but . . . Even a bottomless credit card isn't fun when you're shopping alone, especially when you have a memory of shopping while young and in love. I had more fun when Laurent and me took his clunky old Renault to that megawarehouse Ikea, just north of Paris.

We kept making a zillion wrong turns and ended up making a hysterical day-long adventure of it. Had ourselves a little cheap-o lunch in the store cafeteria, a couple of tiny bottles each of *vin blanc*, and laughed our tails off as we debated endlessly over a set of twenty-nine-euro sheets. (I won, there was no way I was going to sleep on blue plaid sheets. It's all white or bust for this *jeune femme*.)

Walking home from Bonmarché through the Tuileries, the sky is huge and blue. I am tired and fading. I just can't detach from those memories of Laurent—that day at Ikea we ended up spending, like, a mere 180 euros, split it, and thought ourselves wildly extravagant. We were giddy, setting up a real apartment together! Yeah, well, that never happened. I could just wring his neck. Silly fuckwit. Still not quite over that breakup, I guess. Oh, *screw* him. He didn't have the intelligence to adore me properly. How haughty does that sound? Yikes. I gotta curb my reading of courtesan diaries; I'm getting "too big for my britches," as my grandmother would've said. But you know what? She actually would've loved all this: all my new disciplines, the opulence, and the adventures.

My grandmother was, as my mother used to like to say, "a woman with unself-conscious sexuality who possessed a disregard for the mores of society." In other words, she was racy. Love that. "It must be genetic, I guess," I laugh to myself as my eyes glance

unconsciously over to the *glacier* where this whole gloriously extravagant new life-o-mine began. Man, what a difference six months
can make. Now look at me. Head-to-toe sha-sha: that Hermès Birkin
bag; a taupe Dior chiffon sundress with ruffled hem; Louboutin
slingbacks, and my new La Perla lingerie. What fun! I'm *so* not taking any of this for granted. Nope. I'm one lucky girl—even if a bit
lonesome. I used to get lonely when I had none of this, and one thing
I know, between lonely and poor and lonely and rich, this is better.

Bzzz. Bzzzz. My purse is vibrating. Oh, *merde.* Is it that Japanese vibrating ball shaken into action? And I fumble through my
purse in hot pursuit.

Phone. *Phew.* Would hate that tiny magic sphere's battery to go
to waste without partaking in a final round. Love that little devil!

I check out the caller I.D.: FRÉDÉRIC DE FALLOIS. Cool. Bring it
on, honey. When I push "answer," it instantly hits the mental play-
back of him moaning as he came the last time I saw him. Christ,
what a scene that was!

"*Allô?*" His voice is low, molten gold.

"*Oui, chéri . . . c'est moi,*" I say, in a voice that I *think* sounds sexy.
Could be off-base on that, though. And yes, I agree, "*chéri*" and
"*chérie*" are *so* overused in this language, and really have started to
have all the charm of a day-old baguette.

"*Tout va bien, ma beauté?* I was just taking a pause at work and
was curious what you were up to?" he says. I hear the sound of ri-
fling through papers in the background.

"I'm just taking a promenade in the Tuiluries *maintenant.* It's an
enchanting afternoon. *Et toi?*"

"You are so close. I'm in my office at the Embassy. Would you
care to stop by and see it? I have a little present for you." (Little?
Yeah, I know, buddy. Been there, fucked that. But what the hell? I
am kinda bored.)

I fall silent and let him wait for my answer—I really shouldn't
indulge his spontaneous whims without making him *sweat* and
work. Which, in fact, was exactly what I was doing, the last time I
saw this gorgeous creature.

"Are you free?" he asks, getting impatient.

"Free? No . . . we both know I am *very* expensive!" I joke, realizing I'm smiling.

"Please come now. I beg you," he says, with such intensity that my lower regions virtually burst into flames.

"Hey, that's my line," I kid. *"Mais. D'accord.* I will be there in ten minutes. And Frédéric, don't have one of your minions meet me. You be waiting at the grand entrance yourself, or I shall simply turn on my heel and find amusement elsewhere. *À tout à l'heure."*

I press "end call" before he can argue. Not that he would. By the way, ladies and gentlemen, that was a small-town American girl bossing around a Big Shot French Minister—as though it were the most natural thing in the world for me to do. What am I thinking?

And therein lies part of the charm of being a courtesan: calling the shots. It is about power. Having the ridiculously easy to attain power over powerful men. And since we're in France, that would more or less only be possible via sexual intrigue. *Bien sûr.* So, like a moth to a flame—no, more like a moth to a bonfire, actually—I slink over to the Quai d'Orsay by way of the footbridge over the Seine.

I'm thinking: ha-ha! *This* is the fun part. It's not about getting new exorbitantly expensive sheets and furnishings; it's about knowing I make this man nervous. He's probably frantically shooing people from his office, having calls and meetings postponed, hastily taking another one of his blue magic pills. At least he'd *better* be!

I arrive precisely fifteen minutes late . . . still considered on time by French standards, and actually referred to as the *"cadeau de politesse"*—the gift of politeness. Having touched up my makeup under a tree in the Tuileries, and discreetly spritzed *parfum partout*—and I do mean *partout* (everywhere)—this little sex-kitten-to-go is ready, *come* what may. Nice choice of words, right?

I approach the huge wrought-iron gates with a confident stride, keen to utter, "Monsieur de Fallois is expecting me." But there's no opportunity for that announcement, since the gates open at once and I see Frédéric descending the stairs while two richly uniformed military guards stand flanking the entrance, swords in hand. (Hey, if that hot soldier from Vaux le Vicomte is here, drag him along, and we'll make this a ménage à trois!)

Dammit, again Frédéric looks fucking *Amazing* (with a capital A!), taking the stairs two at a time—eager bastard—clad in a light summer-weight gray wool suit with a white crisp shirt and pale yellow tie—he has to be the hottest man over fifty France has ever produced. *Vive la France*, indeed!

As he waits on the last step, watching me approach, I shake it like a runway model. (Or at least, I'm trying to.)

"Bonjour, ma belle. What a treat to see you in the sunlight. You are lovely," he says, as we do the ubiquitous double-cheek air kiss. "And you smell divine."

"Bonjour, Frédéric. So do you. What fragrance is it that you wear?" I ask, as we enter one of France's most prestigious buildings and breeze through the intense security; Frédéric waves them off with a wave of his hand. Gotta say, it's pretty sexy to see total power wielded with just a gesture.

"Merci, but I wear nothing," he says, leading me through a labyrinth of elegant corridors. Underlings fall into a hush and bend over in small bows as we pass. So chic.

"Yes, as memory serves you do *wear* nothing," I retort, suddenly thinking, "You know what? It is seriously insane that I am even *talking* to this hugely important minister dude. Once again, power *is* like a drug—having the same effect on *me* as those little blue magic pills have on *him*!"

"And this is my *bureau* (office). Please . . . sit wherever you like, and would you care for something to drink, my dear Alexandra?" he asks, as he cleverly closes and locks all three doors that connect to other offices.

"What a gorgeous office, Frédéric!" I practically roar, blown away by his enormous and well-appointed office. Cringing from my own constant lack of editing expressions of awe, I swallow hard and vow to play it cool. Placing my coat on a powder blue chaise, I take refuge in a sumptuous armchair. And offer a somewhat less teenager-y utterance. "And yes, thank you, I will have a . . . Perrier *avec citron*, if you have it?"

But bloody hell, what a killer place to work. The room could very well double as a ballroom if you took out the long, commanding Louis XIV desk: two enormous chandeliers hang from the three-meter-high ceilings; the walnut walls drip with ornate carvings and are edged in pale gold. Elaborate antique Chinese vases line the marble fireplace mantel, and a plethora of overstuffed antique armchairs and couches fill the room. A positively masculine arrangement of tall phallic calla lilies sits in front of each of the five floor-to-ceiling windows, each revealing breathtaking postcard-perfect views of the Seine and the Jardin des Tuileries.

"Perrier? *Vraiment?* No Champagne today? *Viens*, I will have some if you will join me?" he asks, holding up a bottle of Dom Pérignon. (C'mon. Find me anyone who can refuse free top-shelf Champagne? Then again, don't. That's not a person I even want to meet!)

Bottle in hand, Frédéric stands *contrapposto*—the definition of masculine and commanding—in front of one of those drop-dead cool office minibars: all mirrors and sparkling crystal-cut glassware and bottles of liquors. In that devastating suit, it's dashingly chic—*très* James Bond of him. And I suddenly see myself as Miss Moneypenny over here—dull as paperwork. Better shake into something resembling seductive and ditch the Elmbook girl, all stunned and ga-ga impressed.

"Better idea: You pop the cork and pour, and I will start looking for this present you spoke of," I practically purr, moving to his side and sliding my hands in his front pants pockets. Standing behind him, both hands deep within his pockets, I trail warm fingers over his strong thighs and slowly bring them to his crotch, caressing him through the fabric, my thumbs on his sex and my fingers stroking his balls.

Bingo! Jackpot! The man took the magic pill. Now we're talking, mister.

"Is *this* my present? I would be very happy to *receive* it, darling," I whisper, taking him firmly in my hand while leaning over his shoulder and gently biting his earlobe.

Pow! The Champagne cork flies across the room as Champagne explodes all over the floor. We both burst out laughing that he has allowed something so very *déclassé* to occur. Note: Uncorking Champagne is akin to an art form in France and is done quietly and slowly, so that only a whisper of gas escapes from the opened bottle.

"*Mon Dieu! Pardonne-moi.* You're *very* distracting, my Alexandra . . . Here, please take this," he says, ever so sweetly, smiling and handing me a crystal flute. At the same moment, he absent-mindedly drops his and it shatters all over on the beautiful parquet floor, sending crystal shards everywhere, glittering like diamonds. He's a painfully embarrassing 0–3 in the Champagne-serving department now. Ouch to the ego in the great suit.

"Easy, boy . . . Allow me to take over. Come, why don't we leave the mess and you can show me the view?" I laughingly command, as I fill another flute for him, place it in his hand as if it were a grenade, and jokingly wrap both of his hands securely around the stem while holding his gaze in mine.

He lets a sweet smile overtake him, surrendering himself to be disarmed. I throw him a reassuring wink that says, "Trust me, it's all fine, baby," and lead him by the arm toward the far window, where a saffron yellow damask armchair awaits. By the way, all of this may have been the smoothest negotiation process that has ever unfolded in this room!

"Wait . . . I really *do* have something for you," he says, turning back for a moment.

"I have something for you, too—get over here!" And with our eyes locked, I step out of my dress, boldly, hands on hips proud and wearin' nothing but my heels, a sheer lace thong, and a smile. (I'm not even drunk, by the way, except from this intoxicatingly *fun-fuck-me* seduction. *I don't know what he had in mind, but this works for me.*)

"You're awfully brave," he says, somewhat stunned, as he rushes back over. "What would you do if Jacques Chirac came into the room right now?"

"I'm only interested in *your* coming at the moment and I noticed that you locked all the doors," I reply, peeling off his jacket and dropping it to the floor.

Ferociously Frédéric tears off his tie, plows through his shirt buttons, and only gets hampered struggling with his cufflinks.

"I'll do that. Take off those . . . *everything*," I demand, pointing to his shoes. (It so kills the spontaneous desire if I so much as catch a glimpse of a black dress sock on an otherwise naked man. Black socks are the assassins of all passion, you have to admit.)

I take off his cufflinks and toss them by my dress. He fumbles, balancing on one leg, feverishly working at the laces, and scrambling to pull off his socks, as a bead of sweat appears on his brow. What are you, twelve years old, mister? Just take a seat and remember to breathe, boy.

Once *chaussures et chaussettes* are safely off, I push him back onto the armchair and, still in my killer Louboutin slingbacks, place an extended leg out, my heel just to the top of his dark blue boxers. He looks up at me with those panty-melting blue eyes as his hands run wild over my outstretched leg. Passionately succumbing to lust, as only a Frenchman can, he takes my hips in his strong hands, pulls me to him, and thrusts me into his face.

Oh, Jesus Christ. This room, his eyes, that move, his warm breath on my sex, and me—it's all I can do to keep standing. He softly kisses me there again and again . . . my head drops back from the sheer aching of both wanting it *now* and wanting it to last for hours.

"May I?" he asks, resting his chin on my *chaton*, looking up at me through half-closed lids.

"You may." (I have no idea what he's asking, but "yes" is the only answer I can even possibly form in my mouth.)

With raw wild force he takes my delicate underwear in his two hands and tears it violently apart at the center. Wooph! That's a new maneuver. Kinda insane not to just slide them off but, yeah, *damn hot* of him to rip them open like wrapping paper on a Christmas present. Sliding a warm finger inside me, he starts stroking me slowly, with tender gentleness as his eyes watch me. He clearly loves the sight of me melting into pure bliss. Dizzying tides of pleasure overwhelm me, and I literally collapse on his shoulder as he keeps touching me with increasing intensity.

"No . . . no . . . please . . . wait . . . ," I beg, completely on the edge of coming, my nipples hard and swollen.

In what feels like gestures made through water, I pull him up off the chair, fall back into it myself, and yank off his boxers with one hand as I take his sex in my mouth with the other. He instantly moans, his eyelids falling closed as he arches his back, pushing deeper into my mouth. Sucking him in slow, gliding strokes, I watch the expression on his face pass into a state of being utterly, rapturously lost.

Goddamn sexy; I just want to catapult him into such an orgasm he can't help but scream out. There is something so magnificent about watching this perfectly refined icon of authority submit to everything I suggest . . . so, let's *really* go for it, Monsieur. I grab his hands and place them on my shoulders as I slide one of my hands down to the ripped-open threads of my thong. With my vision all blue and hazy, I give a last flick of my tongue to the tip of his hard cock and start luring him and it down between my breasts.

"I'm going to make myself come for you. And I want you to watch," I declare, as I caress his cock in my hand and touch myself with the other. I'm going to slide right out of this chair, I'm so wet. Just hearing me say it brings me an unknown pleasure I can taste. *Literally.* Frédéric's mouth falls open and his eyes grow large, as he watches me with intense fascination. Guiding his hand to his hard cock, I put my hand over his and show him that I want to watch *him*. I struggle to keep my gaze on him as I edge closer and closer and hear his deep moans quicken as he swells in his own hand. A small drop of shimmering come drops from his sex and falls on my nipple. His hand grabs frantically at my breast, spreading the warm moisture as he claws and squeezes it, adding a final white-knuckle painful pinch. I am *gone*. Writhing and twisting in frenzied shudders of ecstasy . . . doubled—*no, tripled*—by the awareness that I absolutely should not and cannot yell out. The sight of me unleashing this exquisite pleasure brings him to a fucking huge orgasm, so overwhelming and deeply forceful, he clearly can't stop himself.

"*C'est bon. C'est bien ça. Ohhhhh . . . Laaa!*" he yells, still caressing himself as he shoots come all over my neck. After a few moments of catching our breaths and letting the blood rush back to emptied brain cells, we look at each other and burst out laughing. In fact, we can't stop laughing together, in waves of surprise and complete, wild satisfaction.

"*Wow!* You *yelled*, cowboy! You know that? Hilarious. I got ya!" I joke, still sitting beneath him.

"*Pas vrai.* I did not," he denies, with such feigned indignation. I just sit and smirk.

"Fine. Right. Whatever you say, *mon capitaine!*" I give a mock salute.

I feel the *eau de Frédéric* quickly drying on my throat. I always did like *comme des garçons,* but this is pushing it!

"Perhaps I did. It was beyond my control," he says, shaking his head. His expression of clearly feeling off balance and puzzled gives way to pride, as he beams in the blue light of dusk. He straightens up, pulls on his blue Façonnable boxers, and heads toward the little bar to retrieve a towel. He warms it under the silver sink's faucet and makes his way back to me while I just wait, bemused and watching.

"Here you are. I thought you might need this to . . . tidy up . . . the . . . that. . . ." His sentence drifts off—there's just not an elegant way to phrase it.

"My 'pearl necklace,' as it were?" I say, dropping the warm towel on my neck and savoring the sensation.

"*Génial!* And that reminds me . . . your *cadeau!*" he says, clapping his hands once and striding toward his desk. Frédéric opens the bottom left drawer and takes out a small black box.

"This seems an entirely redundant gift—but I do hope you like it," he says, placing one hand behind his back, bending at the waist, and handing it to me as a servant would offer a *carte de visite.* Damn nice presentation, boy!

With still shaky *après* orgasm hands, I open the black box imprinted with "Mikimoto" and push up its lid. A beautiful choker of luminescent black pearls rests on white satin; each pearl is as big as a large marble and gorgeously opalescent, even more shimmery than the glimmer of come I notice on my breast.

"Really! *Another* pearl necklace? It's lovely! How funny. I have to say, I like them equally well!" I gush, excitedly taking them from the case and trying them on. My hands can't quite manage the closure. Frédéric springs to my side, steps behind me, and assists while gently running his warm hands over my skin.

I can feel a joyous, contented smile spreading over my face. A truly pure smile, not intended for anyone but me. In this moment, having shared such an intimate part of myself, I cannot help but feel vulnerable and closer to this man. I know I shouldn't, but I am powerless after this afternoon with him not to feel some unique tie to him.

And now I am aware that perhaps I was wrong about him on at least one level—in fact, Frédéric doesn't need to direct or control sex for him to be happy. I begin to understand that he probably acted like that the *first* time so as not to feel it was anything but a physical experience. I've seen that seems to be a running theme for first sexual forays with these men.

Now things are different. Something about seeing each other in the daylight, looking into each other's eyes the whole time was incredibly emotional, and dare I say, soulful. I know. I *know*, you think I'm treading dangerous ground even thinking so much, considering that my lovers are married. But I see now that though I don't think they anticipate it or are prepared for it, an emotional connection has been born, and that connection is indeed a key element to being in a liaison with a courtesan. That alone will keep them coming back for more.

Finally, having secured the necklace around my neck just so, Frédéric places his hands on my shoulders. A shudder runs through me. So strong, he can feel it reverberating through his fingers. He wraps both hands around me and pulls me in close to his bare chest. I can feel his chest hair on my back and his heart still beating quickly against me. Yep, he's in deep now, kids.

"Alexandra . . . If I were to invite you to my *maison de campagne*, my country house, this weekend, would you join me? We could ride in the mornings, have a charming picnic in the sun under a tree . . . sleep in each other's arms . . . *Donc, dis-moi?*" he whispers into my disheveled hair, as we both look out at the setting sun, vibrant red across the Tuileries.

"That sounds sublime . . . truly I would love to. But I could only see you *dimanche* (Sunday), as I have a dinner *samedi soir*. Would that still suit you?" I speak to the window, seeing his reflection start to appear in the glass as the room begins to fall into darkness. Frédéric whips around with surprising speed and steps back to recapture an air of dignity.

"Alexandra, if you decide to continue to stay with Jean-Albert, well . . . I shall feel quite deceived," he announces, while attempting to look authoritative standing there in his boxers and that damn wedding ring. I put my hands up to my shoulders and give him a look of tenderness and questioning. Instantly, his face softens with emotion, and he holds out his hand to me. "It is my intent—no, *my deepest desire*—to have you for myself. I will not share anything else with Jean-Albert," Frédéric proclaims, releasing my hand, regally taking a seat in the armchair, and languidly crossing his legs. (Buddy, you'd be a lot more commanding if, say, you had on clothes.)

"Frédéric, the way you say that is more than slightly offensive. As though I am an object . . . a company, a . . . ." He interrupts me as he leaps up and starts to put on his pants and belt.

"I just simply can't imagine you going back to his bed . . . it's too . . . No, Jean-Albert cannot," he snorts, looking at me angrily, tightening his belt.

"Is this really about *me*, Frédéric? Or the fact Jean-Albert *once* slept with your wife . . . a long time ago. Am I wrong?" I try to say it casually, though once the question escapes my lips it sounds a lot more venomous than I intended.

"*Pardon?!* He slept with my wife? Alexandra, what are you saying?" Frédéric looks awash with a mixture of fear and disbelief.

Holy shit. Oh my God! He didn't know, and I just let that *chat* out of the bag. Big time! Backpedal. *Vite!* Christ. How to do that? Anyone have an "erase voice track" button? "Grace personified" this is not. By a long shot. *Major courtesan faux pas!*

"I don't know, or did you sleep with *his* wife? I was simply haz-arding a guess there. All I know is that you two seem to have some extreme rivalry, and I assumed it must have involved someone sleeping with someone's wife." (Keep going, Alexandra, this sounds semiplausible.) "I mean, you're both magnificently wealthy and ridiculously successful in *different* fields, so what else could it possi-bly be about?" I say. I finish dressing and try to slow down a gigan-tic impulse to race to the exit.

"Hmmm. Consider *yourself* on probation, Alexandra. Remember, I'm in politics and have acquired quite a discerning talent for know-ing when people are lying, *donc, fais attention,*" Frédéric says, with a piercing stare that softens a moment later. "Oh, Alexandra, I see I shall have to make a profound effort to win you away. Give me *di-manche* with you in the country, and I am confident you will leave Jean-Albert by Monday morning . . . and here, don't forget the box," he says, taking the Mikimoto box from the floor and handing it to me.

"You have your work cut out for you Sunday, *chéri*. And thank you, but I don't need the box," I reply, tying my hair in a chignon for my "yes, I'm the reason Frédéric howled a screaming orgasm through the hallowed halls" departure from the Embassy.

"Take it . . . there's a card for you in it," he insists, smiling and looking at me with gentle eyes again.

"*D'accord et merci*. Really, the necklace is just stunning," I say, run-ning my hand over my new choker. "And the afternoon was . . . magi-cal. Until Sunday then, *à bientôt*, you gorgeous creature." I try to end on a high note and give him a long, passionate farewell kiss. He takes my face in his hands and looks into my eyes deeply. "The pleasure was mine . . . you are my greatest pleasure . . . *au revoir, ma chérie*." He walks me to the door, turns the lock, and opens the door wide.

"Thank you for coming," he says, pretending to be professional by formally bidding me adieu in the public hallway.

"No, thank *you* for *coming*." I smile broadly, extending my hand to shake his.

His eyes twinkle with a stifled laugh. I tilt my head as if to say a final "got ya again" and step out into the long hallway, just as an older, distinguished man passes us to the left. I have an idea and launch into a discord of false pretension, feigning having been in a serious meeting—*sans sexe*. While attempting to look earnest, I belt out with all the authority I can muster (given I'm still sporting a bit of come on my ear), "In closing, Monsieur de Fallois, the French constitute the most brilliant and the most dangerous nation in Europe, and the best qualified in turn to become an object of admiration, hatred, pity, or terror. But never—*never*—indifference."

My pretentious proclamation hangs in the air until the gentleman enters an office down the hall and disappears. The sparkle instantly returns to Frédéric's eyes the second we're alone again and, his gorgeous smile filtering his voice almost into a whisper, he leans in to say, "Now who's the prose thief? That's Alexandre de Tocqueville describing his motherland in the early nineteenth century." Frédéric nails me.

"*Oui, touché*. But don't forget this brilliant line, 'Much more genius is needed to make love than to command armies,'" I say with a big smile. Thinking, memorizing fabulous quotes is almost too easy.

"I'm lost. I know I've heard that quote but my mind is currently working at a slightly reduced speed of efficiency due to loss of fluids. Who was it who spoke that line?" he asks, perplexed and still scanning his memory.

"Ninon de Lenclos, my dear. Now I am one up on you in quote thievery—and I still have a significant edge in Champagne serving. Your work is indeed cut out for you." I laugh, turn, and trot off as he watches me, shaking his head. I believe I have left him both charmed and mystified—a very good way to leave a man as you walk away from him, by the way.

I scan the corridor for more dignitaries, but I am alone. Oh, thank God. No one. I just want to get the hell out of here before someone else spots me; I am so sporting a "just was a bad girl—and one helluva sassy demon" glow. I have to admit, that's becoming my "look of the season," way more than the bohemian chic all the magazines are pushing. Ha-ha!

Making my way past the security check, I give a big jaunty wave to the three uniformed guards, in such a way as to make it very clear I wasn't exactly here for a cup of tea and a chat. Right. Check out the new necklace, boys, and see the box, Miki-*fucking*-moto!

I saunter out and down the long staircase to the avenue, passing the two young uniformed guards standing at the gate. I give them each a breathy *"bonsoir,"* a wink (nobody winks anymore—it's a rather cool move actually), and throw my head back, freeing my hair from its loose knot, in a celebration of life. My crazy bananas *life*.

Yeah. Pretty damn amusing. I just scored a seriously fabulous necklace, and all I did was make *myself* come. Oh, right, and there's a card. Gotta check that out. God, Frédéric is quite brave to write something—anything—that could be tangible evidence of his cheating. Ha! So American of me to think like that. The French wouldn't dream of allowing that idea to hinder their seduction rituals.

Opening the black box, I see a small white envelope attached to the lid. Must be the Certification of Authenticity card that comes with all these high-ticket treats. I'm starting to have quite a nice collection of these babies. Yep, and what's this? I pull out another plastic card just beneath it.

Centurion American Express.

Oh, man, another Black credit card. Funny thing is, I really can't think of a single thing I want or need. How wild is that? Walking back to my flat, I pass through the Tuileries at dusk. The fresh evening air is blowing through my hair, my fingers caressing the smooth cool pearls of my necklace. Life is damn good. I hear, *Bzzz, Bzzz*. Check my phone. No call.

Inbox. One *texto*, from Frédéric.

```
Miss U already. Sunday won't cum soon enough & Monday
Jean-Albert will b very unhappy . . . F.d.F.
```

Silly boys. When they're ten, they're fighting over a skateboard; when they're fifty, they're squabbling over a mistress.

LES CADEAUX
DU MOIS

How does one calculate the entire price of furnishing an apartment? The bill from the *antiquaire,* Chloe Chevalier, for *just* six "important" pieces of furniture from the Empire period came to 134,000 euros. And the bill from Bonmarché: 21,450 euros. I'm hideously embarrassed; maybe I should stop toting up this list, if not for tax reasons, then for reasons of turning a blind eye from self-consciousness.

As a finale, I must add that amazing Mikimoto neckace. Value: I have no idea of the price. 100,000 euros? More? Maybe. Beats me. Don't really have the time or inclination to immediately check out its price tag the way I did in the first few months. Mind you, that's not a sign of becoming jaded and spoiled; I am just busy and, frankly, my mind has acclimated to all the gifts and free financial rein (and, *non,* that was *not* another riding metaphor).

NOTABLE OBSERVATION UNIQUE
TO LIFE AS A COURTESAN

When one is in her twenties and the mistress of a man three decades older, one instantly feels older as well. And not necessarily in a good way. Like your life just shot ahead, and you went from stolen kisses with nubile young men barely able to shave—and imagining your wedding and the distant idyllic notion of having a family—to looking into the eyes of a man weathered by life, with chest hair maybe even going gray. Surrounded by his world, where everyone you meet is careening closer to retirement than middle age. It's bizarre— as though your life went into fast-forward and you missed those priceless landmark moments of life, and—poof!—you just instantly have this extravagant life you didn't earn or achieve. I guess no one ever said being a courtesan was going to be easy.

A FEW MORE COURTESAN SEXUAL TIPS *POUR TOI*

Gentleman on top: Many women love this position, as it feels the most intimate and allows greater freedom for touching, kissing, and hugging. It was also the preference of nineteenth-century French courtesans, who had to accommodate their elaborate hairstyles, hats, and endless corsetry. Assuming you are less encumbered, you can also add to your repertoire the following ideas for reaching the divine *petite mort*.

With him on top and inside you, place your knees over his shoulders to increase penetration and stimulation of the G-spot. If you want to really shoot for coming together, when you're in this position, reach between his legs and tenderly squeeze and release his testicles in rhythm to his thrusts. Many men say this increases their erection (and we all know to feel him swell inside you is the path to pure ecstasy).

For men with very large penises (even just reading that line gives you pleasure, admit it!), try lying on your back with your legs flat against the bed; this will increase your tightness and prevent him from penetrating too deeply—and yes, there is such a thing!

Be vocal: And I don't mean just in verbally expressing what you desire from your partner, though this is absolutely essential, and it will make for far more intimate and fulfilling sex. I know it sounds unnecessary or silly, but do remind yourself that you are worthy of having all your sensual needs met. Of course, it takes some time to feel comfortable asking for what you want in bed. And certainly, you don't want to leap into bed with a list of demands, nor act as a director the first time you seek to experiment with all your new knowledge. Take slow, gentle steps, starting with tenderly taking his hand and placing it where you feel will excite you the most. Gently show him with your own hand the gesture and pace you want him to follow. If you feel shy or timid, remember men find watching a woman touch herself exceedingly sexy. In fact, it's often a fantasy from their youth, so move freely and with confidence. Every man wants to be a better lover, and to make his partner have an orgasm; you just happen to be the one with all the skills, so enjoy your talents and teach him lovingly.

The other meaning of "being vocal" is to literally express your pleasure through sound. As much as your pleasure pearl, the G-spot, your voice is one of the keys to sexual pleasure.

Think about it. It is hard to abandon yourself to lovemaking when your lips are sealed tight, right? So relax and let go, verbalize some of your bodily sensations as they arise. This will also accentuate the pleasure he feels—it's a massive form of arousal for your partner to hear his lover moan and writhe in pleasure. And of course, your sounds of pleasure give your partner feedback about what delights you. (A win-win situation entirely.) Voicing your pleasure through sighs, whispers, moans, and yelling enhances your own excitement, and your body will follow the cue and accelerate you toward orgasm.

CHAPITRE QUATORZE

One is not born a woman, one becomes one.

—SIMONE DE BEAUVOIR

*G*otta say, going from dinner with Jean-Albert Saturday night—which of course stretched into a rushed morning of skedaddling him out of my apartment on the double-quick so I could be ready for the 9:00 A.M. pickup by Frédéric was a dicey tag-team affair with a little unforeseen issue to manage. Let me just say, I finally get the appeal of the bidet.

Truth is, a bath may cleanse one's exterior of the telltale scents of a rival's markings, but a bit more work needs to be done to *really* shake out the evidence. Allow me to be crass here a moment, but I did find myself taking Marie-Hélène's once quickly dismissed advice of jumping up and down on my bed to expedite the exit of dear Jean-Albert's deeply sown seed. Do you even get what I'm trying to say, ever so metaphorically? Here's the less chic version: after sex with one man, and pending the arrival of another, jump up and down to expel the last man's come, and head to the bidet to tidy up to perfection. There, I said it. I'm blushing. You too? Hey, no one ever said this would be easy . . . for either of us!

A wonderfully sweet time *samedi soir* with Jean-Albert got shortshrifted mentally, as I found myself slightly more excited preparing to see Frédéric. Could be because I sensed Frédéric was on the edge of losing it, meaning any guardedness and all propriety. Read—I am *très* close to making this man obsess madly about me, and I, twisted girl that I've become, want to push him over the precipice and see what's *really* inside him. Or it could be that France and all its traditional naughty pursuit of secret pleasures have penetrated my core, and I'm now just destined to seek scandalous adventures at every turn. Hey, they've made it work as a way of life in this country for eons. Regardless of its origin, I was *definitely* up for an excursion into trouble.

Already cloaked in many a carefully laid spritz of *parfum*, I pull on a pair of sleek Hermès camel-colored riding pants and a crisp white cotton shirt, weave my hair into a long braid, and slip into the shiny new pair of chocolate brown knee-high riding boots—a necessity that I'd scampered out to get last evening while Jean-Albert prepared my apartment with candles in every nook for our romantic night. It's a damn good thing I live around the corner from Hermès now, or my "can't possibly go to the country without riding boots" run could've screwed up the timing of our *grande soirée*. Juggling men is going to take some doing, though clearly I'm more than a little up for a challenge these days!

Frédéric rang me at 9:07 A.M. to let me know he was waiting downstairs in his car. His voice instantly extinguished the previous ten minutes of what has become my now-familiar early morning reality flashes. I had been feeling a little pang of, "Oh gosh, if Jean-Albert found out what I'm up to he'd be crushed." Still, MH claims it's a good thing to keep them all working for my affections.

Though her advice is consistently correct, I, with my Midwestern sense of decency (don't laugh, there's still *some* left), don't quite embrace the idea of hurting anyone just for my amusement or benefit. And God knows, I almost gave Frédéric a cardiac when I stupidly let slip the "Jean-Albert slept with your wife" line . . . Curses! Talk about flubbing up!

All this self-analysis is washed aside as I realize, "OK, I'm due for one escapade to the country . . ." time to shift gears and dash to my awaiting Minister. Whoa, *Minister*? That's got all kinds of weird pseudo-religious connotations to it. Let's try another title—what about my awaiting Prince of Politics. *That* works.

I toss all the necessaries into my purse: my cell phone—turned to "off" now—a Lancôme compact, credit cards (not that I'll need them), breath freshener, an extra pair of silk panties (almost a given these days), Serge Luytens *parfum*, Chanel sunglasses, Dunhill cigarettes, lipstick, Cartier lighter, apartment keys, and we're off. I bound down the five flights of stairs in a mental state I can only describe as "giddy."

Good boy. Frédéric's out of the car and standing like a doting footman at the door of my building, waiting for me patiently. He feigns a bow and says, "My elegant siren, you look lovely. I am honored to spend the day with you."

Okay, I'm lovin' that. Older men, I tell you, they got charm *down*. A young guy would've been like, "Hey, whass up?" Which is just so wrong, and the definition of nowhere, *non*?

A quick double-cheek air kiss, and then Frédéric pulls me in for a real one, and man, oh man, this *homme* can kiss like a demon. The contrast is brutal to the fading memory of Jean-Albert's departure just half an hour earlier—sadly, he still kisses with that "trout gasping for air" effect. Seriously, I tried to teach him to relax those tiny lips, but oh God, he's got some sort of lifelong commitment to jamming his tongue between those wannabe lip shelves. It's occurred to me midsmooch that it's not *unlike* a python trying to skewer his prey. Then again, that same move does work quite a bit better when his head's between my legs. Fair enough. Yet another reason why a woman needs three men! And now I've got two under my belt, *literally*.

Climbing into Frédéric's silver Aston Martin is like crawling into a space shuttle—in a good way. Damn sexy car. Damn sexy man. Nice combo. We zip off into the countryside, making for the outskirts of Chantilly, about an hour just north of Paris. Whizzing down the Périphérique and careening onto the Autoroute de Nord, conversation is as fast and fun as the car. Very.

Frédéric holds my hand when he's not downshifting and kisses the tips of my fingers at the stop signs along the way. Two gold stars there, kiddo. We speak of love and passion—his choice of topic—and he asks whether I think it's possible to love and/or be captivated by two people at once. I think I get where he's going with this line of questioning: He's either asking me if I can deal with his wife long-term or asking if I think I can or intend to be both with him and Jean-Albert at the same time.

I answer freely, instantly aware Marie-Hélène would scold me harshly for doing so—but is she in the car? *Non.*

"I think there are many kinds of love, and each has its own unique appeal and hold on the people involved. Sometimes what we call 'love' is truly an appreciation or respect for what *once was*, when physical passion has gradually died down and become tender devotion. People often keep relationships going based not on the current dynamic between them but on either memories *or* dreams for the future. I could be all wrong, but it seems—and I can only speak from experience about young couples and their naïve choices, as I've fallen into the same well-meaning place—I, like many people, have chosen men based on their potential. What *I want* or think he can one day become. Over time, I've learned to not wish for someone to be anything but what they are in that moment. And to never assume someone can change, or even wants to, just because you wish it for them. And then, on the flip side, is the problem common for couples that have been together for ages: they married young, grew up together, created a family, and pursued a life as soul mates, with great intentions of forever. Sadly, with all the rigors of raising a family or growth that pulls them in different directions, that love often fades into a civil partnership. It's like that quote—and I think you dig my reservoir of quotes, don't you?" I look over at Frédéric, who nods and says with a chuckle, "Oh yes, carry on, my wise young one." I pause to light a cigarette and survey the landscape rolling by, and then present him with the nugget: "By Rochefoucauld: 'Life has taught us that love does not consist in gazing at each other but in looking outward together in the same direction.' *Pas mal*, huh?" I say, thinking, "I have *got* to stop with the quotes. Even I am getting bored with them!"

"*Oui, c'est ça*. It's quite true, love is a meeting of illusion, fantasy, and a hint of reality, that distinct and unique mixture that each person conjures up in their mind. Then, if they are fortunate enough to happen upon a person who possesses the same mentality, it clicks like lightning and locks you to each other with passion." And Frédéric looks back at me after a quick check in the rearview mirror.

I steal a glance at him, thinking, "Hmm, interesting, I just bamboozled him, and he didn't even see it. I *completely* didn't answer his question, and in a very French way just offered a bunch of ambiguous high-flyin' ideas into the wind. Maybe *I* should be the politician. Maybe all these big shots aren't really as clever or masterful as the public wants to believe they are. Maybe, like movie stars or celebrities, society indulges them with credit they don't really deserve. But damn, doesn't matter to me if Frédéric's not a genius, or is just simply smart and fortunate; he's stimulating my mind and body to fire on all cylinders.

It's very rare that a man keeps you titillated, intrigued, and in a constant state of dizzying desire—desire for him, but also a desire to better yourself, to delve deeper into his mind and your own. I wonder if I could refuse Frédéric this afternoon. Might be a study in discipline on my part. Nah, why play games? Plus, I'm really getting into this sex with eyes locked thing, even if the expressions are possibly not the most flattering of facial contortions.

And with that reverie thoroughly enjoyed and exhausted, we turn off the back country road onto a small dirt *allée* half hidden by the bending branches of a large willow tree.

"This is it, *chérie—la maison de campagne de ma famille*," Frédéric says, unconsciously leaning in toward the windshield, as though this will bring us there faster. Sweet.

The car slows to a crawl as the sound of cicadas in the tall dry grass wafts in our open windows, nature's orchestral welcome.

The smell of late-morning dew drying in the warming sun is

mixed with the unmistakable scent of horses, so crisp is the smell you can practically feel a warm satiny muzzle against your out-stretched hand. What is it about the smell of country air, horses, and hay that's so purifying? And I could use a little purifying these days, right?

We pull into the circular drive that still sports a smattering of small pebbles that surely once were strewn with great care. An elegant eighteenth-century cream two-story stone *manoir* is nestled between ancient tall oaks that stand like regal guards. Trails of ivy cling to the lower-floor windows and writhe around the deep gray shutters, climbing up the portico over the double-height front doors. Tall cone-shaped firs dot the island lawn, surrounding a decaying stone bench that faces out across the expansive vista to the south.

"Frédéric, what a lovely house! It's positively delightful," I say, catapulting myself out of the low seat.

"No, *you're* delightful . . . the house is merely charming," he replies, opening the trunk and lifting out a large wicker basket.

The air smells like the pure earth, and with the sun caressing every plant, and caressing me, I can't help myself from twirling around like a child. When I see that the enormous lawn gives onto a pergola of tall arching oaks embracing an ink-black stone pool, I clap my hands with joy. (Have completely tossed out grace personified for childlike joy. Marie-Hélène would be horrified.) Is this my life? Because it feels very much like a dream.

"What shall we do first? Lunch? Ride? Where are the horses?" I chirp.

"My dear Alexandra, the horses are in the stables, *juste à droite à deux cent metres*, the house is open. I shall set up a *déjeuner* fit for my queen under my favorite tree. You have free rein to do as you please, go wherever you wish. What's mine is yours," he says, planting himself in front of me, tipping my chin up, and looking deeply into my eyes.

"*Charmant de toi* . . . What's *me* . . . is *yours*." Oh, so stupid of me. Clearly left my clever banter in the car.

"Music to my ears. I was very sure you'd like it, and as I said, Jean-Albert will be one very unhappy man by tomorrow."

"*Ça suffit*—that's enough about Jean-Albert. I want to see this favorite tree of yours. What makes it so special?" I ask, following him out onto the sage green grass.

"Actually, *mon père* planted it the day I was born, and I had my first kiss there at *dix ans*. I lost my virginity under it at *quinze ans*, and, well, I proposed to my wife beneath its branches," he explains, glancing at me to see how that last bit goes over.

"Lovely, I am touched you are including me in this profound history." (I am employing some of that misplaced grace here, since I never do like to hear "wife" references—way too much reality.) "Hey, stop right there," I command, flopping down butt first on the grass. (Grace in obvious retreat.)

"Have you forgotten how to be a kid? Time to lose the shoes and feel the damp grass between your toes. Ditch the *chaussures*, boy!" I demand, pointing to Frédéric's fastidious Berluti suede lace-ups.

"I do have to say, you're quite a fan of making me take my shoes off, young lady." And he puts the wicker basket down and quickly pulls off his shoes and socks.

"Let's go barefoot all day, and leave them there until the moment we leave," he suggests, with big sparkling eyes, like he's a wild man living dangerously. I play along.

"Now you're getting the hang of it, baby." Picnic provisions in the crook of Frédéric's arm, we skip off hand in hand to the famous oak tree, which is brilliantly located at the choicest spot—the central helm overlooking the lichen-encrusted garden pool. (Midskip it occurs to me, if Frédéric's wife and Jean-Albert could see us gallivanting in this storybook setting—all barefoot and jubilant—they'd both probably vomit.) Frédéric sets about unpacking his secret stash of lunch fixins (Elmbrook word, sorry), while I spread out a gorgeous damask tablecloth the color of clotted cream for us to sit on.

"*Chéri*, this tablecloth is Pierre Frey. It was surely meant for a gourmet dinner, with flickering candles—and not to get ruined by grass stains *en plein air*," I point out, the impoverished student in me rearing her ugly, pragmatic head.

"Please, this tablecloth should only have hoped to be so lucky as to be the magic carpet to this gorgeous day. Think of this finale of pleasures as its death wish," he offers with a chuckle, as he places a trio of Limoges plates, of increasing size, in front of each of us.

"*Et voilà, votre déjeuner*, Mademoiselle," he announces, as he presents the basket's contents, laying them out one after another, in a very precise, French DNA–innate fashion. And, yes, he loves to "announce." God, if I ever got this man a portable mike he'd be in ecstasies. "*Nous commençons avec huîtres de Breton . . . un peu de citron pour celles-là*"—fresh oysters from Brittany, and a little lemon to go with them—"*de rigueur baguette et un pain de campagne*"—the ubiquitous baguette and a large round loaf of bread with a dusting of flour—"*pâté de sanglier et un merveilleux foie gras, quelques cornichons. Le fromage: un Camembert, un chèvre avec poivrons, un morceau de Brie; et saumon grillé, mais froid dans un moutarde génial de miel; et toujours, pour le dessert, de pêches, cerises—un kilo parce que c'est mon fruit préféré, et ensuite, deux sablons a même chose ma mère faisat pour moi pendant mon enfance.*"

God, what a spread! You care to get it translated? Your call. If you said yes, here ya go. The first is an acquired taste, generally only applicable to those with French passports: wild boar pâté; a marvelous foie gras (your standard goose liver); tiny pickles—oh, God, they have an American name, I've forgotten; weird moment, am I more French now than American? Whatever, continuing. The cheese: Camembert, a little goat cheese round with peppercorns, Brie, cold grilled salmon in a genius mustard sauce with honey; and for dessert, peaches, cherries, a kilo—because, he says, they are his favorite—and finally two big butter cookies like his mother used to make for him as a child. I'm full just listing the menu again.

"*Mon dieu*, Frédéric, you are amazing. I'm most impressed and . . . intrigued; you have somehow managed to anticipate my *every* want," I tell him, placing a thick cotton napkin in his lap and caressing it over his lap teasingly until I feel him harden.

"Marvelous news . . . Then I hope you also approve the wine. I've chosen a Sancerre to accompany the *huîtres,* and a very fine bottle of Château Haut-Médoc 1997, for the *pâté,* or if you prefer we could sail through the whole thing on Dom Pérignon?" he asks, pulling the chilled bottle from its terra-cotta cooler.

"You, my dear, are on a roll. I will gladly partake in whatever you wish," I say, leaning over the array of plates and dishes strewn everywhere to lay an adoring kiss on those tantalizing full lips. The sweetness of the moment, the fresh crisp air, the warm sun, the unmistakable aroma of a French picnic . . . it all sweeps me away, and my thoughts are catapulted to a fleeting memory of a picnic with Laurent on the cliffs of Étretat last summer. Divine as one could ever fathom as we had driven all day, arriving at just the moment of *le crépuscule,* the exquisite violet light that exists only in that nebulous expanse of time between day and night. When that scintillating golden light unique to France metamorphosed into a pale pink shot with gold wash, he pulled me to him and turned my head so my line of sight would be precisely in line with his.

Enormous pearl gray seagulls swooped and dived, all cawing loudly for a crumb or a spare hunk of cheese. We threw half a baguette into the air—the largest gull caught it with beautiful precision, and swept down to feast on the craggy cliffs below. We sat, me between Laurent's legs, both of us facing out toward the sea. We silently watched the sun set, drinking in the peace after the long drive and the laborious climb up the cliff—and as if given a gift for our efforts, witnessed the rare and fleeting moment of the magic green rays that burn for only a few seconds—*les rayons verts*—illuminating the whole sky, just as the sun hits the horizon. And now, here, Frédéric . . . with me, this all feels somehow almost as precious. Like a sweet romance, like he's my boyfriend, and yet I keep having to remind myself, that no, this is not a love story. It can't be. And you know what? Sometimes that sucks. I make a conscious effort to embrace that "let it go" well-born theory of MH's, and play through.

Frédéric and I devour everything lying before us. From the chalky cold oysters to the last cookie, hands stained with cherry juice, breath flammable from stinky cheese, and big smiles to match our swollen tummies. Dragonflies dive-bomb the abandoned salmon while the sun moves across the sky, now casting us in shadow.

"Sublime . . . that was madly decadent. I'm afraid after all the *vin* I'm in no shape to ride a horse," I say falling onto my back, dissolving into just watching the leaves overhead dance in the breeze.

"I'm afraid I'm in no shape to ride anything, you included, my sweet delicious plum," he concurs, lying down next to me. "I never do this, just wallow away an afternoon. You're a very welcome addition to my life, Alexandra. *Je suis très content avec toi.*"

He pulls me close, and with my head on his chest, softly recites a La Fontaine fable to me as lily white petals from a flowering magnolia fall in rings around us like nature's confetti.

A beautifully peaceful afternoon as we fall asleep, lulled by the wind in the trees and the hum of bees lapping up the leftover wine, the enchanting calm offered by nature herself.

Hours pass as quickly as the clouds. As the sun begins to ebb, we rouse ourselves slowly, pile the disarray into the basket, and leave it just inside the door of the *manoir*. Frédéric explains that the Grimauxes, who live over the hill, are the caretakers, and they will see to it. Ah, yet another soothing element to this lifestyle; no cleaning up. Anything. *Ever.* "There are people for that" is the standard mantra. I will never get used to that. I think that would be the day I would officially get that "spoiled and jaded" stamp on my forehead.

We drove back to Paris with gentle smiles, light chatter, and reveling in that state of contented, quiet tranquility, like only a country picnic in the sun can give you. Both of us are surely aware that the absence of *any* sex, twisted or *normale*, brought us a greater sense of intimacy. And while it may have been his goal to "win and sway" me away from Jean-Albert, I don't think Frédéric was fully prepared to have feelings. Maybe I'm reading too much into all this, but despite my profession, I am a die-hard romantic—but you come to your own conclusion.

Dusk was falling like a heavy cape as we pulled up to my building. Frédéric had been lost in silent thought since we passed back into the heart of Paris, and I had just let him drift off without my usual "What are you thinking?" inquiry (which, by the way, never results in an honest or great answer, so drop it from your repertoire if you can!).

Under the street lamp just buzzing into a golden glow, he walked me to my door. As I opened my mouth to start to thank him, Frédéric took hold of my shoulders and hugged me with surprising force, murmuring with his face deep within my hair, "I want you to know, I would do anything for you, Alexandra. Never do I want you to be sad or in want of anything. No matter what happens, know that I adore you . . . You make me feel like a teenager again, like I haven't a care in the world. And frankly, it's starting to hurt to have to let you go each time . . . to watch you walk away. Tell me you won't walk away from me. Even if you feel you have reason to be angry with me. Tell me you'll not just leave," he pleads, taking my face in his warm hands.

"Don't worry. I'm here, darling. I'll be here tomorrow and the next day and many more after that." And I kiss him with as much reassuring tenderness as I can put into a meeting of lips.

"*Vraiment? Bon . . . mais, n'oublie jamais, je t'adore.*" And he watches as I turn the key in the lock and step into the courtyard, and the heavy door glides closed.

Well, looks like someone we know has huge abandonment issues. Guess we've stepped over that precipice rather speedily, eh? And on the other side is a whole lot of fragile, needy clinginess *of a jeune homme charmant* trapped in a man's body, one with graying hair. How touching.

Chez moi, I slip into a long bath, try not to think too much about Frédéric, and send Jean-Albert a loving *texto* to assuage the hint of guilt:

    Chéri, tu m'as manqué beaucoup j'espère te voir demain
    soir. XXX. Alexandra.

(Darling, I miss you very much. Hope to see you tomorrow night, kisses . . .)

Blatantly obvious damage control there.

The next morning I'm awakened by some *manifestation* (political demonstration) under way on the Place de la Concorde. Have to hand it to the French: For as much as they let adultery slide under the bar of propriety, they do get all up in arms about the slightest political debacle. Rare is the day when there's not some hoo-ha crashing down on the government. Call me bonkers—and you wouldn't be the first—but I have some starry-eyed hope my efforts with Frédéric will soften his harsh policies. How's *that* for being egotistical?

Marie-Hélène rings at noon to book a lunch for *mercredi* and to catch up on news.

"So, my Alexa, seems you have a handle on the 'man in each hand' strategy. Are you ready for me to throw in another one, to keep them all in the air and off balance? Men are like stocks, my dear. Diversify your assets to increase your dividends." There's the sound of a smile in her voice.

"Well, OK . . . who's the next contender? And, fair warning—I don't want any more men who know each other. It feels slightly incestuous, and I can't make another choice screw-up the way I did, blurting out to Frédéric that Jean-Albert had slept with his wife! Did I tell you about that little snafu? He had *no* idea, and was positively enraged!" I still blush just thinking about that faux pas *extraordinaire*.

"Oh dear, didn't I forewarn you to pay scrupulous attention to details in these affairs? I think we may have a disaster on our hands. Didn't you hear? It's in the morning *Figaro*?" Marie-Hélène asks.

"Hear what? What's happened? Is this about the *manifestation* I can hear raging outside?" I ask concernedly.

"I hope it's not what I think it is, but . . . Frédéric has closed Jean-Albert's treasured Samaritane department store, claiming it's a fire hazard. But the entire population knows that's complete nonsense, and I fear it may be a vicious payback to Jean-Albert—for years of animosity between them, and well, now I can't help but think for possibly discovering the newsflash of Jean-Albert sleeping with his wife, via you, Jean-Albert's other precious holding."

"Oh, my God! Do you think it's possible?! Wow, come to think of it, Frédéric did say again and again, 'Jean-Albert will be very unhappy by Monday,' and begged me not to leave him no matter what happened. Christ! He had decided it before our picnic, and . . . oh no . . ." I can't finish my sentence.

"*Écoute:* This is in no way your fault. It's about these childish men battling over possessions and egos. All the more reason for you to step away for a moment and meet the marquis I have in mind for you. Thankfully, he's not in the slightest connected to big business or politics. Just a bon vivant aristocrat with tremendous wealth, a tremendous château, and a passion for 'collecting' . . . and who still happens to be single!" she explains, exhibiting her miraculous skill of glossing over any crisis with the next acquisition.

"Hunhhh. I'm feeling more than a little sick over this. They may call this 'polite society,' but heavens, its members are absolutely cut-throat with one another! And to think, I was having illusions my affair with Frédéric would soften his hard edges. *Pfff.* Okay, yeah . . . maybe a marquis will provide a welcome distraction. By the way, *please* tell me he's not a troll!" Maybe that ability to transition seamlessly to the next affair *is* contagious. Hell, with MH every decadent idea is infectious.

"*Non, au contraire.* I think you will be quite delighted. The marquis . . . his *prénom sans titre* is Louis-Philippe . . . is just thirty-nine years old. He acquired his title and estate early in life. Rumor has it his parents were killed in a car accident on their way to see him in boarding school. *Très tragique, n'est-ce pas?* Only son. Inherited generations of his family's flourishing sugar business. *Vraiment,* virtually every cube of sugar in France has passed through the family refineries. Now he has very little to do with the day-to-day business, so he bides his time indulging his exquisite taste in the arts, travel, music, and literature. He is a passionate and erudite collector of art and antiquities. Is that not divine? And, you see, this is all quite perfect timing, as Louis-Philippe needs to marry soon and carry on the family bloodline. If he were to die without an heir, the château, title, and fortune would fall to the French government."

"*Quel* conundrum," I say, a little wearily, hardly able to shake up any enthusiasm, given the Samaritane scandal. "Okay. You still didn't say he wasn't Quasimodo, but I know you're always looking out for me, so yes, you can arrange for us to meet, or tell him whatever is the necessary next step. I don't care. Let me know. I will still see you *mercredi* for lunch, right? We can discuss it then, when my bones will with luck have regained some solidity. *Je t'embrasse,* MH."

How's that for apathy? I'm pretty much the queen of it at the moment. I mean, *fuck.* Thousands of people just lost their jobs at Samaritane. Paris lost a priceless, iconic landmark . . . a major fixture on the face of this beautiful, historic city. And for what? To satisfy men's silly tit-for-tat, stab-you-in-the-back games. I'd better check in with Jean-Albert and get his take on this. His *point de vu* will be telltale if this is personal . . . *and personally a result of me.*

I hit CALL JEAN-ALBERT. And feel something along the lines of nervous fear as the line rings.

"*Oui.*" He picks up after five agonizing rings.

"*Bébé, tout va bien?* We'll see each other tonight, *chéri, dis-moi oui, mon ange?*" I ask, absurdly throwing in as many terms of endearment as can be jammed into an opener.

"Alexandra, today is a dark day. After all my contributions and generosity to that pompous ass Frédéric de Fallois, he has gone and shut down Samaritane. I am livid. If you love me just a little you will never, I repeat, *never,* speak to that criminal again," he says darkly, his burning fury almost coming through the phone and singeing my ear. Generally, when it comes to conversations with men, I prefer *other* body parts to melt.

"I understand you must be terribly angry, dear heart. Why do you think he went through with it after your agreement?" I ask, tossing in a nervous cough for good measure, as though this is the first time I've thought of it. I know I am blatantly pushing the issue to the nth.

"You? Me? The past? I don't know, I can't really speak about this now. I may be in too foul a mood *ce soir* to be any fun for you," he says, obviously switching the phone to his other ear. "Just know, I cannot have you be in any way polite or even civil to him again. I saw how he made it clear at Vaux that he intended on seducing you, oh, *merde*, enough, I must go. I have to prepare for a press conference. *À plus tard, mon amour.*" And Jean-Albert clicks off.

Yeechh. I am in the middle of this, even if 30 percent . . . probably is more like 75 percent, but Jean-Albert doesn't know I fucked up royally and revealed his dalliance with Frédéric's wife. Oh, gosh, if that *merde* hits the fan, I'll really be up *merde* creek (word for the day: *merde*).

A COURTESAN'S LIST OF
TO-DOS

As Baudelaire put it so well, "She must astonish and bewitch . . . appear magical and supernatural . . . she must borrow from the arts in order to raise herself above nature, the better to subjugate hearts and stir souls."

The following are suggestions to enhance your power to seduce and enchant:

- Pick your best body part and make it your trademark. If you have a magnificent neck, make it the focus, celebrate this unique aspect of you. Same with your arms, décolletage, ankles, fine wrists, slim hips, etc. Marguerite de Valois was one of the very first women to expose her divine décolletage, thereby ensuring that throughout history she's been renowned for possessing the most beautiful and legendary breasts! For Josephine Bonaparte, it was her lovely arms which she chose to accentuate by always leaving them bare.
- Move with feline grace and, above all, unhurriedly (I'm still working on this one . . .). Movements and gestures should be fluid, graceful, and languorous, silently stirring desire and suggesting sensuality. Saunter or slink into a room, with a light, nonchalant, and carefree attitude. Add a coy smile or a gentle, bemused laugh to your

entrance—both of which can be supremely seductive as they draw people to you instantly, making them curious about what you're thinking. Remember, many of the most captivating and successful seductresses were not true beauties by any means, but were famous for entering a room with a mesmerizing aura and holding every man's attention. Examples: Coco Chanel, Pamela Harriman.

- Don't be afraid to show your independence. Not only does it separate you from the crowd, but wild independence has a provocative effect on men. Telling them their presence isn't necessary per se puts them off balance, and at the disadvantage of having to prove their worthiness, and we know men love a challenge. Independent women exude a sense of adventure, confidence, and spontaneity while also attracting men's natural desire to want to tame something.

- Once you have a man's interest, and the initial honeymoon period has started to wane: Play the coquette! Men need to feel the hunt to stay emotionally engaged. Send contrary signals; run hot and cold. Plunge a man into confusion with your indifference. Better to be ambiguous, or even unavailable, so as to frustrate him, to stimulate his passion. As we all know, the more you pursue a man, the more they run away, and the reverse holds true as well. The less you seem to need a man, the more he will be drawn to you. Just listen to Marcel Proust: "An absence, the declining of an invitation to dinner, an unconscious harshness—are of more service than all the cosmetics and fine clothes in the world."

CHAPITRE QUINZE

No man hath it in his power to overrule the deceitful-
ness of a woman.

—MARGUERITE DE NAVARRE

Two weeks have passed, and I haven't quite shaken the guilt trip of the Samaritane closing extravaganza. Though interestingly, Frédéric rang and offered me a different kind of *trip:* to accompany him to St. Petersburg for some meeting of head honchos of the world's political elite, followed by a gala at the Hermitage. Tough to refuse, as I would *kill* to see the Hermitage. But I also well know Jean-Albert will *kill me* if he discovers I traveled with Frédéric, so I declined graciously. Which is rather generous of me—to both of them, but mostly to Frédéric—considering he definitely played dirty, and, to be honest, I am not at all charmed by his ruthlessness. Frankly, the enchanted picnic is forgotten. Who knew he had tricks up his sleeve and a *très* sneaky agenda? To be totally honest, I just can't decipher if Frédéric is not only "playing" Jean-Albert, but if he's "playing" me, too. Frédéric *seemed très* sincere but, hell, it's his job to persuade and ever-so-smoothly get what he wants—by whatever means necessary. Note to self: Dalliances with politicians are tricky business. But let's clear this up right now: Monica Lewinsky I am not, not by a long shot! I believe all she took from her affair *avec*

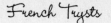

Clinton was a weight problem, a come-stained Gap dress, and a book of poetry. *Amateur!*

I was just heading out for my standing weekly *déjeuner* with Marie-Hélène when a text message came in. Can't be her canceling by *texto* as I know for a fact Marie-Hélène is committed to never *lowering herself* to "such a common means of mass communication."

Holy fuck. It's from Laurent:

```
everywhere I go on this planet, u r with me, I miss u.
pls 4give me.
```

Wow! He always did give good *texto*. God, after all this time and all the pain, is it possible that that boy can still open my heart and take hold of me with a dozen words!? I think of that sexy little half-smile he always had on his face after making love. Just what does he mean, "everywhere on this planet?" Where the hell is he? Greece again? Maybe his gorgeous older Amazon *femme* didn't pan out. Like hell I'm just going to zip off a forgiving reply and have him hurt me all over again. No, *merci* my life is overflowing with men who are so bananas for me they'll battle over monuments and millions because of me. I am quite a prize, Monsieur Love Me and Leave Me Laurent! No lost kid from Toulouse is going to get me back with such a pittance of effort. Hrmph!

And now I can take pleasure in knowing that finally *he* may be sweating it out, anxiously awaiting my reply.

Well, keep waiting, kiddo!

I managed to put him out of my mind (lie!) and zip off to that lunch with Marie-Hélène, where and as per usual she swept me into her maelstrom and persuaded me of the genius of her plans. Man, is she good—I always seem to leave her having agreed to yet another scheme. While she would probably like to imagine she was Madame de Pompadour in a previous life, I'm not all that sure Marie-Hélène wasn't the first female snake oil salesman. And considering her affection for all things *reptile,* this is maybe not so much of a stretch of the imagination! I swear this woman could sell dental floss to a toothless man.

Thus, once again, swayed by her pitch, I agree to a rendezvous the coming Saturday night to finally meet this Marquis de Sugar . . . or whatever his name is.

For crying out loud, you have to agree, all these names are a mouthful: Marquis Louis-Philippe de Tassin; Marie-Hélène de Saint Florent; Monsieur de Chip on the Shoulder, etc. Never do you come across a Marquise Amy or Vicomte Bob. These meter-long proper names are dramatically complicated—as much, in fact, as their owners are! And it all only adds to feeling like we're in a play by Racine. I just hope I'm not killed off in the third act!

Anyway, Marie-Hélène's got it into her head that, in addition to snaring the Marquis, I need further schooling in my sommelier skills, as if the endless reading and lessons by Jean-Albert in the nuances of wine weren't enough for this young courtesan. So, it's all booked: the Marquis, MH, and I are to be treated to a *dégustation privée*—which is the complete opposite of the "disgusting" it sounds like. In this case it means a private wine-tasting lesson by one of the world's greatest sommeliers, Monsieur Gaspard Navarre, of the famous George V Hôtel on *samedi soir.*

Well, if the Marquis Aristo turns out to be a fatso, at least I will have acquired some useful knowledge from the night, right? Hate to head into an evening with not a chance of coming out ahead in some respect. Spoken like a true courtesan, don't you think?

With Frédéric on ice in Russia, I only had to deal with Jean-Albert in the days leading up to Marquis D Day. Understandably, Jean-Albert had been a distracted crab, and my sympathy was all I was requested to offer. And that mostly by phone, save for a single tea rendezvous and a stroll through the Parc Monceau.

Which is a damn good thing, because I'm going through one of those "sex? I can take it or leave it" periods with him. Is it hormones or the swirling emotional tsunami of playing in the big leagues of big shots? Probably both. Not to mention that the actual physical aspect of all these sexual adventures is beginning to get to me; what used to feel like healthy romps of body-toning aerobics is starting to feel like being put through the ringer. I'm depleted of my reserves, and hell, just plain man-handled. Of course, in some ways it's my own doing (those crazy angles and positions I choose!), but these men with their trim little waists and sharp hip bones are positively making my inner thighs into mincemeat! Not exactly your standard "on the job work hazard," I know.

Samedi arrived despite my secret pleas to God that the Marquis happened upon a suitable wife *par hasard* in the interim. Marie-Hélène arrived *chez moi* at 7:30 to fill me up on more Marquis info and Champagne. The latter was more appealing. Standing next to me in the salon, unconsciously smoothing her hair in the mirror, MH relinquishes further details: "While I very much support your continuing with Frédéric and Jean-Albert—*tu connais, ma devise est 'toujours: il faut profiter'* "—hard to translate precisely, but more or less means: you know, my motto is, always benefit from it—"Louis-Philippe is possibly, if you so choose, a gold mine," she says, re-uniting with her *flûte de Champagne* on the mantle.

"I thought he was a sugar refinery?" I wait two beats for a laugh. Am rewarded only with a bemused smile. So I hold forth, "I know, I am game. But if he's so great, why don't *you* marry him?" I add, with a raised eyebrow.

"Alexa, I should think you should know better. One, I am quite well where I am. I prefer the *varied* options life has to offer me and the gifts *varied* men have to offer me. And two, I hesitate to men-tion, but I am of the belief that my days of a family life . . . specifi-cally, my days of fertility, have come to a silent close while the band has continued to play on. A doctor confirmed as much recently; it just wasn't meant to be," she says, looking suddenly older than her years, her voice a tonic sadness.

"Screw that doctor! Well, not literally, of course—but then again, *maybe*. I bet he or another could help you with your fertility if you really desired a child."

"No, like a *vraie femme parisienne*, I will accept what nature has destined for me, be it these laugh lines, good metabolism, or never experiencing motherhood. But you, my sweet Alexa, if you wish for a child, the Marquis is the answer. You could leave behind—or keep, for that matter—the other men, and have everything you ever dreamt of. To start a child's life with a title and a fortune is a gift few can offer their children. The silver spoon, I believe you say in America." At this point, she is almost whispering.

"I grew up with neither title nor fortune, and I believe the love my parents had for each other and for us was a far more valuable gift than had I been anointed the Marquise de Elmbrook, and had the means to have bought up every pair of Nike tennis shoes I coveted. But I do truly appreciate what you're saying regarding children— and your being so open with me. You are my gift," I say, surprising myself by leaning over to kiss Marie-Hélène on the cheek.

Our cheeks brush, and a faint, mesmerizing fragrance floats up from her neck and demands I linger a moment longer. Mmm, no wonder men fight wars, go through fortunes, and lose their heads for women. Damn, we *are* soft, entirely delicious creatures.

I pull away slightly, just enough to still feel her skin's fragrant warmth.

"I've never asked you what *parfum* you wear, Marie-Hélène; I have to say, it's absolutely captivating. Really, the smell hits me at my core; it smells like pure sex, man and woman, clean and unsullied, so complicated—I could succumb to dangerous things given an evening in your midst." Now I am unabashedly flirting. After speaking of children, and feeling a melancholic tone arise in her, I'm hoping to take her back to reveling in the beauty and power that are so dear to her.

"Your imagination is a delight, Alexa. Never lose that. The *parfum*, is, in fact, especially made for me by Frédéric Malle. You must know of him." I shake my head no. "He is a brilliant 'nose,' and has a charming *boutique privée* right near here on rue du Mont-Thabor. The whole process of developing a couture fragrance takes ages. He spends months deciphering just what notes speak for a woman's *esprit*. No two are ever alike, of course. And mine—you will enjoy this—is based on the essence of a love panther. *Oui*, it is the only animal that emits perfume to lure its *victims*. Other animals may exude an aroma to draw *mates*, but the love panther, only for *victims*!" she says with a devious smile truly worthy of her *parfum*.

"Zounds! I'm more than a little awed by that story . . . but I'm learning that with you my awe never ends," I say, shaking my head for drama and punctuating the moment with a toast of Champagne. "So shall we allow yet another lucky man to bask in our glory now, be it just for a few hours?" I inquire mock-haughtily, raising my flute, quite sure this is the persona she wants me to take on.

"*Bien sûr*, my rosebud. I should tell you, I think after bringing the Marquis into your orbit, my guidance with you will be very close to complete. You've swept from an unsure novice to a rising star, and now . . . you are very much assuming the position and full blossoming of your womanhood . . . in control of all your powers. *Félicitations!*" Marie-Hélène looks me in the eye, tapping my flute.

"Say it's not so. I will never allow you to cease to offer, nor me to stop following, your sage and generous advice. And isn't a rose more beautiful and sought after, *before* it's in full bloom?"

"Ah, true, but only in regard to flowers and fruit that are then allowed to ripen in a hothouse kept with great care." With that she doles out a small sample of that kittenish laugh. "Indeed, Alexa, you may be too clever for the men you encounter; be careful with that. Remember also, many things you were raised to believe are different in France. All truly delicious passions are more enduring and sublime with age: women, men, wine, cheese, architecture, etc. On that note, let's go indulge and tantalize our palettes with *les plus grands vins de France*! The George V and the Marquis await us!"

We hurriedly touch up our lipstick and powder, grab our ludicrously overpriced purses—mine, a Dior *chocolat* leather gaucho bag with dangling keys; hers, a pale green ostrich Kelly bag—and make our way down the stairs, headed for Hugo, who is waiting below in the car.

The Champagne has added a sparkling delight to our moods, as does the always thrilling ride through Paris on a summer evening. Watching the sky transform from a pearly orange sorbet to vivid violet just as the Tour Eiffel bursts into a shimmering festival of white glittering lights. I *love* this city. Whoever is in charge really pours on the romantic nuances. Hold that thought: Frédéric's among those in charge—strike that compliment. He's verging on being a persona non grata in my book these days.

Arriving at the fabulously *raffiné* George V hotel, I am surprised to realize I'm rather excited to meet this marquis. I mean, I've heard about him for so long and, in such depth, as to only leave the question of is he left- or right-handed. Or tucks his sex to the left or right, for that matter. (BTW, men who "go right" generally are smaller in length but greater in circumference; *little* known detail that holds *wide* appeal. Did you get that pun? Of course you did!)

We hasten to the revolving door, where Marie-Hélène pauses and gestures that she's to pass through first.

"Age before beauty, my dear," she announces, to explain it.

"*Au contraire.* No one would surmise the first, and everyone would confirm the latter is rightly your title," I demur.

"See? You're now surpassing my witticisms. *Génial.* The night is yours!" she adds, whirling through the doors. We zip through the lobby, arm in arm, me noting that ubiquitous aroma of wealth at every step. Very possibly due to the enormous and opulent floral arrangements that the George V is renowned for, as much as for the very mediocre rooms that carry price tags equal to the cost of a Cartier watch. But for God's sakes, the florist must have a budget of half a million euros a week to create all of the towering arrangements that fill the palatial hotel. Bouquets two meters tall loom left and right; rubrum lilies intertwined with shoots of bamboo mingle with phalaenopsis orchids in hues of mauve, buttery gold, and shell pink. We skip the dark, *boiserie*-lined bar (too obvious a choice of venue given our *métier*) and ensconce ourselves in the luxurious dining room of overstuffed silver and gold Louis XVI chairs and tables set for dinner. The Marquis is due to arrive at 8:00 P.M., and if he's so much as a hair late, I'm well prepared to give him the cold shoulder. Given that I'm clad in a pale plum Ungaro one-shoulder sheath, it shouldn't be a problem.

Just as I pop open my silver cigarette case from Jean-Albert, I sense the sudden sweeping arrival of male energy—testosterone so dense it almost extinguishes the candles.

The Marquis speaks with a precision as exquisite as his pinstripe gray suit, *"Bonsoir,* Madame de Saint Florent and Mademoiselle Alexandra.*"* Then, turning to me, "It is a distinct pleasure to make your acquaintance. I am the Marquis Louis-Philippe de Tassin. But please do call me Louis-Philippe. It has been an arduous wait *de vous rencontrer.* Indeed, I have longed to meet you since the memorable yet all-too-fleeting glimpse of you at the ball at Vaux le Vicomte. You made quite an impression that evening, on everyone and *everything*—I am sure the gardens, walls, and mirrors are still extolling your charms." He adds a nod of his head in my direction and extends his hand toward me.

(That, kids, is old world aristo flirting at the top of its game. In turn, I try to play my hand with as much skill as I would employ if this were indeed a game of whist in the seventeenth century.)

"I'm delighted that we finally meet *ce soir,* as that auspicious evening I surely wouldn't have been free to offer you my full attention. The occasion of an intimate *dégustation de vin* is a far more preferable opportunity, as that fateful evening I wasn't sure if I was the spider spinning a web or the fly caught in my own net," I murmur through a smile, as he kisses my hand gallantly. Yeah, I'd say that worked.

"I can assure you, we were all caught in your web, and willingly so." The corners of his mouth turn up into a coy smile. Then, turning his attentions to Marie-Hélène, he showers *her* with more of those de rigueur flamboyant compliments that pass for a greeting in *le haut monde de Paris.*

With the two of them exchanging niceties and gossip, I steal the moment to drink him in as deliciously deeply as I sip the Champagne.

Hell's bells. (Don't worry, I didn't let that slip out loud.) This one's sexy in a wacky way I would've never thought I'd go for. In a word, actually in two words: shaved head. Hmm. Not Telly Savalas as Kojak–shaved, but way more modern young cool. And throw in some major pricey clothes, and "hot damn" comes to mind. You know the film *Titanic*. (God, I am aware my American roots have been unearthed there, but hey, this is the perfect description of the marquis: a dead ringer for Billy Zane, who was also in the film, once you got past the youthful beauty of Leonardo.)

He's tall, tan, and very fit, and has well-shaped, dark eyebrows that form a gorgeous frame to dazzling blue-green eyes of the come-fuck-me variety. Watching him, I can see he's being ever so much more animated in his theatrics; he's completely aware that I'm studying him with admiration, and he's clearly pleased. And he's fastidiously turned out, too: buffed nails on beautiful long fingers (I have a thing for hands); a platinum Audemars Piguet at his wrist; a gold family signet ring; and that excruciatingly sexy couture suit. Having learned a bit in that department of late, I can gauge that it is Armani simply by the shoulder. Shoes? Always check shoes; they can be the deal breaker. Nope, in this case, they're the end-all, be-all: Berluti. Hilarious. All my men wear Berluti. I should buy stock in the company. I almost burst out laughing, thinking how funny it sounds to say, "All my men wear Berluti, or they wear nothing at all." But it can't really be my silly version of the famous Chanel quote by Marilyn Monroe, "I wear Chanel No. 5 or nothing at all," because my men aren't exactly wearing nothing at all even when naked. They still sport those damn wedding rings. Ah, but not this one. Single!

Louis-Philippe refrains from joining us in a *flûte de Champagne*, informing us that it may be a detriment to properly savoring the wine that awaits us. A connoisseur with class. Sexy. *Always*.

Marie-Hélène and I try to pass off this minor oversight on our parts by abandoning our bubbly and stubbing out our cigarettes.

"Well, we shouldn't keep the world's finest sommelier waiting, should we? Undoubtedly, some jewels have been decanted in advance and are beckoning our . . ." (That was me, attempting to recover some wine-oriented knowledge, as he interrupts.)

"Our mouths, our tongues, our noses, our eyes. Yes, let us descend into the *cave pour la dégustation*," he says, with such sensuality

I'm finding it hard to stand up. Marie-Hélène flashes me a look that says, "Told ya. He's killer. Marry him . . . *now*." And you know what? I am having a serious brush with a *coup de foudre* (love at first sight), if I can say so this prematurely and naïvely.

The head sommelier with the world title is waiting for us patiently in the entrance of the dining room. A rotund man of about forty-five, who you would not be incorrect in mistaking for the Cajun chef Paul Prudhomme, receives us with a delighted twitter and more than a little flip of the wrist. Read: chic gay man, very well in his skin.

The Marquis—oh hell, let's just call him Louis-Philippe—makes the introductions, as the two men are already "well acquainted." (Meaning Louis-Philippe must have some God-awful impressive wine collection.)

Despite having been forewarned that the sommelier, Monsieur Gaspard Navarre, has a lame right hand, I still, like a fool, unconsciously reach out to shake it. Christ, somebody shoot me. So inelegant of *moi*. Everyone looks in opposite directions, as if to pretend it didn't happen. Thanks, gang.

"Fair warning, Mesdames *et* Monsieur, we shall be taking a labyrinthine passage through the inner workings of the kitchen and down through some narrow, winding stone stairs to reach the famous *cave*, or wine cellar. If any of you are claustrophobic, now may be the time to reveal it," the sommelier announces in a charmingly playful tone.

"Very well, follow me, *s'il vous plaît*." And he hastily leads us out of the shimmering candlelit dining room and down a brutally UV-lit white corridor that could very well be in a hospital if it weren't for the framed photos of "*Serveur du Mois*" and other images of commended staff members. By the way, this lighting is such hell for what is the first minutes of a first "date"—so painfully bright you could count my eyebrow hairs or do surgery *or both*. The four of us all zip along, each surely thinking, "Herein lies the secret inner workings of the elegance we see in the dining room? I prefer the final effect; get me outta here."

Our sommelier turns to his left and is met with pristine white double doors, with the omnipresent circular windows. He pauses and allows us to enter before him, while uttering, *"C'est la cuisine.* As it is the first seating *pour dîner,* all eighty-seven chefs and sous-chefs are working at top speed at the moment."

Holy mother of God! As glorious as the ball was at Vaux le Vicomte, for all its detail and excellence, this is somehow even more astounding. Perhaps because it's completely meant to be *behind the scenes,* and yet it is awe-inspiring in its beauty and organization. We all just stop in our tracks at the sight before us—almost a hundred men, each in a starched white chef outfit, apron and tall stiff chef hat, *bien sûr,* weaving around each other with such extraordinary, meticulous efficiency, expertly masterful in each of their distinct specialties, moving from station to station.

To the left, fifty glossy white porcelain plates are warming under steam, while on the right, seven huge copper *poêles* (pans) simmer a varied assortment of choice *poisson:* a *saumon avec câpres* wallows in a beige *beurre;* a *bar* slowly roasts, as its fanlike fin bakes to a crisp; two dozen *coquilles Saint-Jacques* brown in another. An older gentleman is entirely consumed with his task of trimming the plates with swirls of sauce—a Bearnaise here, a *crème à ciboulette* there—as nearby one very young man looks up nervously from his task of shelling platoons of peas from their velvety envelopes into a large, gleaming, steel bowl. It's a magnificent sight, and I'd be just as happy to hover here all night watching the five-star *cuisine* come to life, but Gaspard the Sommelier hurries us through. I fall behind the others, walking as slowly as seems polite. My eyes dance from the pastry room on the right, where shiny trays of éclairs and glistening fruit tarts cool on silver racks, to a final image of two large men heaving a stone tray of piping hot croissants and *petit pains* from a blazing hot brick oven, placing them one by one on a marble *plateau.* The huge scale, eye for detail, extreme care, artlike excellence of expertise! Heaven must have a kitchen like this!

The four of us pass through another set of white double doors that open onto a small foyer, with only a low, ancient wooden door to the left.

"Mind your head and take the shallow stairs one by one," the sommelier warns.

We each descend the rough circular stairs, holding on to the weathered oak banister for dear life. Marie-Hélène's and my heels click and echo against the rough stone worn with deep hollows from decades of wear. After another large wooden door, with rusty hinges and a blackened keyhole, we have arrived at the famous secret *cave*.

The ceiling must be four meters tall, the room maybe fifteen feet square. It's here that row upon row of the world's most precious wines and Champagnes slumber and age with dignity. The old, stamped wooden crates announcing the elegant wines' titles and posh vineyards adorn each wall of shelves, as though an ancient library of Bacchus's favorites: *grandes bouteilles*, magnums, grand crus, millesimes of Pomerol, St. Estèphe, St. Émilion, Haut-Brion, Puligny-Montrachet, Château d'Yquem sauternes, Macons, Bourgognes, chardonnays, Bergeracs, Pouilly Fumés, Margaux, Côtes du Rhône, Languedocs, Haut Médocs, Moët-Chandon brut premier, Deutz Brut Rosé . . . the list goes on and on.

I stand, rather speechless (rare for me, we know), as Marie-Hélène greets another sommelier, the young apprentice Pascal Garrone, a discreet and friendly-faced Italian man who has a charming shyness—a quality I haven't seen much of these days.

Pascal has already decanted several bottles and placed them on the rustic pine farmer's table in the center of the room. Each is aligned with four appropriately specific *verres* (wine glasses) ideal for each wine. The table also holds a few platters of thick, toasted, crusty slabs of bread slathered with a hearty gray foie gras for us to nibble on in between tastings. They are accompaniment, and also perhaps palate cleansers. One could wager they'd not be serving a host of stinky cheeses to wage war with a wine's distinct *bouche et nez, évidemment*.

Louis-Philippe stands next to me and thoughtfully whispers

faintly, "Thank you for coming this evening. If anything strikes your fancy, tell me, and I shall buy you a case—or maybe the whole vineyard!" He laughs softly, and winks.

Winks?! Hey, we all know I love a good wink. And God, does he smell as good as he looks. Chanel Antaeus, I think. I'm battling a wild urge to run my bare hands all over his smooth head and bite his neck. A smattering of discipline and decorum still prevail, I'm happy to find—miraculously enough. His sexy cranium's safe, *for the moment*.

Master Sommelier Gaspard de la Limp Wrist, *literally* (oh, I'm going straight to hell for that comment!), ever so kindly pours us each a small glass of a *vin blanc*—a Mersault, Hospice de Beaune 2004 Bourgogne—lifting it to the light, assessing the color, and giving it a single rotation to "open" and gauge the fluidity. Small sips all around, and the sommelier holds forth his appraisal: *"C'est un jeune vin très intéresant; arômes subtils qui combinent des fleurs blanches et des fruits exotiques, ce vin se révéle avec des notes souples et généreuses. C'est un vin parfait d'accompagner, par exemple, une sole meunière."* (In short, "It's great wine, drink it.")

We all listen with attention and continue to take light sips, trying to capture the bouquet and the notes he's referring to.

I wonder if they notice me smiling into my glass. If they do, they probably think I'm enraptured by the scent of the grape. Sure I am. But I'm also thinking of my life of eight months ago, when I'd grab any *vin blanc* that had a pretty label and cost less than five euros at my local Monoprix grocery store.

As the younger sommelier, Pascal, assumes the role of decanting *la prochaine bouteille du vin* to titillate our senses, Master Gaspard leads us to a very small wood door at the back of the *cave*, situated above four tiny stone stairs.

"As we let the *vin rouge* breathe a bit more, would you like to see one of the greatest underground passages of Paris?" All four of us nod like plastic toy dogs won at the traveling circus.

"During World War II, when the Germans were descending on Paris, this secret passage provided a clandestine escape for the precious few who were made aware of its existence. It extends all the way up to the Arc de Triomphe, and sheltered many important persons, as well as their prized possessions. Even today, very few people know it exists. We have much to sample this evening, but consider this an open invitation to return to climb the low passage, when time allows." And Master Gaspard returns to the table of wines while the rest of us gawk in amazement.

Louis-Philippe leans in to me and says, "There exists another secret tunnel I shall far prefer to become acquainted with . . . one only *you* can provide access to." And he casually returns to chatting up Marie-Hélène as though that were a common thing to say to a complete stranger. Well, well, ladies and gentleman, looks like we are off and running, with yet another highly sexually charged demon on our hands. I wasn't prepared for a right out of the gate innuendo. But then again, who am I to play the moralistic virgin? Sometimes I just forget this all goes with the territory.

We make our way through a few more offerings from France's greatest vineyards. The next wine is served in tall, wide-mouthed crystal goblets. Monsieur Gaspard resumes the lesson: *"Un Château Cheval Blanc 1982, Saint Émilion Grand Cru . . . Une très belle année. Impressionnant pour sa douceur et son caractère raffiné; le nez vert avec des notes de tilleul, pêche miel, et vanille. À garder longtemps et pas très cher, à environ 850 euros une bouteille."* (Sure, it's a downright *steal* at 850 euros a bottle. Does that make each glass about 270 euros? Yikes!)

Some more of that scrumptious pâté on toast is passed around in tandem with the wine. I find it is such a brilliant combination, I am tempted to pull up a chair and park my *derrière* right there all night, devouring and drinking with abandon, ignoring Marquis, Marie-Hélène, and all. Probably wouldn't go over well, so I'll stick with observing some version of what I believe is called "etiquette." But wouldn't it be fun to just live life doing *everything* you crave? Mayhem would rule, which, in fact, isn't so far from what passes for social mores in this city that seethes with hedonism.

Another bottle is served with aplomb, a *vin rouge* Gevrey Chambertin 2000 . . . *"Blah, blah . . . au nez encore fermé sur des notes*

poivrées . . . couleur subtile . . . blah . . ." Alright, this is all insanely
marvelous, but I'm getting a smidge drunk, slightly missing the
finer details of the delicate *bouquet*—while entirely losing the ability to translate, let alone stand upright.

Moments? Minutes? *Hours* later? Beats me. The tasting con-
cludes with another glass of I-forget-what, with Louis-Philippe ordering case after case, with Monsieur Gaspard in tow, as they march
about the cave, raving about the mythic Petrus Pomerol, praising a
Château-Pichon-Longueville '89, *c'était une grande année* (that was a
very good year for . . .) I feel like leaping up on that farm table and
yelping, "You know what? *This* is a grand year for *me*. For *everything*!
Let's hear it for this little chickadee hick who somehow fell in with
the beau monde de Paris and is rocking the hell out of it!" (Somebody get me off my high horse—feel free to knock me off—and it
might be wise to bring me a huge glass of water, too.)

The three of us (two members of France's aristocrat "de" con-
tingent and a young drunkish girl from Illinois) lavish our sincere
thanks on our wonderful and warm sommeliers. We bid our adieus
in succession, making the two-cheek kiss exit to Monsieur Gaspard's and the silently lovely Pascal. (By stupid luck, my insobriety
has obliterated what would've certainly been another reach for his
hand. Phew!) And we make our way back through the *once* madly
engaging kitchen that now feels very much like a twirl on a merry-
go-round set smack dab in a cooking school. A lesson there: Stick
with one's first impression and engrave it in memory—*especially
when drinking is involved*. This also is applicable to the old "beer
goggle" approach of how possible mates look increasingly tempting as the bottles empty and the night stretches into the wee hours.
In short—what was once a hideously unfuckable troll can appear
the reincarnation of Cary Grant after a few too many *pastis* and the
sun coming up. *Don't* go there. The morning wake-up call will be
so vicious as to make you want to claw your eyes out, as you make
toward the front door attempting a silent exit . . . even when it's
your apartment. (I may have to start taking antidigression pills soon,
right? Sorry.)

Back in the heart of the hotel, breathless but energized, the Marquis, Marie-Hélène, and I take advantage of the sumptuous armchairs in the George V dining room, and immediately order from *les cartes* placed in our eager hands. The menus given to women never show the prices—as if our little fragile minds or wallets couldn't withstand the blow. *France. Frozen in time!*

Nevertheless, I seize the moment, on behalf of women everywhere, to make my first expertly informed foray into dining excellence by opting for the *sole meunière* accompanied by a glass—yes, *another*—of the acclaimed perfect accompanying *vin blanc*, the Mersault, Hospice de Beaune 2004 Bourgogne.

And am rewarded with the maître d'hôtel's duly impressed, "An extremely fine choice, Mademoiselle." Fun!

The three of us make light-hearted banter about the wine for a moment, and then segue into slanderous gossip. That is, if you can call Marie-Hélène's outburst scandalous: "I should say, the unveiling of the Grand Palais's new roof was simply an abomination! The reflective quality and smaller dimensions of the panels well warrant a public outcry!" Truthfully, the raw, low-brow chatter was confined to Louis-Philippe and me. *Quelle surprise.*

When MH went to powder her nose, Louis-Philippe launched into this arena, while taking my hand in his hand . . . *in his lap* . . . *his firm, warm lap.*

"While you can be assured I adore the company of Marie-Hélène, I would very much like to slip away with you and indulge my *bouche et nez* in pursuit of your *bouquet intime*." (And no, he's not interested in deciphering the manufacturer of my *parfum*.)

"Is that a promise, a threat . . . or an invitation? *Écoutez, Marquis*. All good things come to he who waits." Yuck, that may be my worst quote ever. Well, his rehashing of the wine adjectives fell slightly short of original, so what the hell.

"May I invite you one day soon to come be my guest at my château in the Loire region? I should think you would find it very much to your liking. You are a woman who has a taste for all things beautiful and a passion for acquiring valuable objects of desire. My fantasies are already sweeping me away to spending a day with you *a camporella*." He flourishes his hand at me, as though I have given him my personal bio and list of hobbies that claims I collect Renoirs or something. And, just for the record, if you discount a teenage obsession with Bonnie Bell Lip-Smackers, I don't collect anything, buddy—except, maybe now, *men*. Or maybe that's exactly what he's referring to. God, who knows. As ever, I will just play along.

Marie-Hélène rejoins us, and espressos are served immediately, along with a small tray of *petites madeleines, tarte de citron,* and *fondant de chocolat*. That's another thing I love about Michelin-star dining: You can take an elegant, "*Oh, non, mais, merci*" on dessert and still load up on sweets, as if it were an obligation to honor the chef.

"*A camporella?* I don't suppose that's *camping* Cinderella style? Glass slippers under the moonlight?" I say, clearly still two sheets to the wind and fresh out of witty retorts.

Marie-Hélène returns and interjects, "Dear Alexa, it's Italian. Have you no Italian in your repertoire? Louis-Philippe, I demand you retain an Italian instructor for Alexandra at once. Sweet girl, I shudder to imagine you reading Machiavelli in anything but its original Italian. You concur, of course, Marquis?" she asks, with a flick of the wrist that denotes her request is implicitly understood and will be carried out forthwith. That would be MH vastly exaggerating the gravity of the situation to reap me the benefit of Italian fluency. Smooth lady. And I am still sipping *vin blanc* over here, stunned and more aware than ever that I am still the neophyte to her seamless, worldwise ways.

Louis-Philippe nods acceptance of this command, signs his name to *l'addition*, and discreetly tucks a five-hundred-euro note inside the leather sheath. Nice tipper. If all else fails, I should become a waitress at one of these high-end *restos*. Nah, *pas possible;* there *are* no female *serveurs*/waitresses *ever* at gourmand restaurants. Strange, really, when you think about it.

The three of us stroll arm in arm—the Marquis in the center— out of the opulent restaurant, and all heads turn in appreciation at the confident stride of our trio, dressed, coiffed, and tailored to couture perfection. However fleeting all of this is, moments like this, I do prefer to be the subject of admiring eyes than the bearer of them. I do realize that it's a lot of work and effort to put on all this extravagant regalia and prance around being fabulous.

Truthfully, it was a helluva lot easier to be the old low-maintenance me, the no makeup, jeans, and sneakers girl. No zillionaires ever gave her much attention, and that was fine. All this coiffing, adorning, and fussing every night is tremendous fun; it feels like playing dress-up, but I'm all too aware that these same people, for all their appreciation of the new and improved me, wouldn't have given me a glance earlier today as I dashed to *la poste* to mail a package to my parents, wearing glasses, corduroys, and a T-shirt, a cap jammed over my dirty hair. Image is a big part of the *haut monde de Paris* game, and frankly, I can't imagine playing it forever. I've got better things to do, like that damn thesis on Boucher that haunts me when I let the clouds clear and the rays of reality illuminate my mind. But come on, when rare opportunities like Vaux le Vicomte or this evening pop up, it's bloody impossible to refuse. So much to learn, to discover about myself and the inner workings of this culture and its men. And I *know* I will get back to studying. Maybe tomorrow. In which case, best to now "take it on home," solo, so as to be fresh to concentrate *demain*. (Insert shock at self in employing self-discipline given sexy, dashing man at arm's length. Oh, hell, making him wait will even fuel his passion further. So it's a good decision all around.)

As a hazy moon held court above, Louis-Philippe escorted us out of the hotel and over to Hugo, *le* driver, standing (God, how long has he been standing there?!) by Marie-Hélène's gleaming Mercedes parked a mere ten feet from the front door.

Taking my hand and raising it to his lips, "Darling Alexandra, will you not allow me the honor of seeing you home? I promise to be well behaved," begs Marquis de Semi-Pushy of the terribly irresistible eyes.

"Ring me when you promise to be *badly* behaved." And I wink and slip into the depths of the backseat next to MH, leaving the marquis on the sidewalk to curse his choice of strategy.

The second the car speeds away, Marie-Hélène and I fall into gales of laughter.

"Oh, you . . . You are a little vixen, my rosebud. A very well-played *soirée*, Alexa. First, self-deprecating, then coy and disinterested, aloof yet witty, and as a finale, devilishly racy. You have left Louis-Philippe in a state of splendid torture and unquestionably placed him directly in your back pocket. I know him well, trust me. He's seriously smitten."

"*Bon.* So am I. I find him handsome beyond words. Elegant . . . refined . . . and the best part: single! How marvelous not to feel the slightest hint of being 'the other woman.' " I clasp my hands in celebration, as we pass by Place de la Concorde. By the way, don't you think it's slightly amusing that allowing my honest all over the map comments to just pour forth works with these men? Let's hear it for the appeal of schizophrenia! It's a good lesson to learn that there's no sense trying to pretend you're "all feminine" or "all business" or "all" anything. Cool.

"Wonderful. *Mais, n'oublie pas* (but, don't forget), with men at this level, they can have whomever they wish, whenever they wish; thus, you must continue to exhibit detachment and autonomy. In the rules of seduction, dazzle the other with your blinding light. Place yourself on the horizon like a beacon, a shimmering mirage. Create a playful yet exasperating quest for him to seek and pursue. In the words of another well-known marquis, Marquis de Sade: 'Man is prey to two weaknesses. Wheresoever on earth he dwells, man feels the need to *prey* and to *love*.' "

"I'm guessing that's not *pray*, but *prey*, right?" I say, as Hugo comes to a stop at my door.

"With *you*, my most treasured rosebud . . . all men *pray* to be your *prey*," she roars, rolling up the window, still laughing.

As I head up the steps to my flat, it occurs to me that all of this endless advice on how to play men is getting slightly tiresome and starting to feel very "us against them." And it's not: their souls are just as fragile as ours are, but with steel swords between their legs that sometimes command them to make foolish choices. Kind of like women's inability to pass up a good sale on shoes. Oh, c'mon, don't try to pretend you haven't bought at least one pair of shoes that didn't even fit just because they were on sale! And men, silly little boys that they can be, can rarely pass up a pretty woman who captures their attention in a unique way.

And as for Marie-Hélène's Marquis de Sade quote. Funny, it's probably true, but it reminds me of Baudelaire's line: *"Il faut toujours en revenir à Sade pour expliquer le mal."* ("One must always return to Sade for an explanation of evil.")

Maybe, just *maybe*, all this playing with men's minds and sexual weaknesses is a bit evil. I mean, just what am I accomplishing by not even responding to Laurent's text message? Not that I've forgotten a single letter of it, like it's tattooed on my brain. Then again, my nonresponse *is* terribly French, and this kind of behavior seems accepted and ingrained throughout their history. I just came to this country; I didn't make the rules. So as they say, "when in Rome . . ."

(Footnote: How much rationalizing is going on here? Oh, about as much as one is likely to have bad breath after eating Roquefort and smoking a Gaulois—*beaucoup!*)

COURTESAN SEXUAL TIP
DU JOUR

- *Rocking your hips:* When making love while lying on your back, place your feet spread, knees bent, and rock your hips *back* (instead of rocking your hips forward, which gives deeper penetration). I know it sounds confusing, but if you simply lie on your back, and arch your back slightly, it will be obvious exactly what I mean by tilting your hips *back.* This "hips back move" narrows the opening and really clamps down on his penis, giving you both far more pleasure. If you're feeling generous—and frankly, really great lovers always

focus exclusively on their partner's pleasure. It's the entire idea
behind tantric sex . . . which is certainly worth delving into!

• *Discover new erogenous zones:* For some women it is possible to reach *la
petite morte* through caressing of breasts, nipples, *derrière* (OK, anus—
there is no pretty word for it, *désolée*), and in very rare cases, without
any direct contact to erogenous zones, but instead through
stimulation of other areas like the neck, inner arm, inner thigh, etc.
Can you fathom how amazing that would be?!

Experiment with every part of your body; some women find they
can come quickly during sex when their partner does something simple
like a soft bite on the collarbone, putting his fingers in your mouth for
you to suck gently, his warm breath exhaled over your nipple.

It's been said the famous nineteenth-century courtesan Cora Pearl
could reach *la petite morte* simply by letting her long hair cascade over her inner arm . . . Imagine how exciting taking lunch in your office with the door
closed could be?! Each woman has her own personal triggers, the pleasure is
finding what they are for you.

CHAPITRE SEIZE

Passion arms us against sentiment.

—ALEXANDRE DUMAS

To be honest, I don't entirely agree with the above quote. Though, admittedly, it definitely has its moments of application. Women, even courtesans like me, attach to men sentimentally. How could we not, with all our maternal instincts and the hormones that make us nurture and want to protect? In fact, men would make better courtesans, with their ability to keep emotionally *de*tached. But hey, women, at least for the moment, have that market cornered, not to mention like hell we'd drop credit cards in a man's lap to guarantee his attention.

But back to my ever-increasing tornado of men and revelations. My little shiny-headed Marquis sent flowers the following day: a huge bouquet of calla lilies. Chic, but had to give them to the concierge (as I have also with all the arrangements Frédéric sends), as I expected Jean-Albert to come by for a drive-by visit on his way to Asia for a business trip. Anyway, now the concierge's apartment is positively overflowing with enough flowers to festoon the winner of the Kentucky Derby (very American thinking on my part, eh?)

or, as she likes to say, in an obviously more Frenchish comment, "It is like living in the gardens of Versailles." My *chapeau* goes off to her there in the well-phrased department. I think I'm draining all my reserves of witticisms and French references on these *soirées* with the aristo crowd, and by the time I make it home, I'm lucky if I know my *droite* from my *gauche*.

Jean-Albert's off to Shanghai to open yet another one of his hi-falutin luxury shops. If I tell you this company specializes in hand-bags, is that too much of a clue? Too late. Anyway, don't need a million bouquets from other men all over my apartment. Jean-Albert's already sporting a shaky ego, fearing he's losing me, so best be gentle with him. He presents a bulletproof exterior to the rest of the world, and sometimes I think I'm the only one who knows his secret self.

And as for replying to Laurent's message? I'm still not sure what to say. Have even thought, that perhaps it wasn't even meant for me. I mean, really, we all have accidentally sent messages to the wrong person, and it's not like he's been in constant contact with me and I'm besieged with love letters and calls. Really, with my luck, I'd respond in equally adoring terms and he'd write back: "Sorry sms was 4 someone else." God, my little heart couldn't take that! So I'm focusing on my Marquis, who frankly looks like the catch of the century and at thirty-nine *ans* surely knows who he is and what he wants!

Even if I was initially a hair disappointed that Louis-Philippe's note with the flowers fell a bit short of the enchanting poeticism of both Frédéric and Jean-Albert, now I'm thinking it shows he's less a ladies' man–playboy and more sincere. Or maybe I'm all wrong, and that for all his physical allure, he's just a moron. Oh, I'm kid-ding. But having been on the receiving end of a great many beauti-fully written *mots d'amour* these days, my radar is highly tuned to seriously compelling correspondence, so I'm basking in his previ-ously exhibited charm and taking this as a tentative until I show him I'm assuredly interested. You judge . . .

Ma chère Alexandra,

If you would join me at La Maison du Caviar, *jeudi soir*, I can promise you a night you will never forget. I will send a car for you at 20h.
Je vous embrasse tendrement. À très bientôt . . .

Louis-Philippe de Tassin

You have to admit, it's a tiny bit drab. I mean, it's polite,
concise . . . inoffensive at best. Oh, all right, I'm giving him a hard
time, whatever. I hear you; not every man has to write like
Flaubert. But if he makes love like he writes, truth be told, I will
surely fall asleep midfuck. *Joke!* Oh, you know it's not . . . Actually,
it's starting not to matter how much money these men have, just
that I feel *something*. It's complicated to explain. Something that
makes you feel like there's nowhere else you'd rather be, that the
moment is somehow unanticipated and/or profound. There's only
so much caviar one can eat and, frighteningly enough, I already had
a ball giving that all-U-can-eat-caviar consumption a go with Jean-
Albert at Prunier a few months ago.

So it's not about that invitation; it's that I do sincerely think
there could be something significant with Louis-Philippe. With his
penetrating gaze—I do so love *penetrating* of all kinds—to clarify,
almost all kinds. Don't let me get ahead of myself here; more to the
point, don't let me get behind myself, if you get me!

My Marquis is all the things I have always adored and everything
I have come to realize I enjoy. Sure, we can start with sexual, add elegant, refined, single, young, wealthy, impeccably mannered, highly
intelligent yet playful, a self-created character with a strong presence. (Truthfully, a lot of these aristo kin rest on the family name and
fail to develop much of a personality, and frankly, as in-breds, they
very often have a loose nut or a frighteningly spooky appearance. I
may very well get booted out of France for saying that, but someone had to!) But Louis-Philippe has this spirit, a life force that I'm
absolutely taken with. Frankly, Laurent had it, too, a palpable enthusiasm for living—in truth and expressively, always seeking new

adventures. Actually, in the original Greek meaning, "enthusiasm" translates as "God is within us." How wonderfully poetic is that?!

As a consequence of all my musings on my Marquis while indulging in a warm lavender oil bath this morning, I could see my heart just racing, literally creating a tide in the bubbly bath water, when I thought of him. You can't fake, manufacture, or feign that. No siree!

While with Jean-Albert it's a true appreciation for him and honor to be with him, when it comes to the sexual arena there—despite his skills, I need not admit to you—most of my desire there is created by my own mind. And with Frédéric, he's as sexy as they come (pun intended), but his appeal to me is more fantasy-based and fueled by the power we each have and the limits we make and break. Even on our picnic, it somehow felt that he was intentionally going from one extreme, of the Hermès saddle sex, to the sweet romantic picnic, as a strategy. Hard to explain, but when you remember that he *is* a masterful and manipulative politician, you do have to consider it. It's hard to forget that so much of his interest in me seems to be about or connected to an ongoing power struggle with Jean-Albert over possessions and prestige. In contrast, Louis-Philippe is just a gift, free of any ploy or game. Now I just have to not blow it, and snag him!

But until then, in the keeping all plates spinning department, I've got Jean-Albert tonight, and Frédéric is still in Russia, so there's no work to be done there, and the Marquis is booked for Thursday. Daring boy, he really does have his work cut out for him with his "a night you won't forget" comment! With the exception of just standing me up, I think that's gonna be tough for him to swing.

D'accord. I should get going over to the Bibliothèque Nationale and put in some long-overdue work on that thesis . . . Hmmm, hmmm. (Insert: loads of puttering around my apartment, tidying unnecessarily while humming. Almost to the extreme of rearranging my sock drawer.)

Okay, I think it's apparent that the thesis has as much appeal right now as a root canal. I mean, really, how did I ever just sit in the dark bowels of the library for hours on end, day after day? Yes. It seems I will have to *inch* my way back into that mind-set. Hey, I *could* call Isabel, the other *très* neglected aspect of my previous life.

She picks up on the first ring, and having spotted my name on her caller ID, launches right into conversation, "Alexandra . . . I'm *so* glad you called. I *knew* you would. So, can you believe it? Isn't it surreal?!"

"Hiya sweetie. What? . . . You mean Samaritane closing? I know, that's madness," I say, wondering why that's thrilling her to bits, and equally just happy to have her be so nice to me again.

"Samaritane? No, who cares about that? I mean *my* news . . . didn't you get my invitation?" She sounds as perplexed as I just did.

"Is it an invite to the next *défilé*? No, I haven't checked my mail in days," I answer, thinking it *could* be fun to return to "the scene of the crime," the Hôtel Crillon after–fashion show party where I met Jean-Albert, but this time arrive *with* him. That'd be de-leesh.

"No, I'm talking about the invitation I sent you to . . . my wedding!!! Mathieu and I are engaged!" She's so breathless and exuberant, she might be doing back flips.

"Holy shit, girl. That's fabulous. Really? Wonderful. *Ohmigod*, tell me everything!" And we slide, both of us grateful, back into our old rapport. I couldn't be more relieved, as the first couple of minutes there we were as out of sync as two blind ballerinas.

"Oh, I know, it's all happened very fast. But when you know, *you know*. You liked him, right? He's just the *best* thing that ever happened to me. I'm over the moon." Her voice has endearingly fallen into a coo.

"Oh, honey, he rocks. He's great, gorgeous, genuine, and so funny. This is huge news. How did he ask you? And when? When? When will you tie the knot, you wild woman?" I am so elated for her *and*, I realize, to be speaking to a woman who's so pure, passionate for life, and for once not giving advice about manipulating men but instead just appreciating them. (Tiny slam to MH, *pardonne-moi*.)

"He asked me the weekend after I got promoted. Oh, don't think I told you that. I got bumped up another notch here. I'm now working directly with Nicolas and am ennobled with a 'chief of design' title. Anyway, we went to Mathieu's family's house on Île de Ré to celebrate two weeks ago, and he just asked me spontaneously, as we were swimming in the sea at midnight. Isn't that the *most* romantic thing you ever heard?"

"Yeah, pretty much! God, how fabulous. You deserve all this. I cannot get over how your life has just shot stratospherically into wonderful bliss," I add, sincerely stunned. I lean against the wall, gazing out over Place Vendôme.

"You should talk! I know you're living a dream life of luxury—at this ball and that château. You're the talk of the town. Is it exciting? Are you in love?" she asks, with touching hope.

Without realizing it's about to happen, I lose the strength to stand and slide down the wall, as my feet give out from under me. Whoa. Didn't see that coming. Apparently, I'm *not* in love and *not* at all well. Kicking off my stupid mules and pulling my knees to my chest, it all comes pouring out before I even realize I'm speaking.

"Love? No. Sadly, not in love. In *appreciation*. In *heat . . . in deep* and in heaps of gowns and jewels, but love?" I right myself with some of that good old American "look on the bright side" resiliency. "It's OK, I'm having a blast, and it's fascinating. Not at all ready for the big leap, but I'm so glad you've found the One. How cool. Have you designed your dress yet? Of course you are designing your dress, right? And you haven't told me—*when* is the big day?" I ask, lurching to stand up, while reaching for my cigarette case on the side table.

"Two months away! Had to be an early autumn wedding. Remember how you and I always said it's the most gorgeous time of the year in Paris to be married? And we have an engagement party the Saturday after next . . . You know me, it's all completely rushed and gonna be haphazard chaos. But I am just out of my mind with happiness. Oh, *merde*, I should go. Have to work like a *chien* now, with the new job title and to pay for all the coming celebrations. Call me this weekend. You and I have to sit down, put away some Champagne, and plan this gig. I so need your advice on everything, from the flowers to the music. You're the only woman I know with impeccable taste in those things. Ring me, love you . . . *bises*."

The line goes dead. *And so do I.*

I was lost in silence for several minutes. Really lost—I didn't know where to look, where to put my hands, where it was safe to let my mind go. Then I did something I have never done before . . . and sure as hell won't do again. Not proud of this, but despite it being all of 11:00 A.M., I beelined for the kitchen, popped open a bottle of chilled Veuve Clicquot, sat staring out at the skyline, and got good and drunk.

It gets worse. Once the bottle was completely drained, I staggered into the bedroom, and in some misplaced act of defiance put on my old, beat-up jeans and a gray Gap T-shirt I've had for a millennium (and looks it, complete with baby vomit stains from my au pair years), threw my wallet into my crappy old backpack, and descended onto Place Vendôme with a vengeance . . . Albeit a veering-all-over-the-place vengeance. Like a loon on a mission to escape and simultaneously "fuck the rules," I hit Cartier like a bomb.

Ignored stunned reaction from sales team regarding my *ensemble.* There's a stretch of the word *"ensemble."* Eyed a pink diamond necklace, very similar to the one I saw Kirsten Dunst wearing as Marie Antoinette in the movie, and asked to try it on.

Some advice here: never, I repeat, *never* shop while smashed emotionally or by alcohol or both. At the time I thought it riotous and *très, très* cool bohemian of me to swan into Cartier, looking like fuck-all and then . . . Oh, God . . . Yes, I did tell the terribly unamused saleswoman, "Put the necklace, *moitié et moitié* on these two cards." (That's half and half *en français.*)

And I added, "Just keep the box; I'll wear it out." Well, well. That's all a bit nuts, wouldn't you agree? Certainly made a splash at Cartier with that move. More of a tidal wave, really.

Having charged—I'm too embarrassed to tell you exactly how much—let's just say five figures to each, Frédéric and Jean-Albert, I careened over to Boulevard Haussmann and saddled up to the counter at . . . McDonald's, and ordered two filets of fish and *grandes frites.* "Yea . . . I definitely want a French fries, yea. Definitely should have fries . . . ," I stammer, sounding very much like Dustin Hoffman in *Rainman*, I might add.

Good God! Devoured the fries drunkenly while wearing jeans with hole in knee and twelve carats of pink diamonds. Still with price tag hanging off the back. Chicer moments I have had, *to be sure*. At the time it all made sense. That's the thing about drunken decisions made in heightened emotional moments; they always seem like you're having some genius epiphany of pure wisdom when, in fact, you're doing the dead opposite.

I guess I walked home. God only knows what other trouble I could've gotten into had I not drunk, shopped, and ate myself into unconsciousness. All I know is, the next thing I remember is Jean-Albert calling around dusk and me nattering, "I'm sick . . . sorry, I can't see you tonight, baby. Call me from Shanghai." And that going over like a lead balloon.

The next morning, I surfaced into consciousness, or a hazy version of it, still wearing the aforementioned ensemble and very much less amused with self and my spontaneous shopping spree.

I scrubbed away reality in that gorgeous antique copper *bagnoire* and pulled myself together, at least physically. "Oh, screw it," I told myself. "I'm allowed a little descent from the endless scrutiny and pressure to be Mademoiselle Perfect. I mean, in the grand scheme of things, I clearly had a little 'crash,' and while some people might opt for a noose around their necks, I go for pink diamonds. So I did a little damage at Cartier, let's not kid ourselves: These men don't even see their credit card bills. Hell, Marie-Hélène would probably claim this was a good way to keep them both off balance. All I know is, I'm backing up from the married ones and honing in like a rocket on Louis-Philippe. I deserve a sincere single man just as much as Isabel does. There's no good reason why my little Marquis couldn't become a real boyfriend. Maybe even the One. Just occurred to me: Then I'd be a Marquise. Hilarious. Don't even much care for that 'cut' of diamond; I'm much more an 'emerald-cut' girl. Spoken like a true courtesan, huh?"

I rang Marie-Hélène at noon, and though I thought I'd edit my recap, I ended up telling her the whole ugly truth *and* what spurred the whole Ferris Bueller's Day Off—that is if he were a young courtesan in Paris—adventure. As I had guessed, she was all for the necklace, the madcap afternoon, and even canceling on Jean-Albert. I swear, I could tell this woman, just for kicks, I am plotting a takeover coup of the Louvre and she'd say, "Marvelous idea! Run with it! Remember, that should really be done wearing something military . . . say, the crimson velvet waistcoat from Dolce and Gabbana's last collection . . . Oh, and be sure to be finished by Thursday—we have a salon appointment!"

Here's what she said about my antics of the day before: "Alexa, acquiring the necklace for yourself was a perfect statement of your impetuousness. Sending those kinds of signals is shrewd, as it reminds these men that you cannot be controlled, and their desire for total control will plunge them deeper into confusion and obsession with you. Postponing a rendezvous with Jean-Albert was also—perhaps unconsciously—clever of you." More like made in a state of *unconsciousness*, I sat there thinking. "Your greatest power in seduction, almost your 'trump card'—as you say in English—is your capacity to shut them down, make them chase after you. Delaying their satisfaction is always a *bonne idée*. Make them afraid that you may be withdrawing. Run hot and cold, and while it may frustrate a lover, and he may act angry, it's a sure sign of his enslavement." Do *not* get this woman started; she could rationalize everything from "Let them eat cake!" by Marie Antoinette to World War II.

Though Marie-Hélène did hasten to add, "But of course, you must know, I think you did yourself a disfavor with your choice of attire." I just laughed. "I knew that'd be the single detail that you'd be horrified by! Yes, I think I got that 'cold-hot' thing down; frankly, it's a bit like the old phrase in fishing, "catch and release." Snag them hook, line, and sinker, and then throw them back, gasping for air. And frighteningly enough, with Jean-Albert kissing like a trout, it all comes rather naturally." I say, laughing.

"Not the most refined reference I've heard you utter, my sweet. But I get your meaning. Still, steer clear of those American slangisms (Wha? I let that attempt at American slang slide), as the Marquis is younger and not likely to be as charmed by them as the older gentlemen are."

"Noted and *d'accord*, master. Fear not. I've drifted off the podium of the grand courtesan. Tonight I intend to use all the powers at my employ to enchant, captivate, and ensnare the handsome Louis-Philippe. We are due to have dinner at La Maison du Caviar. And I should tell you, he has set the bar quite high by assuring me it will be a night that I'll 'never forget.' You know him. What do you think that entails? And please feel free to offer any last-minute advice, as I've clearly placed him in the leading contender position," I say, catching sight of myself in the mirror above the fireplace. I'm a bloated wreck; it will take some doing to appear fabulous by nightfall. My face is so hangover-puffy, I look like a blowfish.

Never at a loss for words, MH continues with great seriousness: "The wonderful thing about the Marquis is that he has the money and the imagination to come up with anything. It would be unwise to even wager a guess. Remember, he's looking to marry, so retain a certain elegance and taunt him sexually rather than utilize your lovemaking skills to astonish him."

Hearing her speak such a blatant idea into my ear as I see myself in the reflection, I feel distinctly aware of the surreality of my life. Does anyone else on earth receive advice like this? And is it even weirder that it has become so *normale* for me? For all her varied advise, Marie-Hélène is rarely, if ever, wrong. As much as it all sounds brutal and manipulative, it's as though she has reduced behavioral patterns between men and women down to their raw essence. Of course, there are patterns and differences due to culture, society, and genetics that can be studied, and applied to what we all want from life and our relationships with the opposite sex. So, as many times as I am tempted to discount MH's theories and commands, she's got a lot of wisdom under her belt. Under her one-thousand-euro Chanel belt, that is.

Marie-Hélène ends with, "And do ring me at the first available moment. I shall be on pins and needles waiting to hear how it goes, *chérie. Bonne chance!"*

"You know I will. *À demain."* And with all that settled, I breathe a sigh of relief. Click my cell phone to "end" and notice a text message still typed into my phone.

What the?!

Miss u madly. Where r u? I will cum to u. mch love. A

Hmm, don't remember getting that, but I was two sheets—*no, a dozen sheets*—to the wind last night. I scan who it's from and when it was sent, and oh, mother of God . . . *I am "A"! I sent it . . . to Laurent last night!* Apparently in an alcohol-induced, romantic state of unguarded honesty at the ludicrous hour of 8:12 P.M.

Piss. Ugh. Not very clever of me but too late. And as I think we all know now, I meant it. I want what Isabel's got. I am crazy for the Marquis, but, I'm going to admit, however incredible it would be to land him, there is something terrifying about the idea, too. Part of it is a fear that I would have to be at my most perfect and fabulous all the time, and that's hyperstressful, to say the least! Of course, a huge part of me floated away on the fantasy of Laurent ringing and beckoning me back to him. Wow, that would be a knight-in-shining-armor moment. Wouldn't that be great? No, really, it *could* happen. Should I pack a small bag? Should I cancel on the Marquis now? Well, something has to shake out after I sent that text message off into the world. (Should be interesting to see just how he eagerly he responds, and if he comes to me or asks me to come to him. No, no, don't get ahead of yourself, Alexa; remember that he still has a lot of work to do to win you back. Right. I'm not the naïve girl I used to be, and whenever he calls I have to play it far cooler than that text message dripping with sap I sent. Now it's my turn to make him jump through a few hoops.) With my newfound talent for switching gears (read: turning a blind eye to reality), I amazingly found the will to sit down, clear my thoughts, and spend the afternoon *chez moi*, reviewing all my notes and working on my thesis.

Looks like I have about a good three months of serious work to put it all into some kind of order. If I focused I could possibly finish the damn thing by Christmas. God, would that feel good. And if things, say, spun out well with one of these men, then I could segue into something resembling a real life.

At 7:00 P.M., I'm pleased to discover, all the anxiety of yesterday has somehow floated out the window on a breeze, and possibly landed on someone else's unsuspecting shoulders on the streets below. (Sorry buddy, if the burden fell heavily on *your* head; haven't the time for it—have a date with a *marquis*!)

To be honest, with the exception of my drunken shopping spree—for damn sure—I have recently acquired the skill of assuming all the lighthearted frivolity of Scarlett O'Hara in *Gone with the Wind:* "Oh, fiddle dee dee, I can't bother myself with that right now. I'll worry about that tomorrow." In clinical terms, this tendency could be labeled "reality avoidance." While it's occasionally useful in anyone's life, in a courtesan's it's a necessity. Thus it is that with nothing but pure excitement, I hustle around doing the dressing to the nines routine for dinner with Louis-Philippe.

Hmm. The "future wife" look? That's easy: a distinct *non* to anything black or blatant. A *oui* to a sleek slate-gray *pique* strapless dress, falling midknee, by Chloe, with its smoke alençon lace bolero paired with a demure matching gray silk slingback. A big fat "no way" to the pink diamonds in lieu of the far more discreet Mikimoto choker and, just for fun, Nicolas Ghesquiere's oyster suede dragonfly bag with an appliqué of Swarovski crystals and freshwater pearls. Man, once Isabel told me about this bag, with its jewels based on a brooch designed by Balmain himself, I knew it would fall into the can't-live-without category, of which I'm acquiring quite a healthy family of must-haves, dare I admit. God, have I clearly fallen into luxury consumer mode or what? Well, perhaps it's only natural as I "consume" the man (Jean-Albert) who creates the best luxury consumer products! Thank the lord, Jean-Albert is out of town, and there's zero chance of running into him at dinner *ce soir.* Then again, am so confident of my ability to chat my way around and through any given situation these days, it might've added some excitement to the night. I'm getting so twisted—the old me wouldn't have dreamt of a sticky situation like that as being amusing. And may I say that I'm wearing the absolute perfect outfit of my dreams, as I put on my makeup in my beyond dream apartment and am off to meet a most sought-after dream of a man. So, twisted girl that I may be, it's all good, right? (That's rhetorical, by the way, so shush.)

A final sip of a predate chilled Sancerre, a last cigarette and a breath-restoring gargle of mouthwash, and we're off and running, kids. The driver has arrived, and now I make my way downstairs to launch off on what feels like a first date. Wait, it *is* a first date! Wild that I almost forgot that, so much of the last few months has felt like, well, more like being called on stage and less like a date between a boy and a girl. Yep, no doubt about it, the Marquis already has a tremendous edge in that this all feels more genuine and sincere than my assignations with either Jean-Albert or Frédéric. Thank God.

The bespectacled old driver is waiting at the door and announces, while opening the door to the gleaming new slate-gray Rolls-Royce, "I'm Hugo, and I will be delighted to be at your service this evening. Marquis de Tassin is awaiting you at the restaurant."

I employ Courtesan Car Etiquette and slowly slide onto the backseat, then glide—legs together (yes, demure, albeit for a microsecond), ankles intertwined, hands clasped and placed on lap—all very "royalty hath arriveth," *non?* Oh, and all the while swallowing a laugh that we've got yet another Hugo driver on our hands. Just curious, here: When they hand out the drivers' licenses, are they just all preprinted with the de rigueur name, "Hugo"?

As the Maison du Caviar is just a stone's throw from the Champs-Élysées, there isn't much in the way of time to get nervous, or for anything more than to remind myself, "Wife material; you gotta pull that off, Alexandra. That's a helluva lot more of an achievement than *lover*. Good, I so enjoy a challenge."

Hugo pulls right up to the restaurant, and I'm surprised there is no valet outside, as is customary. I'm deposited at the door with an

"Enjoy your dinner, Madame. I will be here if you should need anything at all" from the ever formal Hugo du Jour.

I enter the restaurant expecting the usual warm gold lighting, enhanced with the soft peach tones that are so common in expensive restaurants. (Reason: It makes the traditionally old and haggard clientele appear more appealing, while allowing dark corners for illicit rendezvous.)

But tonight I am met with almost complete darkness. "Weird," I think. "Is there another restaurant by the same name? Have I shown up early or . . ."

A heavy taffeta curtain is whisked aside as the flickering light of hundreds of ivory tapers spreads a shimmering glow throughout the entire room—which is completely empty of tables save for one, majestically adorned and placed in the center of the restaurant. The resonating voice of Louis-Philippe reaches me mere moments before his hand is slipped into mine, and the music of Mozart's overture for *Cosi fan Tutte* is set in motion by a string quartet of young men tucked into the bay to the right.

"Alexandra. You look radiant with celestial light. I hope you will be charmed by the notion of dining *juste nous deux*. I have taken the liberty of booking the entire restaurant to create a more intimate venue for our *premier soir ensemble*."

And Louis-Philippe leads me by the hand past a line of four impeccably turned-out waiters in white jackets, standing in silent, respectful attendance, and the maître d'hôtel, who gallantly offers, "*Bonsoir*, Mademoiselle. It is a pleasure to see you again. May I wish you a lovely dinner." He pulls out the velvet-backed chair from the table set for two.

"Louis-Philippe, this is positively divine. I am so touched. You need do nothing more to ensure that this is a night to remember," I say sincerely, unconsciously putting a hand to my heart.

"Ah, but the night has just begun, my beautiful Alexandra. There's so much I want to discover about you, I fear I may deluge you with inquiry after inquiry. Indulge me, if I may be so bold as to request such deference," he says—so formally!—while simultaneously nodding to the sommelier that the chilled Cristal 1994 Champagne is suitable to be poured into the crystal flutes.

Go ahead buddy, chop-chop! At this point I kind of wish I were on a lazy Susan–type chair that I could just spin around on and take in every square inch of what has been created purely for my amusement. I *want* to say: "How damn cool is this?!" But it's replaced with "My dear, I'm sure you're aware it is often what a woman *doesn't say* rather than what she says that speaks of her true soul."

"*Vous avez raison.*" (You are correct.) "Who was it that said that phrase?" he asks.

"Me. Just now, I believe. Be as original and forthcoming as you please. Feel free to ask me whatever you wish. I don't suppose you have committed to memory the thirty-five character-revealing questions that comprise '*Le questionnaire de Proust*'?" and I smile, sure that he has—just as much as I'm sure that this bottle of bubbly goes for about five hundred euros in a restaurant of this caliber.

"Oh, but of course, I have, and I adore that you are willing to make it a game. I *so* love a game. *En fait,* Proust was a family friend of my grandfather's and for as much as my *grand-père* pretended he was ill at ease being mentioned in the historic masterpiece *À la recherche du temps perdu,* he instilled in me a great appreciation for Proust and his observations about society. I cherish his perspectives on the inner workings of the mind and the role that memory plays in our pursuits of . . ." he trails off, searching for the perfect word.

Knowing as a courtesan that every word I say is as crucial as how I look (and also looking to amaze him) I steal the moment.

"Pursuits that provoke *concupiscence* . . . lustful or otherwise," I say, with a wink. Okay, that's the last damn wink I can throw at this man! I swear I've become a hideous winkaholic. That's gotta come to a screeching halt before I overkill its charm. And BTW, here's a free definition for you: "concupiscence," powerful feelings of desire.

"*Exactement, chérie, c'est le mot juste.*" (A literary expression, meaning "the perfect word.") "You are certainly as intelligent as you are *belle . . . extrêmement.*" And he tips his flute to mine.

MENU

Mademoiselle Alexandra Ward & Marquis Louis-Philippe de Tassin

Selection des vins

Amuse-Bouches: Beluga caviar   *Cristal Champagne 1994*
avec crème fraîche

Entrée: Risotto crémeux   *Pouilly-Fumé 1994 (Ladoucette)*
aux crevettes et herbes fraîches

Plat: Dourade en feuillete   *Savigny Les Beaune 1996*
avec câpres et pignons   *(Dubois)*

Dessert: Mangue en coulis sur   *Château Y'quem*
un nougat glacé au miel

Espresso, San Pellegrino

Ching! Yes, that is both the sound of delicate crystal meeting and of a cash register. You got that right!

Phew. That worked. With the charming quartet easing into Schubert's Symphony No. 7 soothing all my senses, my contented glance settles upon the hand-calligraphed dinner menu placed at my right. As our two names lead off the beautifully embellished *carte*, it's clear that everything, down to the choice of *eau* (San Pellegrino. All Euro-trash men order this water, swear to God!) has been prearranged *pour* our *dîner privé*. That is *so* sexy. I do love the effort these men put out to please a woman.

Over the scrumptuous banquet detailed above (and I've discovered, BTW, that one can never tire of beluga, *it's just not possible*) both Louis-Philippe and I spiral into serious swooning. And I might add—wildly enhanced to levels of which I have scarcely previously experienced, with both of us responding to the other with answers to Proust's questions. Conversation had a rare precision that was simply intoxicating, thereby evoking a lot more of that *concupiscence* we both dig!

Here's a sampler of the results, enough to give you a take on him:

	Moi	Louis-Philippe
Favorite heroine from literature:	Phaedre	Manon Lescaut
Favorite man from history:	Leonardo de Vinci	Lorenzo de Medici
Favorite heroine from history:	Elizabeth I	Jean d'Arc (Joan of Arc)
Favorite painter:	Surprisingly not Boucher, but Egon Schiele	Caravaggio
Your dream of happiness:	This moment	"When the woman I love agrees to marry me"
Principal trait of your character:	Passionate curiosity	Ardent
Favorite poet:	Rilke	Châteaubriand
Quality you most detest in yourself:	Impatience	Caprice
Quality you most like in yourself:	Commitment to an idea	My *joie de vivre*
Quality you most appreciate in women:	Independence	Self-assuredness
Quality you most appreciate in men:	Humor	Commitment to honor
Your favorite composer:	Mozart	Bach
Talent you most wish you possessed:	To play the violin	To live simply
How you would like to die:	Making love after a long beautiful life	Peacefully, at no burden to others
Favorite color:	The pale green of a tulip stem	White—the sum of all colors

I don't know what your desired responses from a man would be, but Louis-Philippe's pretty much secured him the starring role in my fantasies of the future. And as we know, I had hatched just such a plan for such a man and he stepped into the role beautifully. By the time the last chocolate-covered espresso bean had been nibbled and the final drops of Champagne had been sipped, we were both so bloody sure of a well-made match that had he suggested we get hitched at sunrise, I would've pushed for *sooner*. More of that impatience of mine there, obviously.

As I stood to thank the maître d', it occurred to me: What an incredible lack of sexual innuendo there had been, and what a welcome surprise it was. To captivate each other so intensely without the slightest seductive or suggestive word falling from his lips *or* mine. Just an intellectual rally of ideas, references, and anecdotes—in the last few days that had become more valuable to me than a plethora of pink diamonds, and even more delicious than the beluga.

But don't get me wrong—I'm hankering to get this man naked *tout de suite*, and frankly, I kinda miss the crazy, sexually surprising situations that have come my way in the last nine months. *Coming* being the operative word. Oh, I know, it's a bit vulgar of me, but it seems it's true: Once you kick your sexual desire *and curiosity* into high gear, there is no shifting back to low gear. If there is a low gear, mine has fallen off.

Louis-Philippe and I leave the restaurant, and as we're stepping into the car I look back at the famous Maison du Caviar and smile, thinking, "Yep, never in my life will I forget that extraordinary experience! A whole restaurant to ourselves? Like a scene out of movie, where you say to yourself, 'please . . . like that ever happens!' It *does*." If I kept a diary, Anaïs Nin would have nothin' on me. OK, I take that back. I wonder if Marie-Hélène has ever kept a diary; would *love* to get my hands on that!

The evening closes with a little detour from what I thought would be read as my demure request to be dropped at home, but of course would be game playing. I agreed to his suggestion of a long walk by the Seine, where we strolled hand in hand while a white sliver of a moon lingered just above the delicate spire of Saint Chapelle. Truly, so exquisitely lovely an image, it almost pierces one's soul with delicious torture. *Vraiment,* is there *ever* a night in Paris that isn't astonishingly beautiful?!

On Pont Neuf, bathed in the silvery rays of the moon, standing beneath the regal equestrian bronze of Henri IV, we pause to sneak tender kisses and bask in the warm night air. The city is quiet save for the cooing of doves in the courtyard of Passage Dauphine and a handful of late-night revelers singing on Pont des Arts behind us. I lean against him as we both look up at the moon, shimmering like a piece of jewelry set against the black velvet of the dark sky. Louis-Philippe wraps his arms around my shoulders and whispers, "I never dreamt I could find myself falling in love with *une femme américaine.* You're quite a surprise, my dearest Alexandra. Does the idea of Alexandra de Tassin scare you?"

Prepare yourself for my answer, given in the French methodology of response, i.e., "never direct."

"My sweet boy, one question we didn't ask each other from the *questionnaire de Proust* is, 'What is your *devise* (motto for life)? Perhaps you will find it reassuring that mine is 'do something every day that scares you,'" I say, turning to face him and smiling playfully.

"Oh, how terribly dangerous and wonderfully surprising! Though I hope you appreciate my commitment this evening to being the consummate gentleman, I shall hold you to that statement, my dear libertine. And perhaps you will also enjoy my *devise: Il faut vivre passionnément et non pas seulement exister.* One must live passionately, not merely exist."

That, my friends, you have to say, is a helluva first date. I went home, put on my favorite silk charmeuse nightgown with antique lace, and began writing down all that had recently happened to me in Paris. I didn't stop writing until I fell asleep, pen in hand.

A perfect way to slip into sleep after a perfect night!

* * *

P.S. No news from Laurent. My fury and disappointment is greatly reduced by the magnificent idea of a future with the marquis that clearly is unfolding before me. God, how I wish I hadn't sent that text message back to Laurent! For someone (that would be me) who has learned the skill and pleasure of having power with men, crap, have I blown it there with Monsieur Real Guy (that would be Laurent, obviously)! Come to think of it, maybe this power play and game of seduction *only* applies to men of Jean-Albert and Frédéric's ilk. Nah . . . men are men, right? Regardless, if I have *any* regrets regarding all the wild and spontaneous things I've done in the last nine months, I *only* regret sending that message! That's a huge statement, *non*? Must learn to adapt the age-old philosophy of "don't drink and dial" to the new and improved "don't drink and text." Oh, and I should add in "don't drink and shop," "don't drink and answer the phone," "don't drink and dress" . . . *bien sûr.*

COURTESAN TIPS
FOR THE HOME

- You must cultivate your surroundings to echo your sensuality. If you invest in no other room in your home, spend generously and lavishly on furnishing your bedroom. Create sensual environments with sumptuously luxurious beds and boudoirs. Every detail should add to the alluring ambiance: a deliciously beckoning bed or rich, sumptuous linens and duvets; a bounty of luxurious pillows to fall back into. And need it be said: four-poster and canopy beds are de rigueur? They may very well have been created solely for their extraordinarily pragmatic uses during sex, giving you something to hold onto and/or to tie him to—while masterfully mounting your lover and driving him blind with desire with your Japanese squat trick.

- Fill the room with the fragrances most arousing to men (amazingly, the number one choice is vanilla).
- Create soft, sensual light. Add this soft lighting everywhere: candles at dinner, bedside, and by the bath. Switch to pink and gold-tone lightbulbs and shades. Watch those angles of illumination. Be very careful: A woman should never be lit directly from below, as it creates a scary monster cast to one's face. And ditch all that pragmatic but heinously unsexy bedside paraphernalia! Lose the Kleenex, Chapstick, thick hand cream, and sleeping aids. Replace with scented candles, gorgeously packaged massage oils, and a marble dish or leather case stocked with a bounty of sexual toys and treats: feathers, satin ribbons, strands of pearls, vibrators, and vibrating spheres if you can find them!
- Stock the fridge with at least two bottles each of a fine Champagne and a chilled white wine such as Sancerre. Stock the freezer with a bottle of vodka and plenty of ice cubes. Nothing is less chic than when a man brings you Champagne and you haven't enough ice to fill your ice bucket. Tacky!

The liquor cabinet should always be filled with a couple of bottles of red wine; I recommend a good Bordeaux or pinot noir. Keep Perrier, tonic water, and Evian on hand, as well as a fresh lemon and lime at all times. Have an array of easy to nibble—easy to be fed—*amuse-bouches.* A very important concept to learn, and something Europeans have known for ages: tantalize the tongue with extremes. Serve dishes that offer contrasts to each other, stimulating the mouth and senses. For instance, follow sweet with savory, a cold watermelon soup with a flaky *millefeuille* of *chèvre frais, épinards,* and *saumon.* Serve a creamy risotto with crisp olive and tarragon focaccia. Whether it be an *après* sex snack or a twelve-course meal, from silver dishes of cashews to handfuls of frozen grapes fed by hand, always have sensual foods on hand and at the ready.

CHAPITRE DIX-SEPT

From your ardor alone,
Embers of satin,
Duty exhales,
Without anyone saying at last.

—ARTHUR RIMBAUD, "ETERNITY,"
TRANSLATED BY FRANCIS GOLFFING

arie-Hélène was all but putting together my wedding registry after I gave her the lowdown on my big date with the Marquis. I believe the word "triumphant" would not be going too far to describe her enthusiasm. I couldn't say what tickled her the most about the idea of marrying me off to Louis-Philippe—my snagging the gold mine, sugar refinery, or if she thought him just another notch on my belt.

Maybe she just enjoys her Svengali-like power to encourage me—more like command me—to follow the course she's set. Whatever her motivations, I am one happy little rosebud with an eye to the future for the first time in a while. Life seems to have miraculously fallen into place for me. I'm getting back into the thesis, and I have added keeping a journal to my literary pursuits, while still keeping Frédéric and Jean-Albert in the loop, albeit through turning chilly on them. Which, weirdly enough, is working like a charm, and is of course, just too easy to accomplish.

Wish somebody had told me about this surefire way to keep a

boy's interest, oh, about ten years ago—I always thought it was about all the *effort* you put out, when it is, in fact, all about the *lack* of effort you put out. But I must clarify: the theory I am referring to here really applies to men who are *not* healthy, decent individuals. Lovely, sincere men don't play games or fall for them. Which is perfectly applicable to my darling Louis-Philippe—I so love that he's just straightforward and putting it all out there about wanting to marry. That certainly is far more thrilling than when I met Frédéric and he announced he was setting out to *acquire* me from Jean-Albert. I was caught up in the glamorous evening, the moment, and his power; otherwise, I might have just poured Champagne down his pants. The fact that he remembered me from earlier, passing by his office pushing a stroller, was the clincher that made that night seem magical, and as though fate were playing a role. But now I'm dead set on destination Marquis—and the rest? They're going on the back burner and getting no encouragement. So, adhering to MH's make them chase you theory, I made a rendezvous with Frédéric for a lunch and—check this out—stood him up. Balls? Yes, I have acquired a large pair, as I further hone advanced courtesan seduction skills. And I'm here to tell you that they work! Hilariously enough, my never even properly canceling on Frédéric resulted in his sending me, the next day, a Cartier Tank *montre* (watch), valued at a hefty 11,400 euros, in case you're curious. Delivered with a little note:

Mon Amour,
Time stands still when I am not in your arms. . . .
Time was excruciatingly endless as I waited to lay my eyes on you. . . .
Time is yours to choose when you will allow me to bathe in your ethereal beauty again . . . .
Je pense à toi . . . comme d'habitude,
F. d. F.

An 11,400-euro watch?! "Time is money" is more like it. Talk about rewarding bad behavior! Man, oh man.

Free of the two geezers (aren't I being sassy now, with the young king of my heart, Louis-Philippe, filling my thoughts), I busied myself with my research on Boucher, my new daily Italian lessons (by the way, learned that sex *a camporella* means essentially sex al fresco or sex outdoors—no huge surprise there), and I finally spent an evening with Isabel.

The *soirée* with her was huge fun, and thank God, since after that Grand Véfour dinner cum mess I was pretty sure we'd lost our link. *Pas du tout.* Phew. We had a ball, plotting out the engagement party and all the wedding details for her pending nuptials. Gabbing away with Isabel, I carefully kept my mouth shut about the Marquis and my growing interest in him. I didn't even drunkenly let the Frédéric affair and fallout pass over my lips, nor even a single word about Laurent. Could it be I'm learning discretion and sagacity? Possibly, but I wouldn't put all my money on it quite yet if I were you!

Obviously it was best to focus on her and downplay (into nonexistence) the fantastical nights and jewelry and . . . Well, *you* know. It was so much fun to hang with her again, and I didn't realize quite how much I'd missed her until I came home that night, realizing my cheeks literally hurt from laughing, and that the only extravagance of the night was the bottle of Dom Pérignon I'd brought to accompany the cheapo sushi we ordered in, so we could toast her.

Once home I did have a tiny mental quandary, trying to fathom whom I will invite to escort me to Isabel's two celebrations. Let's see, for *escort du choix*—Jean-Albert would frankly be the most relaxed and cool, probably earning a wider following of fan club members with all his wit and charm. But then I would be on the receiving end of too much judgment, like, "You know he's married?" and "She's got tons of jewels from him, can you imagine?" And possibly it would make Isabel uncomfortable, given that she essentially works for the man. So he's out of the running.

And it may be too soon to bring the Marquis, not to mention that he seems a bit of an elitist, and God only knows what he'd think of a wedding reception that's held in a museum in the Marais and not set in a family château. Speaking of which, I agreed to go this weekend with him to that château of his in the Loire. Not that it took much arm twisting. I'm so hopelessly caught up in the idea of him that I'm quite ridiculously already practicing signing my name as "Alexandra de Tassin." God, what am I—*thirteen*? But, it is an absolute pleasure that he's so attentive and has just all the time in the world to call during the day and chat. It's so unlike Frédéric and Jean-Albert, with their curt barks and listening with one ear routines. And, Christ, if I can score a watch without even showing up, hell, you can be sure that, until I have a ring on my finger, I'm gonna keep up the courtesan tactics.

As the weekend adventure approached I pulled an all-nighter—something I haven't done in months if you don't count sexual shenanigans, that is—polishing my history! I read up on the family name, "de Tassin," and the region in France where the Marquis is still treated like king. I also recorded some personal *histoire* in my own journal. It's an amazing experience to relive all these events, especially the beginning, with Jean-Albert. I will always be indebted to him for setting me on this journey that's educated me in so many ways. Rats, what a pity he's still in Asia; I would've been happy to smother him with kisses tonight . . . Poor soul, he doesn't know what he's missing. Well, maybe he does; that *could* be why he's started sending flowers *every day* now. I'm having them sent directly to the children's hospital in the *banlieue* (poorer outskirts of Paris). The concierge finally got inundated and it's a lovely idea to imagine that they brighten those sweet little children's days.

So when *vendredi après-midi* finally rolled around, I was in a fine mood, and packed for the weekend in the country.

Truth be told, the extent of my French country château excursions was sitting on the lawn of Frédéric's *manoir* in Chantilly! So I really had to do some thoughtful packing and organizing for this trip. No more relying on a killer designer dress to lift this Elmbrook girl into becoming a convincing and/or enticing Parisienne. Nope. With a nod to Louis-Philippe's inherent elegance and a thirst to show my truer self, I've tossed the expected light cashmere twinsets, a bounty of scarves and foulards, Hermès riding pants and boots, and a healthy offering of basic crisp white shirts in varying styles (Anne Fontaine, the *maîtresse* of white shirts, for day; a breathtaking one by Gianfranco Ferre—the master of white shirts—for evening; and a Gucci as a fallback).

With two cocktail dresses, one black and one white, and matching *talons*, a smattering of lacy Sabbia Rosa lingerie, and I think that should do it. I mean, it's just a little romantic getaway to the countryside; no chance I'm going to need to pull out all the stops in a gown or jewels, as I will probably be taken on a tour of his stables and be standing hip-deep in *merde de cheval, n'est-ce pas?*

Louis-Philippe arrives at 5:00 P.M. as expected and promised. What's not expected is that instead of the two of us driving off in some sexy little sports car, we're shoving off for the three-hour ride from Paris to Indre-et-Loire in the Loire (obviously) in that beastly huge barge of a Rolls-Royce with Hugo at the wheel. Which, of course, is still a treat but also *not*, in that (and let God not strike me dead for complaining here, but . . .) (1) There's no privacy when you have a driver. You have to self-edit and skirt some things, like sexual banter, witty sparring, and/or gossip. And for a girl like me that loves a good "no holds barred" chat, it loses a fair amount of charm. Literally, I would prefer to have been sitting in a crappy Citroën alone with him for the privacy of it. Do you believe me? I kinda do. (2) There's something a bit unmasculine about a man who hires some joker to drive him everywhere. Driving, especially on back-country roads, can be very commanding and sexy good fun. (3) Call me a purist, but driving a British Rolls-Royce through the French countryside is like eating Indian food in Tokyo. We're not exactly going to blend in, and it just feels as wrong as it looks.

All of this quickly offset by the pleasure of seeing Louis-Philippe. As I climb in next to him in the backseat, I notice he's wearing a very dapper black pinstripe Yves Saint Laurent suit (trust me, it's obviously YSL, I can tell by the lapels) with a pumpkin-colored pocket square and a pair of Berlutis as shiny as his shaved head.

Knowing he hasn't come directly from work—impossible when he doesn't work!—I find it utterly charming that he is dressed to the nines to impress me. Wait a minute, what am I thinking? All this care in his appearance probably isn't an effort made for me. He's a marquis, and dressing the role of a dandy, with scrupulous attention to his attire, is certainly more expected of him than, say, of the local *boulanger* (baker) on the corner.

We fill the travel time speaking about Italy—he fulfilled his promise and set me up a week ago with a private tutor—which has me making a few bravely foolish attempts at speaking in Italian. I thank him again for the tutor, and tell him that my Latin studies at university have really helped me to grasp the root of many of the words I'm learning. So, on a whim, he casually tosses out an invite to go to the Palio in Siena as a venue for me to give my new Italian a tryout. How cool is that? If I say I'm studying canary diamonds, ya think he'd buy me some?! I swear, with these men, you so much as mention a vague idea about something, anything—a place, a painting, a hotel—and their comeback is, "Then let's go!" or "Would you like to own one?" It's craziness. Frankly, I don't want to look like a greedy demon, or even talk about material wealth, this weekend. As a possible future wife, it'd be bad form and, after the pink diamond fiasco, I know the wealth factor isn't the real allure of a man, and so I tell Louis-Philippe that I'm starting to keep a journal, an idea he responds to with an energetic, *"C'est une très bonne idée. Verba volant, scripta manent."* Meaning—in Latin—"Spoken words fly away but writing remains."

How sexy chic is that? And he follows up with, *"Tu as soif?"* (Are you thirsty?) "I had Hugo make a batch of Saigons, and we could have a little nip." He pulls a pair of matching black-leather hip flasks from the pull-down cabinet.

"Saigons? Can't say I've tried one," I reply, taking one of the flasks and unscrewing the silver top. The fumes—trust me, that's the prefect word here—the fumes of this potent high-alcohol-content beverage fill the car instantaneously and almost strip the paint off the interior.

"What's in it? Is it named 'Saigon' because it hits you like a bomb?" I ask, not even kidding.

Taking a big swig, he answers, "I don't even know . . . Hugo?'"

"Sir?" responds Hugo, so quickly that I know that he can't have missed a single word. Have *I* mentioned, I loathe that?

"What's in a Saigon?" Louis-Philippe asks, looking suddenly less the connoisseur and more the spoiled kid.

"*Eau de vie*, lime juice, and a dash of ginger ale, sir," Hugo recites automatically.

"*Voilà!*" and my Marquis sips away as the hours pass and intelligent conversation flies out the window. Fine; I could use a bit of mental downtime.

With the weekend traffic, we get a bit delayed, and arrive at the château at almost 9:00 P.M. Louis-Philippe has half-drifted into a nap, with his smooth-as-silk head resting on my shoulder. Mmm, even his head smells sexy. My thoughts drift tipsily to, "Damn, this boy is fun. Wouldn't it be a kick to be his wife? The world our playground, the access to information and beautiful places and interesting people to meet. Yeah, I'm pretty damn glad I didn't stay in Elmbrook and get a job as a manager at The Limited at the local mall." (At age ten, that was, I assure you, my *big* dream!)

Admittedly, I also spend a fair amount of time staring at his crotch and trying to gauge what could be in store for me there. Am I wrong? Or is it always a toss-up? At least men get a general sense of what awaits them before we unveil. We women have to decode the forever misleading silhouettes created by fine tailoring, loose trousers, and suit jackets. Almost never, I've discovered, do you get a realistic idea of what a man will look like naked. Unfair! It's robbery, I tell you! Hugo finally announces that we are pulling up to the gates of the château, as much to awaken Louis-Philippe as to be tour guide to me while my groggy, sweet Marquis begins to shake off the mind-numbing alcohol.

"*Parfait*. The lights will just have been turned on and the château will be at its most enchanting for you, darling," he says, taking my hand in his. Good move, I *do* love holding hands. The car passes through a set of huge wrought-iron gates and past a pair of video cameras that someone failed miserably to hide discreetly behind the vines climbing the tall stone walls surrounding the grounds.

"Is that really necessary? The cameras? I mean, it's not like you're Brad Pitt, baby?"

Oops! Maybe the mental downtime sapped that wife-material elegance I thought was so at my disposal.

"Brad Pitt doesn't have *my* art collection, darling Alexandra," the Marquis retorts, putting me quite neatly in my place. A place called "endlessly in over my head and out of my element"!

A long, slow drive down a classically French *allée* of tall plane trees that sway slightly in the early evening breeze. A gas lamp lit beneath each tree, casting light up into the canopy of leaves overhead and throwing mosaics of shadows on the shiny hood of the car. We pass a gatekeeper's outbuilding—now unneeded—a carriage house, and a long, low building of rose stone with a slate roof.

"Hugo, pull up to the house, leave the bags, and then deposit the car back there in the garage. We won't be needing it until *dimanche après-midi*." And, Louis-Philippe adds, pointing out the long structure to the right, "That's where I keep my favorite six cars. I will have to show you; I recently installed a mechanism that, after you drive in, rotates the cars 180 degrees, so that you need not be burdened with backing out when you choose to leave," he says casually.

Favorite *six cars*? Burden of backing out? Oh, this is gonna be good.

ANOTHER COURTESAN SEXUAL SECRET TO
ADD TO YOUR REPERTOIRE

Eyes wide open: *Oui.* "Open-eyed sex" sounds easy, but there are a few moments when your inhibitions can make you want to keep your eyes closed as a buffer to your more sensual actions. The next step to increasing sensual pleasure is to try to *let go* and watch, consume your lover with your eyes. In fact, it will sincerely deepen your level of intimacy and increase your excitement in lovemaking if you keep your eyes open during sexual play. It is a very simple idea that is wildly underused: If you try no other techniques, just keeping your eyes open will give you a greater sense of connection and closeness to your lover. Even when you are indulging in making love to yourself (well put, *n'est-ce pas?*), you will find that the act of seeing your own body flush, swell, and react to your touch increases your arousal exponentially.

When you keep your eyes open during sex your attention is fully focused, adding yet another sense to the touches, tastes, and sounds that are building and accentuating your pleasure. Gazing gently into your lover's eyes throughout lovemaking adds another dimension to your sensuality, your sexual confidence, and often will bring you that much closer to orgasmic happiness. "Orgasmic happiness"? Don't you think people would book all their vacations there if such a place really existed?

NOTABLE OBSERVATION UNIQUE
TO LIFE AS A COURTESAN

As a courtesan, if you should catch the flu or fall ill when you are expected to be available, your lovers-*protecteurs* have no interest or time to offer to take care of you. Which is a bit disappointing. But hey, you're not exactly family.

However, they *will* send their top doctors and nurses to tend to you round-the-clock, and their assistants will spend half a day shopping for a "get well" basket guaranteed to be stocked with a dozen magazines and books, freshly squeezed *jus d'orange*, chocolates from Pierre Hermé, Guerlain Vega perfume, scented candles from Côté Bastide, and a fluffy white robe from Dior. I even received a Prada hot water bottle once—which I returned immediately for credit, and cashed in for shoes. Let's face it, a designer hot water bottle is absurd! (Plus, truth be told, I already had one by Chanel.)

CHAPITRE DIX-HUIT

All night I drank love's wine,
Just as all night the pond drinks the full moon.

—RAINER MARIA RILKE

After crossing over the wood-plank bridge that straddles the moat (yes, I said "moat") the Rolls-Royce glides to a stop in front of what I can only say is *the* fairy princess castle of my childhood dreams and drawings. Magnificently lit, Louis-Philippe's château could practically be mistaken for the Louvre, for all its grandeur. A dozen tall windows line four stories of bisque-colored stone. The gigantic castle stretches all the way across my field of vision and up, up, up toward the twinkling stars, which are starting to make their evening performance.

Sixteenth-century spire-topped turrets adorn every corner as more than a dozen enormous chimney tops vie for attention. An elegant coat of arms is carved into the pilaster over the double doors, reminding me this is, amazingly enough, a *home*. A fucking *astonishing* home. And it could be *my* fucking astonishing home, if I play my cards right and dole out the proper appreciation while masking the jaw-dropping-staggeringly-difficult-to-grasp reality—that the dude with the shiny head and breath that could melt bronze (the Saigons' fault, to be fair) sitting next to me is not just the owner but the descendant of a long line of princes of the blood of the French aristocracy.

Maybe you already know, but I just recently discovered from my readings, that this "prince of the blood" distinction is a vastly more prestigious title in aristocracy than many others, since others can be *noblesse de robe*, who acquired their titles from relatives who were court officials or judicial office holders. There is also the slightly more prestigious *noblesse d'épée*—the nobility of the sword—meaning their titles were earned by military accomplishments but also *could have* been purchased by the rich bourgeoisie—which is, of course, less admired in France than sitting on your ass and/or fucking for a title. Which, come to think of it, is pretty much where I stand tonight. Seriously, even if the place were empty and we just slept in sleeping bags, I'd be hog-wild game for this place. My musings are interrupted by Louis-Philippe's voice: "Would you be interested in seeing the property and hearing a little about it? The light is so marvelous right now; it would be a pity to just head directly indoors." At this moment, the double doors open and two men in dark gray uniformed waistcoats take the bags inside while respectfully saying, "*Bonsoir,* sir"—and with a nod in my direction—"Mademoiselle Alexandra, *c'est un grand plaisir de vous souhaiter une bienvenue au château de Tassin.*"

The staff. They know my name! I swear I could hug each of them. Just when I thought I had become a bit faded, I can't help thinking: "Quick! Somebody get a picture of me! I have to show it to everyone I ever met!" Do you know how wrong that would be? *Hideously.* And yet that girl inside me just keeps doing giddy somersaults.

"*Ah, merde,*" says Louis-Philippe, "they always forget. I detest when they use the word *bienvenue.* I've told them a thousand times, *les autres châteaux vous accueillent, seule le château de Tassin vous reçoit.*" (Other castles *welcome* you, my castle *receives* you.) Ooph! Smells like pretension to me. Reeks of it, in fact! Whatever, get over here, stinker!

With nothing to do, not even unpack, as again, "there are people

for that," Louis-Philippe leads me about ten meters back, to take
in the full glory of the château de Tassin from a more commanding
perspective.

Is my hand sweating? I'm pretty sure it is, and I don't even get
sweaty palms, but I should be rejoicing that thankfully my body
has opted for damp palms over a situation that really warrants crap-
ping my pants. (And I know, that's way Midwestern inelegant of
me to even think, but I'm OK with that, since I told you, I'm
telling you the truth at every turn!)

And so the tour begins: here are the facts I was told about
château de Tassin:

"The château was originally constructed in the sixteenth *siècle*
(century), during the reign of François Premier. (Right. My family
house was built during the *reign* of Nixon, so we're about even
there.) The main building comprises a central Renaissance gallery
that serves as the music room and is bordered to the north and south
by intricate stained-glass windows (My house is bordered by the
Devons, with their mangy barking dog on one side, and on the other
by the Johnsons, with their agoraphobic son.) done by the same
craftsman who worked on the Cathédrale de Chartres. (I think the
guys that built our house also did the Home Depot across the highway.) *En bas* (below) are the troglodyte cellars (ahhh, and that would
be what, exactly?), the linen room, a scullery (again, what? If that's
where you keep a collection of skulls of ex-girlfriends, I should
know that right now), and of course, sixteen bedrooms (I'm guessing no bunk beds), twelve *salles de bain* (bathrooms), a grand *salon*
on each *étage* (floor), a *déambulatoire* (huh? I have zip idea what that
is; I'm guessing it's not a ping-pong room), and the art collection is
spread throughout the ballroom (we had Rothko prints in our rec
room; that's similar, no?), a two-story library on the ground floor, a
game room, and a trio of drawing rooms and a few servants' quarters
on the top floor." (We had an attic where we kept broken toys and a
cot that smelled of mothballs.) Throughout this recitation, I continue to nod with a fixed expression of faux nonchalance.

"To the left, if you'll follow me. (My legs are paralyzed from

overwhelming awe; it may be wise to push me along in a wheelbar-
row if you have one.) Here we have a Gallo-Roman hamlet (certainly
wouldn't have guessed that, as I really don't have a clue what that
is—even as I stand here looking at it), and in that building, the wine
press house, we produce eighteen thousand bottles each year of our
private vintage. (Cool—I will gladly take twenty cases; make that
two hundred.) There are the stables off to the distance (well, that's
just pathetic that they're so far away); just behind are indoor training
rings; and obviously this, here, is the bathing pavilion. (Oh, well
thank God. No bath is complete without a pavilion.) Behind the gardens is a greenhouse, where we keep the seedlings and bulbs for the
next year's flora and foliage (Ah. I always wondered if I'd ever hear
anyone actually say "flora and foliage" or if people just write that in
nineteenth-century British books.) and about eighteen hectares
away is the hunting lodge, set deep in the woods—which, of course,
has excellent shooting territory—do you hunt, Alexandra? No, I suppose not. (Hunt? Just men, and given that I'm even standing here
would attest I don't exactly *suck* at it. Oops, excuse and ignore that
pun, as it's actually something I do—*suck*, that is.) And finally, by the
back gate are the caretakers' outbuildings, for staff and employees.
(What, no chapel? No heliport? How deplorably pagan! How *unmod-
erne;* I'm outta here! This place really is a dump! And I didn't hear
any mention of a tennis court! What a ghastly oversight!) Oh, and I
almost forgot: to the fields to the right, beyond the *boules* courts, are
about forty cows, sheep, and goats we keep for making the fifteen or
so different cheeses distinct to the region. Well, that should do it. It's
charming, don't you think?" he asks, while we head back to cross the
moat, as swallows flitter about the tree canopies.

"It's astonishingly lovely. You are very fortunate to live so well
and *I'm* very fortunate to be invited into your private domain.
Again, thank you for the invitation."

He interrupts the way only rich, handsome men can, without my
cutting them to the quick. "My private domain? No. That is something you have not glimpsed yet, my dear Alexandra." (Christ, please
tell me there's not another château of his somewhere around here!)

"Tomorrow I shall show you, my little libertine, *that* private world. Are you sure you are as much a decadent as you claim?" he asks, looking somewhat serious.

"I should think it safe to say I am well versed and less a novice in this arena than I may appear," I reply. " 'If there's a dare, I'm there' should really be my new motto."

"*Très bien*. Let's go inside. I shall show you around a bit, leave you to bathe and dress, and we can meet in the grand salon for an aperitif at nine?" he asks rather rhetorically, as we step inside and he wipes mud from his shoes on what's surely an eighty-thousand-euro Aubussion rug without a thought. "Does that suit you?" "Like a glove, darling," I answer automatically.

And after a whirl through the museumesque *premier étage*, I'm finally left alone to collapse in a large dressing room designed in the Louis XIV style. Haaahh! This is *so* exhausting. Would I ever feel comfortable living here? Oh, who cares? How cool! It'd be a struggle, but I think "for love" I could endure the agony (dripping wet sarcasm there).

I take a quick bath in a marble tub (note: very cold stone does not make for pleasant warm baths) and then, like a soldier called to war, I pull myself together. Put on my "uniform" (black Chanel cocktail dress) and war paint (makeup in the château version, as opposed to the Paris version, i.e., paler hues), pack my satchel (Fendi satin clutch) with ammunition (perfume, breath mints, lipstick) and a secret poison (cigarettes), and try to blunder my way to the previously pointed out but now completely forgotten location of the battle zone (grand salon).

It's always interesting to date someone whose home warrants a map. Luckily, one of those uniformed staff members (Buster, if your name is *also* Hugo, I don't even want to know!) appeared and escorted me to the salon in question.

An interesting dinner buffet of the *cuisine de terroir* (provincial cooking specific to the region) followed the aperitif and, well, you tell me what you think of the menu:

MENU

Grenouilles à la Vitellise (Frogs' legs with mushrooms. You can be sure I loaded up on the mushrooms here.)

Jambon au foin (Ham cooked in hay. *Hay?* Sure. I needed some fiber in my diet!)

Fromage de porc à l'Ancienne (Pig's head brain. Made further fun, as Louis-Philippe explained, in that it's an ancient recipe and is kept for ten days *before* serving.)

Tarte à la Caillade (Curdled milk cake. Yee-ha! I've been craving that for ages! Joke. Curdled anything isn't really tasty, right? Not generally something I find myself hankering for that often, either. Hey, Marquis-Man, why keep cows around if not for *fresh* milk?!)

If you'll check above, I only said that it was an "interesting dinner." I bet you were with me on this whole experience right up until dinner. I generally adore regional cooking, but I'd say this was altogether too much of a good thing. What are the odds that once I become Marquise of this hacienda we can eat like normal people? Say, fish? Grilled—even in hay, if you must. I just don't like eating the heads and legs of things that once strolled around the gardens.

I survived dinner purely on the intellectual banter and ambiance. Not all bad, really. Better than eating a killer fabulous burger with a man who's a dreadful bore while sitting in a subway car. Man, am I getting good at rationalizing! Good conversation is a tremendous turn-on, and after a healthy discussion of Verlaine's poetry (we both adore it), we launched into debate about genetically enhanced farming (available at better prices, providing more reliable and plentiful crops; I'm clearly for it) versus Europe's resistance to even permitting trials, which would also create jobs (he's against it—*vehemently*). Well, call me a Midwestern girl from the agricultural hub of the USA, but I so dig that kind of sparring. As long as someone has their facts, I'm all for a tussle, even if they hold firm to their position . . . more so still, if they are firm . . . *in all positions!*

On that note, we polished off the cognac, agreed to disagree, and decided to race upstairs, rip off our clothes, and make love to the lulling hum of the cicadas' midnight sonata.

Clarification: we did not "make love," as I really couldn't attest to feelings of love yet, so let's say we made "almost love." He does tell me he's *"tombé amoureux"* with me. Still, it seems a little premature, since we've only known one another a short while. And, by the way, the words "premature" and "short" *so* don't apply to this boy. He's hung like one of the horses in his stable, and with that smooth head between my legs executing a brilliant *bisou minou*, I would have gladly had his name tattooed across my chest by morning, despite his horrendous snoring. (Did you get what *bisou minou* means just by context? It literally translates as "kiss to the tiny kitten." *Voilà;* ask for that when you come to France next time; just as they do with wine and cheese, the male population has this down!)

To be honest, I'm still very much amazed at how much I find this shaved-headed man drop-dead sexy. Part of it must be that his eyes and lips are so beautifully expressive, and they stand out much more when not competing with hair. Frankly, French people can be rather reserved in their gestures and expressions, so I am always elated to find a man like Louis-Philippe who seems so alive, animated, and with a lot to share. And materially speaking, boy, does he have the "a lot to share" end covered!

Saturday was spent having a lovely *petit déjeuner* together of *omelettes aux fines herbes;* warm *brioche* slathered with *beurre;* fresh flaky croissants made in the scullery (found out that's the kitchen); with *confiture* made with fruit from the gardens; and pots of frothy *chocolat chaud*. All eaten leisurely, sitting on the terrace overlooking the bathing pavilion, which I suddenly realized is just a snob way of saying "swimming pool."

Louis-Philippe *let* me (or would the word be *told* me?) to wander the grounds, take any books I wished from the library to read (I was hoping he'd end that with "from the library"—as in "take take": as gifts), or go riding if I wished (frankly, thanks, *non*, I just dig wearing the outfit). Essentially, I was free until 6:00 P.M., while he seemingly spent the day on the phone and fussing with the staff. Not even Jean-Albert spends that much time on the phone, and truth be told I detest a man who's forever with cell phone to ear. Surprising but forgivable. Should add that if he lived in a mobile home and resembled Shrek, I think my "forgiveness" there would be a hint less generous.

And no matter that I was left alone, I enjoyed the day immensely. I played silly fantasies in my mind, like telling the head gardener, "See those two trees at either end of the bathing pavilion? See how their branches arc away from each other, *c'est une image désagréable, non?* Can we not uproot them and switch their positions? It would be ever so much more *aesthetique*." I wouldn't dream of being such a monster, but I am just starting to understand how the rich think and am trying to wrap my head around that while still keeping my feet on the ground. A well-manicured ground, at that!

I stroll through the landscaped gardens that stretch into a series of broad meadows. Past a grove of apple trees so beautiful, as each tree is surrounded by the red rings of fallen apples. Grab two, and eat one in the sun, experiencing a rare moment of pure bliss among nature's free gifts. That is, if you don't consider the concept that each apple here is probably cultivated to such an extreme as to cost twenty euros a pop!

Walking toward the forest, I make a slight detour for the stables to feed the apple in my pocket to the first lucky horse I spot. Along the way the clean, dry smell of the freshly fallen leaves comes to me in gusts, as if a murmuring escort followed quickly by the balmy fragrance of cut wood. Mmm, nature's perfumes fill my lungs as I bask and walk in the afternoon sun, while the château grows smaller behind me.

In the second stall of the stables I accidentally awaken a small white yearling lying in the hay. The golden sun slips through the window overhead; its warm rays capture the delicate performance of dust doing slow waltzes in the air. The picturesque image strikes me as so classically composed it could be a painting by a Flemish master. The charming sight of the yearling, tentatively rising on her unsteady legs to come say hello, unquestionably wins her the prized apple. She laps every bit out of my open palm while looking up at me cautiously under her big soft lashes. Delightful with her shy curiosity, she trails her warm wet nose across my fingers, and when she realizes there is no more she flicks her tail good-bye and settles back into the dry hay. With sticky hands and a big smile, I bid her adieu and amble off to rinse my hands in a cool stream behind the stables. The quick current tickles my fingertips as a tiny brown spotted frog darts from a moss-covered stone to the safety of the water's edge.

I'm so well and having such a beautiful time, I start to wish Louis-Philippe were along to share this with me. Then it occurs to me, *no*, it's that much more sweet to be alone. To be free of any pressure to look pretty, to be able to be silent and take in every nuance, quietly.

Where to next? Everywhere and everything seems a potentially precious encounter. The fields? Yes, I go off to lie in the tall, ripe wheat just tucked away by the cows grazing over the slatted wooden fence. Oh, I could *definitely* get used to all this. For all the material gifts I have accumulated of late, nothing is as wonderfully touching to my soul as this afternoon on my own, reveling in the jewels of nature. What is it about being in the countryside that always makes me feel like a happy child without a worry in the world? I'd almost forgotten how much this, being outside—among trees and streams, animals—is a part of me. I spent every weekend of my childhood at our family cottage in the northern woods of Wisconsin, and I see now how ingrained it is in me to connect with this. God, I so needed this.

I lie for what might be hours in the meadow grasses: facedown on my belly, watching ants, beetles, and big fat bees go about their chores and routines. Such an exquisite state of lucid contentment sweeps over me, I simply wish for nothing. A breath of wind dances through the grasses like a gentle nudge to step out of one dream and into another. I look up to notice that the woods in the distance have fallen into shadow, reminding me of the line by the writer Paul Desjardin, "Now the woods are all black, but the sky is still blue." Precisely; that's a prefect rendering of this vision. How fantastic.

I slowly make my way back to the château, wading through the untamed field, letting the wild wheat and country flowers caress me as they flow past my legs. With a thirst to make a personal gesture and a desire to bring Louis-Philippe a symbol of the calm happiness his beautiful estate has given me, I set about gathering a large bouquet of wildflowers for him. Dashing left and right as my eye falls on this flower and that berry. I pull black-eyed Susans, a couple of curling vines speckled with tiny *framboises* (raspberries), a few mustard yellow buttercups, verbenas, pansies, wild lilies, a few tall stalks of wild grass and fragrant jasmine, the odd dried purple thistle, and at the end, a bounty of Queen Anne's lace to encircle the bouquet, which gets tied tightly with raffia-like pale shafts of wheat. The stems feel cool and damp in my soil-stained hands. I can't imagine a more charming arrangement of flowers has ever existed. There! What an explosion of color, and what a marvelously intoxicating scent. It's the perfect representation of my afternoon: nature's true, untamed beauty. Perfection!

As the sun begins its slow descent, a band of purple runs wild through the sky. The fiery glow mirrored on the long expanse of water in the pool creates a twin chateau of equal beauty and almost too much opulence for the eye to absorb. Opalescent rays of light hit every window of the château, giving the structure such a radiant life force that my mind was persuaded to believe it was practically a living creature. An exquisite apparition, *unexpected, unparalleled, and unforgettable.*

I make my way back to the château, further amusing myself by counting the number of ladybugs that have managed to cling to the stems of my bouquet and which add all the more to its charm. Seven. My favorite number—isn't that charming?

My fine little mood could only be improved by a stolen moment for *à cinq à sept* with my sexy marquis. (That's a French phrase in common use, meaning "making love between five and seven P.M." Of course, *à cinq à sept* is a favorite of the mistress, and generally the appeal is heightened by the act taking place on a chaise longue or staircase. Time constraints give love-making one of its sexier elements, to be sure.) Now, if I could only locate my *paramour* in this maze of rooms and salons!

After much trial and error, I finally stumble on Louis-Philippe in the drawing room, talking to himself animatedly in harsh tones and gesturing wildly. Dude, did you ever see the film *The Shining*? I think you've spent too many long winters alone here; you're almost arguing with yourself!

Louis-Philippe looks up, a slightly crazed look on his face, and points to his head.

Yeah, you've gone bonkers, I get it. Then I notice he has one of those cell phone Bluetooth headsets jammed into his ear. I hate those even more than cell phones. He looks at the wild bouquet in my arms, laughs, and says *ciao* by way of ending the call.

And saying *"ciao"* is even *worse* than headsets—right or wrong?

"Alexandra, have you had a nice afternoon? I see you've been doing some weeding in the gardens. Don't trouble yourself. There are people for that." And he takes the flowers from me and drops them on an open newspaper as if they were a soiled diaper.

Hrmph. I take them back and reply, "I have indeed had a marvelous day. Discovering the delights of your estate, walking aimlessly from one end to the other, has been a total joy. And these 'weeds,' as you call them, will make the trip back to Paris with me, placed bedside as a tangible reminder of this spectacular day. What have you been doing all afternoon? Have you been inside all day, *chéri*?" (There are times when *"chéri"* can lose all meaning and sound about as loving as "dude," and we are on the cusp, *non?*)

"Yes, I guess I have. Frankly, I don't make it around the grounds very much; I have horrible allergies that really only abate in the winter . . . I have busied myself with a little bidding by phone on a Whistler painting on auction in Basel. And arranged some things for your amusement for this evening," he says, coming over to lay a kiss on my sun-baked neck. The tenderness evaporates as he pulls away sharply: "Darling, you have grass in your hair and you smell of the stables. Good heavens, you've taken the outdoors in with you! Why don't you run off and take a bath, and let's rejoin one another in the music room at eight-thirty."

It sounds like more of a command than a request. Frankly, I could hang out and chat about the Whistler painting a while, and you *could* ask me about my day a little more, but that seems to be a nonoption, as I'm starting to sense that you treat girlfriends a bit like you treat "the staff"—they have their uses, but when you don't need them "be gone with you" is the general idea. Fine. I'm certainly not going to force myself on you. Today was my private domain then.

I turn to go, with my treasured wildflowers in the crook of my arm.

"Oh, and my dear, tonight's attire shall be rather formal. Well, at least in the beginning of the fête." Louis-Philippe laughs.

"Wha? *Pardon*. Fête? I am not sure I have brought proper clothes for a formal evening. I thought this was a quiet, romantic weekend, just you and me." *And the staff of fifty.*

Louis-Philippe leads me to an overstuffed faille-covered sofa, again taking the bouquet and dumping it back on the table. (Buddy, no matter how much you try to ditch those, they are comin' with me!)

"My precious, in addition to bringing you here and showing you my home, I thought I'd introduce you to something in my life that is also *private*. From what Marie-Hélène has said to me about you and what you have shared with me, I think you will be most *titillated* by tonight's festivities." He giggles on the word like a schoolboy.

"Did she tell you I love Molière? Are you putting on a small vignette? I am not sure what you are getting at. Oh, do just go ahead and tell me." It's starting to look like I'm going to have to take my identifying with Scarlett O'Hara to the limit and pull down these draperies and whip myself a gown out of them, so please cut to the chase so I can get going on that project!

"To put it plainly, I have invited some guests to join us . . . for an orgy, I believe you call it. I wanted to make it a surprise. You're not in the slightest bit annoyed that I didn't ask you if it was OK, are you?" he asks, stroking my brow. Listen, that gesture of kindheartedness goes better with proclamations of love than announcements of planned group sex, and as for "slightest bit annoyed," you can make that "hugely annoyed."

"Louis-Philippe, are you serious?" He nods with a sly smile. "Well, I . . . I . . . Certainly have never participated in such a thing, and I am not sure the concept *doesn't* scare me, to be honest," I say, watching a ladybug crawl to the edge of a leaf on my wildflower bouquet, spread its wings, and take flight out of the room. *Wait up! Take me with you!*

"It will be *only* the most beautiful people, and I promise and assure you it will be an irresistible, enticingly sensual *mise en scène*. You told me your motto is 'do something every day that scares you.' So, if this 'scares' you, embrace embarking on this adventure with me . . . to the limits of your imagination! I guarantee you it will be fantastically freeing," he says, sweeping his arms through the air in a gesture of persuasion.

"Rain check" comes to mind as a way to steal time and give this some thought. I'm not sure if I can switch mental gears from counting the spots on a sweet ladybug's shell to counting the cocks in a room. This will take some doing. *Sheesh*. In the in-over-your-head department, this takes the *gâteau*.

And he's looking at me with this pressure-loaded expression, having done all to sway me save writing "surrender, Alexandra" in the sky with his broomstick. Oh, *merde alors,* what I would give to click my ruby slippers and get the hell out of Oz! By the way, if you haven't found yourself a courtesan trapped in a castle with a sexy marquis millionaire pressing you into an orgy, I would like to inform you that finding a convincing out is about as easy as emptying a bathtub with a teaspoon while the tap is running. *Pas très simple!*

I realized there was no excuse to be had: after considerable hesitation, my dangerous and omnipresent id ran rampant over my logical side. I somehow fling away all morality and virtue and agree to the evening. *"Ooh la-la, ça va. Mais*, I have nothing *formal* to wear—does it really matter?" I add, as if clothing is the common dilemma of people preparing for an orgy—*talk about absurd.*

"*Bien sûr,* it matters. One must have a discerning eye and pay the greatest attention to every expression of one's self . . . At all times! There is no room in life to be casual about one's taste. Not about a single thing in one's life, from the toothpaste one uses to the quality of silver in the family tea service! You are fortunate in that I have closets full of gowns you can peruse and have your pick. Just open the armoire in your room with the key under the Qianlong vase on the mantel." And Louis-Philippe stands and returns to his desk, as if to say, "Shove off now."

Oh, and thanks for that massively helpful description: "The *Qianlong* vase." As opposed to, I'm guessing, one of those overrated, shitty Ming vases. Right, the work of the Qianlong dynasty is vastly superior, even if I can't even fathom when that critically acclaimed period might have been. And by the way, why would Louis-Philippe have a closet full of women's gowns? Wait, don't answer that. I don't think my heart could take it just now.

I clamber up the long flight of stairs in a daze and give in to the magnetic pull of the bed in my dressing room. Hands to my forehead in a whirl of confusion. Crap, forgot the wildflowers after all. This is all a bit more than I expected, for damn sure.

I don't know about you, but I have never been a big believer that sex is a spectator sport. Does this or doesn't this fall into the "indecent proposal" category? Just how did I get hornswoggled into this?! And just what did Marie-Hélène tell Louis-Philippe that led him to believe this orgy idea was "right up my alley"? Oh my God, just *who* will be "right up my alley" by night's end? My anxiety tightened its hold, and gripped both my mind and heart to such an extent, I thought I might throw up.

All right, Alexandra, get a grip. This kind of thing is *very* European, *very* accepted throughout history. You're being a vanilla girl to be so apprehensive and dubious. Fine. Fine. *Fine!* But copious amounts of Champagne will have to be employed to prepare for this scene. And since it's now seven, I don't see any point in delaying that effect. I push the buzzer above the dressing table—which, the Marquis had pointed out last night, I should use, if I wished to summon the butler for anything. At the time, I thought, like I would ever be so vulgar, and now I'm that girl. Yeeks. Help! How tempted am I to use the buzzer to send out an SOS . . . ? Somebody rescue me! From this castle, the Marquis . . . from *myself*.

The Champagne arrives, along with a silver bowl overflowing with cold strawberries. I ignore the berries, light cigarette after cigarette, and plow through the bubbly with nothing resembling grace. Who cares, I'm alone and standing here naked, fresh from the bath, and aware that I may end the night, *still naked*, but not so fresh.

More Champagne, and I fetch the key from under the vase. With a turn, both doors on the armoire swing open, revealing a vulgar display of couture gowns. (I have a feeling the word "vulgar" will pop up again *ce soir . . .*) Ignoring the question of why on earth these dresses even exist here, I plow through the options, attempting to segue mentally from "wife material" to "orgy escort." *Reality? I miss you!*

I pass on the embroidered Chinese robes, black leather strapless (as if!), and Fortuny gowns in jewel tones, and I opt for a virginal white open work–lace spaghetti strap gown with a nude lining. Cool, I will *look* naked but won't be. Maybe that will be enough and I can casually assume the role of "casually disinterested observer."

Stepping into the gown is a feat, as the alcohol has kicked in *hard* and gravity has become surprisingly difficult to negotiate. And here's the real question: What earrings does one wear to an orgy? Surely there will be ravenous mouths and a flurry of hands, so the chandeliers and hoops better stay in the room. Wish I could just stay with them. Would sending out my dress to inhabit a seat tonight suffice? And I thought it was tough to accompany Jean-Albert to that first dinner at Baccarat. Hell, that was nothing compared to the night I have to look forward to. Jean-Albert, come save me! You know, I bet he would actually helicopter in and do that if I called him. Could be very sexy James Bond. Fuck, he's still in Asia. And how would I explain that I'd gone away with Louis-Philippe? All right, it's 8:20 P.M. Time to stagger downstairs to the music room and charge headlong into God knows what. As for Louis-Philippe, I'm beginning to rethink his appeal—I am *not* charmed by this little concept of entertainment for his "beloved" potential wife. Nope. The fat lady hasn't sung yet on this relationship, but she's definitely clearing her throat.

I slip on the white satin slingbacks I brought to accompany the *demure* cocktail dress that I guess won't be making an appearance after all. Oh, this looks as stupid as all hell! Who would dream of wearing a closed-toe shoe to an orgy? Hey, who would have anticipated an orgy? Right. Fuck 'em if they don't like it. *Terrible pun, as that of course is* très possible.

After my Herculean efforts merely to be clothed—and really how futile does that sound, heading into an orgy?—I claw my way down the long halls and accidentally end up taking the servants' stairs down to the music room. *Merde*, forgot my purse. Like it matters, and like I could find my way back in this state.

Arriving in the music room, I am almost knocked off my feet by the sight of Louis-Philippe. Not that my feet were that steady there, anyway. He's festooned (trust me, that's the aproppriate word) in a large amethyst turban that's bejeweled with a diamond pin securing a peacock feather at the center and a crimson embroidered robe with sable cuffs that's to the floor. He turns away from his conversation with someone, smiles, and asks me, "So, how do I look?"

"Like big trouble," I was tempted to answer.

"Beguiling!" I sputter, astounding the room of people as much as myself with the sound of my voice. What in God's name made me choose that unusual word?! This is already not going well.

The two dozen or so guests laugh and resume their conversations. Louis-Philippe descends on me and whispers in my ear, "I'm burning with desire for you tonight."

"*Bon*, then let's send everyone home and sneak off to bed together," I reply, not entirely sure I'm game for any of this anymore.

"Alexandra, you must admit the guests are all ravishingly beautiful and tempting," he proclaims with more of that arm-sweeping gesture stuff he likes to do. Which, by the way, *does* look as pretentious as you're imagining.

I stub out my cigarette in very possibly some priceless artifact, and gaze across the room at the assembled cast of participants in the upcoming fête *du nudity*. Can't really focus on faces, since I am drunkish . . . Okay, *smashed*. But yeah, they all seem midthirties, rich, tall, and slim and wearing elegant clothes . . . for the moment. Whoops. Strike that. A woman to my left with a cape just untied the damn thing and let it fall to the floor. Now we have one naked girl here, center stage, and about twenty others in various absurd getups. What the . . . ?! Why would that guy wear a bowler hat to an orgy? That doesn't work . . . *at all*. I may be a neophyte to the orgy game, but I know hats are so wrong, right? Christ, so drunk, hardly can stand. Whoops again. Am not standing. Am actually already sitting. Who knew? Isn't it all rather early in the night to start an orgy? I mean, really! I could see, you know, how spontaneously a dinner party might get a bit caught up in revelry as dawn breaks and a few drunken stragglers fall into bed together, wake up, and laugh it off. But, gang: it's not even 9:00 P.M.! And dinner has not even been mentioned.

Louis-Philippe appears to be mingling, and a man to my left, sporting an eye patch, leans in to speak to me.

"Alexandra, welcome. What a lovely addition you make to one of Louis-Philippe's magnificent *soirées*. Would you care for some more Champagne?"

"Love the eye patch. So much sexier an accessory than that guy's hat. No more Champagne for me. Well, OK, one more *flûte*. And what do you mean, *one* of his *soirées*?" I more or less babble.

"The eye patch is a necessary evil, my dear woman. Lost my right eye in a polo accident . . . ," he explains. I interrupt, unable to smother the line that bursts into my brain and begs for an audience: "Sorry to hear it! So, I don't suppose you find yourself saying the old cliché, 'I'd give my right eye for . . .'" And with that I am clearly gone. Gone all wrong and inelegant. Amazingly, no matter what couture gown you're wearing, no matter how many jewels, there's still no guarantee you're not going to be downright tactless and tacky. Louis-Philippe arrives and, noting the semiappalled expression on the man's face, drags me off to a safe corner.

"Having fun, my sweet?" he asks.

"Loads. What now? Does someone strike a bell and we all assume positions?" I ask sarcastically.

"*Une idée amusante, mais non.* People just do as they please, as the mood strikes them, and generally once a few couples commence, it spurs a mood of desire that is inescapable: *volupté générale* (general lust) ensues. More Champagne?" he adds, matter-of-factly. Hello! Someone here has zero capacity for grasping my subtext and undertones. Well, you can fix your lipstick in the reflection from his cranium.

More Champagne supposedly is poured into my glass, though I can't be held to that, as I was too caught up watching an Amazon-like young blonde being stripped of her red strapless dress to just heels and her leopard thong. Now, that . . . *that* is an ass. Wow! This girl's got a far better body than I do. I *knew* there'd be a few drawbacks to an orgy. The man with the girl formerly in the red dress continues to peel her underwear off, and they are tossed into the center of the room. Wow times two! She's, ah, had a trip to Brazil, as in totally hairless and buffed to a sheen. Go, girl! The man's on his knees like a flash and lapping at her, as he takes that ass-to-die-for in his greedy hands.

And, ladies and gentlemen, they're off and running! Clothes get flung to all corners; Champagne corks fly about madly. God, don't let a cork fly over and poke out the single remaining source of vision for Monsieur Eye Patch! But really, I'd love to hear him explain *that* tragedy to strangers: "Lost the right during a polo match, the left during an orgy." I'd kill to hear someone say that! That's almost as great as the taxi driver in Paris, whose name, I kid you not, is, "Fukman." I've gotten into his taxi twice, and each time, I end up cowering in the backseat delirious with gut-wrenching laughter. Mature of me? Not really. I digress. I wish I could say the night became somewhat of a blur, but it's all crystal clear. This is what unfolded: after the leopard thong hit the table, all bets were *off* and all the clothes came *off*. Yes, I suppose true debauchery calls for total nakedness. As couples fell naked onto chaise longues and *canapés* (sofas), others stood, kneeled, or lay nearby, watching with rapacious obsession and feral expressions.

Within the first fifteen minutes I spot one man frantically masturbating as another watches while kissing a woman and spanking a
different man just within arm's reach. . . . Sometimes, naked flesh
is so commingled that I can hardly decipher how many bodies are
involved and whether they are men or women. I'm not even sure
the participants knew or cared. It was all like an erotic homoge-
nization of individual identities. A whirling dervish of orgiastic acts
and carnal pursuits. The room was just saturated with the musky,
throbbing fragrance of sex, as the glow of flickering candles glis-
tened on exposed flesh.

Your basic run-o'-the-mill orgy in a château.

Louis-Philippe saunters off somewhere (charmingly attentive?
non), and I feel distinctly that I could be quite content to just march
off to bed and let these hedonists play through. Then it occurs to
me that this is a very alluring scene of haute couture porn at its most
tantalizing and that I might as well stay and watch. No harm in that.
I may have been the only person who came to this conclusion—and
I'm certainly the only one who's still dressed—but I'm sticking with
it nevertheless. Observing an orgy is strangely like coming across a
bad car wreck on the highway: There is something tragic going on,
and yet you can't take your eyes off it.

A very young and attractive man to my left, standing in an open
cashmere robe, shoots me an enticing glance.

"Bonsoir . . . Je suis Laurent." The mere mention of the name
of my "ex"—though this man looked nothing like him with his
shoulder-length blond hair and blue eyes—was enough to set me
off on a path of sexual fantasy. Oh, and the Champagne clearly
played a serious determining factor, I should add. If one listens
closely, one might be able to hear the death rattle of my integrity
gasping its final breaths.

"I am Alexandra." And some internal automatic mechanism in
me is thrust to the "on" position, as I descend on him like a cat in
heat. I push him back against the windowsill, kick open his robe,
and yank the lace dress up over my head and off to the floor.

With that, I offer, *"Enchantée."* Which is not something you usually say after stripping naked in front of a stranger, but orgy etiquette goes against social rules generally, I'm betting.

I delve deeply into his chest hair as my mouth feeds on every warm hard square inch. My hands knead at his strong pecs while I straddle his leg and start to press my clit hard against his thigh.

He pulls my hair down from its chignon forcefully and grabs it in fistfuls, pulling my mouth back up to his. Biting and gnawing at my open wanting mouth. Ahhh, I had missed good kissing. There's nothing like it to plunge you into a state of almost nymphomaniac craving.

"Alexandra . . . tu es très, très belle," the beautiful stranger murmurs, as he stands up and turns me around to face out the window. I vaguely notice silhouettes below in the garden: a trio of bodies intertwined on the lawn. A man pouring Champagne all over a naked woman, who is squealing in ecstasy. Two men chasing each other to the bathing pavilion, clucking and screaming like a couple of amorous chickens! (Nope, this isn't your typical country weekend getaway!)

My lover *du soir* senses my momentary distraction, and I'm yanked back against a steel-hard cock while he tips my hips in his hands and spreads my legs by kicking them apart. I feel the dizzying heavy throb of desire that only comes from knowing someone wants to fuck you hard and deep. It occurs to me it's been a while since I felt overwhelmed with that sensation, as it's often my role to play seductress. *Pas ici* (not here). This motherfucker is a fiend.

I hear nothing but my own voice, gasping deeply as he enters me from behind with such force I almost feel impaled—*in a good way*. No, make that *in a fucking delicious way*. My hands clutch at the voluminous folds of velvet drapery as he pounds me with a delicate rhythm, taunting in its pace and precision.

"Baise-moi, Laurent!" (Fuck me, Laurent!), I command, my warm breath steaming the window to a temporary fog. You can be damn sure, catching myself saying those words I once uttered with such love, sends me over the edge and beyond the realm of reality. I come three times.

As faceless others yell out in ecstasy and frenzied bodies undulate and shudder in various stages of bliss, Laurent and I steal off to a bedroom and spend hours fucking like demons. Somewhere near daybreak, I slip out of the heavy, weary arms of the dozing Orgy Laurent. Kiss him on both smooth mocha nipples, his forehead, and the tip of his nose, and only with a kiss to his lips does he awaken.

"Oh non . . . Pas partir," he whispers, obviously exhausted.

"Merci . . . à la prochaine fois, mon beau et magnifique Laurent." (Until next time, my beautiful and magnificent Laurent.) I step away and close the door, knowing there would never be a next time.

Realizing I was on a floor of the château I hadn't been on before, I opened door after door seeking a bed to escape to, or even Louis-Philippe to snuggle against. Where the hell did he go? No doubt off with that blond model. Whatever. Like I have a leg to stand on!

Every room was occupied. Hmm. Turns out the blond Amazon with the Brazilian bikini wax ended up in the arms of Monsieur de Eye Patch. I didn't see that coming, nor did I see them coming, now that I think of it! In another room, the man with the bowler hat was out cold but still with that damn hat jauntily astride his head, as he clasped the breast of a fair-haired beauty. A couple of beds were spilling over with three occupants, so I trailed downstairs to Louis-Philippe's master bedroom, cracked the door ajar, and beheld the biggest "wake-up call" of my French adventure—Louis-Philippe tangled in a heated act of oral pleasure with another man.

Okay, is finding your new boyfriend "blowing" another man the kiss of death to a burgeoning love affair? What do you think? I would have to go with a solid "yes." I'm not claiming to be a saint— I did play a minor role as an extra in an orgy for the last ten hours, so my acquiring a sainthood title isn't a strong possibility, but please! Hey, I know historically it's acceptable in France for men of aristocracy to marry even if they are homosexual or bisexual. Louis XIV is one of the most famous examples, and there are countless others. This need not be the moment to "out" French royalty by way of a history lesson, but I do have limits. And this is one. And frankly, now that I'm sober, I don't much dig the idea that my once-future husband now soon to be ex-*amour* Marquis would even throw an orgy in my lap in the first weeks of our "love story." There are a great many things I do not know, but I do know that marrying or even sleeping with a pretentious bisexual bon vivant is not, nor has it ever been, on my wish list of Things to Do in Life. Nope. I double-checked, it's not there! I know some women can swing it, endure and use their marriages as paths to power or success, but I'd rather be penniless and anonymous than know my "husband" was unabashedly craving a steel-hard cock as much as I was.

Despite this sight being the obvious death blow to our young love affair, I tried to exit the room with poise and not fly off the handle, as the me of a year ago might have—no, absolutely would have. What's the point? I backed out of the room, slingbacks in one hand, and slowly closed the door on all that I had once thought was a dream realized.

Later that morning, as I was packing my bags to go (can you blame me?), Louis-Philippe came to my door and swept in with a breakfast tray and a big smile. "*Chérie,* wasn't that just a roaring success? I should say, I hope you are not at all miffed to have discovered me this morning *en flagrante* with Julien. I couldn't find you or I would've adored to have you join us . . . what are you doing? *Mon dieu,* are you leaving? You wouldn't dare! I forbid it!" he exclaims, astonished. *And clueless.*

"Louis-Philippe, I'm sorry, perhaps I'm not quite as intensely decadent as you wish me to be. I admit, after a tidal wave of Champagne, I did manage to partake in the festivities somewhat last night"—way for me to downplay it, eh?—"but . . . I couldn't embrace the idea of being with several people, the anonymity of giving yourself to so many at once?! And I know I don't ever want to play a part in or even witness such an experience again," I say, sitting on the bed with that bouquet of wildflowers retrieved and now, despite slightly fading, tenderly wrapped in a newspaper next to my Goyard luggage, all very *prête à partir* (ready to leave).

"Oh, you're being a tinge moralistic, my darling Alexandra. As a young courtesan, is it not your *raison d'être*—or modus operandi, if you prefer—to enjoy oneself at the expense of no matter whom? I thought you were endowed with a blend of innocence and corruption. That is one of the primary reasons I thought you would be an excellent match for me, that we'd share an understanding of each other's *eccentricities,*" he persists, winking. (Oh, take that wink and jam it up your ass. As with the word "beguiling," I am editing winking out of my repertoire forever. Eesh.)

I'm surprisingly speechless as this all filters in and I become aware that in some weird way, I actually do understand why he'd think that.

He continues, "Not to mention, I thought sharing the world I have created—where everyone and everything is as beautiful, elegant, and astonishing as myself—was a gift to you with your small-town upbringing. It would be the fantasy of most citizens of the world, of this I'm sure!" he proclaims, as though it's mandatory to want what he has. And you know what? In France, in these circles, it almost is.

"As ever, marching to the drums and trumpets, hubris did not hear the light steps of Nemesis at his side," I mumble, laughing to myself at his self-absorption.

"Comment?" he asks, having missed the entire recitation. Pity as I would've killed for him to have that echo in his mind long after I'm gone. Better opt for something more straightforward.

"I may be *small*-town and *small*-breasted, but I am not *small*-minded. It's simply apparent to me now that your lifestyle is more convoluted, shall we say, than I anticipated or desired. I'm certain there is someone more suitable for you—someone accepting of all this sexual freedom and the streams of lovers waiting eagerly in the wings." *Probably literally, there are such people waiting in the château's wings.*

Ever the pedant, Louis-Philippe doesn't listen to me. He's too busy conjuring up the next line of his diatribe. "Alexa, perhaps you might care to reflect on the words of another indulgent marquis, *le Marquis de Sade:* "By giving oneself to everyone, one gives oneself, first to oneself."

Wrong answer! Not only spoken like a truly selfish lover, but God help me over here, wasn't Marie-Hélène recently also quoting Sade to me?

Here is my *unspoken* retort to the Sade quote: "When one realizes that everyone surrounding oneself is quoting Sade, one must take oneself away from said people and give oneself some alone time!"

I stood there patiently, trying not to cry. There was no way I was not going to exit with the greatest dignity one could gather . . . after all this. I stopped listening, and extracted myself emotionally from the moment and just let Louis-Philippe tire himself ranting every self-serving defense he could piece together until the precious end.

Then I grabbed my bag, scooped the weary bouquet of wildflowers under my arm, and gave him a quick dry double-cheek air kiss, as he fell back into an overstuffed chair with a look of shock, annoyance, and undoubtedly, hungover exhaustion on his face. At moments like that, the ubiquitous cheek kiss adds a certain twisted irony that punctuates a great exit with assured flamboyance. *Au revoir*, indeed.

As Hugo drove me to the *gare* to take the train to Paris, I wondered just how I, with all my new so-called awareness, had found myself falling hook, line, and *stinker* for a French playboy player. Hmm. Just far too eager to escape the married lovers and sign up for something that resembled a real story? Hey, it did look very good on paper, you have to admit! I could see now that anything I liked I managed to spin into a vast cyclone of importance and value. I took a man—a stranger—chock full of charm and potential, and manufactured him into the definitive Monsieur Dream Man. *Voilà*. One could also draw the conclusion that drinking copious amounts of alcohol each and every time you see a man may pickle one's mind, resulting in impared judgment or wishful conjuring.

I'm still terribly disappointed, and more than that, I hate to have wasted so much time fooling myself into a fantasy of future. It's *so* humiliating to have to say to myself, "Whoa Alexandra, you really got it all wrong there!"

As I stared out of the train window, the countryside whizzing by, I realized that my wildflowers were actually almost dead, and frankly, starting to stink, and still, I laughed despite it all.

I won't sell my soul for a château and a title. I have to say, that's a rather reassuring thing to have found out about myself.

Even with a new wound to the heart and ego, I am grateful to keep finding the humor in it all. The fat lady has not only sung on this relationship, but she's left the theater!

CHAPITRE DIX-NEUF

When suddenly time stands still and one's existence
blends into the unmoving fullness of the universe.
—SIMONE DE BEAUVOIR, *THE PRIME OF LIFE*

*A*s you can imagine, I arrived back in Paris that evening, hugely relieved to be home safe, my head spinning and none too eager to even so much as hear a man's voice on the radio. Got a text message, *"Gli amore e manco molto,"* which translates into "I love and miss you very much" in Italian. Apparently it's a last attempt by Louis-Philippe to try to charm me back with our new "Italian connection." *Please!* Speak in any language you like, but speak the truth, Monsieur. I erased it without even scrolling down to read the rest.

Poured myself a vanilla martini and slipped into a warm bath, eager to try to drown my confusion in the almond-scented water. You should try it: a dash of *huile d'amande* in the bath is so divine, it makes you feel like you're swimming in marzipan. And all together a fairly effective mood lifter: I managed to not drown self *literally*, yet drowned any remaining concerns with a second martini, remembering the quip "men are like martinis—two's not enough and three is too many." Hmm. Let's amend that—"two *martinis* are *enough* and three *men* are *too many*." Of this I can attest! I laughed as

I bundled myself in an old Gap sweatshirt and flannel pants and climbed into my bed just after sunset.

The room fell into a quiet darkness. On Sunday evenings in Paris, a serene tranquility infuses the city with a gentle peace. Little but the sound of my own breathing and the coo of doves in the courtyard stirred me from my reverie. Mmm. There is a charming quality in silence. For hearts that are wounded, there is no remedy but silence and shadow.

Upon awakening the next morning, I felt an enormous surge of energy, an overwhelming need to take myself off the game board and just work intensely—lose my harried thoughts in the total focus that my thesis demands. No time for returning calls to Marie-Hélène or Jean-Albert—and certainly not to Frédéric. In my mind I just lump them altogether now, and file them under "to be avoided at present." I will deal with all of them later, but if I don't get some real distraction and sense of accomplishment from something, I'm going to leap out of the window. I'm not really serious with the leap threat there, I'm just still a bit of a drama queen. *That* may be the only title I am comfortable with, though apparently the Marquise title is still an option, believe it or not! Check this out: as twisted as he can be, Louis-Philippe is now pursuing me with total obsession bordering on insane. And by the way, I have definitely changed my motto for life, but more on that later. Anyway, Marquis de Sexuality Ambiguous sent me a bouquet of black tulips with a mind-fuck of a note:

My darling Alexandra,

With your dramatic disappearance . . . I feel as though someone has reached into my chest and ripped my heart out. I'm in absolute agony without you . . . now I am sure you are the One . . . my future marquise. You are like the tremor one sees in the air above a flame . . . mesmerizing, impossible to confine, and entirely spellbinding.

Amour,

Yours, body and soul,

Louis-Philippe

Mine in body and soul? Hardy har har, as we say in Illinois! I've never seen a man be less mine in body. And the soul part would be a lot more convincing if, say, he even had one to give away! On first read, it might seem a well-written, sweet letter but we know better now, don't we?! I can say all this not simply for his unforgettable performance at the château, but because like a complete ass with no short-term memory, he stole that great line "you are like the tremor above a flame" from me, when I told him it was one of my favorite lines by the writer Julien Gracq over that fucked-up wild-boar-brains-wrapped-in-hay dinner in that fucking palace of his . . . Oh, don't get me started, buddy. I'm about to send him my copy of the book and mark it for him . . . hell, what's the point? He's just a clueless rich aristo-rat.

Not to mention, if he had any brains or sensitivity at all, he would've sent wildflowers, right? *That* would've been clever. Black tulips? Just a somber reminder of how twisted he is and how right I am to put him in the rearview mirror, château and all. One gold star for this girl with growing integrity. (Not hard when it was at zero, you're probably saying to yourself. Fair enough.)

To be honest, my heart and soul are drained to dire levels. At moments like these, only solitude, the love of dear friends, and intense work can replenish your spirit. Screw the men! Well, not *literally*. I am just going to continue with Italian lessons for the rest of the month (they were prepaid), write in this *journal intime* (diary) I've begun, and work on my research for my Ph.D.

Oh, and I have that engagement dinner party this Saturday for Isabel and Mathieu, and though I never thought I'd say this, I'm happy to go stag. It will be good and refreshing for me to just mix with my own kind, freely and without any of these wealthy hangers-on to worry about. They'd just upstage the event anyway, and frankly, I'm looking forward to just sitting around surrounded by genuine souls . . . who keep their clothes on!

Earlier in the week, Isabel thoughtfully faxed me a sketch of the dress she's designed for her wedding, for my opinion. Since *she*'s the talented designer of the two of us, this gesture was clearly intended as a way for us to get back into sync. At first, I thought,

"What the hell can I offer by way of help?" Then, amazingly, while looking at the sketch what small bit of advice I could offer was blatantly obvious. I found myself applying Marie-Hélène's line to Isabel's plentiful use of lots of lace. You remember—the "women who have nothing to say wear dresses that shout. Women such as ourselves must adorn ourselves with quiet elegance." Isabel totally dug the idea, chopped off the lace sleeves, and saved herself about two hundred euros on Venetian lace to boot! Who knew the advice of a courtesan could be applicable to *cost cutting*?! I also "icks-nayed" the wild idea of her marching down the aisle in a tiara made of wood. Yeah, wood! I know: bonkers, right? That's the thing about Parisian designers: They all get so accustomed to the outrageous, one-upping each other with extravagant ideas, their minds start to think of only the outlandish. After John Galliano put antlers on his bride at the last *défilé*, I can see how she got caught up in thinking a wooden nymph-fairy tiara might work. Had to talk her through the notion that in a few year's time she would look back at the photos and shudder in horror, much as I do when I see my passport photo, all achingly queer with my curling-iron sausage hair rolls and red polka-dot bustier à la Minnie Mouse, taken seven years ago. I've actually thought of "losing" my passport just so I can have it reshot, it's *that* cheeseball, hometown hokey. God, what was I thinking? Scarier still, the look was orchestrated deliberately for the photo! I'll never forget when Laurent caught a glimpse of it and said, "Do you live at Euro Disney with Mickey? Tell me the truth, does he eat pussy or just cheese?" I was so in shock, I fell over laughing. Laurent's the only man I know who can make crass jokes funny, as they were so out of character.

Anyway, I'm just grateful to have Isabel back in my life, and to be thick as thieves with her again, because I missed her madly. As much as Marie-Hélène has been doting, and a close friend, I need to put a little distance between us. I believe I've O.D.ed on men, on everything about them: talking about, taunting, fucking, and playing them. Time to do things for *my* happiness and future. If Jean-Albert works into that, *ça va*. I do kinda miss him. Maybe it

would be fun to invite him to the engagement party after all . . .
Nah. It just doesn't feel right.

In fact, I spent the better part of the week dodging floral
arrangements and calls—by way of escaping into research and a
productive meeting with my *professeur* at the Sorbonne. Truthfully,
it had been so long since I'd really delved into my work that tuck-
ing my backpack full of notes and traipsing into the Sorbonne all
felt like I was "playing" student. Funny, that's how this whole
courtesan life had felt at the beginning, too.

By the grace of God, my *professeur* was amazingly understanding
that I had taken some *time off* for other work. (Little did he guess
that the time off was often taken with *clothes off*!) He assured me
that many Ph.D. students take a pause after years of going full
steam, and when they return to their work, it's generally with newfound passion and greater wisdom. *Passion? Wisdom?* Yeah, I've got a
whole lotta experience in those fields now, Monsieur! But he generously praised my outline and proposal, even offering that if I can
pull it together by the Christmas break, he would feel confident to
have me assist him next year, when he's curating a Boucher exhibi-
tion at the Musée Carnavalet. What a rare one-chance-only opportunity! I'm so not gonna let him—or me—down.

Wild. I used to look at a dinner at Joel Robuchon as a rare, one-
chance-only opportunity. Don't look now. *Maybe I'm getting a clue
and/or possibly a career.*

I finally called Marie-Hélène back on Thursday morning, and
she startled the hell out of me. I told her how the whole Marquis
affair had run awry, and that I didn't much appreciate that he had
attested that she—more or less—gave him the green light for an
orgy. She replied, with marked sincerity, "Oh certainly not. Never
did I say, *or even know*, he was leaning in such a direction. Or in all
directions, as it appears! You know I adore you, Alexa! I believe the
extent of which I spoke of you was that I thought you to be a marvelously intelligent young woman with a *joie de vivre*, a charming if
wicked wit, and an obsequious character. Truly, nothing about your
being sexually open to anyone *he* chose. I am in full agreement with

you on the issue of orgies; a refined woman with a sense of honor wouldn't dream of unveiling herself in such a venue or manner."

I let it all slide, as Marie-Hélène—in her own unique way—has never been anything but helpful, caring, and protective. Though I did stumble a bit on the "obsequious character" comment. You know, "obsequious" means, essentially, "excessively eager to please or obey all instructions"? I wondered, "That's not me, is it?" I'm kind of—oh God, am I going to say this?—I've been told (here goes)—a "wild filly." Yes, I would rather be referred to as a "wild filly" or even a "loose cannon," than "an eager obeyer."

Maybe Marie-Hélène's got a different image of me than I think she has. And maybe it goes both ways. Maybe it's like when a man recognizes that the girl he loves is not the girl he loved—but that he has loved not the person but an ideal, a romantic vision—a personified desire, *a projection of oneself.* Very possibly she's projecting that onto me. *C'est très possible.* Boy, am I thinking a lot those days, *n'est-ce pas?*

In an effort to reestablish my connection to Jean-Albert, and honestly eager for some of that unabashed and endless adulation he lavishes on me, I agreed to meet him for a *soirée* that Thursday evening. Frankly, I didn't care where we went or what we did, just as long as it didn't involve seeing people getting naked while wearing bowler hats or eye patches. Jean-Albert offered an opera-based night out: "My darling, we could have a late dinner at that new Japanese restuarant, Aida, that you've mentioned you want to try. But first, are you interested in accompanying me to an award ceremony at Opéra Bastille? Aida after Opéra Bastille, not a bad theme, *non*? The ceremony will be brief; I just have to shake a few hands and give a few awards."

"*Mon chou* . . . I would happily accompany you to the men's room, so an award ceremony or simply watching *Aida* on television would be lovely," I reply. *Wait!* Is that obsequious, eager obeyer behavior? How nowhere. *That* won't do. A gear change is definitely in order.

"But, actually, I read that dining at Aida is a bit like being locked in a tatami-mat version of solitary confinement while being served three grains of rice and a raw lobster with its antennae still swirling around (my interpretation). Let's go to that new bistro in the seventh, Le Cinq Mars. I'll make the reservation in my name for 10:00 P.M. *D'accord?*"

"Perfect. I will pick you up at eight and . . . I can't wait to see you. I missed you terribly, my dear heart." And he clicks off.

Good. With time to kill, I kick around ideas for a wedding gift for Isabel and Mathieu.

What to give those two lovebirds? In keeping with Isabel's nontraditional ways, they aren't even registering at a boutique as eclectic as Colette, so this will take some doing. Not something over-the-top opulent, for sure. I learned my lesson with the dinner at Le Grand Véfour. Perhaps something like a weekend away in Biarritz? No, too snob a locale. A couple of bottles of cognac from Rhyst-Duperon on rue du Bac, with hand-written labels from the year they were both born? Again, *so* not them. What would be nonpretentious and fun and *them* to a T? . . . I've got it! Since they are completely and hilariously spontaneous and silly together: a karaoke machine. And, I could—or should—add a few bottles of good saki, and a coupon for dinner for twelve from that corner Japanese delivery place they dig. Great.

For the pending arrival of Jean-Albert, I decide to ditch the slapdash student look I've so quickly readopted over the last ten days, and put out a smattering of effort for—*me. Surprise.* It occurs to me that, unlike other times when I'm trying to anticipate what the man I'm meeting will respond to, now I'm kinda OK just dressing for me. I'm fairly sick of dresses and heels, and being on the receiving end of more attention than I need or want. Hence, the low-waisted black cropped pants; flat ballet slippers; a simple black mock turtleneck with that cheap beige poplin trench coat I got at H&M. (To clarify, it's *still* Karl Lagerfeld for H&M, but it was just sixty euros, which *rocks*!)

When I get in the car and he sees what I'm wearing, Jean-Albert instantly goes off on a huge tangent. Think you know which direction? Even I wasn't sure where he was gonna go with it when I first glimpsed his wide-eyed, taken aback expression.

While careening through traffic in that Maserati at surely an illegal speed, he launched into: "Alexandra, you are so right! That outfit is the epitome of quiet elegance. And it's completely free of any blatant designer insignia. Yes! That. *That* is the future—*restrained* and *understated*! After two weeks in Asia, seeing mobs clamoring madly at the store openings for even so much as a keychain, I felt strangely ill at ease. And now, suddenly, I just got it. This luxury goods machine has reached the pinnacle. It's the height of oversaturation; no matter how excellent it is for business, it needs to transition to a new *point de vue*. Yes, the *more* we hear about luxury the *less* we want it now. The word is so overused and the notion overplayed. The bandwagon is too crowded, and truly elegant people will happily get off. I sense it's time to move on, and that very soon we will see a return to more discreet, quieter pursuits of living well. The next movement has to be embracing a discreet wealth, not for presentation but as a tribute to one's self-esteem. Truly refined people have had it with all the bling-in-your-face flagrant labels! Seeing their secretaries sporting the same wallet as they have! Yes, the future is *quiet elegance*!"

What a monologue! "So true! I am in full agreement, Jean-Albert. 'Less is more,' as Mies van der Rohe coined it. You know, growing up in Elmbrook I once took a field trip to his famous Farnsworth House in Plano, Illinois, and even at ten years old that purest philosophy clicked with me. I immediately went home and literally ripped the yellow ruffle canopy (bought from the Sears catalog, I'll have you know) off my bed! . . . But do you really think the consumer market is ready to embrace such a notion? It's in direct opposition to all your PR and marketing strategies," I say, adding in my two centimes and loving that, for once, I can confirm growing up in the Midwest is unquestionably cool.

"I assure you, with the finely tuned machine I have created, I can simply point in any direction and the world will follow. Patrons, magazine editors, and competitors alike. At any given moment or season, they all are lying in wait for my direction. Wouldn't it be novel to seek out new designers—*total unknowns*—and shift the new collections to a cultivated and inconspicuous sensibility. You are my muse. I *love* you for just crystallizing that in my mind," he states with great fervor, punctuating his announcement with a tap of his fist to the dashboard.

I smile at Jean-Albert, at first simply amused at his dramatic pompousness and then registering the reality of what this profound statement from Jean-Albert will mean. Every idea or scheme he has will be set into action, go global, and send out seismic waves that affect millions of people. I'm also remembering what a big hoo-ha production it always feels like to be with this man. And, it's just that I was bored of dressing all frou-frou, and tired of being on the receiving end of jealous glances from other women as they spot this or that flashy purse "of the season" tucked under my arm!

Kinda hilarious—Jean-Albert's attributing what had surely already been germinating in his mind as *my* masterful statement on consumerism. Then again, if *I'm* over all this extravagance, maybe there is fatigue out there for the luxury industry's must-haves and endless quest for prestige. God only knows where I'd fall in a market survey! Something tells me I'd straddle a few categories, being able to check the box for no-income student and million-dollar apartment owner." Does that make sense to anyone?! No? Me neither!

Whatever the source of Jean-Albert's enthusiastic expounding of a new corporate vision, it's awfully exciting and lots of fun to talk about. A great discussion ensues as we both run with the idea and spin it out into all aspects of life, purifying and downscaling everything from interior design to wearing pure essence oils to eating raw food and developing an eco-friendly line of makeup and clothes. Not a bad use of time management and business acumen, eh? Given it was a fifteen-minute drive!

As we pull up to the Opéra Bastille, leaving the car with the valet, I seize the moment with my new-thinking Jean-Albert to share the news of my self-imposed thesis deadline and the wonderful opportunity to help curate that upcoming Boucher exhibit. That new-thinking Jean-Albert apparently got left behind in the car, now being driven off to a garage. "Oh, Alexandra, yes, absolutely finish the thesis, but why struggle? Why start at the bottom of the ladder?" he asks, as we enter the glass doors of the opera house, and all heads turn to stare first at him, and then at us.

"The bottom?! Hardly, Jean-Albert. I would love to curate art exhibits one day, and this is a necessary step." I'm oblivious to everyone around us. Jean-Albert also ignores all eyes and the huddled mass of people clearly tempted but tentative to approach him. He turns to face me with a level of seriousness I haven't seen often in our relationship.

"My dear girl." (Oh God, I do hate it when he—*or his wife for that matter*—addresses me that way; it seems so condescending, *non*?) "Allow me to do something. Please don't say it is extravagant or excessive. Skip the whole, 'working your way up' cliché and let me get you a gallery in Paris, where you can freely express your vision. I have a space that's becoming available in January on avenue Montaigne. Think of it as a gift for finishing your thesis." Jean-Albert squeezes my hand, smiles as if to say, "There, that's done," and darts away to tackle the gathered group of handlers eager to fill him in on tonight's required appearance.

Hrmph! Maybe I've lost my mind, or maybe I've just gained a little of that sensibility he likes to attribute to fashion all the time, but I want to—no, need to—do it myself. Buying me jewelry, even the apartment, is generous in the extreme, but when it comes to my career, I have to do it myself. I remembered telling him at the Ritz that afternoon, that I needed to do it "*seule*" (alone). I have to know in my heart of hearts that it wasn't through Jean-Albert's connections but because of my abilities or it won't mean anything. It won't be an achievement. Just like the closet full of clothes and the massive collection of Empire furniture, I've quickly learned unless it's my hard-earned cash, it's empty of a real sense of meaning.

Well, looks like that chat has gotta go on hold, since Jean-Albert's got his hands full here for an hour. What the hell is this award thing about, anyway? I see Jean-Albert's personal assistant, Clare, finish up a call on her cell and begin to sort some papers in her ever present black folder, containing Jean-Albert's agenda for the day. I sweep in, and after a polite double-cheek air kiss and the usual niceties, ask what the program is. She replies politely but curtly. Why this chick is always so rude to me, I could not say. *Nor could I care less, anymore.* "Each year the company (that's everyone's buzzword for the monster conglomerate that Jean-Albert's holdings) funds scholarships and awards for the most promising young creative minds of France. Tonight, of course, Jean-Albert will be presenting awards for those with musical talents: aspiring operatic sopranos and the like." She cuts herself short, hands me a program for the night, and heads over to scold some photographer for taking pics of Jean-Albert heading into the men's room. Standing alone, I lean against a pillar and vaguely skim the program, when I hear a voice to my left: "Alexandra . . . is that you?"

That *voice.* As though coming from inside my own mind . . . It went on.

"It *is* you! How . . . how are you? God, you look great." And those almond-shaped eyes I once bathed in flicker with light-filled emotion.

"Laurent! Holy shit . . . what are you doing here?" I ask, instantly feeling my cheeks flush red and my heart pound so loudly I can't be sure if I am even actually speaking out loud and not just thinking.

Laughing faintly, my ex—yes, *the* EX—boyfriend, Laurent, says, "Very good to see you're still swearing, even if you *are* Mademoiselle Couture now." He's smiling but rather obviously scanning my hands, checking for that diamond ring he's heard about. Phew. I haven't worn it in a month, and am damn grateful to not be flaunting that rock in his face.

"I'll have you know . . . (Oh man, my voice is shaking.) This isn't couture by a long shot. It's H&M, baby! . . . Now, who really cares? More interesting, why are you here?" (Did any of that make sense? It all just felt like buzzes and whistles in my head.)

"A-hem . . . To receive an award from . . . *your boyfriend,* I guess. Ironic moment, isn't it?" he asks, his smile fading slightly as he nervously jams his hands in his suit-pant pockets like a little boy.

"Really?! Great, which award? Oh, and Jean-Albert is not my

boyfriend, by the way," I begin to say with certainty and am amazed, looking at Laurent, that by the time it's out of my mouth it sounds quite convincing to me, too.

"Yeah, the award for best young composer of France. Pretty cool, really, because it comes with one hundred thousand euros to fund my next piece. Maybe now I can actually upgrade that crap car of mine!" he says, with that charming self-deprecation I remember so well, while running his index finger across the top of his nose—his nervous habit of choice.

Funny, that always made me want to immediately stroke it, too. Still does.

"Wow, Laurent! Congratulations! That's tons of money but . . . ah . . . don't ditch that car. I loo-ove that car!" I say, remembering all our road trips to Chartres, Étretat, Brittany . . . Christ, even Ikea! Wait one goddamn minute here! Why the hell am I being so nice to him? He never even returned my text message after I drunkenly texted "I love you."

He carries on: "We both know my old clunker's not exactly a Maserati, now is it, *bellissima*?" He's adorable, with that smirk and the chiding tilt of his head. Oh, *merde*. He used his old nickname for me. For some unknown reason this boy always loved to give me Italian nicknames. I loved that. Yeah, but he also dumped you, Alexa. Breathe. Just *breathe*.

"You'd be surprised how overrated a Maserati is." I could so launch into a twelve-inch dance-mix long version of how overrated the whole Maserati lifestyle is, but I don't have the time, because I eye Jean-Albert coming toward me—and staring at Laurent and me. Eeks. But I have a point to make here, dammit, and have about a nanosecond in which to make it, so I let 'er rip. "Enough small talk, huh? Wanna tell me why you never even replied to my text message? That move wins you 'France's Biggest Rude Boy Prize.'" I'm attempting to look pissed and desperately trying to scrounge up some of the old anger.

"What?! You're kidding me. *You* didn't return *either* of mine," he says, shaking his head. He looks truly mystified.

"What? I responded to your 'wherever I am in the world' . . .
and by the way, where the hell were you? Still in Greece with the
tall brunette beauty?" (Okay, now we are getting somewhere; real
anger is bubbling to the surface.)

"Greece? Tall brunette? I went to Greece with my oldest sister,
Cécile. And to answer your question, I wrote you that text message
from Rome, actually . . . When the hell did *you* ever write me back?"
he asks, as we both start piecing this convoluted snafu back together
with as much focus as though we were pounding out a Middle East
peace treaty.

"That was your *sister*? Oh . . . I see. Uh . . . Um. Well, I think I
wrote you back about a week later . . . or so. What the hell were you
doing in Rome?" Ahh, cool, that explains why the elegant older
woman I saw with him at CDG looked so right and comfortable.
Siblings. Hmm. Fair enough. And beats me why I think I have a
right to ask, after almost a year apart and the fact that I was fucking
the entire upper echelon of Frenchmen.

"Italy was the last stop on my six-month sabbatical. I guess you
must've written me after I accidently dropped my cell phone into
the Fontana di Trevi. I was trying to take a photo to send you with
the *texto* I was trying to write to you in Italian. I ended up having to
send it from someone else's phone, but I thought you'd translate it
when you saw it was from me. I sent you something like '*Gli amore
manco molto*' (I love and miss you), and then I invited you to come
meet me there, or in Florence, or anywhere you wanted. I guess
the message didn't go through . . . tragic," he trails off.

We both fall silent for an instant, thinking of what might have
been. Feel free to insert sound of the earth stopping its rotation,
with two hearts racing in the background. Followed fast on its
heels by my shuddering in massive regret.

"Oh, *merde*. I did get your *texto* . . . (his mouth drops open as I
turn beet red). Oh my God. Soooo sorry! After readng the first
line in Italian, I just thought it was from someone else . . . and
just erased the rest. That was totally my screwup . . . Oh man,
what an idiot," I add, while both hands magnetically fly to the

sides of my face, creating a very convincing imitation of Munch's *The Scream.*

We both just stand there, smiles creeping across our faces like rays of sunlight through stained glass, expanding and scattering light all over the room. Both of us, in all of our innate clumsiness, created massive miscommuniqués and mangled a flurry of good attempts at reuniting . . . And yet, here we are, we still found each other. Brought together again, by Jean-Albert, of all people!

Perfect. Twisted but perfect. *Very* French.

I continue to exude nervous energy so manic it's frankly surprising there's no lightning in the lobby.

Jean-Albert is hovering and Laurent and I are now aware that there is so much we have to sort through. How in the world will we go about it? Cue: inane chatter spurred by hectic hearts aflutter. Always the one to fill any silence in the room with blather, I assume my role.

"So, Laurent, I suppose we all should file in soon, right? Hey, but tell me quickly . . . are you well, sweet pea?" Yeah, I am now using my old nickname for *him*, as I've said, "All is fair in love and war," and unlike the other occasion I made that reference, this is love.

"*Oui, je suis très heureux.* As you can imagine, this is a big night for me. I have worked really diligently in the last year. Both on my music and myself. And it means a lot that you're here. Alexandra, I want to tell you, I hoped you would be here. Part of me worked toward this award with just the thought that you might be here with him (he nods toward Jean-Albert, who's basking in the adulation of the press), and that I might be able to steal you away for a few moments to speak to you again. I was convinced you had shut the door on me . . . on us . . ." His voice trails off with emotion.

I quickly shoot another glance over at Jean-Albert. He frowns with disapproval and beckons me with a quick incline of his head. Hold that thought, Shorty, I'm not the obsequious girl on call anymore. And Laurent is standing so close I am almost drunk just from the smell of his skin.

Laurent continues, clearly unleashing phrases and ideas that have long been pent up: "I am so sorry that I ran away. It was so cowardly and immature of me. I was so embarrassed at my *com-portement*. You inspired such a zealous love in me—and because I never knew anything like it, I was scared to death of it. I just acted so spontaneously with you, and then wondered if I was truly ready or just lost in emotion. I needed to be alone to discover who I was, out of Paris, away from this safe world. That's why I traveled for so long. I started in Greece, as I said, with my sister Cécile for that week that you and I had long planned. God, it was just hell to be there without you . . . I came back to Paris just after that, discovered you were with Jean-Albert after seeing you in *Le Figaro*, and the thought of seeing you in magazines for months made me ill. I had to escape again. So, I went all over Africa, Eastern Europe, and finally back by way of Italy, completely alone the whole trip, and you know what? Being alone was good for me." (Hurry up, Laurent; Jean-Albert the impatient incoming stage left!) "I want you to know . . . if you'd ever find it in your heart to give me another chance, I'd do it right . . . I still love . . ."

"*Bonsoir*. You are the recipient of the composer award, are you not, *jeune homme*?" Jean-Albert bellows, rudely breaking in and extending a hand to Laurent.

God, what a moment. There I stood with the two men in my life. So dissimilar, each representing a totally different world and a totally different me.

By the way, *très* important detail here: Jean-Albert should never have saddled up next to the devastatingly gorgeous Laurent. Old Monsieur Dried Apple Ears looks like his gramps. Even if he had stacked five-hundred-euro notes on his shoulders, Jean-Albert still pales miserably in the sexy/appealing department. Maybe power *isn't* that sexy. Maybe Jean-Albert represented my variation of an escape route, just as Laurent sought his.

"*Oui*. Thank you very much. It is a tremendous honor, and I'm very grateful," Laurent replies, respectfully, and yet clearly with a strain of anguish that, of all people to interrupt his proclamation to me, it is the old zillionaire I have been sleeping with.

Ughhh! Part of me—hell, *all* of me—wants to slip my hand into

Laurent's and run out of the door with him, yelling, "Bye, Jean-Albert, I'm out of here!" and part of me wants to just be back home in Elmbrook, a million miles away from all of this emotional chaos. Yes, it's safe to say, confusion reigns.

"Time to go inside, *chérie*," Jean-Albert murmurs to me, clearly in a snit after recognizing my "ex" from photos I once showed him. As if taking possession, he puts his arm firmly in mine and draws me toward the auditorium.

As I am reluctantly led away, I look back over my shoulder at Laurent. Our eyes meet in a gaze that feels like someone's ripping us away from each other. Slyly, out of Jean-Albert's sight, Laurent blows me a small kiss, and I smile gently back. It's a gift far more satisfying than diamonds.

We all file into the auditorium and settle ourselves into our designated seats. I sit in the front row, next to Jean-Albert, constantly stealing glances at Laurent two seats away as Jean-Albert whispers into my disinterested ear. "Now that you're finished with your little reunion with your *ancien amour* . . . And frankly, I didn't much enjoy watching that little scene, my dear. Now, tell me again, where was it that you mentioned you would like to go for dinner later? Anywhere you wish. As you know, with a man like me, it could be whatever your heart desires."

Not exactly brimming with sensitivity, is he?

I suddenly feel so detached from Jean-Albert that even *deciphering*, let alone replying, to him seems beyond my ability. I just sit stupefied and speechless. Blah! Listen, mister, the idea of taking you up on your offer of sitting in another over-the-top, sha-sha restaurant with a fussy staff that kisses your ass as photographers congregate outside to snap pics to sell to magazines that will both torment your wife and publicly attest to your prestige as "Monsieur Virile Brilliant Zillionaire who can have any young woman he wishes"?! Oh, that sounds about as tempting as drinking a homeless man's bath water.

I stall by feigning deep absorption in the program.

Jean-Albert rises, gets on stage, and begins to present the

evening's awards. His face has an expression of arrogance and
anger masked by faux timidity. Never a good look!

My eyes dart back and forth from him to Laurent and back
again; it feels as though I'm watching a championship tennis match.
Who's ahead? Who's my favorite player? Who's got the better serve?

As thoughts and glances race about, the rest of me feels calm.
As though time, my life, my role in these two men's lives is standing still. Everything moves in slow motion.

I watch Jean-Albert speak into the microphone and literally hear
only the name "Laurent" pass over his lips, nothing else. I watch in
abhorrence the power-play condescension that Jean-Albert imparts
on Laurent, intentionally mispronouncing his family name and dis-
missively standing in front of him while elbowing him in the chest.
God, what ghastly behavior! Rich and powerful as Jean-Albert is, he
ridiculously still feels the need to one-up and try to diminish
Laurent on what should be *his* night, celebrating *his* unique accomplishments! I feel my head shaking in digust as a flash of insight and
understanding washes over me. How pathetic is this man? In one
fell swoop Jean-Albert's image in my mind was forever marred. Observing his immature, inconsiderate behavior didn't just cool my ardor, but destroyed it all together. I suddenly couldn't see why I'd
ever wanted to be with the little man up on the stage. Any attraction
I still had for him shattered instantly, like a cheap Champagne glass.

My heart went out to Laurent, standing there in his charming
ill-fitting, off-the-rack suit, juggling with warring emotions of pride
in getting his award and amazement at Jean-Albert's blatant arrogance. He endures the bittersweetness of the moment, clutching
his plaque in one hand and the check in the other, listening politely to Jean-Albert hold forth.

It's stunning to me to see the sharp juxtaposition of these two
men side by side. I also see Laurent with a new clarity. I adore that
Laurent is a sensitive soul, an apprentice of creativity. He's inspired more by his delight in reading, thinking, and feeling than by
an ambition to shine in public. *So* admirable. His qualities are truly
something to admire, to emulate. Not to mention dead sexy.

Laurent says a few shy thank-yous and makes a modest but deeply distinguished bow. The whole crowd applauds. Laurent beams, and his eyes fall on me.

Without even realizing it, I instantly feel some crazy force that compels me to leap up out of my seat. I, alone, am giving Laurent a standing ovation, clapping madly and totally not caring that I'm making a complete ass of myself. It feels great!

Jean-Albert fires at me a glare of admonition, but I look away.

Laurent looks at me with charmed surprise, laughing with clear delight as his eyes begin to fill with tears.

Instantly I thought, "Enough! I must escape all this!" Or, as Proust might have put it: *"In the colossal, awe-inspiring, defensive mass of my temple I feel a savage desire to create a place of refuge, a shelter against further misfortunes."*

Jean-Albert is already beginning to announce the next award. I grab my purse, pass Clare with her shocked and aghast expression (oh, go to hell, sister, you've been such a judgmental bitch from minute one), and make for the exit. I need to get out of here, away from both of them, to be alone and figure out what the hell's going on in my head.

As the auditorium doors close behind me, the literal and heavy emotional weight of Jean-Albert's voice is thankfully silenced. *Phew.*

The fresh air and a free taxi are both soothing, reassuring elixirs. Leaning back against the seat, things become clearer: "Nope, I just can't play this role of courtesan to *any* man *anymore*. I have to get off stage and let the curtain fall on my performance. All requests for an encore will be denied, and I am damn sure there's no chance of a command performance!"

All these lovers: Frédéric, Jean-Albert, Louis-Philippe? I have to let them *all* go. Yes. All my soon-to-be exes are Ys—as in *why* did I bother? I know why, but *ça suffit!*

As the taxi makes its way around the Place de la Bastille—where the French Revolution began—I smile to myself, thinking, "and this is where my *own* little internal revolution begins!"

It felt good and right. And definitely, *time.*

CHAPITRE VINGT

I will seek my way again . . . but the goal is in my
heart.
—MARCEL PROUST

hile some people may have delusions of grandeur, I am most definitely experiencing *dis*illusions of grandeur. And you know what? That's a damn good thing. Thank God I figured it out now, at a young age. No sense busting my butt for decades imagining that penetrating the haut monde Parisian society, a life of Maseratis, castles, and the perfect designer shoe is a meaningful endeavor.

You know, come to think of it, I may have just unknowingly sidestepped a very unpleasant midlife crisis down the road! Don't worry, I surely will come up with some other issue to panic about when I hit forty-five. Ladies and gentlemen, lay your bets now on your personal favorite: we've got fears of fading youth, at 10 to 1; infertile career woman, at 3 to 1; born-again Christian, at 2 to 1; and my hunch's on single butch spinster; at even odds. But it is hard to switch hobbies from internal Japanese vibrating spheres to making glue-gun macaroni crafts in a single day.

After the ridiculous orgy with the bisexual Marquis and the awards night tag-team of my ex and future ex, my sanity demanded I stop and take real stock of myself and my situation. Scribbling in my notebook has helped, definitely. It's forced me to acknowledge things I was unconsciously choosing to avoid. No question about it, what I thought was living life I see now was just living recklessly.

But how do I dismantle this house of cards I'd so feverishly constructed? In sharing my story, the exploits of my courtesan life, my *annus mirabilis* ("a year that is remarkable for its great events," for those who didn't make it to Latin class), I have no shame and I have no pride—okay, maybe a *little* shame and a *fair* amount of pride—but I believe laying out the raw truth of it is valuable. What follows is my summation, or perhaps my rationale. You decide. Like a bag of free clothes, take what you wish, what fits and suits you— and discard the rest. Actually, don't discard the rest—jam it under your bed, since you never know when something you thought was totally not you suddenly seems apropos. And boy, can I attest to that, my friends!

I own every useless, luxurious thing in the world. The only thing wanting is the most important thing: *pure love*. I do know what that is; I had that once. With Laurent. And I now realize its more deeply rewarding than all the wealth and material objects on the planet. And you know I know what I'm talking about! In one short year I have had more adventures, more astonishing gifts, more wild, shocking, astounding, disturbing, and awe-inspiring experiences than I thought I'd have in a lifetime.

Life can start to feel like a movie that you've been cast in, but the tricky thing is that it's up to *you* to define the role. Since that idea is not fixed or truly set when you're an anonymous student, that role can be subject to influence and suggestion. Add in naïveté, youth, and any semitraumatic event, and you can slide right out of yourself and into . . . well, being *anything* that seems the opposite of the life that you'd just been living.

When Laurent left me, my faith in myself and my abilities were horrendously shaken and desperately needed to be steadied, so when chance brought Jean-Albert into my life, I leapt at this catalyst to try on an entirely new life. Starved for affection—*or* even mere attention—I got hooked, *literally addicted,* on the constant adoration, veneration, treats, feeling power over men, and being the object of desire. Instantly, I was free to indulge my full appetite for all the things that I, like many young women, had always dreamed of: châteaux; opulent dinners and dresses; jewels; sexual decadence and fantasy—you name it. Not to mention that my ever present vicious curiosity perceived it all as a fast track to greater knowledge. Thus, I felt obliged, and almost commanded, to partake and indulge in all that was laid before me: literature, architecture, interiors, French history, gourmet cuisine, wine, opera, French antiques, new languages, couture, etc. (All good for the mind and soul, but now I would greatly prefer to delve into some of those fields with a more attuned and less rushed level of attention. Some nights it felt like I was cramming for finals!) Having men— especially men of great rank and success—fall in love, cherish, or simply pursue one with abandon gives a woman a power that is completely intoxicating. This fuels *more* self-confidence, which in turn has an even more seductive appeal, which thereby grows exponentially with each man and acquisition, unleashing a cycle of goal-pursuit-conquer-reward-goal-pursuit . . . you get the idea.

Jean-Albert wasn't enough when I realized I could have Frédéric also at no expense (indeed, at a profit!) and then the Marquis fit in as the side dish/bonus prize. How could I refuse?! Playing the role of *femme fatale* to the hilt demanded it!

This cycle, applied not just to acquiring men but also, obviously, to all those ludicrously unnecessary material objects. My new apartment was stocked to the hilt with every conceivable whim, and when I felt no connection to any of it—oh, I was losing my way, all right. The morning after leaving the Marquis, while reading the newpaper, I came across the statistic that 550 million families in the world live on two dollars a day. Can you imagine how vulgar I felt? You can't? Good. It's a ghastly feeling I wouldn't wish on anyone except perhaps those that spend so obscenely!

I shudder at the memory that I once found myself tempted to buy a small Sèvres milk pitcher at Sotheby's for forty-five thousand euros simply because it had once belonged to Marie Antoinette.

Truth be told, it was actually Jean-Albert who was wildly encouraging the idea, but then I thought, "Please, what the hell will I even do with it?" And, oh man, if I ever broke it, I'd want to shoot myself. Now, I just want to shoot myself for even considering it! But my greatest tour de force *de-tour* from reality, was, as we all know, scoring that pink diamond necklace. After pulling off that high jinks I felt as low, bottom-of-the-bucket sad as if I'd just shot heroin between my toes on a lunch break. OK, that might be overstating it, but it was not a good feeling. With every genius morsel and fresh bon mot I learned, instead of just enjoying it for itself, I often felt compelled to unleash it on men like some sort of constant reminder: "See, I am very smart." Thankfully, now that frantic hunger to fill myself with every experience, every tangible and intangible gain, has quieted to a dull roar.

I've learned, too, that intelligence is often best revealed by the questions one asks rather than the answers one gives. And I think we can all agree I have reached my lifetime quota on quoting others. Man, is that getting tiresome! And call me a pedantic hypocrite to use a quote to criticize the use of quotes, but Somerset Maugham said exactly what I mean: "She had a pretty gift for quotation, which is a serviceable substitute for wit." Right? When one has real wit and clever opinions, one shouldn't fall back on the genius of others.

So, you get it. After a year of indulging every impulse, desire, and folly, I am now satiated—and then some. Enough, certainly, to now purge from my life forever what I had sought blindly and willingly until just a week ago. As we know, it wasn't all exactly a ride on the good ship lollipop. But I still believe I am far and away better off for having bravely—some might say, foolishly—embarked on this journey of self-exploration.

Truth be told, it was all a blast—*until it just wasn't anymore*. And that's always a good time to exit something. Honestly, I *am* proud that I courageously went for it. And that in moments of uncertainty and nervousness, I essentially remained true to who I am . . . even when I was playing someone a lot more brave and sassy. I felt tested under pressure and know I held my own, whether it was with Jean-Albert's wife, Frédéric's horse-oriented sex acts, or the Marquis's twisted idea of a third date, I teetered internally but ultimately assumed an unflappable reserve. And to think that last year I out and out crumbled into a shaky mess when I had to give my oral presentation to the dissertation committee at the Sorbonne! *Quelle différence!*

As a final point—*and let's just put this on the record, can we?*—the vast information and knowledge I've gained about men and sex and the interplay between the sexes has been hugely satisfying. *Pun intended!* You can be sure, I have a whole new take on men now. An awareness that no matter how successful or powerful they become, they are still so vulnerable emotionally, very often believing they have somehow fooled everyone, and that they don't really believe themselves to be worthy. Plus, that these men—perhaps all men—get exhausted by the pressures of society to always be in control. They really yearn to be taken care of sometimes, to let down their facade of strength and authority. They're simply little boys with far bigger hearts than it appears, as insecure as they were when they were twelve. Just *jeunes hommes* walking around with grown-up exteriors eagerly seeking approval and understanding, regardless of whether they are a mogul or a garbageman. (Clarification here: didn't date any garbagemen, but think it's safe to extrapolate my theory.)

Once you learn this—and I only just have—you look at men differently: more compassionately and tenderly. You understand *all* men better, from your father to the shy old man who sells newspapers on the corner, to even the losers who sling catcalls at you from construction sites. Yup, even those macho goons, standing around in safety-in-numbers groups, grabbing at their crotches and yelling, "Yo! Ya want some a' this, sista?"—you even see *them* with new eyes. They are less the vulgar and offensive idiots you'd always believed them to be, and more just childish, uneducated boys. Which is really not so different, when you think about it, than aristocratic Frenchmen in their gray Dior suits sneaking off at sunset to meet their mistresses at their *garçonière* (a man's small apartment set up exclusively for trysts)—every country, society, and era has variations on this theme. It's just up to women to identify it, do our best to avoid raising our sons like that, and to steer clear of losing time with men who have made immaturity and insecurity an art form.

It seems that virtually every woman must go through some sort of initiation rite, of falling for a man (or a few!) who are all shiny, perfect, sexy, and too-good-to-be-true, to gain the wisdom to *not* repeat that time waster/heartbreaker. No matter how many girlfriends or family members warn you that "he's a stinker," we still have to ride it out to the bitter end. You don't learn the lesson otherwise.

Stay with me as I wrap this idea up. With this experience under your belt, you are more able to quickly distinguish the heinously false facades, to tell the lost men from the sweet men. The sweet men may appear *at first* to be less grand or ambitious, but are far better intentioned and warmhearted. Just like me and most of the women I know, they are a work in progress. Better to choose those unassuming men—the Mathieus and the Laurents—who are anonymously and quietly seeking their own way in life—than the loudmouth, in your face, "Listen, people! I am the shit!" men who really are just trying to convince *themselves*.

Oh, this may all seem a bit harsh, but look at it as though a handy men decoder has now been inserted into your mind. No more does the big-shot actor appear to be a dream boyfriend when you've met many and see they are almost all brash attention addicts who are cheating on the women in their lives. (BTW: This label is interchangeable with big-shot businessman, office star, class president, etc.) All of which brings up the issue of sex. Oh, it *all* comes back to sex, doesn't it? Which is not a bad thing when you begin to understand that a lot in this world operates on a system of seduction and you can take that awareness and put it in its proper role.

For me, the sexual awakening I've just been through and experimenting with boundaries has been invaluable. The Japanese vibrating sphere, role playing, domination, self-exploration, toys, sex with a total stranger, dabbling with Marie-Hélène. Oh, yeah, it's been a wild ride, and I learned a Pandora's box full of skills, moves, and tricks that have given me such sexual confidence, and such a sense of my own femininity, that I feel like a different person. I wonder if this is how it feels to be forty-five: gloriously attuned and aware of what gives you pleasure, and sure of your powers to seduce, captivate, and be sexually masterful.

Since I was previously so uptight and constrained, I know partaking in all the pushing-the-limits adventures would *only* have been possible with men I wasn't looking to marry. I needed to explore my desires and learn sexual inhibition, free from caring what the man thought, (i.e., no mental energy wasted on "what will he think of me?"). That freethinking and lack of concern gave me free rein to focus purely on the physical, and I learned to look at emotions as a by-product, or even something to be detached from altogether. Sometimes sex with good men is disastrous and sex with bad men is great. And that's why it really is best to sow your oats when you're young, so that when you meet the right man you feel nothing but complete self-assurance in bed. Nothing beats knowing what you want, knowing what makes men crazy with desire, and knowing you've exercised your sexual fantasies sufficiently so as not to be either shocked or restricted going to the outermost reaches of his—or your—fantasies.

You gotta say, "You can't go back to holding hands after having group sex." Nope. Okay. You *could* but it's probably as fun as eating a plastic spoonful of Cheez Whiz after tasting a magnificent, creamy Camembert spread on warmed blinis. (You know, I could add about about one hundred metaphors here to make that point, but I'm employing some new and well-needed discipline. Trust me, it ain't easy: I'm also concurrently strangling a quote that would *so* fit the bill here!)

As in reaching a killer orgasm, timing is *everything*: whether you're just meeting the right man, or you want to expand your own sexual repertoire, or you just wish to heighten the pleasure of your established relationship, there is no better time than now to embark on your journey of sexual exploration. Christ! I sound like a new (and taller) incarnation of that sex therapist—tiny index finger in the air—Dr. Ruth Westheimer! Yes, well, taking advice from a well-trained courtesan may be wiser, actually. So, yes, I am deliciously happy to have learned all that I have about men and sex, but the greatest wisdom is just maybe what I discovered about myself. It's pretty cool to know that I could *occasionally* astonish or captivate what I thought was an impenetrable world, just by resorting to my good ole tomboy Podunk humor. Just by being myself!

If you have to turn yourself inside out to attract someone, he isn't worth it. I am *so* over trying to adapt to what I think a man will want. Marie-Hélène gave me lots of brilliant advice in so many areas of refining myself, but I think she just took it a bit too far at times. To be fair to her, living in Paris can have that effect, trust me.

CHAPITRE VINGT
ET UN

The aim of life is to live, and to live means to be aware, joyously, drunkenly, serenely, divinely aware.

—HENRY MILLER

or fuck's sake! (Sorry, I had to swear as *near* as possible to the above line by Henry Miller, as sort of an homage, if you will. Plus, a kinda cool way to open the chapter, *non?*)

But really, where is my *Exit Strategies for Courtesans* manual? Just how does one gracefully exit the role of grand courtesan? Hell if I know, and I surely wasn't ringing Marie-Hélène for pointers. I did call her, but just to suggest we have another one of our famous *mercredi déjeuners.* I tried to tip her off to the subject at hand by taking a pass on our usual high-end Michelin-star restaurants, with their three-figure lunch tabs, and suggesting she meet me at the totally *Bobo* (Remember? Hipster slang for bohemian bourgeois? You're catchin' on.) Colette with its communal tables.

Marie-Hélène didn't immediately balk, but her antennae were up and all that much more tuned-in when she spotted me waiting for her outside, cream cotton espadrilles, green linen army pants, and a plain cream cardigan. In other words, the absolute antithesis of courtesan at lunch attire.

"Alexa, what have we here? Well, that's a look I hadn't caught wind of yet? Is it Gaultier or something?" she asks, as she glides out of her Mercedes to greet me. By the way, she says the name "Gaultier" as though someone's just jammed a rotten lemon in her mouth. He's a couture designer, yes, but nowhere near frou-frou feminine enough to hang in a self-respecting courtesan's *boudoir*.

"Hey, MH, ah, nah. I think it's by Naf Naf," I reply, giving her a two-cheek kiss.

"*Naf,* indeed, young lady!" she whispers under her breath, playfully scolding me with a swat to my butt as we enter Colette and head down the metal stairs to the *resto*.

We take seats alongside the other diners, all seated together at the long communal tables. I glance at MH, certain she'd find the idea loathsome and impossible not to comment on. Sure enough, she takes the room in in a quick visual roundup. I knew another of her treasured critiques was a comin'.

"Well, well, well, are we in a prison mess hall here? Is this seating arrangement meant as some kind of *punishment*? What might the charm be in sitting so near to strangers whom you wouldn't even wish to have over for tea?" she whispers, raising an eyebrow and placing her alligator clutch on her lap as though it might be stolen.

I know she's just playing, commanded by her role as grand dame to review and assess the surroundings at all times. But she can't fool me. Unbeknownst to her, I've watched Marie-Hélène make her daily stop near her neighborhood *métro* and place cash directly into the hands of all the homeless, who even thanked her by name. I decide to play along.

"Quite so, and take note, it's normal—indeed, expected—to just lean over and put your fork in someone else's plate if you see something you like—sharing food, sharing germs. Builds up the immune system!" I say, drawing a laugh out of Marie-Hélène before she can stop it.

We each order the tuna tartare, a large bottle of San Pellegrino, two glasses of a chilled Sancerre, and a bowl of leek soup.

As the soup and bread are placed before us, Marie-Hélène

quips, "Ah, *bien*, the gruel and bread! This bread is like a door stop. For *my crimes*, I still deserve a better *baguette* then this!"

"With your infinite layers of crimes of passion, you very much deserve a *millefeuille*, my dear!" I reply. (That's a thousand-layer pastry, for those whose French hasn't quite become fluent via my *franglais* musings.)

Lunch goes ahead, very much as I'd expected. After a healthy chat about politics—complete with an amazing story of when Marie-Hélène dated a French arms dealer who used to run submarines packed with ammunition down the Amazon—it occurs to me, from her endless stream of casual lunchtime anecdotes and references to ex-lovers, that MH could provide a nice storyline or two to Hollywood. No wonder I was so seduced by her tales and lifestyle that I wanted to throw myself into life as a courtesan; she could sway young virgins about to enter a convent, and have them trading their habits for Valentino and Louboutin heels and demanding a *bisou minou* from their *amour du jour* inside a week!

With a couple more of her juicy stories engraved on my memory, I go ahead and order two more glasses of wine to ready myself to broach the subject at hand—my imminent backpedaling in the final sprint for the title of the Courtesan Tour de France.

I give her a blow-by-blow version of running into Laurent and ditching both Laurent and Jean-Albert when I pulled a Cinderella-seeking-her-sanity exit from that awards ceremony. She's heard me speak of Laurent time and again; I know—she knows—we both are aware of what is coming next: I extol the virtues of both returning to being a regular Ph.D. student and opening my mind to the pursuit of finding true love, and Marie-Hélène tries to sway me back to the courtesan team, by way of offering grandiose descriptions of men I should meet, in tandem with listing all the perks and treats she believes I will miss.

"Alexa, I know this Laurent is your *grand amour*, and that it all looks very romantic to return to him after the initial thrill of being a courtesan has, shall we say, worn away to some degree. But you have yet to really maximize all your skills and talents! You have not yet tasted the delicious pleasure of capturing the attentions of a German or Austrian prince. It is an entirely unique experience unto itself! I refuse to allow you to cease your life as a courtesan until you have dipped your exquisite toe into that pool of, literally, liquid gold. At the Vienna ball in the fall, you are assured to be the most sought after by the formidably wealthy Hapsburg descendants. Ah . . . the castles, jewels, and art collections they possess are among the finest in existence! Remember Olga von Bismark? She was dripping in jewels and couture by the tender age of twenty-two."

"Yes, but she married a man who was triple her age, triple her weight, and, you have to say, repulsive at best. Come on, you must admit he looked like some kind of Muppet with those eyebrows so long you could've used them as ropes to climb up his face! Not to mention, didn't Olga von Bismark have to sell it all, and now she's become a religious fanatic, living in Africa as a lesbian?"

"Touché . . . *Mais* the lesbian part sounds like fun!" Marie-Hélène jokes, knowing she's lost that argument and launching into another story of what feels like *The Price Is Right*'s "and for the next contestant, behind door number two . . ."

"Dare I even put forth the temptations of a British lord who has relocated to Paris to find a wife? And did I tell you there is a Count who is a dear friend of Monsieur de Bellemont who has asked to make your acquaintance?" she pleads, while ignoring the tiny low-end piece of wrapped chocolate served with the espressos. (For this woman, it's Debauve et Gallais nougatine chocolates or death! And I *can* see why—Debauve et Gallais is the oldest *maison du chocolat* in France. They continue to make the same chocolates that they made for Marie Antoinette, selling them in exquisite little numbered boxes. How chi-chi chic is that?!)

For all her efforts, it's without the slightest twinge of mental debate that I overrule and squelch Marie-Hélène's plans for me to meet the Brit or the Count de So and So . . . "who's looking to marry." Yecch! Winking, using the word "beguiling," and chatting up aristos who are looking to marry are all going in my "to be avoided forever" bin!

I gotta give it to her, she gave it her all on this last round—her last PR routine presented in its full glory. But I remained undeterred and unswayed. Which left me to spend the better part of the rest of lunch thanking her profusely and sincerely for all her wisdom and generous guidance.

By the time the espressos had been sipped down to just their pale sugar residue, Marie-Hélène had drained her arsenal. I swear she looked at me like a mother hen whose chickadee has not just flown the coop, but announced, "Mom, wings? Flying? You know, this whole bird lifestyle thing is *nowhere*."

I suppose I really sent her a zinger with this: "Marie-Hélène, you know, I loved the experience madly, it was like living my greatest fantasy every day and night, but ultimately, I think I just had to lose myself in order to find myself again. And that's where I am now. Found. And serene."

Hey, you can't really argue when someone says that, can you? Despite realizing I was slipping out of her clutches, I could tell Marie-Hélène was truly touched. Her little apprentice had made quite a splash in this big pond, and she was proud to have been my pilot fish, my guiding force. Though she knew she'd lost a partner in crime, she took it with the dignity she'd always advocated.

"Ah, my dear Alexa. I suppose on some level, I always knew this lifestyle would never be enough to contain your thirst for curiosity and your liberated spirit. But I must say, for an American woman, you came into this traditionally Parisienne position and really turned it on its ear. You broke some boundaries, and it's been a long time since a woman has come out of nowhere and created such a stir. Yes, fortunes and hearts were lost, and you are simply walking away, entirely unscathed. Bravo! I commend you. Please know I respect your decision to leave it all while at the absolute top of the game. My little rosebud has indeed blossomed into a radiant bloom!" she practically purrs, reaching across the table and taking my face tenderly in her soft hands.

How generous and kind is that? This woman has cornered the market on elegance and sophistication. I count myself fortunate to have been welcomed into her private salon of learning. I suppose it's somewhat like the French take on British finishing school, but of course, change the syllabus to add some more sexual proficiency classes than serving high tea!

Marie-Hélène and I wrap up the afternoon with a sacred promise to still meet every other *mercredi après-midi* for lunch. Though I *did* make her agree to slum it with me in the student cafés, and she actually agreed—only if I'd make the effort to still wear a "dash of lipstick." *Pas de problème!* It's a silly but painless request, and somehow I love her for it.

Marie-Hélène and I link arms, exchange heartfelt smiles like that of old war buddies parting on Liberation Day, and walk out of Colette together into the late afternoon Parisian sun.

Standing together on the curb as Hugo pulls up to whisk her off to her weekly appointment at the Guerlain salon, we hug and give each other the ubiquitous two-cheek kiss with distinct and marked affection.

Marie-Hélène's parting words?

"Alexandra, if you do write about me in your *journal intime*, I give you total permission to quote me freely. For all the bits of wisdom we cherish from those that came before us, it would be nice to leave our mark as well, don't you think? And, Alexa . . . Don't you dare ever wear diamonds on the *métro*, you hear me?" And off she scoots with a smile and a low-waisted movie-star wave, gliding into that chauffeured Mercedes and off to yet another classically Parisian afternoon of self-indulgence.

I stand on the corner, arms wilted at my sides, watching the car pull away, thinking that Marie-Hélène may be the last great courtesan this city will ever know. And maybe, one of the greatest women I have ever known. Quintessential grace personified.

And how do you think extracting myself from the life of Jean-Albert went over? Take a guess. I didn't have a clue how he'd deal with it, either. I half hoped he'd cling to me, fall at my feet claiming I was the only woman for him, that there could never be another, and that he'd throw himself in front of a train for me. *Right.* A bit much to ask for, but I was thinking something of that caliber was reasonable, if for no other reason than to end our story as dramatically as it had begun.

I was dead wrong, and in the end, I think it might've been trickier for me to leave him *if* he had been terribly gallant, professing lifelong love and his intention to leave the wife for me. *You* know what I'm talking about. I was looking ahead to that almost inevitable—no matter how fleeting—moment of looking back on all this ten years down the road, perhaps when life hits a snag and I have the clothing budget of Mahatma Gandhi, and being tempted to romanticize it all, thinking, "Dammit, I was such a fool to leave. I had it all. *Curses!*"

Well, we can all rejoice, because that's not gonna happen. As with all the rest of this motley crew of characters (and I adore how they'd all be positively aghast at that description!), the true essence of each person's soul and decency always reveals itself in the end. *This* is how it all shook out.

I called Jean-Albert one afternoon, more to *fermer la porte* and move on than from any real concern. I asked how he was, after apologizing profusely for my rather hasty, silent departure from the Opéra Bastille awards night.

"Alexandra, you have disgraced me greatly. First by cavorting in a dalliance with Frédéric de Fallois, and then by that shocking departure at Opéra Bastille. No one has ever made such a public display of apathy and ingratitude to me."

"Jean-Albert, I agree it was inelegant of me to exit without saying good-bye that evening. Can you, on some level, understand that to see you and my ex-boyfriend and the way you treated him was all very much disgraceful to me as well?" I say, holding my own 100 percent.

"No. I have no time to think of such things. You do realize I am running an empire, and I need someone at my side who is at *all times* committed to presenting the best public image. Heightened emotions can play no role on the public stage that I live on. That is just a simple fact. You were wrong to act impulsively, carelessly revealing the naïve American girl in you to everyone in attendance. And since you embarrassed me in front of a great many people, I would look entirely the fool to run back to you. You see, *I would—* you know I do love you—*but I cannot,* for the sake of my reputation. My status requires that any further meetings between us need to be conducted out of the eye of the public. I am truly sorry to have to shift our love affair to that level, but at least for the immediate future, I can't be seen with the sole woman who's dared to overtly humiliate me. So you will agree to my request to meet, for the time being, in private. I could come pick you up tonight and show you that space on avenue Montaigne for your gallery."

Kind of a nut-job, wouldn't you say? He starts off as Grouchus Enormous and ends with that mammoth real estate offer again. He so doesn't get that I'm not just lying silently low, I'm *gone*! So I'm compelled to lay out for him—*more like spell it out for him—*

A-u r-e-v-o-i-r!

I took the high road, remembering a backlog of about one thousand beautiful and adoring things Jean-Albert has said, done, and offered me. I *do* owe him a great deal of tenderness. Interestingly, as I think back to all the treats and gifts, I think the most wonderful of all were the love letters. Heartfelt and sincere? I think so. Regardless, they are my treasures, and all I really want to keep. Thus, the following fell out of my mouth:

"My *dear* man"—it was high time I threw that address back at him—"I have to tell you that I think our affair has run its course. You know I adore you and have had some of the loveliest moments of my life with you. I just think our paths are diverging. You are at the pinnacle, the summit of your career and I am just beginning the climb." He interrupts, as per usual. Insistently, he begins his tactics of persuasion.

"Alexandra, this is why it's foolish of you not to let me help you. With just a donation to the Musée Carnavalet, not only can I ensure that you will assist curating that Boucher exhibit, I can arrange for you to co-curate. And you could go on to launch your own gallery by next summer—if you let me help you. You are aware that I have one of the greatest art collections in Europe; I have all the connections in the art world that can instantly shoot you to the top. For God's sakes, you're being a stubborn martyr, Alexandra. Sometimes pride is better left at the door."

"I'd rather keep my integrity and self-respect *and fail*, if need be, than just have success all handed to me. Can't you understand that, Jean-Albert? You are a self-made man; isn't that a vital source of pride to you?" I ask kindly but with indignation.

By some strange misalignment of neural synapses in his mind, he doesn't get this point. *Pfft!* Went zipping right over his head—like that private jet of his.

He just marches on with offers, reproaches my decision, and even retracts the "we have to meet privately for a while" idea. But it all goes *entirely* off the wall when he says, "What if I buy you an actual Boucher painting? There is one coming up at auction at Maastricht next month. I was going to buy it for you for Christmas. Can you really refuse that gift? And me with it?! Alexandra, what do I have to give you to keep you in my life? Just name it." His voice is now mournful and weak.

Okay, you tell me. Maybe I've flipped too far to the other side of the scale of morals of late, but is that not almost a bribe? I am quite sure bribes and love shouldn't mix. (Much like wearing pink and red. And don't say Yves Saint Laurent mixes them, it's still ghastly! I clearly haven't quite shaken the courtesan mentality yet, have I? No, it obviously will take more than a week to fully molt this skin.)

I go on to sing the praises and the virtues of poverty and struggle, and that goes over with Jean-Albert about as well as wearing a full-length sable coat to a PETA dinner!

About half an hour later, the conversation has come to feel like I'm talking to a six-year-old who's covering his ears, bellowing, "I can't hear you! I can't hear you!" It comes to this:

"Sweet man, you can offer me the moon and the stars, but I need to pull away, change my life, step away from the spotlight, your shadow, the haut monde, and just be anonymous and make my own way. Whether it makes sense to you or not, please respect my decisions. One of which is that I have sent you the deed to the apartment today by messenger; I am returning it to you, along with the credit card. And I will leave the apartment in two weeks' time. I just need to find out if I can return to my old flat; then I will send you the keys and . . ."

Interruption 2,493 from Jean-Albert, and as it occurs I tell myself, this is the last fucking time this man cuts me off as though what he has to say is more important than what I have to say. Buddy, listening is one *art* you haven't acquired.

"Oh, God no, Alexandra. You are serious? That's madness. My dear"—again with the "dear"?! Christ, if anyone calls me dear again—in any context—I may slaughter them—"I am older and wiser; you will be back. Go off and make your little stand of independence. But promise me you won't be so self-righteous as to *not* come back when you realize your error. Fair warning: a man like me doesn't wait long for a woman."

A great deal of crabbiness due to hurt ego going on there, eh? And what a healthy dose of condescension! I'm *so* sick of that. I smother an urge to yell into the mouthpiece: "Bring me normal men or bring me death!" And instead opt for: "Well, don't exactly turn the hourglass, so sure I will return." (I swear it sounded better in my mind. *A lot better.* Still, I'm fine with it. Point made, and for all *he* knows, it could be a popular American retort. I should've come up with something like the French sculptor Rodin's, "Nothing is a waste of time if you use the experience wisely." That woulda been far better.)

We both hang up the phone utterly exhausted with each other, and truth be told, it feels slightly reassuring that in the end I see that he may have *adored* me, but he doesn't *get* me. In either sense! And man, is that ego working against him!

I dash off an e-mail to Frédéric—similar in feeling to the Jean-Albert chat, but frankly it's all just an act of closure, or as they say in French, *"tourner la page."* Obviously and gratefully, the affair with

Frédéric lost some serious steam when he was in Russia and I was "in orgy." And as luck would have it, he's now deeply immersed in a super messy political scandal.

How's that for cliché of him and callous of me, to say that as though he's just stubbed his toe? *Mais oui*, Frédéric de la Horse Sex has been accused of taking political kickbacks for favors. Oh, *quelle surprise* there, eh? Please! Everyone in France knows he did it, but now, in the modern age, they are obliged to at least feign *shock* and disapproval *for a while*. Hell, it's more likely he'll end up president of France because of it than saddled with any criminal charges. Such is France. Deliciously twisted to the core. And if you count yourself a hard 'n' fast goody two-shoes, immune to temptation, ooh la-la, I give you . . . oh, one year max . . . before you find your-self at the Sonia Rykiel sex boutique stocking up on various scented love oils, lace garter belts, and fishnet stockings for a ren-dezvous with that François you met at Café de Flore!

Let's just say, you don't see many nuns in Paris . . . and if you do spot one, more than likely it's just a "one-off" fantasy ensem-ble, and she's off to some clandestine rendezvous with her lover as she teeters on her black ankle-strapped Chanel I'm-gonna-fuck-you-hard pumps.

And the funny thing is, you think I'm kidding.

Au contraire, mon amie.

ÉPILOGUE
Three Months Later

Absence diminishes little passions and increases great
ones, as the wind extinguishes candles and fans a fire.

—LA ROCHEFOUCAULD

Before I could so much as put in an hour on my thesis, I just wanted to release myself of everything that belonged to my courtesan's life. Mission: de-courtesan my life. I arranged for the pink diamond necklace to be put on auction, and I sent the check from the sale, as well as six enormous boxes of clothes, to a charity called SOS Femmes Battues, an organization that assists women financially who are battered, down on their luck, or even homeless. That felt right. *Very.*

Truth be told, I didn't give away every single thing. A few precious items got sequestered to the "save but just as memento" category: the Balmain bag with the pearl and crystal closure, and that very first gray silk bias-cut dress Isabel gave me that I wore to my fateful meeting with Jean-Albert . . . Oh, OK, I'll admit that some jewels were impossible to part with: I put the diamond ring, the necklace, and the earrings in a safety deposit box, to be tapped if I should ever hit on hard times. Hey, I *earned* those, and you can't argue with that! I followed the trip to the bank with a little trip to the costume jewelry boutique Agatha on rue Bonaparte to pick up a pair of faux diamond studs that were positively a dead ringer for the two-carat numbers I used to wear—yeah, plopping down a mere twenty-four euros for them felt divinely fun, as now I can sport the same look for *beaucoup moins cher*. Frankly, the feeling of wearing the new crystal versions isn't so massively less thrilling than wearing the ones that cost as much as a sports car, as at least now I don't have to worry about having to leap into the Seine if I were to lose one!

The final detail of my ex-courtesan life to wrap up? I had all the Empire furniture loaded up in two trucks and sent to auction at Drouot Auction house. And when that monster *chèque* came in, I sent it directly over to Jean-Albert's office with the note below.

Dearest Jean-Albert,

You will always hold a special place in my heart, my sweet *chéri*. . . . Thank you most sincerely for making so many of my dreams come true. You're an extraordinary man, and I am forever grateful to have shared in your life. . . .

   I will finally say it:

Je t'aime,
Alexandra

Not bad in the grace department, huh? And don't be shocked that I said "I love you." I *do* love him. For who he is and who he was to me. One mustn't forget, for a man like that to so publicly and privately devote himself to a young American woman—that's rare, and I am honored that he chose me. What's more, Marie-Hélène relayed to me that he's supposedly suffering and not looking too well, so I do feel compelled to offer a sweet parting word or two. Can't imagine where or when our paths will cross again, but I feel good knowing that I've done my best to ensure there are no ill feelings, just cherished memories.

Remember that plan of chucking the glamorous apartment and moving back to my old flat in the 6th arrondissement? That hit a big fat snag—the city tore the building down. Yeah, tough to move back in and snuggle up among the rubble. So, like a freshly anointed vagabond, I took up Isabel's offer and crashed at her and Mathieu's flat on their spare futon.

Frankly, it was kind of great to be thrown into the midst of their daily lives as they prepped for their big wedding day. Watching them was a constant reminder of what real love is and helped me shift mentally back to normal-couple reality. (As in—love has nothing to do with mind games, sex with saddles—or with strangers. *Always* good to remember!)

Not to mention it gave me a lot of fabulous *amie* moments with Isabel as she and I scoured the city, negotiating like crazy paupers to keep the wedding on budget. Spent the best time chatting up a host of interesting characters, exactly the kind of people I had been isolated from of late, who would have been referred to by Jean-Albert and his crowd as, "There are people for that." That soul-dulling phrase I had been so accustomed to hearing at every turn. As we bought up votive candles by the case in the Jewish neighborhood, wholesale white tulips by the gross from a flamboyant transvestite, and argued the best deal on fireworks (Isabel's idea) with a little old Chinese man in the Gobelins district, I felt a part of the ebb and flow of normal life again. I liked connecting to people, waiting in lines . . . even fighting for a good seat on the *métro*! And I was really grateful that Isabel and Mathieu had extended me the invite to stay on at their love garret while they went off on their honeymoon to the Maldives. Theoretically, that would give me two precious weeks to hornswoggle myself a new apartment. Except that never happened.

On the big wedding day, Isabel and I met up with her sister, the other bridesmaid, and all set off in a taxi to the chic Musée de la Chasse et de la Nature in the Marais, where the ceremony and reception were to be held. The three of us jammed in the backseat like sardines, Isabel's gown cradled in oodles of tissue, tucked into a silver Balmain garment bag and draped carefully across our three giddy laps, we almost blasted the poor driver through the window with our shrill enthusiasm.

"Isabel . . . can you believe this? You—the most nontraditional girl in Paris—are heading to the altar!?" her sister bellows as we careen onto rue du Temple.

"Yes . . . It's amazing, I'm not the slightest bit nervous . . . In fact, am more concerned with the surprise I have for Alexandra," she says, pulling a "don't kill me but I have a trick up my sleeve" face.

(Oh, you know what I mean!)

"Listen, girl, if you throw the bouquet at me so full-on blatantly that it takes my eye out, I will tell everyone about the time you accidently peed while dancing at Baron and then pretended you'd spilled your drink on yourself!"

"Horrors! No need to unearth that one. . . . Especially since there's a strong chance I will repeat such a performance tonight!" she jokes, as we pull to a stop and are virtually propelled to disembark from the cramped taxi. Only then do I think: (1) That ride was a helluva lot more fun, being all squashed in there laughing together, than had we been all uptight driving here in some ritzy boat of a hired limo or Town Car, and (2) What's this so-called surprise that she's cooking up? *Hmm*.

After helping Isabel with her gown, assisting with her hair and makeup preparations, and the traditional pre-ceremony glasses of Champagne, I left her to hastily ready myself. How nice to no longer be the self-obsessed creature laboring over my image. I just pulled my hair back into a loose chignon with a spray of tiny violets tucked in, swept a bit of color on my lips, and climbed into my bridesmaid gown. No mean feat, as the violet-hued one-shouldered gown entailed a rather complex arrangement of straps in disarray and where every seam has been distressed and burned at the raw edge, cascading down into an uneven train of trailing threads. It looked at first glance—or to the untrained eye—as though it were a purple parachute that may have been shot down during some nasty jet fighting. But was, in fact, in couture-speak, intended to represent "a virginal damsel fleeing her depraved captors in a castle tower." *Voilà:* Isabel's wedding theme, as you may have guessed (or maybe not!).

As I make my way past the guests all taking their seats, I think, "But you know what? This dress is damn sexy in a medieval sort of deconstructivist way. Don't know when I will ever wear it again, but adore the way it so perfectly skims my shoulders . . . ," my thoughts trailing like my hands that unconsciously caress my neck and down to my décolletage.

Just then, I feel—or am I imagining?—the gentlest tender kiss to my bare neck. Then the soft exhalation of warm breath. I'm *not* dreaming! And my head falls back, suddenly and knowingly, as strong hands embrace my waist and guide me to face those familiar lips.

Laurent. My love. My surprise from Isabel. My God . . . how great!

There he stood, so breathtakingly handsome in that same dumb off-the-rack suit he'd worn to the awards ceremony, a pair of nameless dress shoes that could only be described as "the farthest thing from fabulous Berlutis," and his personal smell that someone should study and package as it makes me blind with desire! On second thought—no, I like having that smell all to myself!

Not so surprisingly, Laurent pretty much charmed my pants off in record time. (And we all know, I can get naked at the drop of a *chapeau*!) And I wasn't even wearing pants actually, so make that "charmed my dress off" over my head. As soon as that beautiful wedding ceremony ended, after rings and "I do's" were exchanged, Laurent and I were racing around hand in hand, taking back stairs and slinking through locked doors. Yep, shagging like minks in every hidden nook and dark closet of that gorgeous *musée* loaded with its secret stairs and *salles*.

We had a lot of time to make up for, *n'est-ce pas*?!

The two of us miraculously fell right back into step—into that glorious rapport and rhythm, as if our split had lasted only as long as a hiccup and our love had kept escalating despite the year we were apart. I now think it's possible that with time, experience, and new wisdom, you can love and appreciate someone *more passionately* in spite of the fact you are not in each other's actual presence. I think it's a result of something called "enlightened maturity." Whatever it is, it exists, and it's cool as hell! As I once told you, there is no off-ramp for love. Perhaps the last twelve months apart were like a brief pull over at a roadside rest stop, giving us each a little time to pull ourselves together. Whatever. Now we are on the love autobahn!

I know what you're thinking. At first, I wondered, too, if my leaping back into life with Laurent with such abandon was just another of my now familiar escapes. Then, about twelve seconds later, I realized, nope, I just simply love this man. (So, if that's what you were thinking too, you can ditch that notion like Brie gone bad.)

In the days after Isabel's wedding, as the ecstatic newness of Laurent and me being back together shifted from delirium to the beautiful day-to-day reality, of course we had a few issues to tackle . . . and a couple of land mines to sidestep. But, thankfully, everything that I thought would be a potential issue or hurdle to scale gratefully fell by the wayside.

The fact that we managed to work any issues out *tout de suite* made me all that much more aware of how much each of us had grown emotionally. We seemed to have learned what we really love and need.

In case you're curious: The first almost land mine to deactivate was the idea that Laurent didn't exactly cherish the notion that I had been the lover to at least two older big-shot millionaires. And you can throw in that I had certainly indulged in some extremely unique sexual antics. How'd he deduce the latter, you ask? Well, after all the trade secrets, dares, saddles and whips, squats, Asian vibrating balls, taunts, and games, a woman doesn't in any way, shape, or form come across in bed as the same type of lover. No, not with my new array of skills, positions, angles, tightening moves, and enthusiasm. All of which were like a neon flashing sign that this little chica had become a helluva lot more sexually free and uninhibited.

Laurent actually said, jokingly, although clearly with a biting truth: "Alexandra, while I was traveling to the four corners of the earth, what the hell? Were you at sex camp!?"

Um, kinda!

We talked about it, and I tried to calm his wounded masculinity like this: (This is *not* in the slightest a direct quote, by the way.) "Well, now, buster of the hurt ego. Admittedly, I didn't 'close up shop' and vow a life of celibacy, but if you were really to look at this matter maturely, you should count yourself damned fortunate that while you were quite busily attending to your own very pressing problems the woman you love was honing her own skills, tending to her own garden. Admittedly with the help of some very wise fellow gardeners! But now, when you finally decided you were ready to return and give your best, the woman in question has also bettered herself in ways that will illuminate your life with great new pleasures."

Really, though! Such as, now, I can speak to him in the Italian that he so adores. I can shower him with brilliant anecdotes and a wealth of knowledge from all my readings, wine studies, and literary and history research. And among such delights, he now has one wildly talented sexual mate who has a safety deposit box so loaded with diamonds that he need *never* feel a pressure to buy her any. Truly, I think all young men certainly dread that heinous expense, and that he need never feel the burden to make a lot of money to buy me things. All pleasure, no pressure. C'mon, how is that not a coup? Add in that now all of Paris, friends and famous alike, will see him as the man who was so amazing that Alexandra, grand courtesan of Paris, left it and all the trappings behind for him!

I smiled a rather gratified smirk when all that was met by his expression of silent, wide-eyed, happy gloat. No question about it, being on the receiving end of all those speeches of persuasion by Marie-Hélène also happened to teach *me* the art of persuasion. I *so* love an unexpected return on profits!

Oh, and the other possible ticking bomb that might've annihilated our renewed love fest? Of course, Laurent harbored some natural fears that after such extravagances, I had gotten addicted to a lifestyle he couldn't offer, not even with his new hundred-thousand-euro windfall! No question it was just a matter of time before *that* issue came up, so I tried to bring it up first, in order to head it off at the pass, as we say in the States.

Over another bottle of our good old fave, cheap Muscadet *vin blanc* (which actually still has its charms), once again I gathered up the material for my defense and set him straight before the bottle was even halfway depleted. Or should I be saying half full? Oh, never mind! This is not an existential moment, thankfully that was all earlier!

Anyway, I launched this to soothe his fears. "I know you may fear that I will miss or even dash back to the life I just left. Sure, all the luxuries were wonderful fun, but they were never things I sought passionately, never anything that can replace the real joys of life. Listen, Laurent, I will never forget one particular day, when I was sitting in my apartment drinking fabulously expensive Champagne, surrounded by all my new gorgeous museum-quality furniture, my closets bursting with couture, the phone ringing endlessly with opulent offers of trips and fashionable balls. And the diamonds . . . feeling the actual heaviness of so many diamonds around my neck. And I just felt *totally* empty! Life had no meaning. And I knew it never would without chasing my own version of success, expressing my own creativity . . . and without you. Here's the bottom line: If you sell your soul, even just for a second, no matter how much money you acquire, you can't buy it back! And I felt I was edging mighty close there toward the end. I never need to have that kind of extravagance again. I've had it. I know what it feels like, and, oh—with the exception of the sheer pleasure of sleeping on divine sheets—it's really not so great!" I fell back into my chair laughing at the realization that quite possibly the bed linens are the best part! After my little presentation, Laurent bursts out laughing. We are both so madly intent on making sure everything's okay now. So many things are making us laugh. And we both know *now,* that if either of us ever feels any tinge of anxiety or fear, we can bring it up and deal with it. Sure, we both made mistakes, each of ours incredibly different, and perhaps very common to our gender, but the greatest gift in the world is another chance to get it *right.* And we both know it.

To forgive and not to forget, but to *remember*.

So Laurent and I spent those two weeks inseparable from one another; going for long brunches at the cheap cafés on the trendy rue Montorgueil, tagging along while the other ran errands. (Which he charmingly calls in English, "errandses"; I never correct him, because it's so damn charming to hear him say it.) It was like rediscovering the Paris I fell in love with and the man I fell in love with, at the same time.

Life as a courtesan seemed like a dream I'd conjured up and lived out only in my mind—I was no longer seeing any of the same people, nor eating at the same *restos* . . . I wasn't even in the same arrondissements—it was like somebody had slipped a one-way ticket back to reality in my backpack, and I couldn't believe how good it was to be back. Everything tastes, smells, and looks better when you're in love. Money can't do that—it can on occasion, come close, but it has no staying power, and the fleeting happiness it gives disappears when the last drop of Cristal Champagne has been drunk and that great Dior dress goes out of style.

So when Isabel and Mathieu were due to return, it took nothing more than my saying to Laurent the following: "Hmm, I suppose I'd better get packin', huh, sweet pea? Can you imagine when the happy couple comes home, Mathieu carries Isabel over the threshold and I'm hanging out doing a pedicure with a seaweed facial on?! Nah. I'd say it's time to go."

"So, then . . . I'll go get the car . . . and we'll go . . . *home*," he says. His eyes are smiling.

"*Your* apartment? Cool. I have an idea," I say, dragging my luggage on top of their futon to pack.

"I bet you do, little lady. Lay it on me, *bellissima*," he demands with a smirk.

"We make another go at that Champagne risotto tonight."

"Okay, deal. On one condition," he says with faux seriousness.

"Ah, but of course. Whatever it is, I grant you it, my sweet prince," I joke, sweeping my hand from my breast as I dip into a small curtsy.

"Really? You've just agreed to marry me," he says quickly, with a hint of nervousness.

My jaw drops open and I burst out into a laugh of delight. "Oh, what a girl will do for Champagne risotto!" I fall back onto the bed, and he climbs on top of me, straddling me with those long, strong legs and pressing his hard sex against me, the two of us almost in tears of joy, looking deeply into each other's eyes, and knowing that this time, it's *absolument pour toujours*.

A *final* priceless quote—*I assure you, the last one!*

Our old *ami*, Rainer Maria Rilke, hit it on the head:

For one human being to love another; that is perhaps the most difficult of all our tasks, the ultimate, the last test and proof, the work for which all other work is but preparation.

ACKNOWLEDGMENTS

I don't wish to burden you with my debts, but I am compelled to extend my sincerest thanks to the many vital and supportive souls who have been invaluable to me during the creation of this book.

Many thanks to my family (whom I shall honor by *not* including their names in this rather racy tome) and to my friends, to whom I owe so much gratitude in this last year, my *annus mirabilis*.

Globally, *mes vrais amis*—Renaud Vuaillat, Olivier Gayral, Jean-Albert Lievre, Alberto Garrone, Franck Melenic, Ross Marsh, Jeremy Gilbert, Frédéric Beigbeder, Katie Chebatoris, Charlotte Tarantola, Beth Bowley, Julia Balio, Cameron Shay, John Kelly, Kent Kurtz, Carter Pottash, Augustus Gertz, Jean-Philippe Chretien, Nicolas Portolleau, Floris Houwink, Yannick Boudou, TWD, John Sykes, Kathy Greenberg, Sabina Fogle, David Ingram, Nancy Flavin, Fabian and Lorene Edelstam, Frédéric Chevalier, Marianne Freire, Nancy Wetzel, Sara Krauskopf, Terrance Gelenter, Gillian Doria, Paula Wood, Alain Morice, Adrian Gilbey, John Baxter, Wendi Merrill, and my guardian angels: Michael Connor and Jeff Ely.

A most gracious *merci beaucoup* to everyone at St. Martin's Press—Sally Richardson, my editress extraordinaire Elizabeth Beier, Courtney Fischer, and Michelle Richter. And to my Hollywood team—the fabulous Lauren Lloyd and Jessica Wiltgen of Lloyd Entertainment at Gold Circle Films and Amy Schiffman at Gersh Agency. And an enormous thank-you to Bob Greenblatt and Danielle Gelber at Showtime for all their enthusiasm and faith in this decadent little tale. A humble and heartfelt thank-you to the Oscar-nominated director Oliver Hirschbiegel for his interest and encouragement.

To Dr. J. McGinnis, for her exceptional care and helping me to bring my most beloved and treasured Oscar Maximilian into this world.

And finally, the greatest thanks goes to the most faithful, generous-hearted soul I could ever dream of imagining, my best friend, the marvelous Helena O'Neal.

Learn the rules of love à la français.

Spend the morning after with Klein, a trés chic fashionista who flees the stylish confines of New York City for the elegant arrondisements of Paris. There she'll encounter one hilariously bad relationship after another until she meets— peut-être—Monsieur Right.

"Paris Hangover will hang around your dreams long after Klein kisses you good-bye— on both cheeks, of course."
—Jacquelyn Mitchard, author of *The Deep End of the Ocean* and *A Theory of Relativity*

Paris Hangover

A NOVEL

KIRSTEN LOBE